Fire in the
Mountain

By

Lily Ennis

Fire in the Mountain
By Lily Ennis

ISBN: 978-0-473-22190-4

Dedication

For my husband Geoff

Prologue
15 February 1944

Alfred winced as he cowered in the sodden grey mud of the foxhole. The B-17 flying fortress had again missed its target of the monastery on the hill and the purple cold of the night sky lit up with the red and orange incandescence of the explosion. Alfred watched the rain flash light and dark sparkling wet against the glow of the fires.

Everything around him seemed to be happening in slow motion making him an observer and not a participant. Harold writhed in pain next to him with one leg bent at a hideous angle, the other blasted off at the knee. His blood was at one minute black and the next red. There was so much of it. He could smell it, and worse, taste it in his mouth. Harold panicked and grasped his stump screaming. The piercing sounds of falling bombs and the thunderous boom of explosions stayed outside Alfred's consciousness until Harold's gurgled screams brought him back. He wriggled to Harold through the bloody urine soaked mud keeping well below the top of the dugout.

'Alf, Alf,' he shouted. 'It's all right mate, you'll be all right. You hear me? You hang in there.'

'It's gone, it's gone,' Harold screamed, his words punctuated by the piercing sounds of the battle outside the foxhole.

'I have to staunch the wound,' Alfred shouted back louder than he meant to.

'I don't want to die here,' Harold panted. 'Don't let

me die in this godforsaken hell hole.' He slumped onto his back with a grimace. 'Tell Lily I love her.'

'Tell her yourself Harry,' said Alfred. 'Nobody died of a missing leg. Come on mate. We'll soon have this bound up. They'll send you home now. Out of this shit hole.'

Home thought Alfred. It seemed a comforting thing to say. He needed Harold to stay strong and he wasn't about to let Harold see his choking fear. For that was sure to infect him with despair and desolation. Grunting, Alfred hauled Harold onto his backpack. Harold fading, offered no help.

'Got to stop the bleeding mate,' Alfred yelled.

Alfred shrugged off his own pack and flopped it onto the ground. He fumbled to loosen the straps and grappled for the first aid kit. Alfred was only rudimentarily familiar with its contents. He choked down his nausea as adrenalin kicked in and pulled out a large triangular bandage and some gauze.

'Stay with me Harry. Hold this on it.'

Alfred placed a thickly folded gauze bandage on the end of Harold's appendage hardly daring to touch it. He took Harold's hands and gently positioned them on the still gushing limb. The closest to this Alfred could remember was the time he'd hit his thumb with a hammer and the thumb had instantly swollen and throbbed with every heartbeat. But at least with each pulse the blood had stayed within his body. Harold was losing his with every heartbeat. He wound the bandage round the limb until the bandage ran out. It couldn't be called a leg now. It's Harold's appendage.

Alfred became aware of the battle outside the foxhole;

bombs shrilling through the smoke-thick air, screaming men struck in pain and fear, the sounds and smells of the rain, the stench of blood and urine and the smell of death.

He looked up ahead of him. At the top of the hill the ancient abbey barely stood. It had been smashed to ruins. Fifty nine ally fighter bombers had dropped 1450 tons of high explosives and incendiary bombs on it. There should have been German intelligence occupying the sentinel position. Now it was said that only civilians and monks were in occupation. It was rumoured that no treasures remained, that thousands of manuscripts and papal documents had been trucked out last November to the Vatican. There had been an agreement between the warring factions that Benedict of Nursia's abbey would not be bombed.

Alfred never saw it in its full glory. It was by now little more than shards of crumpled masonry which flashed pink and white in the light of the incessant bombing. Whilst there had been only civilians and monks in occupation two days ago, now the Germans had taken up residence, fashioning the crude demolition materials into foxholes of their own. Through the heavy rain Alfred could see flashes of Polish gunfire on the eastern part of the hill and all around him the New Zealand Corps and the Fourth Indian Division were burrowed into the sides of the hill, rifle fire flickering through the blue smoke and rain.

Alfred called across to the foxhole to his right. Charlie, Charlie, are you there mate?'

'Yeah mate,' Charlie called back. 'What is it?'

Alfred scrambled out of the squalid cavern that he had

shared with Harold for twenty hours and sprinted over to Charlie.

'Harold's been hit. Lost a leg, broken the other one.' He grunted the words out.

The rain had become heavier and with it the temperature dropped. Cold rain fell heavily from Alfred's helmet onto his face as he shouted to Charlie.

'That's our planes goddam it. Bloody hit and miss. What do they think they're doing? They're killing us.'

'We can't do anything while those bombs are missing their target,' Charlie replied. 'Can't try for the abbey. Plenty of Gerry on that east ridge but orders are to stay put for now.'

'Sooner we get off this hill the better,' Alfred barked.

'Just sit tight mate,' Charlie replied. 'You see to Harold. I can hear the sergeant relaying orders now. We'll soon know what's happening.'

'I need dry bandages to stop the bleeding,' said Alfred. 'I've wrapped it up best I can. God it's a mess; so much blood. Poor bugger. He's in agony. He needs a medic. Relay that message along the line for me Charlie.'

Alfred scrambled back over the potholed sloping ground to the relative shelter of the foxhole. Harold wasn't screaming anymore. It calmed Alfred but the quiet inside the dugout now was not peaceful. He felt out of his depth and he wondered if he would do the same for anyone other than Harold. Grudgingly he concluded that he probably would.

Alfred and Harold had shared their hopes and dreams since they'd met in the tiny army camp at Waiouru. Both had been wiling away the early years of the war as

7

students in modest local schools in small town New Zealand. Both had been less than truthful about their age when they signed up. In a short eleven months they'd become men. They learned to drink and smoke and how to satisfy a woman.

Alfred allowed his mind to take him home. He'd had a sweetheart of course. Sophie was at school with him and lived three farms down the road. She was the sweetest fairest girl in the district.

He glowed inside as he recalled his last summer at home. At the church picnic on the flats by the river he and Sophie had stolen away for an hour to be alone. It was deliciously naughty. They swam together in the river then lay on the grassy flats above it as the sun dried their clothes.

Sophie's wet dress clung to her so that the outline of her tiny waist and small perfectly formed breasts, nipples erect, teased him. How he wished he'd been brave enough to nuzzle his face between those breasts. He'd delighted in his swelling manhood and pressed himself against her hip. His hands caressed the sides of her body and he could feel the swell of her breasts. She'd let him kiss her. A first for both of them. Alfred thought about that long hot kiss. It seemed a lifetime ago. He had given himself completely to it and became lost in its languid promise. That kiss was as good as a promise. Sophie was his sweetheart and he was hers. She wouldn't like to know that he was stuck in a watery grave on the side of a hill with bombs raining down on him and the smell of death all around.

He looked over at Harold. He had the dark haired Lily to go home to. Harold had been forthcoming about his exploits with Lily. She had freely shared her body with him without comprising her virginity. Lily was the girl Harold was going home to. The thought strengthened Alfred's resolve. He would see Harold right through this night, off this hill and beyond. He focussed on his friend lying there hurt but brave with new determination.

'All right private, what's going on here?'

Alfred snapped out of his reverie. The sergeant scrambled to the edge of the dugout.

'Harold needs a medic Sir,' Alfred answered. 'One leg blown off and the other broken. He's out of the water a bit. Need a medic Sir.'

'We're retreating private.' The sergeant ignored Alfred's request. 'I want you to make your way down the hill. The boys at the top are coming back down now. Assemble on the true right of the river. There's cover under a stand of trees just beyond the bend. You should be able to make it before first light.'

'Yes Sir. Sir?'

'Yes?'

'Is there a medic along the line Sir?'

'No time for that private. Now move.'

Alfred strained a look above the dugout. The thick grey clouds closed in on the night sky which, when the incendiary bombs set off fires, back lit them with a yellow glow. The rubble masonry still flashed white and pink and orange. The rain was not letting up.

Below the monastery men were scrambling out of their shallow foxholes. They were no more than shadows as far as Alfred could tell. It was difficult enough negotiating the sloping terrain without the added burden of the rain and the heavy army packs and rifles but he could see some men were helping the wounded to safety. Seems Harold was not the only casualty.

'Come on Harold old chap,' Alfred spoke reassuringly. 'Let's get out of here.'

Harold screwed his face up and grunted. The pain was too severe to even scream. He heaved his body into an upright position.

'I don't want to drag you Harry.' Alfred took command. 'We can't knock your legs mate.'

'You go Alfie, you go. Save your own arse. Leave me.' Harold huffed out the words.

'Not on your life. What the hell would I tell Lily? That I left you in the dead of night on the side of a hill in some foreign land because I was too busy saving my own arse? I don't think so.'

The intermittent explosions provided enough light for Alfred to scan the hillside for vacated foxholes. Trouble was, he was above the holes he needed to get into and could not determine the empty ones.

Alfred knelt before Harold and put his arms around his waist. 'I have to sling you over my shoulder. It's the only way.'

Harold screamed.

'I know mate, I know. Hold on tight.'

Harold's stump was as red and black as if there had been no bandage at all. Blood was seeping into the cold rainwater which pooled at the bottom of the foxhole. They couldn't get free of it.

Alfred stumbled backwards with the dead weight of Harold. Blood poured out of the stump and Alfred felt it seep hot onto his body. Harold moaned as Alfred lurched out of the shelter of the hole and stumbled down the slope. Slippery under foot, Alfred took more care than he would otherwise have taken, slowing their retreat. His adolescent frame struggled. Not that Harold had gained any fat during his time in the army but his muscles had developed considerably, as had Alfred's.

He located a dugout about one hundred and fifty feet from where they'd been holed up. He lowered Harold gently across a shape on the ground. It was Jack; he thought it was Jack. His head lay cocked to one side, his helmet askew and half of his head was missing. Alfred thanked God for the poor light. He was already sick to his stomach. He noticed that Jack's pack was not with him. His foxhole buddy would have made his escape with it along with Jack's rifle.

'Are you still with me Harold?' Alfred called out. 'Think about Lily. How lucky you are, eh mate. We're getting down. I'll get you a medic.'

Harold slipped in and out of consciousness, too racked by pain to respond. Alfred heard the whistle of an incendiary bomb. It seemed so close as to be on top of him. What did they say? If you hear the whistle then it hasn't got your name on it? The whistle was replaced by a thud and a spontaneous explosion which lit up the sky. Alfred could not see through it but was peppered with the mud and debris fallout. He lunged over Harold, shielding him from the force of the explosion.

'Aah, aah,' Harold moaned.

'Sorry Harry,' Alfred grunted. 'Steady mate, keep it going. You're doing well. Not long now, help me mate. Up you come.'

Alfred took several deep breaths to summon his strength for the next push. His heart raged in his chest.

He lifted Harold off Jack's body and slung him onto his shoulder. He could taste Harold's blood and urine imbedded in the thick serge trousers. And then he realised it wasn't just Harold's urine. It smelt like death. He could hear nothing around him. There was nothing but getting Harold to safety.

Alfred hesitated just a moment to leave the dugout. The bomb that had just exploded had been so close to them it may as well have dropped on them. What were the chances of another falling in the same place? Close to zero he calculated.

He lurched from one slippery foothold to the next. He gained momentum and perfected a technique that seemed to be working. He passed empty foxholes and some had dead men in them. He was deaf to shouts of his comrades and to the screams of the wounded.

Harold had gone quiet. He wasn't even moaning quietly any more. Alfred wasn't sure if this was a good thing or not. He knew next to nothing about fixing people up. He hadn't seen much action in this war and seen less wounded. But he spoke loudly to Harold anyway. It bolstered his courage.

He lunged to the relative shelter of another unoccupied dugout and dropped Harold onto the ground. Harold let out a moan. A good thing. Alfred was somewhat relieved.

'Nearly there mate.' Alfred was reassuring. 'Let's have a look at the lay of the land.' Alfred tipped his head back so he could see beneath his helmet. Dark and rain. There seemed to be less light down here. He could see the flat black sinew of the water down below flash a thin reflective light as the illuminated sky allowed. It looked good, beckoning and reassuring somehow. Safety. From where he crouched it didn't seem so far. And as the sergeant had said, achievable before sun-up.

'Okay Harry,' Alfred shouted. 'One last push to get us onto flat ground. You can do it mate. Think of Lily. Okay? She wants you home Harry.'

Alfred wrapped his arms around Harold's waist and heaved him onto his shoulder, blowing short outward breaths, garnering the strength for the push to a standing position and the last downhill push. As he stumbled out of the hole it was immediately coveted by a private from the line above.

The vegetation grew thicker now as they neared the toe of the slope. Although it was easier for him to gain a foothold there was a risk of knocking Harold's legs on the scrubby branches. He took a more sideways route to the flat ground. More men shuffled, stumbled and ran around him now. But there should have been 1600 more. The fact didn't escape Alfred.

At last he made it to flat ground. The pressure on his knees and thighs receded and he wanted to rest but his duty was to Harold. He trudged on in the rain and dark, with his pack on his back, his mate on his shoulder and his rifle in his hand. After half an hour he made it to the cover of the trees beyond the bend in the river.

'Private.' The Corporal acknowledged Alfred. 'Well done. 'Who is that?'

'Sir. Private Harold Jones Sir. He needs a medic.'

'Sorry son, Jones is gone.'

Chapter One

Lana felt her neck and face heat to crimson as Paul took centre stage. She thought she'd be better prepared. Lord knew, she'd had plenty of warning. Weeks in fact since she'd received the speaking programme. And while she'd initially been stunned to see his name on the list of speakers she was sure she was ready to face him. She'd delved into his past and learned he was a geologist. While she'd been tootling her flute these past decades he was figuring out how the earth was made. She assumed that he was married with children. Wasn't everyone? Would he remember her? Would he want to remember her? When she flushed red at the very sight of him, it all came flooding back. Thirty years ago became yesterday. Her heart thudded in her chest. The thunder of it echoed in her eardrums to the exclusion of any other sound. Paul had the same effect on her when she was sixteen. She kept perfectly still hoping he wouldn't notice her.

'Lana.' Her colleague dug her lightly in the ribs. 'What's the matter?' she whispered.

Lana turned to Emma. 'What?'

'You're gasping,' Emma replied.

'Oh, am I? It's nothing. Just a bit hot in here.' Lana reached for the neck of her merino jumper and fanned it in and out of her chest. It did nothing to take the blush from her throat. The room was a comfortable several degrees warmer than the frigid Icelandic summer outside the hotel.

The audience clapped to welcome Paul. Lana quietly joined in not wanting to do anything to draw Paul's eyes to her. She was seated a third of the way back to the right amongst three hundred other delegates from around the world. She could have sat in the front; up until this point she told herself she had the confidence to, but simmering close to the surface was fear. What if he recognised her and didn't want to meet up with her? No; better to meld into the crowd for now. Besides, she might not be as impressed by him as she once was.

'...of managing a lahar hazard in a volcanic setting.' Paul introduced his lecture.

How on earth was she going to concentrate on what should be an interesting lecture with Paul Harrington delivering it? She dropped her head a little and shut her eyes. She conjured up the last image she had of him. It was astoundingly easy, as if it were yesterday. He was sixteen, as tall as her, a shock of black hair, gorgeous white-toothed smile and that school uniform; brown trousers, brown jumper, and brown Charlie Brown shoes. His soft brown eyes looked up from his dipped head so that his lids looked bigger than they actually were, so shy was he.

'...in the New Zealand Central Plateau region,' he explained as he directed the red pointer onto Mount Ruapehu on the large screen.

Lana opened her eyes. Where was that boy? She realised she couldn't remember his voice. She could not reconcile the voice that confidently held a room of peers with that of the boy she'd loved. She stared hard at him as if by searching his face the young Paul would materialise and match the vision inside her head. The man that stood ahead of her was taller than in the picture and he had lightly greying temples. His jeans were faded around the knees, his shirt fashionably hanging out. He seemed easy and confident in his topic.

'...entrained into the front of the lahar,' Paul continued.

She hadn't thought of Paul for decades so why on earth should she have butterflies? She knew he was not the same boy and she was not the same girl. She shouldn't feel a thing for the man on the stage, should she? He was new to her now. They were no longer teenagers. They had changed, and their lives had histories.

Lana reluctantly recalled her adolescence. She was no beauty and she had no wish to reminisce on that. Paul was sweet on her but he was painfully shy; as was she. But they were girlfriend and boyfriend. They had held hands and kissed knowing that one day soon they would give themselves over to ultimate pleasure. If they had been brave enough to share their bodies with each other back then maybe she wouldn't have these butterflies. If their relationship had ended with a proper conclusion she wouldn't be having hot sweats. But it hadn't. It was unfulfilled before circumstances tore them apart.

Well, that was a lifetime ago. He didn't seem so shy now. But then, neither was she. And she had to admit she felt more swan than duckling these days.

She wouldn't avoid him for the duration of the conference. She had no intention of doing that. The mature thing to do would be to confidently approach him and congratulate him on a well presented informative lecture. If that were true – she hadn't heard a word he'd said. She just needs a little time to compose herself, enough time for the red to leave her face. After all, she knows he's here but he doesn't know she's here.

Therefore the advantage is hers and she'll be composed and delighted to see him and he'll be shocked to see her.

'...early warning system patched through to several agencies.' Paul moved around the stage engrossed in his lecture. The passion for his work was evident in his wild hand gesticulations. He alternated between thoughtful repose and excited animation as if he was trying to analyse the slides on the spot instead of having a carefully rehearsed speech at his ready.

Lana ticked off her significant events in the thirty years since she'd seen him. One; twenty years as a flutist in the Sydney Symphony Orchestra. Status: retired. Two; married to the now deceased Russian cellist, Yuri. Status: widow, still grieving. Three; completed science degree, still studying. Status: perpetual student. Four; no family. Status: childless widow. It rang hollow.

No family. The phrase echoed loudly in her ears. She bet Paul had a lovely wife and a lovely family. She suddenly felt inadequate. Who was she kidding? Look around you Lana. What do you see? Career scientists – weather beaten old men and young men who are going to be weather beaten. Women your age? Not so many. And a new batch of fresh-faced confident women pursuing a career, as did she, only to leave child rearing too late.

Paul's one of them – a weathered career scientist. The sheer fact that Paul is the keynote speaker at this conference suggests he has a lot of respect in his field. Undoubtedly he has achieved a lot, been all over the world, worked in exotic places and hasn't even thought of Lana Letov Marshall for a single minute in all those years.

'... risk of breaching the bund.' Paul aimed the tiny

red dot at the lower right corner of the photo. Lana was familiar with the volcanic region of which Paul spoke. Tongariro National Park was Lana's research laboratory. Mount Ruapehu provided the glaciers that she was studying.

She wondered what path he'd taken to get himself here. It seemed incredible that their paths should cross in a conference room in Iceland when they both studied different aspects of the same volcano back home.

'... preventing a loss of life. Thank you very much.' Paul concluded his lecture. A loud applause ensued snapping Lana out of her reverie.

***

Paul enjoyed the experience once he found his rhythm and the audience warmed to him. It wasn't his natural environment but he'd had to give many lectures over the course of his career. It was a requisite, a trade off for taking grant money so he could fulfil his academic needs and it was a small price to pay. He could usually get weeks in the field or months on a contract and then a few quiet months to write up his research without having to answer to anyone. It was only at events such as these that he felt the pressure to conform to social conventions.

Before every lecture he had to psyche himself up by doing his own form of meditation. If he'd analysed his own performance as acutely as he studied the world around him he would have realised that his command of the subject was what held him together on stage.

He glanced around for Lana and saw her sitting about a third back, a bit to the left. A stab of heat coursed through him. He couldn't have predicted the sudden anxiety that flushed his body. He wanted to go to her now, sweep her into his arms and feel her soft body melt to his touch. She still had luscious dark hair that framed her beautiful oval face. She looked a little flushed and agitated but he saw her blue eyes sparkle across a sea of heads when she deigned to lift it. She didn't seem too interested in the talk with her head slightly bowed and sometimes with her eyes shut. It was a strange reaction given that all he had done was walk on stage. He presumed she had recognised him. She could have at least sat a little closer. She would have known he was speaking. At least she was there. The dryness in his throat gave him pause. More than ever he felt not only every eye on him, but now, with Lana in the room he must give a seamless performance. He reached a trembling hand to the glass of water on the lectern and took a gulp. He felt it calm him. He would deliver his lecture and worry about Lana later.

***

'We should sit near Paul Harrington,' said Emma. 'He'll be at one of the front tables. Isn't he delicious? Do you think he's available?'

'I have no idea,' answered Lana tersely. Emma's plunging neckline did not escape Lana's attention. She'd only just met Emma so she didn't have the measure of her yet. After the conference they were to fly to New Zealand together where Emma would spend a year at Lana's university. She was a good ten years younger than Lana and in their short acquaintance Lana

19

understood that Emma knew how to carry her long blonde hair and willowy figure.

She hadn't managed the confidence to seek Paul out and didn't want a reunion in front of her Canadian colleague. 'There's room at that table by the wall. We'll still have good views of the convener.'

'Good views is not what it's about Lana,' countered Emma. 'You have to network. That's what these gigs are for.'

Lana sighed as Emma led her towards the front of the enormous dining room. It was the conference room converted for tonight's dinner. The room was resplendent in cream and gold with exquisite side lamps affixed to the walls and heavy crystal chandeliers running through the centre of the room. Drops of gold brocade softened the walls, and the carpet was embellished with delicate gold and turquoise patterns. It took Lana back to her orchestral days where she wore insignificant black and let the concert halls swallow her up. But this short walk through the room brought the butterflies back, for Emma commanded the attention of every person present.

Lana had taken a great deal of care in her grooming. The apple red dress with tapered shoulders straps and sweetheart neckline was stunning enough on its own but when she wore it on her five foot six inch svelte frame, teamed with strappy black heels and red necklace with matching earrings, she felt positively radiant.

'May we?' asked Emma touching one of the chairs.

'By all means. Please do,' offered a stout older gentleman wizened by a life spent out of doors. Not an unusual feature amongst geologists Lana observed.

'Thank you. I'm Emma and this is Lana. I'm from Canada about to spend a sabbatical in New Zealand.'

Introductions were made around the table and Lana shook each proffered hand firmly but not too aggressively. She was conscious that she looked pleasing but did not want to stand out in the crowd. Many years in the orchestra had taught her to dress well and to always present herself in the best possible light. It was a difficult habit to break. She noted that some of the female geologists were uneasy in their glamorous dresses. Some dressed awkwardly and when others got the dress right they clomped about bow legged on their unfamiliar heels as if they were boulder hopping whilst surveying a stream. Even when Lana was out in the field on a windswept plateau she was mindful of her attire.

'I'm sponsored to be here,' explained Lana taking a seat next to a ruddy blonde Australian. 'I secured a grant from the Tongariro Natural History Society to attend. They're a group of volunteers who do conservation work in Tongariro National Park.'

It was Lana's duty to expound the virtues of her benefactor at every opportunity. And as Emma had rightly pointed out, this is the time to do it.

'I've had many holidays trekking your bush,' said Tim.

'What field are you in?'

'I'm studying a glacier called Tuwharetoa,' Lana replied. 'It lies directly above the Crater Lake on top of Mount Ruapehu. It has some large crevasses at present which may calve shortly. It could have a significant effect on the lake level and on the unstable rim of the crater.'

'You must know Paul Harrington then,' Tim remarked.

Lana was stunned for a moment. She had expected to meet Paul here tonight of course. The room was not yet full and she had surreptitiously searched the room for him but she hadn't noticed him.

'Well, yes. But not lately,' she replied. 'That is, I did know him at school but haven't seen him since.'

She did not know this new Paul Harrington and she had no wish to have a reunion with him in this social context. It would be too public. She'd much prefer a quiet place, just the two of them so they could recount the intervening years, and even the years they had shared together.

'Oh how funny,' said Robert with a lazy North American drawl. 'And with you studying glaciers in the North Island. The country must be bigger than I imagined. Paul and I were working on the same project in Columbia. Have you caught up with him yet? Does he know you're here?'

'No,' said Lana shifting in her seat. 'On both counts. How long were you in Columbia?'

'Several months,' said Robert. 'About two years ago. We practically lived in each other's pockets. I'll bet he can help you with your research. His first field of expertise is volcanology. He's become interested in lahars only in the last year or so.'

'Have you kept in touch?' asked Lana.

'Yeah, a bit. Mostly by emails. We send each other academic papers and such like.'

Lana noticed that Robert's ring finger was empty. She wondered how to ask of Paul's marital status.

'And your families were with you overseas?' asked Lana.

'No, my wife travels as an international sales rep so it was never practical for her to come with me. And Paul's family stayed put in New Zealand.'

That went well. Lana was pleased at her line of questioning. How many men did she know actually wore a wedding ring anyway? So Paul was married with a family. Exactly what she expected. She was pleased for him but not as pleased as she might have been if she had still been happily married to her fabulous Yuri. She felt like a one person play, acting cool, saying the right things, the expected things one is supposed to say in new company.

'And you had no scientific paper to present to this conference?' she asked Robert.

'Not yet, Robert replied. 'I've got something in the pipeline. Anyway, how could I shine next to Harry? The lahar he spoke of, how relevant is that to you in your study? Surely it's just downstream?'

'Yes it is,' said Lana, aware that the conversation had turned from the personal to the academic. 'The lahar path follows the Whangaehu Valley which is directly below historic glacial terrain. I'm in my first master's year and I've only been up to that locality a few times so it's not surprising that I haven't run into Paul.'

Lana let the academic conversation buzz around her as she sipped her red wine. The glass was bulbous on a tall clear stem and the wine was hot and irresistible. Its sweet familiar bouquet calmed her. She gazed without much interest at Emma who appeared to have the attention of everyone at the table, flicking her long

23

blonde hair off her face and draping it over her tanned shoulders.

After he had eaten his entree Robert left the table vacating the seat next to Lana's. She took a sip of the red wine savouring its warmth before letting it slide down her throat to sit at the top of her belly. Then into her peripheral vision a male figure paused behind the empty seat next to her and softly laid a hand on the back of her chair. He bent his head and addressed her in a warm clear tone.

'Hello Lana,' said Paul. 'May I sit with you for a bit?'

Lana spluttered. It was the voice she had such trouble with earlier in the day. She clumsily set her glass down on the white tablecloth barely registering that a drop of wine sloshed over the side. She stood instantly to greet him but was at a loss what to do next. Kiss him on the cheek? Hug him? She shot out her hand. He shook it firmly, and held it for just a bit longer than was acceptable.

'Well, Mr Harrington certainly remembers you,' exclaimed Emma. Lana wasn't sure if it was a sneer or pleasure written on Emma's face. 'Why don't you introduce us?'

'Hello Paul.' She smiled at him. 'I really wasn't sure if it was you. I had no idea of your career.'

'We were at high school together,' Paul explained to the table. He broke off to introduce himself to Emma and the others he didn't know. 'I haven't seen Lana for what, thirty years? Time has been kind to you.' He smiled at her.

'Thank you,' she graciously accepted. 'You look well too. Please, sit.' She gestured to the empty seat and poured him some wine hoping he didn't notice her hand tremble.

'Did you see Robert?' she asked. 'Your friend from Columbia. He was sitting here.'

This was going all wrong. He was supposed to be shocked at finding her here. Not the other way around. The practiced conversations in her head were coming to nothing.

'I had a very pleasant reunion with Robert this afternoon,' said Paul. 'I've left him sitting in my place at my table.' He nodded his head gesturing at a table somewhere that didn't matter anymore. 'Do you mind?'

'No,' said Lana. 'Of course not.' She returned his smile.

Paul received much adulation and compliments on his lecture. Lana let him bask in the success of it. Emma was very keen to make his acquaintance. She seemed to steer any conversation Paul might have had for Lana to her but it didn't escape her that Paul immediately brought the conversation back to Lana. Well, it had been thirty years after all.

He sat close to her with his leg almost touching hers but not quite. She was aware of his masculinity, his thick dark hair; his close cut goatee and aftershave she could swim in. He sat comfortably, straight backed. He didn't have a paunch that one might expect at his age which she put down to his active lifestyle. He paid Lana the closest regard and he held her gaze with his hooded liquid brown eyes as if she were the only woman in the room.

'And how are you Lana? Have you had a good life?' Paul spoke quietly intimating that her answer was for him only.

It was a sweeping question. Had she had a good life? This was hardly the place to be circumspect. And she had propelled herself into the past this morning when he had appeared before her like a ghost out of time. It all seemed too much to even begin to answer. She always did pretty much what she wanted. She'd enjoyed her previous career in the orchestra. She had not known tragedy, apart from her husband dying in a car accident five years ago. She did not want for anything. She was not carrying too much emotional baggage; never been to counselling anyway.

'Yes, I have had a good life,' she said, as if that summed up thirty years. 'And you?'

'I guess so,' Paul said. 'No complaints anyway.'

'I didn't know you were a geologist,' said Lana. 'A doctor no less.'

'I've been overseas for much of my career,' Paul explained.

'Ah yes, Columbia.'

'That's just a small part,' he said, 'the most recent overseas assignment.'

'So you've worked at many Pacific Rim volcanoes?' asked Lana.

'Yes, I've mostly concentrated on plate boundary volcanism.'

'What brought you home? Family?'

'Sort of. And the time was right. In the early years I didn't think of home a lot. My work was exciting; new countries were exciting. But over the last few years I began to think about home more and more until eventually it dominated my thoughts. So here I am. Home.'

'So why the switch to lahars?'

'Gap in the market?' He smiled coyly, not giving her any more. 'So come on, tell me, what are you doing here? What have you been up to? Family?'

'Ah, no. No family.' Lana was a little reticent.

'No? No little Lana's running around? Oh, shame.' He seemed genuinely sorry for her.

She was puzzled by the warmth in his reply. She gave him the standard explanation.

'I had a career in an orchestra. I was married. Yuri died. There is someone at the moment. I've come late to study. I felt the need to be useful. Do you know what I mean? You've done incredible work over the course of your career. You've discovered things and that knowledge is used to find out more. It must give you tremendous satisfaction.'

Paul searched Lana's eyes for everything that she had not said. She'd told him the sum total of her thirty years and yet told him nothing.

'Lana I'm sorry. You're too young to be a widow. I really am very sorry.'

'Thank you. We were very happy. It was Yuri who introduced me to the outdoors. We used to go into the Blue Mountains on entomology expeditions.' She laughed. 'Can you believe it? He collected bugs!' But she suddenly stopped laughing. Yuri weighed heavily on her shoulders.

When the main course arrived the conversation around the table was dominated by the cuisine. Lana was given the meat dish. Emma and Paul on Lana's left and right respectively were given the fish dish.

'Would you mind swapping with me Paul?' Lana

asked. 'I'm not vegetarian but I can't do seared meat I'm afraid.'

'A delicate palate?' Paul chided. 'Of course, I don't mind. It is actually cooked you know.'

'So they say,' she said.

Lana was glad of the diversion of dinner. She was determined to keep the conversation light and away from their shared past, for now anyway. She questioned him on his lahar research and diverted the subject away from their lost years, lost love and lost dreams. She felt him relax as he became immersed in his field of expertise. Now he was articulate and eloquent and he gesticulated with punctuation for effect.

'Do you get up to the mountain often?' he asked.

'I last went up in April,' said Lana. 'Stayed on the east side of the mountain for a week. Loved it. I need to go back up soon. I want to measure the crevasses on the Tuwharetoa Glacier. There are some serious cracks up there at the moment. I need to see if there has been any deepening over the winter. I'm going up at the end of September.'

'Let me know exactly when eh?' said Paul. 'I'd be keen to help.'

Lana had been about to put a forkful of fish into her mouth but her hand froze and the fork poised in front of her mouth. This morning she wasn't even positive if Paul Harrington, PhD was the same Paul Harrington, teenage love. Now he was cramming thirty years of unwanted memories into her head and inviting himself into her world.

'Ah, sure,' she stuttered as politely as she could. She put the fork back down to her plate and reloaded it. She felt herself blush.

Paul smiled. 'Honestly, I've been going up to the lahar path about every six weeks weather permitting. Since both our research is on the same side of the mountain we may as well collaborate.'

'I don't know how useful a post grad would be to you.'

'You'd be surprised.'

'Why don't we discuss it tomorrow? You could join me for an early morning run. Not far, only a few kilometres.' *What did I do that for?* she thought. *It blurted out without any thought. God, one minute I'm nervous about reuniting with him and the next I've practically set up a date.*

'Ha, you must be joking.' Paul laughed. 'Isn't it enough that you scale the highest peaks in New Zealand? No wonder you look so fit and lovely.'

He said it with such ease. She could only assume that he meant it. She graciously turned to him and accepted his compliment as if she had just played a piece of Bach without error and the conductor had nodded his praise.

'I'm not staying for the rest of the conference,' said Paul matter of factly. 'I have a flight out at one in the morning.' He reached into his back pocket and pulled out his wallet. 'Here's my card.'

Lana took it and studied it. Email, mobile and university contact address. Auckland. She realised that she hadn't even asked where he lived. But she had not given much away about herself either. Best not, not here at a table of strangers. She wasn't and never had been an open book.

'I can give you my email,' said Lana. 'I don't have a

card I'm sorry.'

Paul pulled out another of his cards and Lana wrote her details on the back.

'Lana,' said Paul softly. 'I'd really like to see you again.'

He was doing it again; inviting her to drown in his silky deep brown eyes, his voice liquid gold to her ears. Lana smiled at him tightly, politely, noncommittally. She had a life and there really was no room in it for Paul Harrington.

***

Lana's bedside alarm buzzed at five thirty waking her from a fitful sleep. She snapped it off quickly so as not to wake Emma. She had turned in not long after dinner. Paul had left to pack and catch his flight. She was happy to be alone with her memories. When Emma swiped her door card in the small hours Lana had feigned sleep.

She snuggled back under the covers for a few minutes, her eyes open, with only the faint glow of the alarm clock to break the dark. She listened to Emma's contented breathing and reflected upon her conversation with Paul last night. He didn't appear surprised to see her; delighted and charmed but not surprised. He looked good for his age and she smiled at that. She was pleased for him. The evening with him was ephemeral, no more than a fleeting coming together of two past lives, intangible, gone. And he was gone now, back home to his wife. It hardly seemed real at all.

She quietly threw back the covers and swapped her summer pyjamas for tight fitting lycra shorts and running top, pulled on her socks and quietly closed the door on her sleeping room mate. She ate a breakfast of toasted muesli and tinned fruit with black tea – nothing different from home so far. She was a creature of habit. She looked forward to her run around Reykjavik.

Lana left the hotel a little after six. A half hour jog should see her run three point five kilometres. She never was a super athlete. She checked her watch and set off along the Grottisgata. The city streets were practically empty. Dawn had broken into a white sky with painted charcoal clouds sketched onto the canvas. It was still and she was aware of the first shrills of birdlife permeating the air.

The morning run was Lana's thinking time. There was something about the rhythmic steady pounding of the road that enabled her to formulate an idea and follow it through. It was on a run that she'd had the notion to change her career after Yuri's death. She had found it impossible to play especially poignant pieces of music without choking back tears. Some of her professional repertoire had brought tears to her eyes so special were the pieces to Yuri that her breath was stolen from her and she could not do the music justice. She was letting her colleagues down. Her gut wrenched with some of the Bach pieces and the grieving seemed to be never ending.

The meeting with Paul last night had shaken her and the fast clip of her jog reflected her agitated frame of mind. The encounter made her reflect on her life. But she didn't want to reflect on it. Didn't want to feel that to spend twenty years playing a flute was nothing more than self indulgent.

Her marriage to Yuri was everything she had hoped

for. They literally made beautiful music together. She was already playing in the orchestra when Yuri secured his place as fourth cellist. It was love at first sight but felt as though they had already been together a lifetime. She felt relaxed with him and although their cultures sometimes kept them apart on a spiritual level, their music, hot and passionate, bridged their differences. Marriage was a natural step to take and she'd never had to work hard at it. She put up with his interest in entomology with humour and he suffered her insane penchant for martial arts with quiet pride.

They were each so passionate about their professional lives that the line blurred into the personal. Having a family was never a priority, not the time for it, or the inclination for it. There was too much music, so serious about the music. But now that Yuri was gone; Yuri, a more passionate soul than Lana, she believed; now there was no legacy of Yuri. Lana felt just a little sad at that.

It was a shock to suddenly be alone again. It took tremendous courage for Lana to change her path. It would have been easier to stick with her peers and friends and see through the grieving process with those friends she regarded as family. But once she had made the decision to return to New Zealand and do something useful, as she termed it, there was no turning back. She found a university, an undergraduate degree course in science and a house, in that order.

And then there was Alex. She'd met him by simply walking into his accounting office. She needed advice in light of recent inheritances and financial upheavals and he was there to give it. It was eighteen months before they slept together. He had three grown children and an ex-wife who he had no contact with and a pleasant house in a pleasant suburb. All very comfortable. They shared each other's bedrooms when it suited, which was usually three times per week. There was an unspoken agreement that they were a couple. Yes, it was very comfortable and for the time being, satisfactory.

Lana visualised the map she had seen of the inner city. She didn't really mind if today's run was longer than normal. In fact she preferred it. It gave her time to think about last night.

She wondered what had gone through Paul's mind when he looked at her and saw tiny lines at the corners of her eyes. Of course she had noticed them on his face but it was different for blokes. It gave him a rugged and authoritative look – something she had no wish for her own lines to convey. And of course his stubble disguised any feathering on his face.

She raised a hand to her cheek and with her fingertips gently dragged at the skin below her eyes, fleshing away any signs of aging. Did he search for the sixteen year old girl he had loved? Did he wonder where she was and what she had become? He had appeared at ease, infuriatingly so, and she scolded herself as she remembered her blush and stutter.

Her tempo remained steady as she strode along the Saebraut. The sea breeze was fresh and there were small whitecaps on the green waves. Her dark hair blew back from her face and she lifted her head slightly to feel the wind on her damp hot face. Her face. *After all these years, he sees me long passed my prime. You're not that pretty so you'll have to be clever. I don't want to remember that. I haven't had those thoughts for decades.*

How dare he remind me?

It was absurd to care what Paul thought of her anyway. She simply did not have the time physically or spiritually to rekindle her lost love. Not that Paul had given any indication of the desire to do so. But if she was entirely honest it would be too easy to weaken to his charms if he did intend to charm her. As Lana approached the hotel she resolved not to take Paul up on his offer.

Chapter Two

Lana shrugged off her raincoat and hung it dripping behind the door of her tiny office. One of the benefits of being a post-graduate was the private space that was allotted to her by the university. She didn't mind that it was only as big as two telephone boxes. She had personalised the space with photographs of New Zealand birds and alpine flora and the musical score of her favourite Minuet and Badinerie by Bach. She conceded that it could have been a little more personal. That is, a photo of Yuri maybe. A colleague could walk into Lana's office and not learn a thing about her by reading the walls.

Julie popped her head around the door. 'Hey there,' she said. 'Welcome back. How was the frozen north?'

'Hi Julie,' Lana replied. 'It was beautiful.'

'Learn anything?'

'Of course,' Lana laughed. 'I learnt it's all about networking. And amazingly, I had a reunion with an old high school flame. Have you heard of Dr Paul Harrington, volcanologist?'

'Name rings a bell.'

'He's working out of Auckland and studying the lahar path,' Lana explained. 'He gave the keynote address.'

'How exciting for you,' said Julie, fishing. 'Isn't it?'

'No, not exciting, interesting,' Lana corrected her.

'Whatever you say.'

Lana frowned and pursed her lips at Julie's inference.

'What have I missed here? The mountain still on status one?' she asked.

New Zealand's mountains were rated on an activity

level from one to five with five being eruptive. Mount Ruapehu and White Island were on a level one alert and had been for years. It meant there was a little seismic activity but nothing to be alarmed about.

'Yeah, everything's normal,' Julie replied. 'We've had heaps of rain in the last couple of weeks. It should be filling up the Crater Lake nicely. When are you planning to go up?'

'The end of September. The snowmelt will have started by then and the track in should be clear of snow. In the meantime I've got my thesis to work on and then a short report for the Natural History Society, plus the presentation of that report. So that will keep me out of trouble for the rest of the winter.'

'I want Emma to accompany you.' Lana pulled a face. 'Don't be like that Lana. She can help you more than you'll help her. Think of it as having your own personal assistant and not the other way around. You know the area. She doesn't.'

'I know,' Lana sighed. 'It's fine. And you're right. She's very knowledgeable on dating techniques.'

'Knowledgeable but maybe not successful,' Julie quipped. 'Thirty four and still unmarried.' Julie laughed as she turned to leave. 'I'll let you get on with it then. Good to see you back.'

Lana unpacked her workbag and switched on her computer. She pulled out her lunchbox. Alex had made her favourite egg sandwiches. She smiled and put the box on a shelf. Alex looked after her well on the nights they spent together and a packed lunch was one of his rituals. She knew he'd have the same lunch and at twelve on the dot he'd ceremoniously place his pen on the papers he was working on, like a tribute to having made it through the morning, and leave the office for lunch. She, on the other hand, would often find her lunch box unopened at two in the afternoon, having been preoccupied in something interesting. Left to her own devices lunch would be a boiled egg and a dry bun.

She stooped as she logged into her mailbox and typed in her password; flute1. Then she left the room and padded along the sterile corridor to the small tearoom that constituted the lunchroom for the entire Natural Resources Institute.

'Hi Lana.' Emma poured a coffee and stepped back from the sink bench.

'Good morning. Settling in? Julie showed you around?' She didn't wait for Emma to reply. 'You're going to accompany me on the next field trip I hear. It will be at the end of September. Does that suit you?'

'I'll have to check my diary. What are we looking at? Two? Three days?'

Lana poured her coffee and took a sip. 'Yep, something like that.'

'Have you heard from your Dr Harrington?' Lana noticed goading in Emma's tone.

'No.'

'Hmf!'

'What does that mean?

'You will. He seemed smitten with you.'

'He is not smitten with me.'

'Well he sure acted single around you. You sure he's not married?'

'It's not our business,' Lana retorted.

'Then I shall make it my business. If you don't want

37

him, I'll have him.' Emma tossed her head and strode out of the tea room.

Lana took her coffee back to her office and settled in front of her computer.

Of all the mail coming in, and there was a lot today, there was only one new person. She double clicked.

Dear Lana
It was good to meet you last week. I hope you had an enjoyable time. I am happy to assist you in your research. Do you still plan to go up the mountain at the end of September?
Paul

Lana sat back in her chair and put her hands behind her head pulling her damp hair back as she did so. She stared at the screen and tried to read between the lines. It sure didn't say much. Or maybe it did; it just didn't give anything away. Exactly like he didn't give anything away at dinner. She analysed the message.

It was good to meet you. Good. Noncommittal. Implied that the experience was not bad or disagreeable. Unambiguous.

I hope you had an enjoyable time. In his company? Did she enjoy meeting him? *I hope* conveyed a modicum of concern for the other person. He cared that she had an enjoyable time in his company.

I am happy to assist you in your research. I am happy to. Non-assertive. The ball's in your court. I want to come into your life, but only if you would like that.

Assist you in your research. I know more than you. You would be wise to accept my offer of help. Your

38

research is important and you will require assistance. *Do you still plan to go up the mountain at the end of September?* Where will you be in September? I have made myself free at that time.

Paul. A statement. Cool and not too friendly. Not friendly at all. Lacks feeling. Scared to show any emotion. Playing it cool.

Lana considered her options. She could reply in the affirmative and that could be done in two ways; in a professional non-committal way as per Paul's email, or in Lana's naturally buoyant verbose way. The second was to reply in the negative. And that could also be done in either of the two methods. She simply did not know what to reply so she sat on it.

During the next week Lana became immersed in her thesis and tutoring obligations. She still did not know what to do about Paul's email. She had deliberated and agonised over a reply and got nowhere. So she delayed saying she would get back to him when she had firm plans. What was there to gain? Academic help, sure. But she could get that anywhere. A reunion was highly likely to get emotionally confusing. He had a family. He said he'd come home for family reasons. She would not be the scarlet woman. Life had settled down for her after the upheaval of Yuri's death. And there was Alex now. But there was no denying that dinner with Paul in Iceland had been emotionally unsettling. She wished she was a stronger person. Another email came in. As soon as she saw his name in the inbox Lana jolted and the familiar redness crept up her throat and butterflies hit her stomach like the monarch migration. Paul had changed tack.

Dear Lana,
You must be very busy. I am keen to do a few surveys of the lahar path within the next couple of months. I wonder if you would assist me with this work? Perhaps it could coincide with your own mission to the mountain? Please respond. I need to organise another helper if you are unable to assist.
Regards, Paul.

There appeared to be more lines to read between.

You must be very busy. I'm sorry you have not replied to me, which ordinarily would be considered rude but I am gracious in giving you an excuse as to why you have not replied.

I am keen to do a few surveys of the lahar path within the next couple of months. I am also very busy and this is proof.

Would you assist me with this work? Let me see you in this professional capacity.

Perhaps it would coincide with your own mission to the mountain? You have work to do and we could help each other. I will fit my schedule around yours.

Please respond. Reprimand. Point taken and guilt assumed.

I need to organise another helper if you are unable to assist. Although I just told you off I softened it by qualifying it with a reason.

Regards. I'm trying to be more cordial and friendly than my first email.

She would tell him immediately that she now has firm dates and she was very sorry not to have replied earlier.

She sat back in her chair with her hands behind her head and read her reply email over and over and over. It was crucial to have a clear meaning for each and every sentence. She did not want anything misconstrued. She would wait until the end of the day to send it in case she needed to change it. Its meaning would leave Paul with the impression that she was not too eager. She put the email into drafts.

***

A nasal voice came over the intercom announcing the museum's closure in fifteen minutes. A thick-set muscular man scrutinised the room. Two exits, both without doors. A Sherman Firefly tank occupied two thirds of the room. To one side two mannequins dressed in army fatigues posed for an enemy encounter holding Lee Enfields at the ready. The balance of the room displayed photos depicting battles where the tank had been used. A tattered New Zealand flag hung on one wall.

The man was alone. He stepped over the thick red security rope, slipped onto his stomach and rolled under the tank pushing a small knapsack ahead of him. He waited a second, held his breath and listened. Nothing. He scrambled to the far side of the tank, quickly scaled it and shimmied down the hatch into a cavernous void. It was dark and the air was stale. His heartbeat echoed in his eardrums.

One floor above him a second man surveyed a large open space divided only by free-standing exhibits. From his position in the centre of the room he could see all

41

three exits. He knew one door led to a stairwell. He'd come in this way. The room was dark but the displays were well lit so one could focus on each exhibit without the distraction of those alongside it. To one side of the room was a diorama depicting the thick jungle of Malaysia with an open jeep, trees, a mannequin soldier struggling through the undergrowth and camouflage netting. The whole space was only about twelve square metres.

A family of four stood in front of the exhibit. It was the man's first choice. He checked his watch, all the while listening for the footsteps of security staff. Four fifty pm, no footsteps. He could not afford to wait for the family to move. It was time to employ the contingency plan. He casually made his way to the far side of the room skirting past the plinth with a bust of General Freyberg and past the glass case which housed gas masks, to a small alcove with a display depicting a field hospital circa World War II.

Its feature was a female mannequin dressed in the blindingly white uniform of the day, starched and pressed as though its owner had never tended to wounded men with missing limbs and didn't intend to. There was supposed to be a sheet over a small operating table. Joe said it would hang to the floor so he could hide under it.

The man checked his watch. Four fifty three pm. There was no contingency for a failure at the nurses' station. No time to go back to the Malaysia diorama, family or not. He thought he could hear security in the distance. His stomach churned. He had to make a decision quickly. He looked around for another exhibit with a vehicle he could hide under. The beauty of the open jeep in the Malaysia exhibit was the depth of foliage around it. He would not have had to cling on at all. He could have just lain there camouflaged by plastic leaves. But there was nowhere else to hide.

In front of him was an assemblage of flags and banners occupying free space hung in a semi circle arrangement. He dashed to one end, pulled down a flag and leapt back into the nurses' alcove. He laid the flag upside down over the table. The missing flag barely left a gap so if a guard noticed anything it would be when he looked into the tiny nurses' station. And given that it was not a major feature on this floor there was a good chance the guard wouldn't even check in there. He positioned himself under the table where he had a good view of the plastic nurse's legs and the carpet approximately three metres in front of him.

At four forty five pm in the red room the man made a study of a lean green 1940 BSA M20 motorbike. Mass produced and extensively used by allied forces in World War II it had a 469cc single cylinder valve four stroke and a three gallon fuel capacity. It was being ridden by a plastic mannequin in battle fatigues. The man waited until an elderly couple left the room and he quickly moved to the wall behind him. There was a tunnel along the length of the wall with one end open near an exit door and the other end open near the other door. He slipped down onto the floor into a push-up position and lifted his feet up inside the tunnel then inched his hands backwards along the floor. He slid his long slender body all the way into the tunnel. And waited.

At five o'clock a hooter sounded echoing a hollow

resonance throughout the buildings two floors. The display lighting switched to a glaring white light. Security officers walked sure-footed and slowly throughout the building glancing to their left and right. The man under the operating table in the nurses' alcove heard the guards enter the bathrooms and come out again. One security officer entered the large room. He took a leisurely stroll around the perimeter of the room. From under the table the man saw two shiny black shoes pause about two metres away from him. The shoes did not turn to face him. The man started sweating. He was sure his beating heart would give him away. The shoes moved away. The man exhaled a silent sigh of relief.

The three fugitives heard the guards leave the building and exchange pleasantries with the cleaning crew as they came in. For the next two hours the museum would echo to the high pitched hum of vacuum cleaners.

Joe sat inside the Firefly in the near dark. A shaft of cold white light beamed down from the entry hole at the top of the tank. There was plenty of room inside for him to spend two hours having a big enough cavity for five gunners. The armoured walls were eighty five millimetres thick and Joe was beginning to feel the cold of the walls seep into him. The tank had a top speed of forty seven kilometres per hour and weighed over thirty two tons. Joe would have liked to have been a gunner. This was the sort of tank he had plastic models of when he was a kid. But they were used in the type of war that by the time Joe had signed up would never be fought again. Shame thought Joe. Driving tanks like this was the reason young lads joined the army in the first place.

He had entered the army as an officer and they had sent him to university where he stood out, obliged to wear his military uniform and his beret at a just so angle. It was at university that he developed a feel for the collectables market and it took him all of five minutes to realise his special interest lay in military collectables. And right now the market was hot. Everyone around him talked of real estate but that required equity and long term commitment. He was young. He had no equity and wanted fast, high returns. This exercise, planned with military precision, was low on outlay, and short term with high gain. Tonight's work will only take about nine hours. But that wasn't all.

Joe had chosen his accomplices carefully. Tom was in the military before Joe had joined and he had ensured that their paths crossed. He was a medic, already having served in three peace keeping tours by the time Joe first set foot on base. Joe still marvelled at how he managed to get Tom on board. He positioned himself under the narrow shaft of light and sent a text message to Tom.

Tom's phone vibrated silently in his pocket. It was a tight fit inside the tunnel but he was the slimmest of the three men so he didn't object when Joe allocated it to him. The cleaners were still in the room so he left the phone buzzing against his hip. He couldn't answer the phone without a major repositioning and right now that was not an option. His arms began to stiffen, stretched uncomfortably in front of him. He waited.

He had experienced adrenalin rush situations before. That was what the army promised – not an ordinary career. As a medic he could perform complex tasks under extreme pressure and stay focused on the job at hand. Maybe Joe had seen that in Tom. Joe appeared to look to Tom for guidance but if that were true why did he fail to talk Joe out of this mad-capped scheme? And worse, how had he ended up actually helping him? Joe had a knack of making Tom feel special. He could be charming in a way that made Tom eager to please him. The adrenalin peaked as he slipped into his hiding place but spiked again when the phone had buzzed in his pocket.

Presently the room was clear. He nudged forward in the tunnel to free his arms then reached back to his trousers and grasped the phone. He fumbled and it dropped, landing in the tunnel and thudding on the plaster of Paris. Tiny beads of sweat peppered his forehead. Retrieving the phone, he shimmied back inside the tunnel and with shaking hands read the message. Joe had heard from Ant who was in the nurses' station and not happy.

Ant sat on the floor beneath the stainless steel operating table, a Republic of South Africa flag draped over the table shielding him from view. *Of all the people to need a plan C it had to be me he thought.*

Ant's nickname used to be Amp. His first trade had been an electrician and he had done a lot of work for government departments in rural conservation areas. There he realised a love for alpine flora and fauna and he spent all his spare time in the mountains. Eventually he managed a career change and worked in biodiversity for the conservation department. Unfortunately the income was no match for private contracting and he soon found himself up to his balls in debt. He met Joe through a colleague who had a short tempestuous relationship with

Joe. Ant played an unwilling sounding board to Christine's ranting of Joe's faults and Joe and Ant had a good laugh at her expense. Their friendship consolidated and they spent time together in the wilderness every so often. This scheme seemed like a good idea at the time.

He was but one cog in the wheel, he knew that. But he felt with his specialist knowledge in electrics he should be looked after by Joe. Without him they would all be stuck here until morning when they could walk out as easily as they had walked in without any valuable booty at all. A wasted risk that would be. He felt vulnerable under the flag. It took a few minutes for the trembling to stop. The cleaners were bound to notice the flag had been moved. He considered his options. He could stay put. For: it had proved an effective hide from security; he had leg room and was reasonably comfortable. Against: the flag was his doing. It should not be missing from the display and it should not be draped over the table. The cleaners should vacuum right up to the table and the plastic nurse if they were diligent workers. Discovery was assured.

Joe had said there were two cleaners and that they took a floor each. Correct so far. Ant analysed the feasibility of scuttling across the room to the Malaysia exhibit without coming to the attention of the cleaner. She was matronly and the vacuum cleaner was slung to her back. His steps would be covered by the high pitched scream of the machine. She had her head down concentrating on pushing and pulling the head over the floor. He reckoned he could easily hide amongst the exhibits and get himself across the room to the jeep. Seemed like a no-brainer to Ant.

He sent a message to Joe informing him of his situation. He slipped quietly out from underneath the operating table on his hands and knees. He lifted his head to find his face buried in the skirt of the plastic nurse's uniform. His heart leapt and he fumbled to straighten her dress back over her knees. He flattened himself against the wall of the alcove aware of the clamminess in his palms.

The cleaner had her back to him. It was now or never. He crept from one exhibit to another, paused, checked that she still had her back to him and dashed to another display. He got across the room to the relative safety of the exhibit in less than five minutes. He hopped over the safety barrier, dropped to the floor and rolled beneath the jeep. His heart was beating so loudly it threatened to drown out the vacuum cleaner and he needed a piss. But all in all, it was a good result.

He let himself relax safe in the knowledge that he was completely hidden from view. He looked at his watch. He had plenty of time yet. No need to add to the risk. When the cleaner disappeared from views Ant made a move to the stairwell. He could hear the second vacuum cleaning screaming its shrill on the floor below. It sounded as if it was at the other end of the building. He ran in the opposite direction to the switch room, sneaked open the door and slipped inside. A bank of switches faced him. All he had to do now was wait for Bing to tell him when the cleaners left the building, leaving the alarm in exit delay.

Bing crouched in the tall straw coloured tussock at the rear of the building. He had a good view of the main entrance. This was the entry the cleaners had used. Two had entered the museum the same time as the security and other staff left just after five o'clock. He texted the information to Joe.

He snuggled into his thick jacket against the changeable spring weather. He figured he would be out here for the full two hours it would take the cleaners to do their job and leave. So he settled in with his flask of coffee and prepared for a long wait.

At six fifty eight pm having observed the cleaners leave the building, Bing sent a text to the men giving them the all clear. Then he slung his backpack onto his shoulders and started the twenty minute walk home.

Joe and Tom crawled out of their hiding places. The main lights were out now and thin beams of light focussed on all the pedestrian areas. It was not lost on Tom that as boss of this undercover operation Joe had the most comfortable hiding place. They regrouped as agreed at the switch room on the ground floor adjacent to the stairwell.

'So far so good,' said Tom wiping trembling hands on the side of his trousers.

'Well done Tom.' Joe rubbed a hand on the small of Tom's back.

'All right Ant?' asked Joe opening the switch room door.

'I had to improvise. You said there was a sheet over the table,' Ant complained. 'I pulled a flag down off the display and used that'.

'Yeah yeah, okay. Calm down. We haven't done enough for a debrief. How's the nerves?'

'Not bad,' Ant replied. He had set his tools out in front of him. The switch room had banks of electrical circuit boards mounted along one wall and a series of monitors sat on a bench.

'Hey look, we might see ourselves on TV,' said Tom.

'Are you serious?' asked Joe. 'Of course we're on TV but no-one's going to see us because we're taking the tapes.'

'Ant, how long?' asked Joe.

'If you two could just shut up for a bit and let me look at this system. Okay, it's no rush job. We get one chance right? So don't touch anything unless I say so. Maybe one hour, maybe two.'

'God, what am I going to do for two hours?' Tom sulked and slung his tall frame against the door jamb.

'Ah Tom, stop your moaning. Sit here quietly. Don't touch any display. We don't know what might be alarmed.'

'I've got an electronic device here that I can use to divert the alarm circuit,' Ant explained. 'Tricks the original circuit so it doesn't know it's been diverted.'

'Diverted to where?' asked Joe.

'It picks up a frequency where there is already a security system operating. In this case it's most probably the bank in the village. Or it could be the petrol station. It will pick up the strongest signal.'

'Can you just walk into a shop and buy these things?' asked Tom.

'Hardly!' Ant answered smiling and tapping the side of his nose with his index finger.

'How do you know it works?' Tom persisted.

'Tom, for God sake will you just let the man get on with his work?' said Joe.

'Just checking. So the museum's security system

becomes redundant right?'

'Right.'

'And we can walk anywhere and touch anything?'

'That's the plan.'

'Good,' said Joe. 'Ant, you get on with it. Tom, you and me sit here and let the man do his work in peace.' He roughly shoved Tom to the floor and sat with him, their backs against the wall.

It was quiet now and the air conditioning hummed gently. The outside lighting fired narrow beams into the windows and onto the carpeted floor.

Ant worked whilst Joe and Tom imitated patience. Every so often they got up and paced the corridor, wiped their sweaty palms and checking their phones for a message from Bing. Ant seemed to take forever.

'All done,' Ant finally announced.

'Fantastic. Good job mate,' said Joe. 'Is there any way to test it?'

'We'll know if it worked the minute we touch the first medal,' Ant grinned.

'Get those CCTV tapes Tom,' Joe directed. 'And look after them. We have to destroy them properly. And put your gloves on before you touch anything.'

Joe led them to the first floor. To one end was the medal display area. Most of the medals were attached to the wall with a security pin. Difficult for Joe public to snatch in a room full of people in broad daylight but easy picking for a night time heist with the added bonus of no security alarm.

Several display cabinets sat in the centre of the space. Medals were displayed with small explanatory labels alongside. Joe made straight for them.

'Look at you my lovelies,' he crooned. 'Screwdriver Ant.' He held his hand out.

Tom froze. This one move would tell them whether Ant had been successful. He gulped down his nausea. 'Why don't we smash it?'

'Number one; it will take a while to discover the theft this way and number two because when they discover they've been had it will buy us time while they try to work out what's missing.'

Joe paused and grimaced at the two men. 'Fingers crossed boys.' He slotted the screwdriver into a flathead screw at the top edge of the case. They held their breath, listened, and waited. Nothing. They exhaled in unison and smiled.

'Ant,' said Tom. 'Is there any chance the alarm really is working and it's going off at the police station? Just that we can't hear it?'

'No chance,' Ant replied with confidence.

'Which ones do we want Joe?' asked Ant.

'Pick carefully boys,' replied Joe. 'I don't want the rarest. Too hard to get rid of. New Zealand medals only. Our market is international. And don't make it obvious. Don't leave a gap. Take the information card with it and spread the other medals over the space.'

Joe picked up one medal. It was the Queen's South Africa Medal issued by Queen Victoria to recognise service in the Boer War. A silver disk with an effigy of a veiled Queen Victoria hung from a brown, black and orange striped ribbon.

'Here's a lovely,' murmured Joe. 'Over six thousand issued, but see this clasp over the ribbon?'

'What of it?' asked Ant.

'Nearly all different,' explained Joe. 'Depends who used to own it as to how important they thought the clasps were.'

'What does the card say?' asked Tom.

Joe picked it up and read the old script. 'It was a nurse, Gladys Hopkin.'

'You can't take a nurse's medal Joe,' said Tom incredulously.

'Tom, you can't take anyone's medal,' Joe pointed out. 'Gladys' little medal is going on a little adventure. Possibly back to South Africa.' He pocketed the silver treasure.

Joe held up another medal. A 1914-1915 Star, a bronze star with crossed swords, a wreath over the top and a crown above suspended by a water marked red, white and blue striped ribbon.

'This is a popular one,' Joe explained. 'Over two million issued but very collectable now.'

'What does the card say?' Tom said again.

'It was awarded to Major Donald Foote for the Gallipoli Campaign.'

Tom screwed the top of the cabinet back in place while Ant started unscrewing the next one.

'Ah, you little beauty,' Joe beamed. 'The New Zealand medal. My personal favourite.'

'Why?' asked Tom. 'What makes that one so special?'

'It dates to the New Zealand wars. First struck in 1869 and this one was awarded to colonial volunteers as well as enlisted men in the British forces.'

He held it up by its navy and orange striped ribbon. It flashed a glint of silver in the pale light. On the front was an image of Queen Victoria and on the reverse a wreath of fern fronds.

'How about this one?' Ant held up a small silver disk with the head of King George VI suspended by twin fern fronds and a black ribbon edged in white.

'The New Zealand War Service Medal,' Joe explained. 'Got market potential. A World War II issue. This is the medal you could get for serving in the Home Guard.'

'True?' Tom came over. 'Let's see.'

He turned the medal over in his hands and read the inscription aloud.

'For service to New Zealand 1939-1945. Brings it home doesn't it? This doesn't seem such a good idea now. These belonged to real people. I mean, Home Guard. It could have belonged to anybody's granddad, couldn't it?'

Ant chipped in. 'Yeah, my grandfather had stories about them. Dad's army guys training after a hard day at the office and then getting drunk on blackberry nip after a march to the reservoir and back.'

'Come on guys, stay focussed,' Joe admonished. 'And Tom, you should have thought a little harder before you came in on this. You're in it now, right up to your neck. Don't you pussy out on me. You two put these cabinets back together while I check out these walls.'

He felt inside his jacket pocket and transferred the booty into a sock. He carefully chose some more pieces, put them into his sock and zipped the pocket. Then he shuffled the stock around so there were no gaps.

Joe sent a message to Bing.

'All right guys, we're done,' he announced. 'Bing

should be waiting by the time we get downstairs.'

Bing startled at the signal. He had spent the time packing, repacking and pacing. He snapped his phone open and read it.

He ran out the door trailing his pack with him. There was barely a moon and lots of stars. He stealed the white double cab Toyota along the dirt track off the main road and kept his lights off. The men exited the rear of the building and jumped in.

Chapter Three

Paul pulled a flathead screwdriver out of his backpack and unscrewed the lid off the plywood box. Holding it to the light he scrutinised the scrawling paper of the seismograph. They were high on the mountain at Dome Shelter where they had a brief reprieve from the bracing air. A shelter was all it could be called, no more, no less; a small hut bare of any adornments for use by those unlucky enough to be caught out by a change in the weather. The seismograph box was kept hidden beneath the floorboards. Data was sent to several agencies off the mountain for analysis. It was that data that scientists relied on in assessing the alert status of the mountain.

'Slightly abnormal,' Paul said settling into a squat position. 'A bit more activity than last month. See?' He showed Lana the peaks and troughs on the paper roll, pointing out a cluster of higher peaks. She edged into him bending to look. She sensed his warm breath.

'Why abnormal?' asked Lana.

'See this cluster here?' Tells me there's something going on beneath our feet.' He bowed his head for a closer look. 'Definitely an earthquake swarm.'

'Which indicates magmatic activity that may or may not result in eruptive activity?' Lana pre-empted him.

Paul grinned up at her. 'Well done Ms Marshall. The masters have taught you well.'

He started to secure the back lid on Lana put a hand out to stop him. 'Aren't you going to show Emma?'

He continued to place the box back into its hiding place. 'She's not here. So, no.'

Lana shrugged.

'You were told to baby-sit her weren't you?' he asked.

'No, of course not. But she should see this. I just thought...'

'Well don't think. If she'd rather be photographing fungus that's her lookout. Come on. I'll show you where the other box is,' said Paul.

Lana plunged her hands back inside her woollen mittens and pulled the hood of her red jacket hard down on her head.

'How many boxes are up here?' asked Lana.

'Used to be just the two,' Paul explained, 'but there's quite a bit going on under here at the moment so Bain installed another one on the other side of that ridge we walked along. Haven't checked it out yet. What I need to do is correlate increased seismic activity to any chemical changes we find in the Crater Lake.'

'But aren't you working on the lahar path? Do you normally check these?'

'The guys from conservation do,' replied Paul as he scrambled up from a crouching position. 'They are theirs after all.'

'Then what are we doing checking them?' Lana challenged him.

Paul gave Lana a wry look. 'I like to keep abreast of developments. Come on.'

She followed him outside ducking her head and pulling the stiff door shut behind her. A breeze was pushing fast moving high cloud around the snowy mountain top. The clouds didn't look to be holding too much water and the sky around them was a thin clear blue. The forecast was favourable for the next few days.

They were based on the leeward side of the mountain for the most part of their field work and rain on the top and west side did not always fall on this east side. The lack of rain here gave the area its desert namesake. The diversion to the southeast upper slopes had exposed them to a chill that Lana was looking forward to getting out of. Her cheeks were ruddy and she could feel the cold biting on her lips making it difficult to talk. She saw Paul walk away and she let her mind flood with summer images. The snow was parched forest, the wind became a hot billowy northerly. Paul became Yuri. They'd spent three days in the Australian tablelands on an insect gathering expedition. They had argued – over nothing she recalled. Yuri had marched off ahead of her while she stewed and considered whether to catch him up or to stand her ground and force him to retrace his steps to her.

Paul marched on ahead of Lana. There was plenty of snow at this high altitude, more snow than bare ground. The spring thaw had barely started but in sheltered sunny spots beneath the ice clear trickles of snowmelt escaped a winter prison, meandering around solid rock, sometimes picking up other trickles and sometimes disappearing underground.

Yesterday when they arrived on the mountain they had dumped their packs in the hut and gone back to a long snow-covered slope carrying vivid yellow pack liners. Lana had never tobogganed down a snow slope before. She chose a short run with a gentle gradient then sat on the plastic pulling it up between her legs. She bumped down the slope squealing at the feel of hard snow sliding beneath her buttocks. Naturally Paul had started at the top of the longest slope. And so had Emma.

She seemed born to it. Must get lots of practice in those long dark Canadian winters, Lana thought. But they had all laughed and screamed and hollered. It broke the day's tension.

***

Lana had been quiet for much of the walk from the carpark to the hut. Emma had ensured that they knew just about all there was to learn about Emma by the time they reached the hut. Lana didn't mind. She listened to them both, their easy banter revealing their personalities. It seemed Emma had a way of drawing people out of themselves.

Lana had delighted in the flora and the landscape as they trekked across the Round the Mountain Track. It was too early for all the tiny white alpine flowers to come out but Lana delighted in the vegetable sheep, a white cushion-like plant that survives snow, frost and hot baking sun. Some large hardy plants looked like cast sheep and would be many decades old. New sheep were mere dots of white each the size of a warbler's eye clumped together on flat barren ground struggling to eke out an existence. Neither Lana nor Paul stood on any foliage but Emma had been told twice to watch where she was walking. She took the reprimand from Paul well. Too well, thought Lana.

Yesterday, as they reached the lahar path an hour into their walk Paul had become animated. He showed them where they would begin their surveys today. Historical lahars down this path had scourged vegetation and for the most part the lahar path was devoid of life. But every now and again a tiny grass had taken hold against a soil-filled crevasse on the warm side of a pebble. That would be enough for a seed to germinate and for the struggle for life to begin.

Today they had been up since first light and retraced their steps to the lahar path where they took photographs and notes. After a few hours they decided to take a break and wander around the tops. Emma had stayed on the lower mountain photographing lava flows.

'Paul,' Lana called from behind him. 'Wait up.'

Paul paused, turned and looked at her. He was well wrapped up against the cold and the barest shadow of stubble threatened to interrupt his carefully groomed goatee and moustache.

'Are you still married?' Lana cried into the wind. Perhaps it was the weather that had prompted her sudden broach of the subject. Or it could have been the flashback of her beloved Yuri that struck a chord of loneliness deep within her, or maybe the wind had stirred her into it. If she did not get the answer she wanted then maybe the wind would swallow her words and she could pretend she had never asked.

Paul grinned widely. 'Is that what's been eating you up? What took you so long to ask?'

She caught him up. 'I've been waiting for you to tell me,' Lana snapped back. 'It's only polite.'

'I was under the impression you wanted a strictly professional relationship,' said Paul with the barest hint of question implied.

'Of course. I do. That is, I mean,' Lana stuttered.

'You mean you do but you don't,' Paul finished for her. 'Lana it's okay. We're old news. I want to know you. I want to know all about you but you've been a closed book.' He went to place a hand on her arm but she bristled and shrugged him away.

'I'm a closed book?' she asked, raising her voice an octave. 'At least I told you I've got a boyfriend.'

'Yeah, but you told me that like you were reading a shopping list.' Paul countered. 'You're not serious with him.'

'I am too,' Lana was indignant. 'You don't know me Paul.'

'I want to know you Lana,' he replied. 'I used to know you. Now I don't know you. I want to get to know you again Lana, please let me.'

She stood bolt upright with her hands at her sides, hands clenched into fists. She shrugged her pack higher onto her shoulders, drew her mouth into a tight line and exhaled quickly through her nose. The cold air stung her face.

'It's you who hasn't told me anything Paul. We've spent twenty four hours together and I know less about you now than I've ever known.'

'Well you did bring a friend,' he retorted.

'She's not my friend.'

'You're not jealous then?'

'Don't be stupid.' Was that a smirk beginning to appear? Was he teasing or? Or setting the groundwork for a move on Emma? 'Of course not.' She gulped down last night's memory. Emma had all but thrown herself at Paul and he had been delightfully flattered and encouraging. But who wouldn't be? She was gorgeous with her bouncy blonde hair and sultry hazel eyes. And to top it off she was intelligent! What a combination to have. 'I'm sorry,' she said. 'I have to go.'

Paul flapped his hands in the air. 'Go where?'

'Up to my glacier. You go check someone else's seismograph.'

'I don't want you going up there on your own Lana. That's not the right thing to do. You know that eh? Even if it wasn't snowy I couldn't let you go up on your own.'

Lana stewed. Her fingernails dug into her palms inside her mittens and she felt the familiar heat flood her face and throat. She'd opened herself up to him and now he was patronising her. Of course she knew that. Did he think she was stupid? The breeze flicked the hood off her head revealing a pink beanie. She reached up to her hood and replaced it, fumbling to tie it tightly beneath her chin. She looked back at Paul. His face softened. Gone were the furrows over his brow and the concern in his serious eyes. The corners of his mouth set in so that a small tender smile emerged and tiny lines emanated from his eyes. Lana suddenly felt five years old. He was right of course but she was not going to give in.

'Okay, here's the deal,' she announced. 'We both go check someone else's seismograph and then you survey the top part of this stupid lahar and I go up the Crater Lake and we maintain visual contact.'

'Not happy,' chimed Paul.

'Got cell phone coverage,' she chimed back switching her tack to a woman's sing song persuasive reasoning.

'Lana, I didn't mean to upset you,' said Paul as he grabbed Lana's shoulders with both hands. He stared intently at her face and saw confusion in her bright blue eyes. She felt his eyes bore deeply, as if he was trying to extract whatever was behind her eyes. Lana said nothing.

The touch of him was thrilling.

'I shouldn't have contacted you should I?' Paul said softly.

'I guess it was a natural thing,' she replied. 'You didn't know I'd be in Iceland at the conference.'

This time Paul said nothing.

'What?' Lana demanded curtly.

Paul winced, 'I knew.'

'What do you mean you knew?'

'I knew you were going to be at that conference,' Paul confessed.

'You're kidding! You knew? How could you? What the hell are you playing at? You knew?' cried Lana.

'Yeah, yeah. Look, calm down.'

She shrugged his hands off her shoulders and took a step backwards. 'I can't believe this Paul. Have you stalked me? Is this all a big set up?'

'Oh no please Lana,' Paul begged. 'You can't think that. I wouldn't do anything to hurt you. I just...' He paused.

'Just what?' she demanded. 'You thought it would be fun to trap me? A challenge for you? Couldn't you have just looked me up on the net? Sent me a note?'

'No, I couldn't; it would have been too impersonal,' he explained.

'And what?' Lana retorted. 'You're not too impersonal in real life? Please!'

'Hey wait up!' They turned to see Emma striding towards them, her hair slung into a loose pony trailing below her beanie. Sunglasses hid most of her face and a scarf nestled into her neck and chin. A very serious looking camera hung from her neck.

Lana ignored the interruption. 'My deal has changed. I'm going to Crater Lake now. Alone.' She turned from them and stormed off up the slope.

***

Lana felt the low grumble beneath her feet as a thunderous roar sounded to the north of them. She froze, dug her boots into the snow and looked up expecting to see thick grey clouds. But there weren't any, only the flighty streamlined ones that had been with them all day. A rumble, deep like thunder, had a gravelly abrasion to it. She turned around to face Paul and Emma.

'The lahar Lana,' Paul shouted already scurrying up the slope to her. 'The Lake's burst.'

He grabbed her arm and pulled her with him towards the sound.

'Hurry you two,' Emma cried out already retracing her steps.

'We're running back to it?' Lana yelled.

'Of course,' Paul replied.

She didn't resist Paul's touch and she allowed herself to be swept downhill with him.

'Do you realise how lucky we are?' she asked. 'We could have still been working in its path.'

'Yeah,' Paul agreed, 'we should be able to get some great photos if we hurry.'

'I mean we could have been killed.'

'But we weren't,' he stated. 'Come on.' He strode ahead down the snowy slope. Emma was well ahead of them now.

Lana shook her head in astonishment and muttered

loudly to herself. 'Oh well, goodbye Lana's glacier, hello Paul's photos.'

'Make a track straight down here,' said Paul as he dug his boots into the slushy snow. 'Down to the track, okay? Careful of the rocks. Put your boots into my footprints. It's not as slippery as you think.'

Paul picked his way down the slope. Lana followed cautiously placing her boots into his footsteps.

'I'm sorry I'm a bit slow. I'm not used to snow. Bizarre given my research topic, I know,' she called after him.

'Save your breath Lana,' Paul answered without even pausing for her. 'You're doing fine.'

As she descended the slope the air warmed and she could hear the gritty boom of the lahar punctuated with the knocking of boulders. Her heart raced. Paul was getting a long way ahead of her and she stopped.

'Paul,' she yelled.

He stopped and waited for her to catch up.

'Can you take smaller steps?'

'Sorry. Nearly there.'

She could see orange marker posts a few hundred metres below them marking the track. They only stood out against the white snow. Further down they weren't visible because so much of the ground was bare earth, a rich orange brown of the desert dotted with lichen-clad rocks.

Finally they reached the track where Lana recognised their footsteps from earlier. The going was easier now with less snow and loose rocks. She relaxed confident in the placement of her feet and they broke into a light jog. She sensed Paul's excitement. This event was what he had lived for these past two years. The lahar was predicted to occur at such time that the precarious tephra dam at the rim of Crater Lake breached. The dam was created in 1995 and 1996 as the mountain erupted and deposited loose ash on the sides of the vent. But the ash had not consolidated and was therefore susceptible to erosion or better yet as far as geologists were concerned, a full scale dam break.

The highly acidic pea green lake water had been seeping through the dam wall at a thousand cubic metres per day. But there had to be a trigger event that would cause the breach. It could have been the glacier calving, in which case waves up to a metre high would contribute to erosion of the dam, or a storm event which deposited more water than usual into the lake. It could be a magmatic injection into the hydrothermal system beneath the lake. Lana knew there had been increased seismic activity and that gas levels in the lake were up. Trouble was, a correlation of this sort did not guarantee a prediction as to cause. And more frustratingly, increased seismic activity did not mean an eruption was imminent.

'What do you think tipped the lake over the edge?' Lana called to Paul as she ran after him.

'I'd like to say a small volcanic eruption but we won't know for sure until the post analysis,' Paul replied.

'Is that the unbiased volcanologist speaking is it?' Lana smirked. 'It couldn't be my glacier calving adding thousands of cubic metres of ice to the lake could it?'

'Probably not,' Paul agreed without a hint that he'd recognised Lana's sarcasm.

'The bund hasn't been tested right? Will it hold?'

'I'm sure it will. If it doesn't then this lahar will

change the course of history of the North Island,' said Paul.

'What do you mean?' asked Lana quickening her pace to align herself with him on the slightly wider rough track.

'Remember where the source of the Waikato River is in relation to the sharp bend in the lahar path? Just below it,' Paul explained. 'And the bund's job is to ensure that lake water follows historic lahar paths down the Whangaehu River. If the whole Crater Lake emptied into the source of the Waikato River and continued to do so after that then agriculture is stuffed.'

Lana smiled in spite of herself. This vernacular was what she had missed married to Yuri. But this was typical of Paul. Eloquent, precise and descriptive on a professional level and yet total heartfelt honesty with a simple little understated word like stuffed to convey cataclysmic destruction.

As they neared the lahar the rumble of it grew louder. Lana pictured films she had seen of lahars. She knew the waters would be thick with debris, therefore more dangerous than merely a flooded river. Monstrous boulders were picked up and tossed and rolled along the river like giant's marbles and when knocked together could be bounced out of the riverbed and kept out with the force of the water. On solid ground they could smash everything in their path.

'Hear that?' Lana yelled. 'Sounds like a cement mixer.'

'I hope that early warning system worked,' Paul yelled. 'It will be all go down below.'

It had been a major exercise setting up an electronic

network that conveyed to all potentially affected parties the possibility of lahar related flooding. Automated traffic arms with bells and flashing lights on two of the state highways should be activated. As a precaution traffic could not traverse the Tangiwai Bridge which had been raised two metres in anticipation of a flood event. Rail links would be halted at the bridge.

As they climbed out of one of the many small valleys that cut down into the ring plain Lana scanned the lower mountain.

'Look, the lahar,' she exclaimed pointing to a shiny snake of a river.

The thin trail of water and mud looked calm and silent from this distance but Lana knew it was fooling her. She could hear it at source and feel it under her feet.

'And there's Emma,' shouted Paul pointing towards the hut. 'We made good time catching her. Come on.'

Rangipo Hut was three hundred metres from them and Emma was approaching it. Nestled in the rocky volcanic landscape it stood out for its straight lines. A snow-free rock outcrop threw a partial shadow over the green tin hut as the sun made its way around to the west side of the mountain. The hut in turn threw a short dull shadow out beyond the open deck and pockets of clean white snow lay in shadowed depressions in front of it.

At the sight of the hut Lana breathed a sigh of relief. It represented safety, domesticity, warmth and food. She desperately wanted to reach it and shut out the grinding sounds of danger. But there was something else in her, a force she did not recognise. She equally wanted to experience the enigmatic draw of danger. She had to see the lahar for herself, to be a part of its wild and untamed raw power. She wanted to experience what Paul felt.

As she drew closer she noticed two men on the deck. Emma emerged from the inside downing a bottle of water.

'Hey mate,' called Paul easing up as he approached the hut. 'Is your party safe? Is there anyone behind you?'

The men looked at each other. Paul noticed an uncomfortable silence as if they were thinking behind blank expressions.

'There's one more of us to come,' said the shorter one.

'The bridge is unlikely to still be there,' said Paul. 'Should your friend be here by now?'

'Yes, he should be,' replied the taller one. 'He may be stuck on the other side of the creek.'

'I'll find out,' said Paul.

Lana climbed the steps to the deck and shrugged off her pack.

'You go Paul,' she grunted, 'I'm just lightening my load. Catch you up.'

'I'm ready,' said Emma lightly tripping down the steps to Paul. 'Let's go.'

Lana noticed Emma rub her hand on Paul's sleeve. It seemed swollen with meaning. She watched them run off in the direction of the lahar before turning her attention to her new hut mates.

She scanned the deck for evidence that more trampers may have arrived since they had left early that morning. Three pairs of solid dust-strewn boots lined up neatly to one side of the door. Motley green army jackets hung in the alcove. She opened the door to the hut slinging her backpack off as she went inside. It took a few seconds for her eyes to adjust to the darkness. A man was lying on his bunk with his forearm over his eyes and no interest in greeting her.

'Hello,' said Lana.

'Uh, hi,' the man grunted.

She quickly made her way into the bunkroom she'd used last night and opened her pack, then transferred her life pack, camera and phone to her jacket pockets. She opened the door to the room Paul had used and counted packs. Aside from Paul's plus Emma's in the main room there were four packs. Seven would be here tonight she thought. As long as no-one comes in from the south. She dashed to the door of the hut.

'Have you guys noticed anyone else up here?' she asked the two men on the deck. 'Behind you or below the hut, off trail?'

'No. No we haven't,' grunted the shorter man. He was abrupt. Lana took the cue and let the subject drop.

'Are you coming to see the lahar?'

'No, we just got here,' he replied.

'It's not far though, a once in a lifetime event maybe,' Lana explained.

'Na, it's all right love,' said the shorter one.

Lana cringed. 'It would be nice to have that fire going when we get back,' she spat back as she eyed the stack of firewood on the deck.

She left them and quickly slipped into an easy jog along the route. She traversed several more narrow rocky gullies and lightly scaled the steep ravines without the impediment of extra weight on her back. She scrambled up a scree slope to the ridge and paused to scan the horizon. Paul and Emma were nowhere to be seen and the din of the fast flowing lahar was filling her ears with panic. If only she could see them. Just above the south flank of the river was a high rocky lava flow. She pulled her beanie hard down on her head and hurried for it.

Presently she skirted the lowest tongue of the lava flow and ascended the leading edge of it. She held her face up to the cool white spray that escaped the confines of the valley. An earthy silt smell invaded her nostrils and she swore she could feel it in her teeth. The power of the lahar was exhilarating. She felt strong now. It gave her its life force. Yuri settled deep within her and she spoke to him in her heart. It was a serenity she hadn't felt before now and for the first time since his death she knew she need not appeal to his spirit for guidance.

She surveyed the scene below her and saw Paul and Emma turn over a body.

***

Bain stepped out of the shower and deftly flung a towel around his waist. He was still red in the face from his ten kilometre run because he hadn't let himself cool off before jumping in the shower. As he went to clear steam from the mirror he noticed his pager silently flashing.

'Oh my God, my God.' He hopped from foot to foot slapping the water off his lean body and threading his glasses onto his head. Dripping a trail on the floor he ran to his laptop and logged on. 'Caroline,' he yelled, 'this is it.'

It was the moment he had been preparing for these past five years. So many proposals had been mooted, consulted upon, chewed up and spat out. Finally the bund got approval from conservation agencies, Maori, geologists, engineers and unbelievably archaeologists who after much digging around with teaspoons declared no evidence of anthropological habitation on this high altitude, eastern slope of a volcanically active mountain. What a revelation. For Bain it had been a major exercise in tolerance. But now his day had come. The buck would stop with him if it all went to plan, equally if it all turned pear shaped.

A petite dark haired woman in her early fifties joined him at his side.

'This is it old girl. It's breached. I have to go. Now!'

Caroline stroked Bain's nearly balding head and laughed. 'Put some clothes on first. I'll fetch your bag.'

She returned with an overnight bag that had been packed and ready for two years. Bain had forgotten what was even in it. 'I know you won't have time to ring me,' said Caroline. 'Just do your job and stay calm darling. You're going in the first helicopter aren't you?'

'Yes.'

'Have you got your pager? Your phone?'

He patted down his clothes and headed for the bathroom to retrieve his pager. When he got back Caroline was waiting for him at the front door, bag in hand. He kissed her on the lips and drove off to her pleas to stay safe.

The East Ruapehu Lahar Early Warning System comprised a network of electronic signals timed to alert agencies working off the mountain that a lahar had been triggered. In Lana's department at the Institute of Natural Resources the warning alerted her colleagues by a pager carried by her supervisor.

Julie jolted as she received the pager alert just as she popped a piece of crystallised ginger into her mouth. It was well after lunch and she had gone past the sleepy mid afternoon stage. Ginger was the short sharp shock to get her through the day. Startled by the pager she all but choked.

She hauled herself higher in her chair and edged it closer to her desk. She flicked the computer to the ERLAWS page. It was password only and she could chat to everyone else in the scheme if she so wished. All those involved would be doing exactly the same. The electricity department, rail and road transport agencies, conservation department, Geological and Nuclear Sciences and Auckland University were logging on. She immediately posted a comment that Lana and Emma were on the mountain, in the vicinity of the lahar and that they were with an Auckland geologist, Paul Harrington.

Auckland University confirmed that Paul was in the lahar vicinity as part of his mission to assess the likelihood of an imminent lahar. They had fears for his safety.

'Shit,' Julie muttered. That meant she should have fears for her students' safety. But Lana was more than a student to Julie. They'd hit it off when Lana turned up as an undergraduate and it was partly due to their friendship that Lana had embarked on post-graduate work. Lana had said that Paul was going to assist her in measuring crevasses in the glacier above Crater Lake. If that were correct and Lana had stuck to that plan then they would probably be above any danger zone. Unless there was a major flank collapse that could lead to the destruction of the glacier, or the draining of the lake that could undermine the adjacent glacier. She groaned as she ran the scenarios through her head. However, they could just as easily have been working on Paul's research when the lahar started. And if that were the case the consequences didn't bear thinking about. She felt the ginger sit in the top of her gut as she imagined having to tell Lana's family of their loss. Funny, after all these years she didn't know much about Lana's kin. And then there was Emma. She'd only been here a short time. It would look bad for the university.

Text rolled up the screen. The conservation department had dispatched a helicopter to the scene and they expected to see the scientists somewhere near the top of the lahar path. The helicopter would follow the snout of the lahar to its end at the west coast with a television news cameraman and two research scientists on board. If they did not see the trio during the first sweep they would alert search and rescue services.

The road transport authority had dispatched patrol cars at the Tangiwai Bridge at the south side of the ring plain. This was the historical path for the lahar and as such, enormous resources had gone into strengthening the roading infrastructure. Police cars were also stationed at the main trunk highway as a contingency. The one and only train to use the rail that day travelled south an hour ago.

Julie imagined the event unfolding. In her mind's eye she followed the tumultuous river down its normal path. A series of monitoring stations were installed at intervals along the route of the proposed lahar, set up by some of her students in collaboration with the conservancy scientists. These would measure the density of the water flushing down, the speed of it and the height of the flow. When the collection traps were emptied the water would be analysed to determine chemical composition. It wasn't strictly Lana's area of research but she was aware of the exercise and vaguely aware of the locations of the equipment. Julie wondered if Lana was in a position to carry out any useful analyses.

Julie sent Lana a text message knowing it would be hit and miss as to whether she received it. Mountain coverage was patchy at best. She put herself in Lana's shoes. Assuming she was safe she would be running around excitedly taking photos. She wouldn't even realise her phone was buzzing if it was buzzing at all. Then she rang home and left a message on the answering machine telling whoever cleared the messages that she might not be home tonight.

***

Fuelled by adrenalin Paul bounded up the lava ridge and surveyed the scene below him. Emma easily matched him and positioned herself alongside, barely puffing. She braced herself with her legs wide and held her camera to the scene in front of them. The noise was deafening, overpowering. A deeper rumble Paul had never heard in his life. To talk over this would be to piss against the wind. Instead he slung his backpack onto the ground and fumbled against the cold to open it. He pulled out his Olympus Tough 8010 waterproof, shockproof, snow proof and crushproof camera. He had picked up at duty free on his return from Iceland. It was all the proofs that sold him on it. But he wished he had his Minolta which was stolen a few months ago.

The lahar was behaving as expected so far as he could tell. Massive dark grey glistening boulders were being tossed around like pebbles suspended by the unusual density of the water then bouncing downstream. The fierce dirty green and white torrent carved hungrily into the gravelly banks of the stream cutting wider and wider into the sides of the valley. As the stream surrendered its banks, the river entrained the debris and added bulk and volume to the discharge. This in turn allowed the larger debris to ride further and faster downstream like on a cushion of air.

Paul took some shots. Those taken towards the mountain top looked straight into the weak sun but he could easily doctor those. Ahead and to his right the light looked good. A rugged barren outcrop obscured his view downstream but directly in front of him the channel deepened and the plunging torrent seemed to disappear into the cauldrons of hell. He flicked the function onto thirty seconds of moving film and watched the mountain disgorge through the safety of a shaky lens.

He motioned to Emma that he was ready to move then scrambled down the side of the ridge. She followed.

'Stay back,' he shouted grabbing her shoulders and trying to turn her back. She shook her head and continued to come at him. 'It's dangerous Emma. Stay on high ground.' He ran from her, avoiding the flow of the lahar and rounding the outcrop that had blocked his view. The bridge was out. Exactly what he expected to see. It had always seemed to Paul an odd location to place the bridge. It seemed to be there only to give maximum thrill to trampers for the river plunged loudly and dramatically between water worn smooth grey edifices before snaking its way down the ring plain between ancient lava flows. Paul had crossed that bridge many times and each time he stood transfixed in the centre absorbing the energy, witnessing the force and drinking in the exhilarating power of the river. It charged him anew just as it charged the ions in the air of the valley. The conservation department had taken a bet that any trampers in the vicinity of a lahar would heed the warning signs on both sides of the valley and not attempt a crossing of the bridge. It was decided to save money and replace the bridge if and when it was reduced to matchsticks.

A small patch of flat green caught Paul's eye. There was something about the green that didn't look like it belonged. He focused hard, squinting to block out his peripheral vision. He identified clothing, in fact, a whole set of clothing, still on a person. It was inert. It was male. He knew they must put themselves in danger to reach it. Emma caught him up. Paul silently pointed out what he saw. 'Come on,' he shouted.

His mind raced as he leapt over the rocky terrain towards the figure, trying to analyse what had happened to the person. The river may have caught the man, tumbled him haplessly around like a cement mixer but then dumped him ungraciously, sodden and ragged above the river. But what was he doing anywhere near the lahar path? There should have been plenty of warning not to proceed into the danger zone. Perhaps he had been on the bridge. It was a possibility.

The angry lahar pulled at the figure as though trying to reclaim what it had given up. The man was in danger of being grasped by the turgid beast and smashed to pieces if he wasn't removed quickly. If the guy had drowned there was a chance CPR could revive him but he didn't need every bone in his body broken as well.

Paul was deaf to Lana's searching screams and blind to her presence high up on the ridge above. He tightened his pack on his back and checked the lanyard around his neck on which dangled his camera then tucked it into his jacket. He looked around to see Emma photographing him. Glancing upstream he calculated his odds. One tossed boulder thrown above him could roll down and kill him. Kill them both.

He scrambled the last few metres to the figure, grabbed it by the arms and dragged the dead weight lumbering over the rock-strewn ground out of the licking edge of the lahar. Emma edged in and helped turn the man over. The arms would not turn with the man's body and there was no help from him. He lay drenched and broken. Emma tugged at the man's arms and checked for a pulse. None. Paul turned him onto his side where he noticed a wound. It was the only tear in his clothing. Emma noticed it as unusual and pushed Paul to one side before tugging the man's jacket up. There was a clean cut, like a stab; deep and not much blood. Paul frowned, unable to fathom its origin. Emma photographed it. The body was abraded around the head and limbs. He took more photos, in case an autopsy required it.

***

Julie wasn't the only one trying to raise Lana. Alex heard the news of the Crater Lake discharge on his way home from the office on the car radio. By then the lake would have discharged half its capacity. He pulled over to the side of the road and rang Lana. She hadn't answered. Frustrated, he left a voice message hoping that she'd finally worked out how to retrieve her messages. It annoyed the hell out of him that she could be so casual. She'd had the phone for over a year and she knew people had left messages because when she'd seen them later they'd ask if she got their message. He snapped his phone shut and beat both palms on the steering wheel. A text. That would have to do. At least his words would come to her when she got coverage.

She said she was going with a colleague to spend three nights on the mountain. Alex was not familiar with any part of the mountain. It never held any special appeal for him. He could not even visualise what walking to the hut meant. Lana had told him it was only a short walk and she had done it before, many times in fact. He frowned as he struggled to remember what she may have told him about the route she would take. Would she have to cross the lahar path to get to the hut? He could not recall. What did a lahar look like? Just a stream, surely – but rock laden and fast. He had not heard from her since she left. But that was not unusual. In normal circumstances he didn't expect to. But surely, in this instance she realised he would worry about her.

Commonsense told him that cell phone coverage was not guaranteed in the mountains. And granted, in this most exciting of circumstances Lana would be doing exactly what was expected of her as a scientist;

79

documenting the event. He could hardly expect her to ring him the minute something happened. He chastised himself for cursing Lana's lack of communication and after sitting at the side of the road with oceans of traffic swimming past in a mad vortex, he pushed his Mazda into the frey and drove home.

***

Lana stopped abruptly in her tracks at the top of the rocky windswept ridge. It was hard to catch her breath for each inhalation brought with it not only the chilly air but the taste of silt thrown up by the lahar. The roar in her ears consumed her. The scene far below her played out in mute stereo. She tried to make sense of it. Paul and Emma were bent over something, pounding, lifting and dipping and pounding again. The thing did not respond and they continued to pound again and again. The wind repeatedly whipped Lana's stray dark hair around her face licking at her earlobes. The screaming of the lahar stole her sense of placement at the scene. Paul's theatre was oblivious to its audience and Lana felt voyeuristic.

From her vantage Paul did not appear safe from the licking tongues of the lahar. She shook herself and leapt erratically over the volcanic landscape inadvertently crushing precious alpine vegetation as she went.

'What happened?' she yelled at the top of her voice as she approached Paul and Emma.

Paul sat back on his haunches letting Emma continue working feverishly trying to instil life into the broken form. Paul looked up at her and shook his head.

'He's stuffed,' said Paul.

Lana shouted, 'Should we pull him away? I'll help you.'

She bent down to grab the man's wet arms.

'No,' screamed Emma. She wouldn't stop.

'Come on love, he's done for.' Paul grabbed Emma's arms and pried her away.

Paul took hold of his ankles and together he and Lana dragged the body fifty metres from the lahar. It was far enough to feel safe from the teeth of the roaring serpent. Emma remained on her hands and knees, head bowed until Paul scurried back to get her.

'No pack?' Lana asked referring to the man.

'No pack,' Paul confirmed.

'Do you think it could have been pulled off by the torrent?' Lana asked.

'Not if it was done up around his waist, I wouldn't think so,' Paul replied.

'You would expect a pack given the distance we are from both the hut and the road, right?' Lana surmised.

'Guess so.'

'So why would a man take off his pack when he can hear and see that the lahar has started? Or why would he not secure all his straps and run like crazy the minute he hears the lahar?'

Emma interjected. 'A person can be stripped bare by the force of water. I'm not surprised at all he hasn't got his pack. I'm surprised he's got his clothes on.'

'In which case his pack will be long gone,' deduced Paul.

'There is a spare pack in the hut,' said Lana.

'How so?' asked Paul.

'There were three men and four packs. Those guys knew I'd seen the extra pack. And they were hesitant to answer when you asked if anyone else was to come. Do you think their friend had already got to the hut with them and then gone back for some reason?'

'Possible,' Paul considered.

'Then why did they lie about it?'

'Well they didn't lie did they? And we don't know if this is their friend.'

'It seems fishy. Something isn't adding up,' said Lana. 'What shall we do with him?'

'Nothing,' replied Paul.

'We can't just leave him here,' Lana wailed.

'Prioritise Lana. He's dead. Nothing we do is going to make it better for him.'

'Paul's right,' said Emma patting him on the arm. 'We need to make ourselves safe. First rule of first aid.' She let her hand linger on Paul's arm then headed for safety out of the valley.

Lana pensively nibbled her top lip. The landscape engulfed her in its raucous tremor. She stood shoulder to shoulder with Paul looking at the body. They were nearly touching. She so wanted to take his arm to give her comfort, to allay the feeling that she was out of her depth, isolated and swallowed up by the enormity of it all. Lana turned to face him at the exact same second he turned to her. She started to speak.

'Paul, I'm sorry.'

He talked over her. 'Lana, I never meant...'

They both stopped and were consumed by a brief but heavy silence. Lana broke it. 'You go.'

'No no, you,' Paul offered.

'I didn't mean to be petty. I'm nervous about meeting you again. It's thrown me back in time. I don't want to go back. I don't need those memories. I'm a different person. You're a different person. And maybe I don't want you to be a different person because you were perfect thirty years ago to me.'

'I'm sorry sweetheart,' Paul softened, frowning. He put both hands out to her and gently touched her elbows, thrusting himself into her space. 'I really didn't think. I was selfish to put myself into your world. I don't want you to recall stuff you find painful. I'm so sorry.'

'It's not that it's painful, just unsettling. It reminds me of my self doubts, the me I hated, the me I worked at so hard to change. The me that doesn't exist anymore.'

'But Lana, how could any of that be true?' Paul asked with amazement. 'I thought you were the loveliest girl on the planet.'

'I never knew that.'

'I was shy.'

'So was I.'

They grinned. Paul tentatively put his hand on Lana's mittened hand and gave it a light squeeze.

'Do you think we could start again now we've got that off our chests?' he asked.

'Not until you answer my question,' she challenged pouting a little, eyes teasing.

He frowned then grinned as he recalled the argument.

'No. Divorced three years. One daughter, 23, on her OE.'

Lana smiled. 'Thanks.'

***

The Hughes 500 helicopter flew in from the north over the top of the mountain. It hovered beneath the sketchy white clouds while Bain, the television cameraman and Blake the second scientist, surveyed the rapidly discharging lake. Bain stamped down the bile that threatened to sour his mouth. This should have been a happy event. Paul could even have taken his place in the helicopter if they'd followed their careers in parallel. Instead he was on a potential rescue mission.

His mind flickered back and forth to times shared with Paul. They'd gone through university together. Paul loved the fact that Bain had attracted the attention of Caroline in the Antarctic because he could ride the snowmobile. Bain was a bit of a petrol head and frequently sent Paul emails from around the world as he toured the factories of Maserati, Ferrari and Lamborgini. Paul would respond with photos of volcanoes, sometimes erupting, sometimes not. Paul had flown back from Guatemala to be best man at Bain's wedding. The photo he had on his mantelpiece after all these years showed the love not only between the bride and groom, but between groom and best man.

He wiped the perspiration off his brow as he scanned the scene below for signs of Paul and the girls.

The pilot manoeuvred downstream as directed by his academic passengers and quickly spotted a prostrate body to the south side of the lahar path.

'Got one, two o'clock,' he announced into his headphones. He whirled the bird into a better vantage point and the three passengers peered out the starboard window.

'Excuse me,' said the cameraman jostling into

position. 'I gotta get that.'

'You can't show that on TV,' exclaimed Bain lifting binoculars to his eyes. 'Doesn't look like Harry. God, don't let it be Harry.'

'I know, they'll edit it, but it should be documented, right?' the cameraman explained. He aimed his camera down to the body.

'Who is it?' asked the pilot. 'Male or female?'

'Hard to say,' Bain replied. 'I'm certain it isn't Harry.'

'I'll call it in – unidentified,' said the pilot.

'Now carry on following this thing,' the cameraman directed.

As the helicopter whipped its course back to the lahar Bain's eyes fixed on the unmoving figure below until it disappeared from view.

***

Lana, Emma and Paul traipsed along the pole marked route in silence up to the hut each ensconced in their own interpretation of what had occurred. The hut was now totally in shadow, beckoning and safe against the distant turmoil of the lahar. They stepped out of the last of the watery spring sun into the frigid cool of the shadow. Lana perched on the deck and gazed out over the eastern ring plain. She squinted in the direction of the distant rumble but the snaking serpent had long since been lost to view. Paul and Emma clomped up to the verandah and collapsed exhausted on the form against the wall.

Lana counted the boots under the bench beneath the

window as she added hers to the row. Three pair. Three people in the hut. She hung her gaiters on the single rope line below the verandah and glanced at Paul. She was apprehensive about going inside. She knew the minute she opened the door of the hut it would be a very different place tonight.

Last night she was apprehensive about being with Paul, a man she knew in her heart of hearts she could trust. Although it was not him per se that gave her cause for concern; it was her. She didn't know what he expected of her but she wanted to be the person he expected her to be. After all, he would have formed some sort of ridiculously unachievable notion of her. She certainly had for him. She couldn't shake the idea that her sexy sixteen year old Paul would grow into anything but her perfect dream man. That's what he was supposed to be – clearly unrealistic. But what did it matter what he thought of her? Wasn't she happy with Alex?

Paul had walked into her life after thirty years and suddenly she was on the back foot. She felt like the awkward schoolgirl she knew she was and that was an image that replayed in her memory no matter how tight she shut her eyes to it. Last night Emma had deflected Paul's attention away from her. And at the time it suited her. It gave her a chance to observe him. He may have been trying to impress her, knowing she was watching him, but nevertheless she was content with what she saw. Emma had flirted with him and Lana pretended Paul wasn't under her spell. He was polite to Emma, there was no fobbing her off tonight. But he constantly tried to catch Lana's eye, like he wanted to include her in their conversation but couldn't figure out how. Or was he in his own way observing her? They seemed to be skirting around each other. Lana felt protective of him, of him and her, of their brief past together. And she was wild at herself for caring. So she glossed over the major things in her life like marriage, love and death as if she was a witness to those, not a participant. And she let Emma play her game.

At least she had got a bit more out of Paul today. Maybe he was on tenterhooks himself. They both were playing it cool. Taking cues from each other. Both scared to reveal anything too personal in case they exposed unhealed hurts.

Lana let Paul and Emma enter the hut before her. The men stopped talking as soon as they entered the room. Two were sitting on benches around a little wooden table in the centre of the room. A third man was lying on a bunk. A crackling fire was lit in the cast iron fire box filling the gloomy atmosphere with blue smoke.

'Howdy,' said Paul.

'Gidday,' the two men at the table replied in unison.

'Look, your mate,' began Paul, 'we found a bloke. Green jacket, brown zip-off trousers. That him?'

The pause between the strangers wasn't lost on Lana.

'Yeah,' said the shorter man. 'That sounds like him.'

'Afraid he didn't make it across the river,' Paul explained. 'He washed up on this side. We managed to pull him clear of the lahar but he's dead. I'm sorry.'

Lana watched the men's reactions. They were blank. When they spoke it was calmer than she expected.

'We should go and get him,' the taller man said to the shorter man untangling his legs from the wooden form.

'He's not going anywhere,' Paul explained.

They were silent for a bit and drank tea out of tin mugs. The man in the bunk gasped every now and then when he made a tiny movement. Then he would wince, grit his teeth and slump his head deeper into his makeshift pillow.

'What's wrong with him?' asked Lana nodding her head in the direction of the bunk.

'He fell and gashed his side,' replied the shorter man. 'Didn't you Bing? Bill.'

'Oh God. Not another one.' Emma went straight to Bill.

'What do you mean by that?' he asked.

'Your friend got stuck in the side with something,' Emma explained. 'Don't know if it was a stick in the river or what.'

'Is there anything we can do for Bill?' asked Lana. 'I'm Lana by the way.'

Emma and Paul introduced themselves.

'Dave and Jim,' Dave volunteered.

'I've bandaged him up for now and given him low dose painkillers,' replied Jim. 'We'll keep him there nice and easy for a while.'

Emma looked critically at Jim. 'Low dose,' she repeated. 'You a doctor?'

'Yes.'

Paul went into his bunkroom and took off his small daypack and jacket. There were three packs already in the room. He came back out.

'Is one of these packs your friends?' he asked.

'Yeah mate,' said Dave.

'Oh that explains it. So he went back for something huh? Wondered why he didn't have it on him.'

Paul stepped into Lana's room where she was taking off her wet weather gear.

'Do you mind if I come in here tonight?' asked Paul.

'No that's fine,' she said. 'I'd prefer it actually.'

Paul raised his eyebrows, surprise radiating from his sparkling eyes.

'No,' whispered Lana, 'I mean I'd prefer it just because I'm not wholly comfortable with those guys.'

'Oh how disappointing,' Paul teased her.

He grabbed his sleeping bag and set up on the lower platform bunk an arm's length away from hers. She studied him. He was casual in his movements, as if it didn't matter to him whether he slept right next to her or at the far end of the bunk.

It meant of course that she should try not to get up in the night and have to fumble with extra clothes. And she will have to wake up looking gorgeous, no sleep in her eyes, no sticky out hair. *What am I thinking? She chastised herself. I don't care where he sleeps and what I look like to him. Alex is probably worrying about me right now.*

Emma appeared at the door clutching her sleeping bag. 'You don't mind do you.' It wasn't a question.

'Sure, of course,' said Paul budging his bag closer to Lana's.

Emma set up her new sleeping arrangements then casually stripped down to her underwear to change.

'I have to phone home,' Lana quickly announced. 'Alex will be worried.' She scuttled out of the room with Paul following close behind.

Again the men suddenly hushed at their intrusion. Lana rushed for the door. She knew she could get phone reception about one hundred metres in front of the hut. She opened the door and was immediately hit by the freezing spring air.

'Blast,' she said as she dashed back in. 'Cold.'

She dashed into the bunkroom, relieved to see Emma had dressed then put on her jacket, beanie and mittens, and went back outside.

By the time she returned Paul had the primus hissing loudly pushing out blue and orange flames up the sides of the billy which perched precariously on top. Alongside he had and three cups set out with dried soup in each. His tight fitting merino clothing emphasised the ripple of his muscles and he wore thick wool socks and a beanie. Lana went into the bunkroom and changed into similar attire. She loved nights in huts. She loved the snuggy thin wool clothes, the candles, the primitive way basic needs were met and she loved the company. Pretensions and egos get stripped away in a hut. Everyone was equal, just for one night. It was everyone in together surviving a night in the wilderness. No-one had another life, just for one night.

She lit some candles and joined Emma at the table. The men budged up, giving her room to sit. Jim removed his glasses and wiped them before setting them back onto his face.

He spoke, 'You stayed here last night?'

'Yes, we're doing some research,' said Lana. 'Incredible luck to have the lahar go off while Paul's here. It's his field of expertise.'

Paul ignored Lana's comment and poured the water into the mugs. For minutes the only sound in the room apart from the sporadic crackle of the fire was the clink of spoon on metal as Paul stirred each drink. He doled out the soup sat down next to her.

'What's yours?' Jim asked her.

'Don't have one yet,' she answered, 'but glaciology is my interest right now.'

'What about you Emma?' Jim turned to her.

'My expertise?' She laughed. 'Believe it or not, it's the age of the Canadian shield.' Jim looked blank.

Paul explained. 'It's amongst the oldest landforms on the planet.'

'So it's pretty exciting for me to be surrounded by the newest rocks on the planet,' Emma crowed.

'What about you guys?' Paul asked. 'You walking around the mountain?'

'Yeah, we were,' answered Dave. 'Things have changed now. With our friend dead.' Jim shot a look at his mate.

'And Bill hurt,' Lana added. 'What a disastrous trip for you. I guess you'll have to radio for help. The bridge is out. You could go out to the south.'

'Probably go straight down from here,' said Dave. 'Through army land.'

'Bill can't do that Dave,' said Jim.

'He might have to Jim,' Dave said with emphasis on the man's name. 'Can you think of anything else?' he said through clenched teeth. He held Jim with a stare.

'He sure as hell can't make a run like that in his state,' replied Jim.

'I won't be running,' gasped Bill. 'You got any more pain killers?'

'Sure buddy,' said Jim. He got up from the bench and walked into the bunkroom.

Dave quickly got up and went to the bench. He made every effort to avoid further questioning as he prepared dinner. He kept his back to them and made much noise chopping and banging. Emma persisted an attempt at conversation.

'Maybe we could follow you down then,' she said, 'if it's quicker that way.'

'Oh I'm not going yet,' said Lana. 'I have work to do.'

Joe addressed Emma. 'Listen to your mates love. You don't want to be tagging along with us. We'll be going through a live firing zone.'

Emma bristled. 'How come you'll get through it then?'

Joe turned his back on them and Emma went to pursue it but Paul put a hand on her knee. 'Just leave it.'

'But...'

'I said leave it Emma,' Paul repeated too calmly.

Lana switched seats and leaned over to Bill. 'Can I get something for you? Drink?'

Bill shook his head.

'Look, we've got tomorrow night in this hut so one of us can be with you until help comes,' Lana offered.

Paul shot a glance at Lana. She read in it that she would be the one to stay and play nurse. Of course, he had his lahar to study.

'I'll make us some dinner,' said Lana.

'No no, you sit,' Paul replied beating her to the kitchen. 'You've had a big day.'

'Same day as you,' Lana threw back. Paul gave her a wounded look.

'I'll help you Paul.' Emma was alongside him in a

92

trice.

Lana thought she had done well today. She had coped with the strenuous clambering and walking, the jog to the lahar and the discovery of a body. It was exactly the same day as Paul and Emma had had. But his one little comment had said you're only a girl and I need to look after you.

She'd been looking after herself for thirty years. Didn't he know that? What made him think she needed him to look after her now? Or that she wanted him to!

She turned her back to the table and stretched her legs in front of the fire. Instantly the heat prickled the skin beneath her leggings and for a moment she let the tiredness overwhelm her. She barely heard Paul softly approach and hold a tin mug out to her. It had a finger of golden liquid in it. He put one arm around her shoulder and he drew her in against the warmth of his body. She let her head lean against his hip, feeling her cheek against the warmth of his skin emanating through the soft thermals. A pulse of excitement surged through her momentarily sweeping tiredness aside. It was the closest they'd been since nineteen seventy eight. She let herself soften under his touch but her wariness was so great she refused her body the anticipation of his embrace.

'This is my tonic after a big day,' he smiled tenderly and swirled the whiskey around in his mug. He inhaled the bouquet before taking a mouthful. He let it swirl around his mouth. Lana watched him push it into the crevasses of his mouth and around to the front of his gums. He didn't want to let it go. And then he did. He closed his eyes and smiled as it made its hot journey to the pit of his stomach.

Lana copied his action and took a sip. It caught in her throat. She could feel the heat going down her middle right into the pit of her stomach. She sighed.

'Was I patronising?' Paul murmured for Lana only to hear.

'Yes,' she replied.

'I guess I was a bit. It comes with being a father. Always looking out for my little girl. Let me worry about you.'

'What's your daughter's name?' Lana asked softly.

'Kate. Kathryn Mary.'

'Nice. It must be nice for you to have a daughter.' She smiled for him. She wanted to enquire more. She wanted to know if he took Kate to piano lessons, if he stood on the side of the pool at school swimming sports yelling his encouragement. Did Kate look like him? Did he miss her? But the noise in the hut was becoming raucous and Lana didn't want to speak over the din.

Jim administered the moaning Bill with painkillers while Dave banged and crashed at the kitchen bench. Emma added to the cacophony as she prepared a meal.

'I'm nearly out of your way mate,' Dave boomed.

'That's all right. No rush,' Paul replied. 'Emma's in charge.'

She turned into the room, a scowl on her face. 'I said I'd help you Paul, not do it all.'

Lana smiled to herself. Lack of privacy was something that came with hut dwelling.

'Well you've got everything under control haven't you?' Paul answered Emma.

He made himself comfortable alongside Lana as Emma huffed at making dinner. He made sure the length of his body touched hers. Lana did not move.

'Tell me about the lahar,' Lana prompted Paul.

He looked at her blankly.

'Yes Paul,' Emma added with more drawl than she was usually wont to do. 'Tell us all about the lahar while I cook dinner for us all.' She waved a knife around before slamming it on the bench and pouring herself a nip of Paul's whiskey.

'Go on. Pretend you're on that stage in Iceland explaining it to the rest of us.'

'I might not be able to stop,' he grinned.

'Good,' Lana encouraged him.

'Well, we're extremely lucky to have a good snowfield surrounding the lake.'

'Why?' asked Dave.

Emma rushed in with an explanation. 'Because the snow gets entrained into the lahar. That adds tremendous bulk to the flow. For every part of water that forms the lahar you can add sixty to three thousand parts of snow.'

Paul looked surprised. 'That's right. You've been doing your homework.' Lana watched Emma preen with the praise.

'That's huge. But light right?' Lana asked.

Paul took up the explanation. 'Light but lethal. Imagine it's like a giant fruit slushy. But it's lubricated on a bed of water so the speed it can travel can be phenomenal. And you saw all that debris in the flow. The debris gets separated out and sometimes one debris type can overflow another. That's cool.'

'Does your team have equipment to measure that?' asked Lana.

'Yeah, and of course half the university will be here

95

right now staked out along the Whangaehu River collecting samples.'

'And my Uni. But we've got the best spot.'

'No doubt about that,' agreed Paul.

'But we don't know what triggered it. It could be volcanic,' said Lana.

Dave interrupted them. 'You mean the mountain could erupt?'

'Now that would be just too hopeful, eh Lana,' Paul beamed a smile to Lana and then to Dave.

'But are you serious?' asked Dave.

'Well, we live in hope,' Paul teased.

Emma stopped her work at the bench. 'Oh my God! I hadn't thought of that.'

'So it could happen?' Dave demanded.

'Of course it could,' Emma replied. 'Here.' She put two plates on the table then joined Lana and Paul with hers.

'When?' asked Jim.

Paul shrugged and finished a mouthful of pasta. 'Don't know. And it's not when, it's if.'

They ate in silence disturbed only by the shrill of the scraping of metal forks on metal plates and the crackle of the fire.

Dave pushed his form back and walked to the door. Jim followed silently. Lana glanced over at Bill. He was still eating, slowly; painstakingly.

Lana and Paul exchanged quiet looks. There was heated discussion coming from the deck but it was muffled. Bill took no notice of it. Outside, daylight was exchanging with dusk and the men were shadows. An uncomfortable silence filled the room.

'Early night for me,' said Lana. She lit a candle, set it into the holder on the wall above the sink bench and boiled water for the dishes.

'I'll sit a while,' said Emma. 'I'll just steal a little of that water.' She poured herself a cup of tea.

'Guess I'm for bed too,' said Paul after he helped her with the dishes.

'I need the bathroom,' said Lana. 'Can I borrow your head lamp?' Paul gave it to her. She clambered into her jacket and boots and went out into the night. The men stopped talking as soon as she opened the door. They were perched on the top step of the deck. She moved past them and they resumed talking in near whispers until she appeared again.

'Goodnight,' she said.

'Night,' they answered in unison.

She stepped into the bunkroom and surveyed the sleeping arrangements. A single candle had been lit and the room was bathed in a dark light. She waited until Paul went out to the bathroom before she undressed. She put on an aqua merino camisole with aqua lace trim to the v-front and matching boy cut knickers. Then she climbed onto the bunk on her hands and knees.

Paul opened the door and caught sight of her.

He groaned, 'Oh Lana, no.'

He closed his eyes slowly. Then opened them just as slowly. Lana froze like a rabbit in headlights. She was completely aware of the vision Paul saw before him. The little merino camisole clung to her body. Every silky stitch moulded to her breasts and shapely waist. Her nipples were hard and the merino emphasised the fact. Her rump was flattered by the cut of the knickers. Paul turned slowly to face the wall to give him time to recover as much as her.

'Thanks,' Lana said as she found the opening to the silk sleeping bag liner and crawled into her bag.

'Okay.'

Paul turned back sheepishly to see a half smile on Lana's lips. He stripped down to his boxers unselfconsciously and crawled into his bag.

She rolled to face him and whispered. 'I don't know about those guys. They don't seem very upset about their friend.'

Paul shuffled closer to whisper back. She felt his warm breath blow across her face and in an instant she felt a tingle between her legs. She wondered if he could tell. He was saying something but it was a blur in her head. 'Sorry, what?'

'I said I agree. There's something going on that we don't know about. I don't think we're in any danger though. How do you feel?'

She reflected. His face was only thirty centimetres away from hers. Wasn't this what she'd dreamed about when she was a girl? To be lying in bed with this man while he pleasured her with his every touch?

Just then the door opened allowing some candlelight to infiltrate. Paul's face was backlit by it and Lana knew that it had enabled hers to be illuminated. Then Emma's headlight skimmed around the room. She blew out the candle and rustled into her bag. 'What do you think of our hut mates?' she whispered.

'Something fishy,' Paul answered.

Emma laid a hand on Paul's hip. 'That's what I think.' She gave a little rub. Paul reached for it and gave it back to her.

'Good night Emma.'

***

'Was this the best we could come up with?' Tom moaned into his hands.

'It was good enough before,' Joe muttered urgently. 'I didn't know the bloody lahar was going to let go, so don't you come at me. If it weren't for your bloody conscience Ant wouldn't be dead.'

They were slumped on the wooden bench under the verandah. Night had fallen. Their new hut companions seemed a smart arse bunch. They couldn't talk in front of them.

The robbery had gone smoothly enough. Bing was waiting for them with the ute when they got out. They'd piled into the wagon and waited off road until morning to head up the mountain. They'd done everything any other tramper would have done; kept to normal everyday stuff. Until Ant bragged about his prize.

He'd pocketed the medal behind Tom's back. Later, when Tom realised what it was and who it belonged to he had become enraged. He'd swung at Ant and the two exchanged blows. Bing tried to break up the fight but by the time he'd entered the fray Ant had pulled a knife. He took it in his side but not before Bing got one in. Weakened by the stab, Ant was a breeze for Tom to head butt. They hadn't meant to kill him and it wasn't the knife wound that did. It was the misplaced fall to the ground that ended with a fatal crack to the head.

Tom glared at Joe. 'I didn't kill him,' he spat.

'They saw the knife wound,' Joe hissed. 'I wish I didn't know that.'

'Stick wound,' Tom corrected him.

'You better hope they don't work it out.'

Tom slumped against the wall. 'I can't believe I'm doing this,' he cried. 'What the fuck am I doing?' He beat his clenched fists on the bench. 'You think we can hide them here? Right under their fucking noses?'

Joe reeled on Tom. 'You shut it,' he whispered harshly. 'It's the last place anyone will look. There always a risk there'd be people here. But they don't know where the stash is. Shit Tom, they don't even know there is a stash.'

Tom wiped his forehead which had broken out in tiny beads of sweat. 'Look at us. Less than twenty four hours and we're fighting amongst ourselves. One dead, one wounded.' He removed his glasses, fogged them with his breath and wiped the glass with the corner of his shirt. He put them back on. 'I'm not happy leaving Bing here.'

'He'll be all right. The brunette's already looking after him.'

Tom shook his head. 'It's not right. We're all in this together. And you haven't thought of something. He could spill his guts if delirium sets in.'

'Nah, Bing's good. Look how he stepped into that fight. He didn't have to. Bing's all right I tell you.'

'You're not worried the minute we're gone he's not going to double cross us?'

'Nah mate. And don't you give him the notion to. He has plenty of silly ideas inside that head without you giving him a hand. Look at it this way. Now we've only got three mouths to keep schtum; you're sweet and I'm sweet. So trust Bing not to sell us down the river. I do.'

He stared hard at Tom. He knew how to handle him. He took a deep calming breath. 'Look mate,' he said quietly, 'nothing changes. Stick to the plan. The medals are well hidden and they'll be safe for a few months. It's all in the timing. We don't want them hitting the market too soon.' Joe placed his hand on Tom's thigh. How he hated doing that. But Tom responded to it, as Joe knew he would.

'I'm sorry Joe.' Tom flicked his mouth into a tight smile, 'bit tense, you know. It hasn't gone like I thought.'

On the contrary, thought Joe. As far as Tom is concerned it's going well to plan. Tom was unaware that he'd been selected by Joe a couple of years ago and it was no accident that Joe had transferred to the same base as his second cousin. Tom was unmarried and as far as Joe could tell he wasn't overtly gay but there was also no indication that the few women friends he had were anything more than friends. So Joe had chanced his hand and become the sort of friend he thought Tom needed. And that meant finding his feminine side.

Eventually Tom revealed snippets of his childhood and recounted family stories. Christmases with his uncles, aunties, cousins and his special Poppa Alf and Grandma Lily, annual duck shooting with his brothers and dad and uncles John, Vernon and Thomas and John's boy Sean at Poppa Alf's rough block off a back road in the Hawkes Bay. It became clear to Joe that Tom had no idea of Poppa Alf's illegitimate daughter Sonya and her son Joe.

'Trust me,' said Joe, 'you're over-thinking. You know

the truth but no-one else does. No-one can link us to the heist. We're just a group of guys on a weekend tramp – just like we've been doing for years. You're doing OK.' He gave Tom's leg a double pat and he saw Tom's shoulders relax as he digested the compliment. He smirked to himself. It was that easy. It always was.

***

Colleen welcomed the female police officer into the reception area of the small town law office where she worked as receptionist.

She preferred to treat the reception area as her own personal lounge, keeping fresh flowers on the desk, the blinds pulled just so and the paintings hung perfectly straight. She wasn't unfamiliar with the police visiting her offices but when the young lady had told Colleen it was her that she needed to see she'd let a small gasp escape.

'May we sit?' asked the constable pointing to a sofa at the edge of the room. They perched uneasily on the edge of the seat. 'A medal owned by your family and on loan to the Army Museum has been stolen. Do you know the medal I'm talking about?' constable Smith asked.

'I know it,' Colleen replied, 'the New Zealand Memorial Cross. It was my grandmother's.'

'It was one of several taken. It's very distinctive and there's an expectation that it will surface in the dealers' market.'

Colleen shuffled a little, her fingers rotating the rings of her other hand. She had known her grandmother but had never known her Uncle Harold for whom the medal had been awarded. She recalled her grandmother's story to her mind's eye. She'd heard the account every Christmas. It was her grandmother's way of keeping the memory of Harold alive.

It was nineteen forty nine. Harold's mother, Elizabeth, held herself with dignity and pride as she allowed the New Zealand Memorial Cross to be hung around her neck. The major, a great big bear of a man with a matching bear of a voice, saluted her then she took a step backwards and bowed her head.

She was one of sixteen mothers, one sister and one father to receive the medal in the town hall that Friday afternoon. It had been five long years since her beloved Harry was taken from her. Elizabeth's husband Tom and her daughter Clarice – Colleen's mother, were in attendance. The New Zealand and British flags hung alongside the dais, limp in the close heat of the afternoon.

Elizabeth had worn her best frock to honour Harry. It had a shapely bodice pinched in at the waist and a little sash at the top of the flared skirt tied to a flat bow at the back.

The tiny cap sleeves showed off her graceful arms. She wore white gloves and her hat, handbag and shoes set off the delicate green of her dress.

The major concluded the presentations and nodded to the brass band which played sombre but rousing music, the notes reverberating off the hard surfaces of the walls and narrow timber floorboards to distort the otherwise note-perfect composition. The major led sixteen mothers, one sister and one father out of the hall. Then medal recipients and their families were ushered to an antechamber. The afternoon drew to a close with polite conversation over cups of tea and dainty sandwiches.

Colleen sat staring at the carpeted floor in front of her clasping her now clammy hands. She knew the story of Harold's untimely demise and that there was a young lad who brought Harold off the hill to safety. The young lad was so naive he hadn't realised that Harry had died in his arms. She always thought he should have had a medal for doing that for Uncle Harry. Maybe he did get one; she hadn't heard.

She reflected upon Harold's friend. Was he still alive? In her mind's eye she imagined the two friends struggling in the mud and cold and wet of an Italian mountainside. She could smell the smoke and taste the mud and feel the weight of death. She shut her eyes and inhaled deeply.

'Thank you for coming to tell me,' said Colleen arising from the sofa.

'I will keep you informed as soon as we have any information.'

Colleen walked the constable to the door and resolved to contact the young lad's family. It was too much to bear alone.

***

Sleep eluded Lana. It had been an eventful and tiring day. So many thoughts ran through her head. At the back of the day's excitement was the unsettling feeling of memories, long repressed, bouncing and jumbled into her brain. She constantly pictured a young Paul and could not, no matter how hard she tried, reconcile him with the man who lay next to her now. She was forced to remember herself thirty years ago. That was something she hated doing. She had never searched for her memories there before. She didn't want to. In her mind she was chubby and awkward; ugly in fact. Well, no-one had told her otherwise at the time. Except Paul. Or at least he had tried. He was so shy that she accepted that his presence alone spoke for him. It may have only taken a few carefully chosen words from the gorgeous Paul to convince her that she wasn't an ugly duckling. He was the only one she would have believed.

She wasn't a shy ugly duckling now. That was some other girl. She was embarrassed that Paul might remember her so. She had tried hard to leave that girl behind. She'd even burned her school photos to make sure she didn't accidently get a glimpse of that girl.

What the fabulous Yuri saw in her she still did not know. Of course she wasn't a girl then, but an independent woman. She'd already been practicing martial arts for five years when she met him. She had a positive attitude to life and she believed there was nothing she couldn't do if she set her mind to it. How lucky she was that he chose her. Yuri would never be replaced, could never be replaced, she knew that. Wherever Yuri was now, heaven or hell, he knew that. He would have wanted her to be happy.

She felt she had completed the very painful and personal grieving process when she took up with Alex. It marked a stage that indicated she was ready to move on. She felt a certain maturity about the decision. But it didn't feel the same as it was with Yuri. She didn't know if it was supposed to. Perhaps it was meant to feel different.

Perhaps Paul was right about Alex. She didn't say she was in love with him. She couldn't say she was in love with him. But she did love him. Perhaps it was telling that they had not moved in together. She hadn't questioned it before, but Paul had forced her to think about it.

There was something undeniably strong between herself and Paul. Possibly stronger than that between herself and Alex. Paul seemed certain of it and challenged her about it and that had shocked and upset her. She looked across to Paul. A faint moonbeam cast pale blue across his sleeping face and onto hers connecting the invisible thread of past they shared. It was as fine as a strand of Chinese silk; invisible when she wasn't looking for it but resolute and unyielding, unbreakable. Why was that? Why should she feel an attachment to this man? It should have severed when he left.

She supposed it was because they did not have the chance to fall out of love or to grow apart. He just left one summer. Gone. Family moved out of town. The wrench had been tremendous at the time but what could they do? They were at the mercy of their families, they had schooling to complete. It was never going to last. It could never be anything more than teen love. They had written a few times and inevitably drifted out of each other's lives. She had not thought of him since. She suddenly felt overwhelmed by her emotions. She was angry that he had forced her to remember, bitter that he had judged her relationship with Alex, furious that he had provoked her to analyse her relationship with Alex, flattered that he had insisted on meeting her and alarmed at her repressed and unresolved feelings for him.

Paul was breathing the sleep breathe. She knew he was not awake. Why wasn't he awake? He robbed her of the ability to sleep simply by lying next to her. Could she not have had that effect on him? She was too emotional, that was her problem. Too intense and too emotional. She was fabulously talented at analysing her faults.

She dropped a slender arm out of her silk liner and lifted her hand so that it hovered above Paul's sleeping, purring head. She lowered her index finger down and delicately traced the outline of his face without touching it. She could feel the hotness of his breath on her hand. Paul gave a little murmur and rolled onto his side to face her. Lana startled. As she withdrew her hand he caught it and took her fingers to his lips. He held her there and she made no attempt to retrieve them.

Chapter Four

Lana woke to a deep-seated grumbling tremor. She bolted upright at the same time as Paul. The room was dappled with the soft white light of a half moon and his face, bare shoulders and torso were partially illuminated.

'What is it?' asked Lana as she grasped the fine silk fabric to her chest with both hands.

'Eruption,' Paul replied.

'Oh my God! Ash?'

'Yep. Initially, anyway. Come on.'

Paul peeled himself out of his sleeping bag and crawled out onto the floor. He hurriedly grabbed his trousers, staggering as he threaded one leg in at a time and stumbled to the door. Lana crawled out of her bag and grabbed her jacket shrugging it on as she made her way out to the living area.

'What's happening?' called Emma.

'Get up,' Paul called. 'The mountain's erupting.'

'We're leeward though,' Lana reminded him. 'Might go right over us without landing.'

'Unlikely,' said Emma.

Lana looked to Paul for confirmation.

'She's right. It's unlikely. We're going to find out any second.'

They fixed their eyes on the mountain top.

Dave and Jim emerged from their room also in varying stages of undress, Jim securing his glasses behind his ears. They all assembled under the veranda.

'Are we in danger?' asked Dave.

'We're on the wrong side of the mountain to see properly,' replied Paul.

'Does that make us safer?' asked Jim.

'Not really.'

Suddenly the low grumble was accompanied by a continuous plume of steam and ash. It rose explosively into the air and with lightening speed projected it several kilometres above the mountain. Stars disappeared as the night sky surrounding the plume was swallowed into its vortex. As the ash cloud dispersed it threatened to block out the night sky altogether.

'Will you look at that!' Emma had joined them with her sleeping bag wrapped around her.

'Amazing,' Lana agreed.

'That's going to blow our way for sure,' said Paul. 'Volcanic deposits trend northeast out of this mountain.'

The ash clouds generated a celestial glow. Lightening straight and blue flashed inside black and white pillows of ash.

'Here it comes,' said Paul with an edge of excitement in his voice. 'Cover your faces. Get inside.' No-one did. They stood transfixed and mute until ash fell around them and onto the hut's roof and deck landing silently and lightly as angels' wings.

'Uh-oh,' Paul exclaimed as an explosion within the giant ash cloud generated the first of the solid eruptive debris. Light clinks pattered the tin roof of the hut. 'This is what I've been expecting. Let's hope it's all small stuff.'

'I have to photograph this,' cried Emma suddenly. She ran back inside shedding her bag as she went. When she returned she was clad in her thick padded jacket but nothing on her legs. She dashed to the edge of the deck and immediately focused her camera.

'Are you mad girl?' It was Dave.

'Emma get back here,' Lana joined in. 'Do you expect me to drag your dead body off this mountain so Julie can send you back to Canada in a box?' She was angry. Everything Emma did said; look at Emma, how beautiful, how clever, look at Emma standing in front of everyone half naked, legs up to her armpits.

'Just a couple more shots,' Emma muttered. But Paul had already grabbed her by the arm and tugged her back. It didn't escape Lana's notice that she remained close to him, almost clinging to him.

'Paul, do you think Crater Lake was emptied by the lahar?' asked Lana.

'I doubt it,' replied Paul.

'So that means the valleys are vulnerable to mudflows,' she said.

'Yeah, that's right. Fast and dangerous.'

'What does that mean?' asked Jim.

'It means we're bang smack in the middle of a multi-hazard zone,' Paul explained. 'We're safe from the lahar. We should be safe from mudflow, but we aren't safe from volcanic eruptions. We've got air fall deposits, pyroclastic surges and falls and unsafe gas levels to consider.'

'Repeat that, in English,' said Dave. 'What do you mean gas?'

'Volcanic debris is ash, rocks and boulders. Pyroclastic surges are the killers. Clouds of superheated gas that separates from the physical flow. Cook you to death in seconds,' Paul explained.

Dave and Jim stared at each other, fear etched on their faces. 'How do you know that's going to happen?' asked

Jim.

Paul shook his head. 'Doesn't work like that. We'll know when we've got one. And there's no outrunning it.'

'The lake will empty of water now won't it?' asked Lana.

'Yeah. The kind of pressure on the plumbing will govern what comes out of the vent next,' Paul explained.

'How long will this last?' asked Dave.

'Could be days,' replied Paul. 'Or weeks.'

'Or months,' added Emma. 'Not to alarm you gentlemen.' She threw a smile to them.

Dave led Jim back inside the hut and Lana waited until she heard them conversing with Bill.

'What are we going to do?' she asked Paul.

'Can't do anything until daylight.'

'Then what? People will be worried. Alex will be worried,' she quickly added. 'We'll need to get a message out.'

'Just have to wait,' he said.

Lana pulled her jacket tighter wrapping her arms around her. She rocked from bare foot to bare foot. The mountain continued to put on a show. It was mesmerising, bursting with white hot energy. She couldn't stop watching it.

'You should put some clothes on Lana,' advised Paul.

She turned her head towards him and took in his bare chest and lean shoulders. His bicep muscles sat taut under the tanned skin of his arms. His dark chest hair looked as soft as down and a delicate swathe of dark hair led from his flat belly to the top of his trousers.

He watched her eyes scan his body. He sensed in

them her desire but her body language was contrary. She held herself upright and still. She did not move. She continued to look at him finally raising her eyes to his face only to find him watching her. She tried to speak, moved her lips and opened her mouth but no sound emerged. She was caught wanting.

His eyes crinkled at the outside corners and his cheeks puffed higher in his face as he smiled his tight but wide closed mouth smile. She felt it was a benevolent smile. There was no mocking in it.

'Yes,' she agreed, not capable of any other response. But she did not move. She was transfixed in the moment. She felt the cool night air and the chill breeze lick at her bare legs. It felt good. She felt alive, really alive. She looked back to the direction of the mountain top. A brownish plume was evident even in the poor light of the ash-laden atmosphere. Paul followed her gaze.

'It's the combination of gases giving it different colours,' he explained.

'Oh,' she gave a little shake of her head to refocus herself. She hadn't heard a word he said. 'You must be cold yourself.'

'Not for the moment. Adrenalin is keeping me warm,' he replied.

She turned from the spectacle of the mountain to Emma who was now standing under the edge of the veranda taking photos. Emma had embraced the scientific moment. No doubt she would publish some of the photos in her research paper, even if it didn't fit her original hypothesis. Lana was sure Emma would steer her research in a direction that meant she could include such precious shots. And Lana had just stood there, slack-mouthed, admiring the view. Frustrated, she knew she should go inside and put on some trousers but she was caught in a spell and was cast. She savoured the moment with Paul. She was witnessing the newest earth on the planet being created as if it were a testament to their reignited relationship. The mountain displayed passion and fire. Paul had given her plenty of encouragement and although she felt the fire within her she was content to let it smoulder for now.

Certainly he'd given her an indication that he wanted more than a professional relationship. He'd displayed to her his aching desire when she had inadvertently paraded herself before him tonight. She realised that the distance he was giving her was restrained.

Why did she keep mentioning Alex? Was she using him as an excuse not to fall in love with Paul? Maybe she was scared of being let down again. After all, if she'd meant so much to him in the first place why did he let her go? He took risks. He risked his life doing the work he did. He risked losing her and he had. What did he have to lose in this mad pursuit of her? Nothing. He was free to love and lose. She wasn't. For the time being Alex was her shield. She was safe with Alex.

A loud shot rang out and Emma bolted to the door of the hut. 'Geez, that was a bit close.' She held her palm to her chest and grabbed Paul's hand. 'Feel my heart.' She placed his hand on her left breast.

'Yes, it's lovely...I mean.'

Lana glowered at Emma although she knew it was lost on her because she was lost in the spell that was Paul.

'Go inside Emma,' Paul said gently.

'But I feel safer here,' she replied. Paul took his hand back and opened the door for her giving her a light push on her bottom.

'Safer here sweetheart,' he said. 'Make me some tea. Will you do that?'

She pouted and went inside.

'Let's sit down.' Paul gestured to the form behind them. He placed his hand at the small of her back as they seated themselves.

'It's Surtseyian you know,' said Paul looking out into the night.

'What?'

'The style of the eruption. Surtseyian. A great smouldering ash cloud soon to explode to something magnificent.'

Paul placed his hand on Lana's bare thigh. 'That eruption is me Lana.'

He turned to watch her face. She looked directly at him with a puzzled expression. She said nothing. She made no attempt to remove his hand. It was warm and comforting and she thrilled to his touch.

'I've never been out of love with you Lana,' Paul confided quietly.

'But how can you retain that after three decades?' Lana replied. 'We grow up, we move on. We can't cling to the past. We change.'

'You haven't changed Lana. You were perfect for me then and you're perfect now.'

'I'm not perfect for you though,' she argued.

'You don't know that. You're making excuses because you've got a nice comfortable life and I've come along and put temptation in your way.'

'You flatter yourself,' Lana retorted.

'No, I just assumed you would feel the same way I do. I'm wrong to assume that, I know. The best I can hope for is that you would acknowledge how much I care about you,' he replied.

'I can see that you do Paul. You've been a perfect gentleman. You've shown me nothing but respect. I can see you want to care for me, but it's hard to believe that we really do have the same feelings for each other after all this time.' She paused and when Paul remained quiet she continued. 'I do care for you Paul. That's the problem. Meeting you again has stirred a fire in me. And I don't know how I feel.'

Ash continued to rain down and the odd tiny volcanic bomb landed on the building with a light ping on the corrugated iron roof. They listened to the pebbles clatter down the corrugations of the iron and land in the gutter. She looked out into the black. 'How did you know where to find me?' she asked in a whisper.

'Remember when you wrote to my university enquiring about post graduate programmes?'

'Yeah.'

'I saw your letter. I was hoping you would choose us and when you didn't I made some phone calls. It's a small world, earth science. We all know each other,' Paul explained.

'So why didn't you contact me directly?'

'I was scared.'

'You?'

'Yeah, me. You don't have a monopoly on feelings you know.'

'Scared of what?' asked Lana.

'Scared you wouldn't see me for one. When I saw your name on that letter I was suddenly sixteen again. I wanted so much to see you.'

'How did you know I'd be at the conference?' Lana asked.

'Simple! I rang your department and asked who was going. Not rocket science.' His smiled infected her. She could see that he thought himself very clever, not devious at all.

'Or earth science.' She sniffed at her joke, smiling tightly.

'Like I said, it's a small world.'

'You've known for a long time that you'd meet up with me. You've had all those months to get used to the idea. All those months to remember the past, our past. Paul, I'm going through that right now. And I'm going through it with you at present,' Lana agonised.

'I know. I'm sorry. I didn't think,' he replied. 'I didn't mean to hurt you.'

She put her hand on top of Paul's which still lay on her thigh.

'I thought if you saw me giving a lecture in Iceland you would be proud of me,' he said.

'Oh I was,' she assured him.

'But you had your head bowed a lot of the time.'

'I was shocked,' Lana explained. 'I didn't want you to recognise me. I was upset that you had missed my prime. And I needed time to compose myself. I didn't want to make a fool of myself.'

'Missed your prime?' asked Paul.

'Wrinkles, Paul.' She fingered the corners of her eyes. 'See? I'm embarrassed now. You were my first love. We

116

were fresh, innocent teenagers with no blemishes on our bodies or in our minds. How vain is that? You see? I'm shallow.'

Paul reached around to take Lana's face in both his hands. His dark eyes drilled hers and then scanned her face.

'You're not alone in that department sweetheart,' he grinned. 'Like I said darling, you were perfect then and you're perfect now.'

Lana inclined her head back a little and closed her eyes. Paul leaned forward and kissed her tenderly on her lips. She parted them tasting his warm tongue and felt electricity surge through her body.

***

The door to the hut opened and Dave appeared. Lana started and pulled her face away from Paul's. She suddenly felt cold.

'Mate, what's going on?' asked Dave gruffly. 'We want to pull out in the morning.' Lana could hear the hiss of the primus behind him and saw the dull glow of a candle as it flickered with the sudden rush of air.

'Look,' said Paul, 'this eruption could accelerate or dissipate or even change to incendiary type projections. There's no real prediction. At the moment it's predominantly ash coming down with some small molten lava bombs. Hear that?' Paul pointed to the verandah roof. 'Those pebbles landing on the roof are molten rock. That means a temperature in excess of twelve hundred degrees centigrade as they spew out of the volcano, then cooling in the air but still hot soft rock when they fall on us.'

'Jim and I are getting out of here tomorrow regardless. Bill will have to stay.' Dave remarked.

'And what is your plan for Bill now?' asked Lana.

'We'll come back up for him when it's safe,' Dave replied.

'Do you think that's wise?' she asked. 'That could be days. He could deteriorate a lot in that time.'

'What do you suggest?' Dave snapped at her.

'I'm only expressing concern.' She stood up and went inside.

She lit a candle in the bunk room and put warm clothes on. By the time she emerged from the room Paul had stoked the fire and was sitting alongside Emma with his mug cradled in his hands. There they were again; those long sensuous legs that ended at her waist and nestled snugly at Paul's hip. He made no attempt to move. Lana stared at his bare chest glowing in the warm yellow half light. His torso had developed beautifully since he was sixteen. Years of physical work and play had chiselled hard pectoral muscles. His stomach was flat for a man of his years. Maybe not too much beer. Maybe he worked out. She realised how little she knew about him. She yearned to feel his rippling body under her touch. She shouldn't have let him kiss her.

She walked over to Bill. 'How are you?' she asked him.

''Bout the same,' he replied.

'Do you have enough food to last a few days?'

'No.'

'Painkillers?'

'Maybe. Jim. He's a medic,' Bill explained. 'He'll see

me right.'

Lana doubted that. 'Is he now? In the army then is he? You all in the army?' But she didn't let him answer. She handed him her cup of tea. 'Here. I'll get another one.'

The hut trembled and groaned in response to an explosion. Lana faltered with the cup.

'Look out woman.' Bill thrashed at her.

'I'm sorry.' She made a desperate attempt to mop the hot tea off his chest and slammed the cup onto the table.

Seconds later molten lava bombs landed on the roof with a heavy pitter patter followed by a rolling clatter as the rock consolidated and sped down the iron. A crash of glass exploded in the hut showering the kitchen bench and floor with glistening shards. Dave and Jim burst inside.

'Where'd it hit?' yelled Dave. No-one answered. They all just stood gaping at the nearly glassless window at the rear of the hut. A faint breeze swirled the ash into the opening. Lana took the broom from inside the front door and began sweeping up the debris.

'I don't suppose this will be the last,' she said.

Paul grabbed a cloth and picked up the rock from the floor. 'Still hot.'

Lana inspected the rock in his hand. It was dark and slightly elongated. 'But cool enough to form a shape,' she remarked. 'Look at it, it's not even flat on the bottom.'

Emma jostled for position. 'This rock is seconds old. It's just been born,' she exclaimed. 'You can't help but be awestruck can you?'

Paul grinned. 'Spoken like a true geologist.'

She took it from Paul and studied it. 'It's special.' She

placed it with great reverence in the centre of the table. 'Do you think I might keep it?' she asked nobody in particular. 'I have a piece of rock from home. It's three point eight billion years old. This piece would be perfect sitting alongside of it.' She cleared the clutter off the table around it. 'The oldest and the newest,' she whispered.

The air inside the hut became murky. Ash continued to float in through the broken window carried only by its momentum. It settled over every surface, pale grey speckles turned dark light and light to dark.

The five of them sat at the small table listening to the grumbling and exploding all around them. The window at the front of the hut was letting in less light now, a sign the air was filling with ash. The explosions were intermittent. During a lull Paul rose and went back outside. The orange lights of small settlements that had been visible in the distance were no longer twinkling. A lifeline severed.

'It's getting thick out there,' he announced as he came back in. 'But I want to go out at first light to do some sampling.'

'You can't Paul,' exclaimed Lana, 'it's too dangerous.'

'Yeah, it is,' Paul conceded. 'But it's my life's work. I can't not get samples. I can get vital information on the chemical changes that occur throughout the eruption cycle.'

'I'll come with you Paul,' Emma drawled. 'If it's safe enough for you it will be safe enough for me.' She smiled her best winning smile.

'Well, uh...'

Lana watched him falter. He couldn't argue with that logic.

'We might get a reprieve in activity, he continued. 'I'll be careful.'

'Yes,' said Emma, 'we'll be careful.'

'You've been on live volcanoes before have you?' Lana asked Paul but it was a statement she didn't want him to answer. She held Emma's eyes. 'You definitely haven't. You can't possibly think about going out there.'

'Lana's right Em,' Paul agreed. 'I'm experienced. I can dash around these hills like a jack rabbit.' Emma was about to interrupt when Paul cut her off raising his arm. 'I know you can run off trail. I saw that today, but this is different. It's unpredictable and you need to make quick decisions. I know this mountain like the back of my hand. I don't need to be looking out for you too. That's settled. You're not coming.'

Lana watched Emma. She seemed to weigh Paul's words carefully and after pensive reflection she reluctantly nodded. Lana was surprised at how quickly she gave up. She expected Emma to have more fight in her.

Lana pursed her lips and huffed through her nose. She realised she'd been holding her breath throughout the exchange. Paul placed his hand on Lana's.

'I really will be careful,' he reassured her.

***

It had not been an easy sleep. Eruptions had been relentless all night. Each time she had awoken to a particularly disturbing explosion Emma and Paul had

121

also jolted into life. It seemed they had snatched less than one or two hours at a time. When the morning light finally woke Lana, it was silent outside. The wood-lined walls of the hut were shadowy. She held her sleeping bag close to her face leaving only her eyes peeking out from its folds. She unwillingly looked at the window. She didn't want to see a thick ash-strewn landscape or swirls of ash flying past. She wanted it all to be a dream. But it hadn't been her imagination. The air was thick and no sunshine was able to penetrate. She glanced over to Paul's sleeping bag. It was empty. She pulled it to her face and breathed in his scent that impregnated the soft down. It was cold. He had left long ago. She listened. Nothing. She quickly sat up and looked around. No Emma either.

'Damn!' She clenched her fists and beat them on her mattress. No wonder Emma had so willingly conceded defeat last night. She had every intention of accompanying Paul and he had bloody let her!

It was calm outside. The hut for once was not trembling. She peeled herself out of her bag and dressed in full thermals with trousers and shirt over top, ready for a day on the mountain should she get the opportunity. Then she ran her fingers through her hair and padded out to the main room. She made straight for the door. She'd held a slim hope that Paul and Emma were sitting on the deck with a hot cup of tea watching the sunrise. But the deck was empty and their boots had gone. How dare they! It was clear that Paul had wanted Emma with him or they would have woken the whole hut arguing about it. She stomped back inside and let the door slam behind her.

The others were not up. There was a light breeze coming through the broken window with ash swirling its way in. She trotted back to her pack and cut up her bright yellow plastic pack liner then fastened a piece of it to the window frame with insulation tape. It gave the room a surreal cheerful look.

Bill was tossing and turning on his bunk, lying diagonally across several mattresses and muttering. She went to him and placed her hand on his forehead. A bit hot.

'Not that one,' Bill muttered. The comment caught Lana by surprise and she quickly withdrew her hand.

'Which one?' she asked squatting alongside the bunk.

'Purple ribbon.'

'What purple ribbon Bill?' Lana pressed him.

'Tom's granddad.'

'Who is Tom?'

'Tom,' he repeated.

'Where is the purple ribbon Bill?' asked Lana.

'Ant.'

'Ant,' Lana murmured to herself. An insect or a name? Antony? She decided to lead the questioning. 'How did you hurt yourself Bill?'

'Ant.'

A name, Lana decided. 'Who is Ant?'

'You shouldn't have taken it,' Bill warned.

'What did I take?' asked Lana.

'Cross.'

'With a purple ribbon?'

'Stop it,' Bill made a thrusting movement with one arm.

'Are you in a fight? Bill? Are you in a fight?' Lana

123

repeated.

He made another thrusting movement and rolled away from Lana. Just then the door to the bunkroom opened and Dave came out. He quickly surveyed the room.

'What's going on?' he asked Lana.

Lana bristled at his tone.

'What's he been saying?'

'Just about a ribbon.'

'And?' he spat.

There was maliciousness behind that one word. It scared her.

'And nothing. Look your mate better see to him if he's a doctor. He's clearly not well,' she implored. 'He's reliving something stressful and it's the fever bringing that on.'

Dave looked around the room furtively. He opened the door to Lana's bunkroom and glanced in. 'Where are your friends?' he asked.

'They've gone out for a minute,' she lied. 'They'll be back any time now.'

She rose from her squatting position and made for the door of the hut. Dave took a half step to one side so she could pass but not so easily that she didn't rub against him.

'Where are you going?' he asked.

She turned, glared at him and slammed the door after her.

It was a trek of some fifty metres uphill over uneven ash-covered, rock-strewn ground to the toilet. A mid-green plastic box battened down with steel guy ropes stood sentinel above the little hut. As she climbed she had a good view of the ash column spewing out of the volcano. She looked down over the east side of the mountain. The ground was covered in a fairytale powder of fine ash. Previously dark brown and red rocks were now a pale shade of grey. It was a different place. She felt like an observer from another planet. She suddenly imagined the little green toilet was a dark blue police box and Paul was the doctor and she was the beautiful assistant.

She was surprised to see she was trembling. The man calling himself Dave, who clearly was not called Dave, was intimidating. He didn't need to be. It was like she and the others had done something to upset him.

She studied the hut from above. It was a simple structure, rectangular in shape with a single gable roof. Apart from the two bunkrooms and the communal living area there was a small warden's quarter attached to the north end. An open deck linked the two. There was a solitary stainless steel sink attached to one end of the deck, quite out of place. Even from here she could see the small yellow cake of soap she'd left next to the tap. A small black polythene water tank was situated on a wooden trestle to the rear of the building. The hut was covered in fine ash and there were trails in the ash on the roof left by the tumbling molten rocks. The water tank appeared to be intact. Both the hut and tank was also secured with metal guy ropes; testament to the ferociousness of alpine winter storms.

On her way back down the hill she heard footsteps behind her. She halted and looked around only to be assailed upon by Dave. He held onto a fist-sized boulder and raised it above his head. Lana immediately bent forward ramming her rump into his body. He lurched forward with the unexpected shock of the impact grunting as he did so. She let out a gnarled guttural scream as she curled her right hand into a fist and using assistance from her left hand to drive it she projected her right elbow into his midriff. She felt her elbow sink into his soft upper belly. He had been surprised by her counter and had not thought to tighten his stomach muscles. Instead her elbow connected with his solar plexus. Dave gasped for breath caught unawares and sucking at the top of his lungs for precious life-sustaining air. He crunched forward heaving as Lana knew he would and his head was perfectly positioned for a smack to the face. She swung her right fist up, pivoting at the elbow and smashed him with a back fist to his face. She felt the back of her fist connect with the gristle of his nose.

It was what she had trained for all those long years. She had always wondered if she'd need to use her skills. And if caught in a situation would she be able to react instinctively? She'd always found it difficult to touch her training partner's head – something about the touch of their eyes, wet mouth, sweaty forehead. It repelled her. But now the adrenalin fuelled the fight, as she'd always hoped it would when it came down to it. Dave howled and dropped heavily to the ground clutching his nose. It began to swell and his eyes watered. She lifted a booted foot and stomped on his head until she saw the first blood streak his cheek. He extracted a mouthful of expletives.

She was pleased to hear it. At least she hadn't projected the bones of his nose into his brain and killed him. She looked at the damage she had inflicted. She couldn't feel safe unless he was unconscious. Her training told her to run or to administer a more permanent resolution to her attacker. But she was prevented from executing further damage as Jim appeared downhill of her. The angle of the incline gave her a temporary height advantage. She was aware that she was still vulnerable to attack from Dave but she had bought herself time. Jim came straight for her. He was unaware that the target he presented to Lana was more vulnerable, in fact the best she'd ever been offered for the sort of attack she contemplated. She summed up her situation in a split second and directed a beautiful straight-legged Muay Thai kick to Jim's groin. He let out a blood-curdling scream as he doubled over clutching himself. Lana grabbed onto Jim's shoulders and with a mighty holler brought her right knee up to his face smashing his head on it as she did so. Her knee connected with his nose which made a dull crack as it broke.

But then the time she'd bought ran out. She felt the earth disappear from under her as she took a wallop to the back of her legs. Dave had found himself in the unenviable position of being on the ground, bleeding from head wounds and possibly affecting any possibility of good decision-making. However, to his advantage he was now below Lana's centre. He grasped her lower legs propelling her face down onto the ground and he dragged her until she was half on top of him. Her worst nightmare. She shouldn't have let herself go to the ground. Now she really would have to get close to her assailant if she was going to win this. Mount, side mount, bridge, post. Words flooded into her head. Why was he still flailing under her? Don't give him space, she heard her sensei over her shoulders. Keep your arms tight. Use your body, dead weight Lana. She tried to relax into a dead weight like she had been taught but she wasn't lying over his chest enough to squash the air out of him and hinder movement of his torso so she flailed her arms and legs, twisted her body around and hit out at him. She had all her weapons free, punching and elbowing, sometimes connecting, sometimes not. She cursed her wasted energy at an unconnected blow. She kept her body writhing from side to side, bringing one leg up at a time and digging in Dave's ribs with her knees.

Her face suddenly was buried in his groin and she bit hard into his thigh. He screamed again and this time jerked her upwards and his legs shot up off the ground. She grabbed the soft flesh behind his thigh and pinched it, twisting it before letting it go. Then her face fell back into his groin directly over his scrotum. She felt the soft flesh under layers of fabric fill her mouth. It was worse than anything she'd ever experienced. She gagged on the furry fabric of his trousers and the sweaty urine odour it harboured. She heaved. She should bite, but it was against her nature. She couldn't fill her mouth with his balls and his blood. She shouldn't think of it. She should just do it. No time to think about it. She knew she shouldn't take her weight off him. It would be all over if she gave him space but the sick feeling in her stomach dominated the rules that she'd learnt to play by.

'Hold the cow still,' Dave yelled as he grasped a chunky boulder. He was scared; she could hear it in his voice. He didn't know that she was completely and utterly spent.

Jim regained his feet and stooped to take hold of Lana's wildly kicking legs. His fingers found her trousers and he pulled the fabric. They gave way and slipped a little pulling away from her. Then she felt strong hands around her ankles as Jim dragged her off Dave onto the uneven cold ground. She wanted to pull her pants up. The cold bit at her skin, but she had to get up. Can't have her back to her attackers, most dangerous place. She panted, unsure what to do. She was aware of Dave's arm raised in the air. She shot a glance at Jim, whose face registered terror. It was enough to make her roll onto her side but it was too late. Now she could see Dave's bloody face and wild eyes behind the rock that struck her head. And then there was darkness.

***

As soon as the early morning explosions eased up, Paul left the hut. He had stolen out quietly so as not to disturb the girls while they slept. He resisted an overwhelming desire to kiss Lana gently on her lips as he left her. He didn't want her worried about him and he figured she would have less time to worry if she didn't know he had gone. It was not quite daylight when he left but he didn't expect it to get wholly light anyway. With luck she would sleep. He knew none of them had got much during the night but there seemed to be a reprieve in explosions at the moment and he couldn't waste a minute.

He made his way up the mountain slope around an outcrop south of the hut. The air was thick. Ash had rested on the snow and dirtied it and it had settled on the steepest barren outcrops turning them pale grey. He noticed that his boots left fresh imprints in the newly fallen ash. It clung to his boots quickly adding surprising weight to them. He looked back and quickly lost sight of the hut but he had a good view of the lahar path far to the east on the lower ring plain. It was a dark flat sinewy line in a grey landscape, there being no moonlight now to illuminate the water and no sun to penetrate the ash-laden atmosphere.

Paul reflected upon last night. Lana's kiss was the sweetest thing. He had dreamed of it since their meeting in Iceland, and hoped for it as she lay the night before in another room. It hadn't let him down. How it had lit his fire. He had dared not move and reveal to her the extent of his desire. As he propelled himself forward he replayed every word of every sentence of their conversation on the verandah. She hadn't rebuffed him. It made him feel warm and deliriously happy.

***

Emma rounded the outcrop just as Paul started climbing. He hadn't seen her, she was sure of it. His footprints were dark against the grey that was everywhere. Easy for her to follow. She zipped her jacket up higher under her chin and hurried to catch him up.

When she heard Paul pull the hut door to at first light she sneaked out of her bunk and followed him. She had barely slept and suspected that they all lay in the dark listening to the tremors of the mountain, all scared to talk, just in case one of them was fortunate enough to grab a few winks. She was on alert for Paul to wake. He wasn't adamant that she was not to accompany him this morning. It was merely a suggestion. It wasn't as though he was expedition leader or anything.

Clearly Lana was jealous of her. She didn't blame her. She was gorgeous, intelligent and had a great body. Paul appreciated that, she knew. She saw how he looked at her.

When she returned from Iceland she'd done a little research on Paul Harrington. Found out that he was a prolific writer of scientific papers over his twenty five year career. Volcanoes were his passion and he'd come lately to lahars. Finding out about his personal life was more difficult. He didn't have a Facebook page, didn't twitter, wasn't linked in. She guessed she'd have to get to know him the old fashioned way. She saw at conference that Lana held some sort of attraction for him but she didn't see Lana as an obstacle. Rather she was her key to Paul and right now things were going perfectly to plan.

She coughed. Minute ash particles sucked in her nostrils. She could taste them on her lips. Glass, she thought. 'Shit.' She swore out loud. She dug into her light back pack and pulled out a bandana, tied it around her face and put her sunglasses on.

Paul was way ahead of her, heading high up to a ridge which was bathed in the filtered morning light. She was surprised he hadn't noticed her. She shuffled into a half jog, half scramble. Paul was right. She was very capable off-trail. It gave her a short adrenalin rush as she recalled cross country skiing at home. Her young nephews would be looking forward to the coming winter. She tried to spend as much time with them as she could teaching them to ski around trees and rocks, to calculate the best line. She gained on Paul easily following his trail.

'Paul,' she yelled. 'Paul, wait.'

Her words echoed closely around her just as a rumble beneath her feet knocked her off balance.

***

Paul shrugged off his backpack and fumbled around for his bandana. He tied it around his head, put his sunglasses on and pocketed a couple of lava bombs. Then he took the lid off a film container and scooped ash into it, and made a note of the time and location.

As he squatted a deep-seated rumble permeated the whole mountain reverberating beneath his feet and right through his body. A shrill scream caused him to look behind just as a massive ejection of steam, ash, bombs and rocky blocks spewed above the mountain. Arcs of white steam trailed the heavy projectiles above the summit as hot air condensed into the cold. Volcanic debris landed hundreds of metres from the centre of the eruption vent and rained down once again onto the lower slopes of the mountain.

He was reasonably protected. He'd been scaling the ridge which trended north east. Therefore, at this moment with the explosion so momentous debris flew more or less over him. He expected to catch the wind once he'd reached the top so paused to cover up before he got there. Now he was too late to traverse it, to get closer to the vent. He gazed back down the mountain to the source of the scream.

'Emma,' he yelled. She was crouched on the ground, immobile it seemed. She had her head on the ground and her arms balled over protecting it.

This was a more fierce eruption than last night. Explosions occurred every minute, less than a minute. Paul was conscious of the change in eruption style. There was less lake water now. These explosions were potentially more lethal to any person silly enough to be on the mountain. He had to retreat and get Emma to safety.

As he descended molten rock pelted down all around him. He looked around for cover, but nothing presented itself. The ash and steam plume emanating from the crater now extended high into the atmosphere. He estimated it to be around ten kilometres.

Thunderous explosions cracked the atmosphere but it was the frequency that alarmed him more than its fire. It was like machine gunfire. But there were no rabbit holes or trenches to shelter in. They were completely exposed. He tried to find an overhang to hide under but it was not the nature of volcanoes to readily offer overhangs.

'Hang on Emma,' he yelled. She was still cowering. He didn't need to see her eyes to know the fear. He felt it too but he told himself it was adrenalin pounding in his ears. He scrambled back down the slope. No sooner had he reached her she pounced up and embraced him. She was trembling. 'We need to get below that ridge,' he shouted waving his arm in the direction he'd just come from. From here the climb looked near vertical and it was only about four hundred metres away. It almost retained its chocolate colour, barely had any ash adhered to it. 'If we can reach that we'll stand a better chance of sitting out the explosions. Okay?' He shook her shoulders. 'Emma?'

She clung harder to him. She couldn't answer.

'Are you hurt?' he asked.

She shook her head.

'Why can't you move?' he demanded. 'Emma. Why? Answer me.' He shook her shoulders again.

She faltered, almost whispering her reply. 'Can't.'

Paul relaxed his grip on her. 'We can't stay here and it's too far to go back. I need you to run with me to that bit of rock face. We'll be safe there.'

Her head darted all around but still she said nothing.

'Emma, I'm here,' Paul implored. 'Hold my hand. We'll run together. Don't be scared, but we need to run now.'

A fresh pelt of rocks fell around them, clipping Emma on the back of her pack. 'Ah,' she screamed and took flight directly downhill.

'No, Emma,' Paul yelled. 'Not that way.'

He tore after her until he felt a crack on his head like someone had flicked him with a finger. 'Ah.' He dropped to his knees clasping his head. His ears rang with the shock of the pain. It was almost too intense to rub. He staggered to his feet just in time to see Emma well in front of him, her long blonde hair bouncing over her shoulders as she bounded over the rocky terrain. She was just running because she could. But he couldn't let her. 'Emma,' he yelled, but his words were eaten up by the raucous blasts. He eyed the relative safety of the outcrop which was becoming further and further away then ran downhill chasing Emma's footsteps.

Suddenly she wasn't in front of him. He slowed, scanning the landscape. Nothing. He followed her trail. They led to a narrow bluff. He peered over the edge. Below the outcrop Emma lay crumpled with her leg twisted out from her body at an odd angle. She didn't move. Hot pebbles continued to rain over the mountain. Paul skirted the bluff and descended the twenty metres to her. 'Emma! God!' She whimpered until he dragged her into a seated position with her back up against the hard rock when she screamed and lashed out at him. 'Steady, steady girl. You've broken your leg.'

'I'm sorry,' she winced through clenched teeth.

'Don't worry about that now,' he replied. 'We're sitting ducks here. We have to move. I'll carry you.'

A fresh volley of fire spewed out of the mountain. A deep rhombus cloud of toxic gases accompanied the expulsions. Within seconds Paul felt the hot sting of andesitic basalt lick his head and arms. This time he smelt the fibres of his jacket as they smouldered under the attack. Emma screamed and clutched her hands to her head as blood spilled down her face but when she saw her hands sodden with the sticky red she became hysterical. Paul slumped forward on his hands and knees and nestled his head against Emma's shoulder.

'Please stop it,' he panted. 'Please stop screaming Emma.' He rubbed her head. He could see her blood oozing silently into the weave of her wool beanie. He put his arm around her shoulders but she would not stop. He couldn't think. He slapped her. Hard, on the cheek. Then she was quiet. She sat stunned. He grabbed her shoulders and made her look at him. Her eyes were wide behind her sunglasses but Paul sensed they were looking through him.

'Help me,' he said. 'You can help me get you to safety or you can stay here and await certain death.'

Finally he saw a flicker of cognisance. She nodded and whispered, 'I can help you.'

'Good girl.' He didn't tell her that he saw stars when he took the last hit. He gave himself a moment to summon strength before he jostled her onto his shoulder. She cried out, one leg dangling and the other kicking into his hip. She whimpered with every step.

The weight of her crushed Paul into the mountain. He felt her soft rump next to his face and her plump breasts digging into his shoulder blades. It reminded him of Lana. She was right. He should not have come out here. It was too soon, too dangerous. The mountain had a lot of anger to dispel yet. He was a fool. What if he died out here? After all he'd done to meet with her, after she'd let him kiss her, after she had given him a glimmer of hope – even though she didn't know her own mind.

He had nearly recovered the ground below the track when the mountain vented its deeper innards. The missiles were bigger, hotter, more difficult to endure. The ground was turning brown under the new round of eruptions. Struck, he lurched forward and fell to his knees with Emma flying ahead of him shrieking until she hit the ground with a thud. He fell onto her trying to ignore the searing pain in his left side, his head still bleeding from the previous hit.

Emma lay still on the ground, crumpled and jumbled like a rag doll, her sunglasses cast aside. Paul wiped the blood from her face and tucked her beanie back over her ears. She was beautiful. Her skin showed no sign of aging; it was smooth and lightly tanned. Her eyelids flickered, the long lashes curled at the ends, as though she couldn't decide whether to open or close her eyes. He suddenly felt protective of her. He couldn't let her face be struck. She didn't deserve that. It was his fault she was here. He should have been firmer last night, should have emphasised the danger. But he wasn't her superior. She was free to make her own decisions. He tucked a blonde tress waves under her beanie. She stirred.

'It's all right, shush now,' he said. 'You've had a knock to the head. We fell.'

She tried to sit up. Paul edged closer and laid her head in his lap. 'Rest a minute.'

'You're bleeding,' she said.

'So are you.'

'My leg.' She clutched at her thigh, straining to lift herself up.

'You can't walk on it.'

She flopped back down onto his lap. 'I fucking know that,' she spat through clenched teeth.

Paul smiled. 'That's the girl. Get angry. Get that fight back.'

She flailed her arms blindly chancing a connection with Paul but he grabbed them and held her tight as she struggled against him. 'Damn you Paul Harrington,' she screamed.

'No use beating me up Emma. I didn't get you into this mess. You're angry at yourself and that's useless too. I don't know what happened to you back there to trigger such a panic, but I'd rather you had the fight in you to get yourself out of this. Now you're going to help

137

me to get you to that rock face up ahead. Understood?'

He could see she was boiling inside.

'I can't walk,' she complained.

'You can stand.'

He helped her sit up then planted his feet far apart to help her stand. But the earth swayed. He focussed on Emma's face, but the landscape around it swam in and out of focus, sometimes receding, sometimes advancing. As she took his outstretched hands he pulled her up. He felt her arms around his neck as she jostled for balance on her good leg. He clung to her for a second. His head would come right in a minute. He felt his cheek grow hot, and then damp. He smelt Emma on him. She nibbled his face. He found her lips and for a moment the sweet warmth of her plunged him into a languid pool. For just a second he blocked out the crackling mountain, the thick air and his light-headedness.

He snapped his head back. 'No.'

'No?'

'That is ... no.' He pushed her back and held her at arm's length. He smiled for her, not to her. 'Let's put that down to head injury eh?'

'If you say so,' she answered coyly. Paul didn't see her smile turn to satisfaction as he hoisted her once again over his shoulder.

He trudged heavily towards the rock face, taking perhaps only thirty steps before a volcanic boulder struck his left thigh and pummelled him to the ground. It felt numb, like a dead leg Charlie. Soon the pain seared through his flesh convincing him he had an open wound. He gently pressed his thigh and was relieved to find the flesh intact but the pain seemed to move to his knee. He couldn't breathe properly. He managed shallow gasps like a fish out of water but it didn't stop the jabbing pain in his back. Emma was screaming. Again. He stumbled off her, tried to stand, but his knee was white hot with pain. He fell hard on the ground.

'What's the matter?' she screamed at him.

'My knee,' he grunted. 'It's stuffed.'

She rolled towards him and rolled up his trouser leg. 'Bite on something.'

'What?'

'Bite on something.'

'Why? What are you doing? Don't touch me.'

'Shut up Paul. I know what I'm doing.' She hauled herself into a sitting position and placed her hands either side of his knee. She cracked the patella back into position as Paul was about to challenge her again. His throat grew hoarse as he screamed. 'That took your mind off your ankle.'

Paul lay on his back and focussed on his pain. He had of course felt the ankle twist but as far as priorities went, it wasn't high on the list. Now that Emma had drawn his attention to it he warmed to its throb. For a minute it was the least painful injury. 'How did you know to do that?'

'I've nearly got my paramedic certificate. Should have it by now but haven't found the time to sit the exam.'

'Where's your back pack?'

She looked around her, surprised. 'I didn't know I'd lost it.'

'We've got next to no protection,' he said. 'Here, take this.' He shrugged off his pack and tucked it behind Emma's head. 'Hold it on your head.'

'What are you going to use?'

'I'm going to get help.'

'You're crazy Paul,' Emma pleaded. 'You can't even walk with your injuries.'

'I can't get you back on my own Em. So either I try to make a dash for it or we both die of hyperthermia.'

Fresh debris fell with the accompanying timbale of the volcano. 'Or a blow to the head.'

'Please Paul, be careful.'

Paul crawled to his good knee and tentatively stood. He gritted his teeth against the pain that was everywhere. Thank God one leg was still good. He shuffled off in the direction of the hut and descended into a depression out of Emma's line of sight when he was struck by a bomb to his head. As he hit the ground he thought how nice it was to be free of pain.

When he awoke it was still daylight, albeit dull, and the mountain was still performing. The atmosphere was thick with muddy haze. He figured he hadn't been out for long. He put a hand to his head. It was intensely sore but to his surprise, not bloody. There was an egg forming. He staggered to his feet and proceeded downhill picking his route carefully to avoid boulders.

Paul took a second hit from a significantly bigger projectile to his back. It hit with such impact that he stumbled sideways down the slope. His ankle was useless. He couldn't arrest the slide. Suddenly he was down on the cold ground, blood spewing from gashed shins. He sprawled facing down the hill with his arms spread eagled ahead of him. The pain in his back intensified with every breath so he tried shallow breathing, panting like a dog.

The mountain raged around him. He had to protect his head. He scrunched into a ball and tried to make himself as small as possible wrapping his arms about his head. He peered up the slope to locate his pack. It was the only protection he had.

Hauling himself onto his knees he scrambled towards the backpack. As he reached it he sustained yet another attack to the head once again rendering him unconscious.

Chapter Five

Two uniformed females in a white Toyota Corolla sedan pulled into the empty carpark behind the museum building. To the west stood the Ruapehu massif capped with snow and entertaining the lightest of streaky clouds about its tops. The sky was a clear, light blue. Sandra eyed it as she parked the car and fleetingly looked forward to some spring skiing in the next few days. Around her neck she wore a lanyard with a set of keys dangling off it and a lacquered photographic identification tag which showed a dark blonde bob on an oval face. The women locked the car and walked to the museum's back door without missing a beat of conservation. Sandra inserted the key into the lock.

'It's unlocked,' she gasped and pushed the door.

'No,' whispered Eileen harshly. She grabbed the younger woman's arm. Sandra saw fear in Eileen's pale blue eyes.

'You're right.' Sandra stepped back from the door. 'Let's have a look outside first.' She backed up from the building never taking her eyes off it. 'Check the front while I go around the side.'

After a minute Eileen returned to meet Sandra back outside the door. 'Anything?'

'Nope.'

They entered the building. The alarm should have been emitting a piercing intermittent beep but it was silent. The women exchanged looks. The alarm if it was on should have been on delay entry. They stared at the alarm panel. No light. Nothing.

142

'The cleaners,' said Eileen.

'Hope so. Better call it in.' Sandra walked quickly to reception, picked up the phone and called security.

'The alarm was activated at 6.58 pm,' explained the man on the other end of the line, 'but there is no indication of a deactivation.'

'Could your system fail for any reason? Power outage or the like?'

'No ma'am,' the security representative did not hesitate.

She thanked him very much and called the cleaning company covering the mouth piece as she gave instructions to Eileen.

'Eileen, I need a list of who was on yesterday. Don't leave reception. We may not be alone.'

After speaking to the security firm and being reassured that the cleaners had set the alarm and locked up behind them, the women alerted the police.

'The police will be here presently,' she announced. 'We'd better remain closed until we ascertain what's happened.'

'You think we've been burgled?' asked Eileen.

'I don't know. Let's find out.'

Eileen hurried after her colleague. 'What's the likely target?'

'Something valuable.'

'It's all valuable.'

'Something expensive then, easy to sell. Something small.'

'Medals!'

They bounded up to the next floor scrutinising exhibits as they made their way to the medal section.

'Don't touch anything. Just look,' Sandra instructed.

'Nothing looks touched.'

The women peered into the glass topped display cabinets. The medals were carefully presented with each medal having a corresponding card next to it. There were no surplus cards.

'Could these screws have been removed?' asked Eileen. 'They're not all screwed home.'

'Hard to say.' Sandra bent forward squinting at the side of the cabinet's top. 'You're right. There are bright makes on the screws. Like they've been screwed recently.'

'Uh oh,' exclaimed Eileen, 'here's something. Or rather, a not something.' She stared at a gap in the wall-mounted medals where several hung on shiny time-ravaged ribbons. 'Someone got lazy.'

'Let's have another look at the cabinets and those screws,' said Sandra.

'Don't suppose you know which medal was on the wall?'

'There's a collections catalogue. That's our best bet. At least we can lead the police straight here.'

'I've just thought!' cried Sandra. 'The electrical room.'

'What about it?'

'It's the security systems room. There's a closed circuit camera. We'll be lucky to get anything I suppose. If they were clever enough to trick the security system they will have taken the tapes.'

They scurried back downstairs to find two constables entering the building. As they reported the results of their preliminary investigation Sandra and Eileen were unaware that a concentrated earthquake swarm was broiling beneath the ring plain on which they stood.

***

By the end of the day an inventory had been completed. It was discovered that sixteen medals had been stolen. Curiously, someone had gone to a great deal of trouble re-spacing the ribbonned medals. So why was there a gap? The police concluded that two people were responsible for the medals theft. One person was meticulous about covering his tracks and the second person stole one medal on impulse without the knowledge of the other; for surely, the careful thief would not have left a gap on the wall. There were no finger prints evident and the police concluded that gloves had been worn for the duration of the heist.

A cross reference with the collections index revealed that a New Zealand Memorial Cross (King George VI), three New Zealand Memorial Crosses (Queen Elizabeth II), three New Zealand medals, three 1914-1915 Stars, two Queen's South Africa medals, and two New Zealand War Service Medals were missing.

A thorough survey of the museum confirmed that no other military collectables had been stolen and that the closed circuit telesurveillence system had been compromised. No pictures of the offenders were available. The police duly noted the missing items and being a matter in the nation's interest, called a press conference.

***

Alex had still not heard from Lana. It was inconceivable that she had not sent a message to him given her situation. However, he conceded, that was the exact reason she had not got a message out. He chastised himself that it was selfish to be angry with her when in fact she was probably at this very minute sheltering out of harm's way and out of phone coverage. She knew he would be frantic with worry. Of course she would get a message out as soon as she could. Therefore, logically, if she had not managed yet to get a message to him it was because she could not, not because she did not want to. But that thought too was driving him insane.

The house felt empty. Alone. Not that he might not have been alone anyway. But Lana would normally have been doing something, well, normal. He'd not be pacing the house, talking to himself, wrangling his fingers through the couple of hairs that were left on top of his head. How many times had he checked his phone? He needed to calm himself. He needed someone to calm him. He needed to talk to someone.

He phoned Julie.

'Alex!' Julie appeared pleased to hear from him. He could hear the lightness in her voice. 'Have you heard from her?'

'No,' he replied. 'I hoped you might have. Are you monitoring events from there?'

'Yes, I'll be here for hours yet.'

'Can I come in?' he asked.

'Of course you can,' she replied with a gush of empathy. As if she knew more than he did. 'There are a few of us here monitoring the lahar and the volcano. We'll soon have word. Oh, and Alex?'

'Yes?'

'Could you pick up some Chinese?'

***

As he joined the early evening traffic Alex pondered his relationship with Lana. He recalled the day she floated into his office. It was a typical blustery spring day and she had appeared before him like a vision in gold. She wore a retro flowery mustard yellow top over jeans and gold strappy shoes with a low heel. She carried a yellow bag over one shoulder that would have been more suitable for a day at the beach. The wind had messed up her silky dark hair and there was a hint of carefully applied but subtle make-up.

She had captured him immediately. She wore a child's innocence and she was immune to the effect she had on him. At that stage he had been divorced for more than two years. He was too young not to enjoy the right female company but at the same time he had come to appreciate being alone. He savoured his newfound and regained freedom. He listened to sports radio and was the master of his own remote control. He had splashed out on the ultimate luxury; he paid a man to mow his lawns. For years he had battled with the lawnmower because that's what blokes do. It was expected. He would work all week only to come home to lawns that had somehow turned into elephant grass and to a wife who pointed out that fact.

But when Lana breezed into the office that day he knew he was ready for love again. She explained her recent bereavement and inheritance along with her plans to start a new life.

After Yuri's accident Lana had turned to her dearest and oldest friend Sarah, even though Lana had friends, especially in the orchestra, who supported her in her grief. But Sarah had been a friend to Lana at school and in the years since. Their lives had taken wildly different paths. A geography teacher, Sarah found recent work heading a natural history society. Alex didn't even know such things existed. Lana had come home immediately after the funeral for a break and to think. She had become enamoured with Sarah's work and lifestyle. Rashly, she decided to settle up her life in Sydney and come home for good.

He knew the relationship with Sarah was not as Lana had hoped. Neither of them had reckoned on the intervening years changing them as much as they had. But for all that, Lana was happy with the choices she'd made. Deeply happy. When she spoke of her studies it was as if she were seeing life for the first time.

Alex had courted her with trepidation and he had been more than diligent in the work he did for her. He asked her into his office many more times than he needed and gradually they became familiar with each other. She appeared to enjoy his company.

Asking her out for coffee was such a natural transition that it didn't feel like a date. He wondered now if she had considered it a date. Passion had never been a strong feature of theirs. They just seemed to fit together like two comfortable socks paired into a ball.

He wondered why he and Lana did not live together. She was a headstrong woman who had resolved to do something she believed in. She needed to follow her dream. She had burnt bridges and was building new ones – bridges that he would cross with her. Let her make her choices. He would not force her hand. She would move in with him when she was ready. He didn't want to hold her back. He was a generous modern man. There were no stereotypes in his world.

Alex felt hollow in his stomach, like he'd been retching all day. It hit him how much he was in love with her. She deserved better than a part time lover. He pictured her again in the sheer silky shirt the first time he saw her and imagined a glistening gold band on the third finger of her left hand. That completed his picture and he smiled.

***

Alex parked the Mazda in the university car park at the rear of the science block and walked around to the front entrance. He paused at the foyer and read the name plate. Dr Julie Bidwell, 1:21. He was about to turn away when something caught his eye. Lana's nameplate, room 1:32 had only her married name. He stared at it for a moment wondering if there was a reason other than lack of space for not including Marshall. Carrying the Chinese takeaway he strode along the bare corridor to Julie's office aware of his footsteps reverberating off the walls.

He knocked on her door. 'Hi there Julie,' he said softly. She rose from her computer to greet him. Alex had met her only a couple of times before. Her short brown hair stuck out from her head, not styled but dragged there by impatient hands and left to the elements.

In her late forties, she had come to academia after an oil drilling career in her twenties and child rearing in her thirties. She fit comfortably into the male dominated world of industry and science.

She smiled and offered him her hand. 'Nice to see you Alex.' He shook it and was surprised by the forthrightness of her grip. He held up the bag of hot food.

'Thanks,' said Julie, 'that's lovely.' She pulled a second chair to the desk. 'Please, have a seat.'

'Any word?' asked Alex.

'Not from Lana, no.'

'From anyone?'

'Only from agencies off the mountain.'

'Do you know who she's with?' he asked.

'A research student from Canada, Emma Purdoe.'

Alex nodded. 'Oh yes, Lana did mention her.'

'And they were to meet up with Paul Harrington,' Julie continued. 'It looks like they did meet. Auckland University says he's on the mountain.'

Alex frowned. 'I don't know him. She never mentioned him.'

'He's a volcanologist working out of Auckland University. They met in Iceland,' she explained.

Alex thought hard struggling to recall if Lana might have mentioned Paul. She said she would be away for three nights with a colleague, but a male volcanologist didn't ring any bells.

'Did they?' he frowned. Lana had told him all about the conference in her usual effervescent way and he knew she had met Emma there. But she hadn't

150

mentioned Paul Harrington. 'What for?' he asked.

'What for what?'

'Why is Lana meeting Paul Harrington?'

'He will help with her research.'

'What does he do?'

Julie had turned back to the flickering screen.

'Julie?'

'He's a world renown volcanologist. Very experienced,' she replied not taking her eyes off the screen.

'Do you know him?' asked Alex.

'Not personally. Know of him though,' she added.

Alex nodded. 'So what do you know about him?' he ventured. He smiled at Julie trying to make light of this new information. 'Should I be worried?'

'On the contrary. As far as I'm aware he'd be very capable of finding safety on the mountain. Remember, the eruptions started at night and they should be in the hut. They're in the historical eruption zone unfortunately, so there's no doubt in my mind that they will have to sit it out in the relative safety of the hut until eruptions subside,' Julie explained.

That was not quite what Alex had meant. His overtly subtle question had been lost on Julie and he considered it would look childish to backtrack.

'There's more Alex, I'm afraid,' Julie continued. 'We had a helicopter report that there was a person on the valley floor of the Whangaehu River system. That's the lahar path. We don't know at this stage whether that person was dead or alive and I don't know exactly where along the river it was seen. Given that they were in the area near the outlet of the lake and given Paul's specialist knowledge I believe they would not have been caught out. They should have very quickly understood the signals alerting them to the imminent breach of the lake. They should have made it to safety. In my heart of hearts I believe they are safe Alex. She paused and her words hung heavy in the air. 'I'm just apprising you of the situation.'

She patted Alex's hand and smiled thinly through serious eyes then continued. 'We don't have accurate numbers as to how many people are on the mountain. As you know, the track is a ring around the mountain with multiple access points. This means that even the conservation department has no idea how many people are in the park at a given time.'

Alex digested this. 'Think about it Julie. If there are three of them together they would stay together, wouldn't they? Especially in adverse conditions. Why would they split up? They wouldn't.'

'I agree,' said Julie. 'If the person the helicopter saw was one of them the others would stay with them.' She did not need to add unless one of them was dead.

'So we can assume that the person the helicopter saw was someone else,' Alex continued his bluff at bravado. 'A lone tramper.'

They descended into an uneasy silence. Julie rose from her chair. 'I'll get us some cutlery.'

Alex swung his chair closer to the computer screen. It may as well have been blank. He pictured Lana lifeless on the valley floor, tossed aside by the raging torrent. There was no one else with her because she was dead. No need for anyone else to be with her. He wondered what she was wearing. Did she have her red mountain jacket on? The one with double sewn seams that was so bulky she had to keep it in the garage. What was she carrying? Did she have a photo of him in her wallet as George Mallory had carried a photograph of his beloved Ruth all the way up to the top of Everest? Was she carrying her wallet? There would be no point in it. Apart from the obvious of course: to assist in the identification of her body.

He startled as Julie returned and snapped him out of his reverie. They ate in silence as the computer screen flickered its erratic light. Alex hadn't noticed darkness fall. The soft white of a street lamp over the car park drew Alex's attention to the black of the single casement window. Julie rose to switch on the light and suddenly Alex was looking at himself in the reflection. He stared right through himself as if he wasn't there; through his pallid skin, his reflecting eye glasses and balding head, through his neatly pressed cotton shirt.

'Let me explain what happens with volcanic eruptions,' Julie said sitting down and clunking her fork on the desk.

Alex nodded enthusiastically. 'Yes. Thank you. That would help.' He managed a weak smile.

'Mount Ruapehu last erupted sixteen and seventeen years ago,' she began. 'The first eruptions were primarily ash. A continuous column rose to between ten and twenty kilometres high.'

'Gosh. That's from here to home. That's twice as high as aircraft fly at.' Alex shook his head.

'I know. Hard to get your head around.'

'The explosive force to propel ash that high must be phenomenal.'

'Yeah,' Julie agreed. 'Now of course all that ash has to go somewhere and in the case of Ruapehu the predominant wind direction comes from the west. Therefore, many of the eruption deposits land on the east side of the mountain.'

'Oh,' groaned Alex.

'Yes. Oh. And true to form there is a westerly flow at approximately forty knots around the tops at the moment. Last time this occurred there were ash deposits between ten and twenty centimetres thick to the north and north east of the mountain. That's very thick. Covers everything. Ash deposits were found as far away as Hawkes Bay.'

'God. So Lana...'

'Lana mush stay out of the ash. It's dangerous stuff. Essentially it's glass. Finely ground particles of glass. If it's breathed in it will perforate the lungs.'

'I assume Lana knows this.'

'Absolutely Alex. Besides, no one understands that better than Dr Harrington.'

'OK, so the mountain was covered in ash.'

'Not just the mountain,' Julie continued. 'The ash affected the local trout fishery and sheep farming. Animals got sick with a condition called flourosis from eating the grass. It happens with humans too when it gets into the water supply. Paul would have seen this in Central America.'

Alex bristled at the continual reference to Paul.

'We think an ash plume was the first of eruption styles this time as well,' Julie explained. 'It was night. I assume that she is safe inside the hut.'

'Okay,' he said slowly calculating Lana's odds.

'The last time the eruptions started there was a lot of water in Crater Lake,' Julie continued. 'We're talking a couple of million cubic metres. It was forced out of the crater and it ran down several valleys, including valleys on the other side of the mountain, as mudflows. We know that perhaps half of that amount had already escaped earlier as the lahar.'

'What's the difference?' asked Alex.

'The lahar has greater water content,' she replied. 'And mudflows can travel at around ninety kilometres per hour. You can't outrun them.'

'So now we have ash fallout and a mudflow. Jesus! Is she safe from mudflow?'

'Almost certainly. The hut is situated between two valleys and it's slightly below a north south trending ridge facing east. It's the best place they can be.' Julie smiled as she reassured him then continued. 'Considering they're on the danger side.'

'So that's it?' asked Alex. 'Ash fall is all she has to worry about?'

'I wish. It gets more complex. As the magma wells up under the crater the explosions start firing out molten rock. It could be small pebbles.' She held up her index finger and thumb into a circular shape, 'or much larger of course. We call these bombs and blocks,' She winced as she considered the consequences. 'And they could be firing out now.'

'Pelting the hut?' asked Alex.

'I would say so.'

'Penetrating it?'

Julie pinched her mouth into a tight line and exhaled deeply. She held Alex's wide stare which searched her

155

face for an answer she was scared to give.

Alex pictured Lana flinching, terrified of being hit by hot rocks crashing through the walls and roof of the hut. He hadn't been to the hut and had only ever seen such buildings in Lana's magazines. A wave of guilt surged through him. He should know more of Lana's world. He realised that he hadn't even asked to accompany her on a single one of her expeditions. He should have insisted on going, one time, this time. Then at least she would be turning to him for comfort, not some stranger who apparently was an expert on volcanoes. Lana would think he was wonderful of course. She was in awe of anyone who was an expert on almost anything.

'I'm sorry Alex,' Julie replied softly. 'I'm as worried as you. Last time this happened huge quantities of steam and gases continued to be emitted after the explosive phases.

We're talking about sulphur dioxide, hydrogen sulphide, carbon dioxide and hydrogen chloride.' Julie ticked them off on her fingers. 'Not nice.'

'And then what happened?' asked Alex.

'A few months after the ash eruptions the magma continued to rise and produce explosions.'

'There isn't going to be any water left in the crater is there?'

'No. It could be empty already for all we know,' she agreed. 'I've just described Surtseyian volcanic eruptions. There is another style that this mountain is capable of producing, called Strombolian.'

'Interesting names.'

'Named for the type specimens in their respective European locations. Strombolian eruptions are short-lived. Last time these occurred two weeks and then a year after the Surtseyian eruptions. We had a fire fountain, if you like, with hot molten lava bombs ejected kilometres from the vent. There was a magnificent display of red and white arcs trailing trajectories.' She trailed off as if remembering the event in her mind's eye.

Alex reeled from her description and Julie quickly sought to calm him.

'Anyway, it may not happen. We can only analyse the past to predict the future. Chances are if Strombolian eruptions are going to occur then Lana and Emma and Paul will be well clear of the mountain. Probably sitting right here writing a thesis on it,' she smiled at Alex.

He returned her smile. 'Can you recall how long the eruptions lasted?'

'Both sets lasted several weeks,' Julie advised.

'Oh no,' Alex groaned. 'She could be stuck there a long time. She won't have food for several weeks.' He shoved his chair back and stood. 'We've got to get her off the mountain,' he cried. 'If she's not drowned from the lahar, she'll be breathing blood from sucking ash, or dead from being struck by molten lava. Or God alive, now starved to death.'

'Alex no, it's not so bad.'

'Where's the bleedin' good Julie?' He lashed out at the back of the chair, 'answer me that. She hasn't got much going for her.'

'Alex. Alex.' Julie jumped up to confront him and laid a hand on his shoulder. 'Calm down. We understand the risks, she understands the risks...'

'Paul Harrington understands the risks,' Alex spat.

'Him too. It's because we understand the risks that we

can address them to mitigate the danger. We're doing our best to monitor the situation and establish contact with Lana. There are a lot of scientists working on this.'

'Scientists aren't going to get Lana off the mountain,' he retorted.

'I wouldn't be so sure Alex. Give Lana some credit. She knows that mountain. And anyway, it's not like she's alone up there.'

'Don't tell me again.' He held up his palm.

She slapped it away and muttered behind clenched teeth. 'Pull yourself together Alex. I won't tolerate this. Either show me you've got bottle or get out.'

Alex hunched over the chair back, beads of sweat on his brow.

'There are search and rescue teams ready to go too. Look, we all want Lana to be safe and off that mountain and we'll do it. Maybe not today or tomorrow, but we will.'

Alex wiped his forehead with his pressed handkerchief. 'Yes, I know. Sorry I snapped.'

'Understandable in the circumstances.'

'You can see me or phone me anytime. My door is always open for you. Let me give you my home number, although you should try here first. I don't expect I'll be getting much sleep.'

Chapter Six

Alfred slunk heavily into the folds of his armchair. He wished he could tuck his legs up underneath him like he used to do before the vagaries of old age stiffened him to concrete. It wasn't so bad being in that position for as long as it took to get a good stretch but it was the getting out of it.

He was routinely tired on Fridays when there was entertainment at the Parkside Retirement Village where he resided. He considered himself to be a young eighty four. He stooped slightly, but only, as he told himself, because he had to use a walking stick thus bringing his once nearly six foot frame down a couple of inches. He still rose at the crack of dawn whether it came early or late in the day. His hair was plentiful, although these days it was white.

Alfred wholeheartedly supported the entertainment put on by the staff. Not that he endorsed the silly games and quite frankly juvenile entertainment the village put on, but it had always been his ethos to make the best of any situation.

But today's entertainment had been an old time tea dance. Never silly and always thoroughly enjoyable. And as women outnumber men in retirement villages Alfred was kept busy on the dance floor more or less continuously. It was funny to think that he had all but missed the decades of the tea dance. It wasn't his experience as a young man serving during the war. In fact, being incarcerated for as long as he was, he was lucky even to see a woman, let alone dance with one. Later, he and Lily had farmed in the back blocks of

Hawkes Bay. There was the odd local dance, but always at night, never in the afternoon when there was milking to be done.

He dozed with his feet sprawled on an embroidered footstool. The cryptic crossword he had been working on in today's paper had nudged him into an early snooze but he stirred when he heard the seven o'clock news pips on the radio.

He forced his eyes open and struggled to focus on the mantle clock to confirm that he had indeed lost an hour. He thought he heard the announcer say that some medals had been stolen.

Damn he thought. *Damn that bloody war*. He hadn't thought of it for a long time. It did no good to dwell on it, but he carried it with him every day all the same. He couldn't not. The war had shaped him as a man. Now the mention of medals would force his mind back to a time when he was a young man. *Damn*.

He struggled out of his chair and made his way slowly down the hall to his bedroom, the stick thudding intermittently on the carpet. He perched on the side of the bed and leaned forward to pull open the top drawer of the dresser. It was the same oak dresser Lily had chosen for their first home. She had kept it polished with oil and vinegar. The bedroom always reflected that sweet smell. He missed it. The drawers had always stuck even though they'd bought it new. He gave it a jerk.

After ferreting around he pulled out a jewellery case. His fingers softy caressed the plush black velvet. He wasn't in a hurry to open it. Memories flooded into his head, swirling into the war portal of his brain so long closed. Keeping the case closed would not hold them back so he opened it.

He unfurled a yellowed newspaper cutting; page two of the Auckland Star, March 8, 1946. He stared at the black and white photo of himself holding his own death certificate. "Killed in action, at Monte Cassino March 15, 1944," the article began. Suddenly the page wasn't there anymore as he recalled his lost hours. It was right what they said about the war; it was a whole lot of waiting around for a battle. He could be waiting months for a battle that might last three days but this wait hadn't been so long. It was only weeks since the advance on the hill and his loss of Harold still cut deep. They were hunkered down in the concrete jungle of the town waiting for the order to advance. The waiting was unbearable. It gave him time to pine for Sophie. And the longer the wait the lovelier she became; her eyes brighter, her hair shinier, her lips fuller and redder which she parted alluringly for him.

Then suddenly it was all on and rifle fire ricocheted back and forth across the deserted street.

'Christ,' he ducked and slid his back down the plastered block wall he was using for a defence.

'That was close Alfie,' said Reg. 'Look out. I'll get the bugger for you.' With that he stepped up above Alfred's sitting position and fired a shot as soon as he breached the wall then ducked back down to sit with Alfred.

'What good was that?' asked Alfred.

'Not much at all. Can't let the buggers think they're winning though.' Reg took a packet of Camels from his breast pocket and lit a cigarette. He shared it with Alfred. He took the last drag and stubbed it out on the cobbled ground. He inspected his rifle, a Lee Enfield. It was his best friend and he treated it as he would his lover. He would not be parted from it. It had saved his life more than once and the lives of his comrades too.

Several bullets left in the round. He may as well finish them off and reload while he was reasonably protected in this enclosed space.

It was quiet now. There were no shots coming from behind. Several comrades had taken care of that by hammering the German offensive from a tiny upstairs vantage off a side alley.

'How much longer do you think we can keep this up Reg?' asked Alfred.

'Well I for one could pull out right now mate. I'd kill for a roast lamb and baked potatoes. In fact I might just do that now.'

Reg was fired up on the thought of what he was missing out on and with great theatrics he flared to the top of the wall and let off several ill-placed shots which were answered immediately. They'd been surprised by the mortar shell that left the officer and sergeant in charge of his platoon dead and Alfred unconscious. When the platoon had recovered the position all they found was smashed concrete, a few twisted pieces of a machine gun and much blood.

What they didn't realise was that a German tank had picked Alfred up, badly wounded and unconscious and there he had stayed for the remainder of the battle. When he regained consciousness many hours later he was in an Italian hospital, never having met his opponents in battle. He found out later that Monte Cassino fell to Polish and British forces with support from New Zealand artillery.

The Gustav Line had finally been breached. Alfred was buoyed and relieved and only quietly jubilant. It seemed an affront to the thousands who had died to be exuberant and now there was the small problem of being a prisoner of war.

Alfred refolded the ragged news clipping and with clumsy hands unfurled a second one. He had no reason to keep it, but it was all he had to remember Harold. He ran his eyes down the script. It described a medal awards ceremony and comprised a list of mothers who received a medal for giving up their son to war.

Alfred was devastated to find that Harold had not survived. He had gone up that hill a teenager full of the excitement and fear of battle. He had come down fuelled on adrenalin and false bravado. He left the hill a man, sullied by the futility of the whole situation. Now he carried images only men should see: of death and dying and fear and hope and salvation. He could not speak of those images. They were his alone to carry and that he did with a reverence reserved only for the dead and dying.

On reflection he had thought he'd changed after that. But he was only seventeen so maybe it was his turning point from boy to man. Maybe there was nothing to change; it was Alfred's rite of passage.

Alfred searched Harold's pockets for personal effects before they dug a shallow grave for him. He was one of the lucky ones; his grave was marked and a brief prayer said over him.

In Harold's top pocket was a dog-eared water-stained envelope postmarked Napier dated two months ago. He pulled out the letter exposing it to the damp dawn only long enough to read the signature. It was from Lily. Alfred put it in his rucksack. He would deliver it to Lily when he returned home. He took off Harold's dog tags muttering a prayer over him as he did so and closed Harold's eyelids. He was at peace now, no more pain, no more laughter and good times together, no more smoking. No more life in Harold's young body.

Alfred felt a warm drop on his hand. He hadn't realised he was weeping. He meticulously refolded the clipping and with trembling hands carefully put it away.

***

Colleen found Alfred easily enough. It turned out he had not strayed too far from the town he grew up in. She was surprised at the speed with which he had agreed to meet with her. There was no hint of hesitation.

She was unsure what would come of the meeting. Two hundred and fifty kilometres was a long way to drive just to tell him that his war comrade's mother's medal had been stolen – not that she hadn't already told him on the phone. But she knew that Alfred was the man who had tried to save her uncle and that Alfred and Harold had been fast friends since the day they enlisted. She hoped to glean a little more insight into her long dead uncle. Alfred knew Harry in a different way than her mother, God bless her, and since her mother was dead there was no reminder of the uncle she'd never met.

She packed her Suzuki Swift for an overnight stay at a motel and hit the road. It should take her four hours on a straight run and she expected to be at Alfred's by one o'clock. *In time for lunch* Alfred had advised her.

Naturally he had offered Colleen his spare room but visions of a carpeted toilet and wall maps of the world drawing pinned to the walls flashed quickly into her mind and she gently refused his kind offer.

She pulled into the village at just about one o'clock. *Thirteen hundred hours* she said to herself in a mock sergeant major's voice. Then she heard her mother telling her off over her shoulder. She really shouldn't pre-judge the man. She didn't know a thing about him. Only about Lily of course.

Villa twenty six came into view. A quick survey indicated spic and span gardens which no doubt the management attended to. She was somewhat relieved to find none of the stupid little placards that people with too much time on their hands liked to populate their gardens with.

No sooner had she pulled up than Alfred appeared outside his French doors. He stood perfectly upright, albeit grasping his walking stick, in what Colleen assessed to be his good clothes.

'Hello,' Alfred beamed.

'Hello.' Colleen returned his smile.

'Did you have a good run?' asked Alfred.

'Yes. Piece of cake,' replied Colleen. 'I should have slowed down and enjoyed myself. I haven't been here for, well, forever it seems.'

'You'll be hungry I expect. Do come in.' He stepped aside.

'Thank you so much,' she said extending her hand for him to shake it.

'Tea or coffee?' he asked.

'Tea please, thank you Alfred,' Colleen replied.

Colleen looked at the beautifully laden table. Oak she noted, which extended at both ends, but it wasn't today. On it was a beautifully embroidered white linen cloth on which two places were set, complete with a spoon at the top of the place setting.

'Make yourself at home,' said Alfred touching the back of a chair.

'Thank you so much. You've gone to a lot of trouble,' said Colleen.

'Nonsense. The niece of Harold Jones? The least I can do is give you lunch.' He shrugged off her remark and leaned across to the middle of the table and sliced some cheese.

'Now. The reason you are here.' he stated.

'Alfred,' she began. 'You know about Uncle Harold's medal of course. I felt, well, that, oh, I don't know what I felt when I got the news. Or now, come to that.'

Alfred remained silent. It was an effective technique he'd learnt during the war to draw people out. People had tried it on him, without much success. The result was that he'd gained a reputation as a good listener, and someone who really considered what the other person had to say.

'Guilty,' she half whispered. 'Maybe. A police officer came to my office to tell me that my grandmother's medal was one of those stolen in the robbery.' She paused and scrutinised Alfred's face. It was impassive.

'I just thought that seeing as you were great friends with Uncle Harry and he spent his last hours with you...' She faltered. 'Well that is...' she reached for her cup of tea. 'That is...' she said after a quenching slurp. 'I don't know Alfred. It would be nice to know a little bit about

166

him.'

'I understand,' Alfred replied.

'Could you tell me about my uncle? What was he like? As a person. Not necessarily as a soldier. I mean, he wasn't a soldier for long was he? God bless his soul.'

Alfred pushed his plate away and leaned his elbows on the table in front of him, stroking his chin.

'If it's not too painful of course,' Colleen added quickly.

'As it happens I've done a lot of remembering in the last few days. Those medals have stirred up a heck of a hornets nest, for me anyway.'

Alfred was pleased to air the subject at last. Having replayed the war in his mind's eye since, the news bulletin events were now in some sort of chronological order that he could easily recall. He smiled as he explained first meeting Harold as a couple of young lads who couldn't wait to have a big overseas adventure.

He carried on for the best part of an hour relating stories to Colleen. He painted a picture of a Harold she had never seen before. Conversation with her mother had never been like this. Alfred knew Harold as a fellow man whereas her mother only saw him as her brother, a boy.

'Alfred, you know what causes me anguish?' she asked with such passion that Alfred couldn't possibly fathom what this niece of Harry was feeling.

'What?'

'Harry was seventeen when he died. Seventeen!' She barely whispered the words. 'He never got to experience the love of a good woman and do you know, I feel guilty about that.

Harry was my uncle, a beautiful man and the love of a

woman was denied him. I often think that if he was ten or eleven when he died he would not know what pleasures there were in store for him. That would make his passing so much more bearable. But, well, you know,' she slowed down. 'There is an awakening isn't there,' she smiled weakly at him. 'In teenagers.'

'Oh yes,' Alfred nodded sagely with a wan smile. 'I do remember. I remember as if it were yesterday. I should tell you Colleen that Harry did experience women.'

'Lily?'

'Well not really. That is yes and no,' he abruptly shut that down. She appealed to Alfred, imploring him with her eyes to continue.

'We both had sweethearts before the war and we were both younger than we should have been when we left for overseas. We left New Zealand virgins but I can promise you we set about fixing that.' He was serious. Alfred didn't even smile at the memory.

'You see,' he continued, 'we found ourselves in a new country, with new women and for the large part surrounded by seasoned men who knew more than there was to tell about the ways of beautiful women. We knew we could die any day, so any risks taken surely cancelled out the thought of death. By risks I mean the clap of course.'

Colleen sat tight lipped and wide eyed. She was shocked at what she was hearing but at the same time mesmerised by Alfred's words. He continued. 'A bit of slap and tickle is not the same as the love of a good woman I know and I'm not trying to make excuses, but don't feel sad for Harry. He died knowing that he had the love of a good woman in Lily and he died having experienced what they would have had together should he have lived.'

'Well,' she shrugged. 'I guess I've been rather naive to think what I thought.' She smiled, 'and all these years too. I suppose my mother had this puritan vision of her brother and it stayed like that until she died. I guess that's why I expected Harry to be a saint.'

'Well Colleen,' said Alfred, 'you just carry on thinking like that. He did nothing wrong, our Harry, nothing. He was a noble man and you can be proud of him.'

'And what of you Alfred?' asked Colleen. 'Do you think of the war?'

Alfred stared through Colleen. Eventually he bowed his head and spoke. 'I block out the bad and remember the good. There is always good you know. Sometimes you just have to dig deep to find it.'

'I'm so glad I came today,' said Colleen. 'I wonder why I didn't come before.'

'Because you didn't have a reason to,' he replied.

Colleen noted the sun feather its long beams low into the room. Time had passed quickly. She took her leave with the promise of talking again, quite soon.

Chapter Seven

Colleen reminded Alfred of Lily. It was a long time since he'd had the pleasure of entertaining a woman whose hair was not grey. He soon found himself propelled back to his first encounter of his beloved wife.

He left Italy at the end of 1945 and arrived back home several months later. The time on board ship was long enough to put some flesh back on his bones. His trousers began to fit better and he even had to employ the little used notches on his belt. The skin on his arms had toughened under the Mediterranean sun and the soft body hairs bronzed under its fierceness. Slowly the fat returned to his cheeks which made the daily shave more pleasant. He only had a small battered shaving mirror to look in. It scared him, his eyes. He saw the same in every man around him – a hollowness, like there was no pinprick of light that gave life to his face.

It was an odd feeling to return to the small town he grew up in. The family farm was on the outskirts of town and he'd been lucky enough to ride Bessie to the town's only school. Lucky because he'd chummed up with lads from way out the other side of town and he may have only met them in passing during the odd rugby match had he not gone to that school.

And of course there were the girls. He had his eye on the fair-haired Ruby that he intended to ask to a dance when he was old enough. She lived out the back of beyond on the other side of town too. But by the time he was old enough it turned out she'd already danced with Steve Thompson, the butcher. Arrangements were made for a hasty vacation for a few months.

He walked the main street, past its narrow shop fronts and wooden cottages. At one time he was familiar with the lives of its inhabitants. Today people he'd known all his life doffed their hats to him, grateful for his efforts, sorry for his experiences and knowing the demons to come. But there was no recognition behind their smiles, until Ruby caught his eye and held it. He saw fear in her as if she'd seen a ghost. He tried to talk to her, to reassure her that it was him. She said she could see it was him, she could see it in his eyes. She heard he'd been killed.

'You can see I wasn't killed,' he assured her. He carried on slowly with his duffel bag slung low over his shoulder and as he passed the narrow shops he became aware of people pouring out onto the footpath behind him. He glanced a flash of reflection in a window. He wore his uniform badly; it touched where it fitted. Surely he didn't look so different from when he left.

He caught a lift in a rural supplies delivery truck that dropped him off at the end of the road to his parent's farm. The driver told him that it was the same 1934 Chevrolet that he had at the start of the war and as they headed out of town Alf could see that time had all but stopped. There was nothing new; no new cars, no new buildings, just the same sad buildings with different signs.

Dust from the narrow gravel road billowed out behind as they clattered along. Finally Bob lurched the truck to a halt, graunching the gears as if the thing were a beast to tame and practically standing on the brake pedal. He made much of the fact that it took the greatest skill to drive such a machine.

Alfred stepped down with his duffel bag and waved his thanks. He loped along the narrow country lane, pausing at the one way bridge to enjoy the rush of clear trout laden waters. He was at once excited and reticent about coming home. He couldn't have anticipated the reaction he got as he walked through town. He hoped it wouldn't be such a surprise for his parents. He hadn't written ahead – didn't want a fuss. He exhaled deeply, squared his shoulders and lengthened his stride.

He rounded a bend in the road and saw his house set back with an expanse of dry stubbled lawn in front of it. It looked exactly the same as the day he left. In the two years he was away it was the picture he held most dear in his mind, apart from Sophie of course and yet as soon as he stood at the front gate he knew he would never live here again.

It represented what he had fought for. It was home and it stood stoically under a regime of freedom. It was solid and dependable and it was always there. It was filled with love and laughter and warm memories and none of those things would disappear.

A typical white weatherboard bungalow, it comprised a single storey with an iron roof and in the heat of the early February summer sun the whole house seemed to shimmer. The casement windows were open to the barest breeze as were the pink fanlights above. He noticed a yellowed lace curtain flutter lazily. Small outbuildings framed the house, also weatherboard and also white. Behind, unruly macrocarpa trees sheltered the dwelling from the strong westerly winds and a rose garden was set to one side of the front yard, mostly white roses, straggly and long past their best.

Alfred bypassed the wrought iron gate and walked up the gravel drive to the front step. The front door was open letting the hot summer air move in and out of the house. He peered in but was temporarily blinded by the dark as it contrasted with the fierceness of the day's sun. It was just as he remembered: dark and calm and safe and home. He heard a rattle of crockery and a high pitched hum coming from the back beyond the central hall.

He sang out as he stepped inside, 'Hi Mum. It's me.'

The humming stopped abruptly. And then he saw a silhouette of his mother holding a plate as she stepped into view. She screamed and the plate dropped to the floor. She came running down the hall wiping her hands on the sides of her apron and came to a halt in front of him. She scrutinised his face then the way he stood as if she didn't comprehend that it was him. Then she embraced him hard and cried.

'Alfred!' she blurted. 'You're dead. You're dead.' She grasped his shoulders and held him at arms' length, her eyes drinking him up.

'I'm not Mum, I'm not.'

'It can't be. They said you were dead.'

'I promise you Mum, it's me.' Alfred smiled and hugged her. He let her hold him, crush him and inspect him.

'Your father,' she muttered. 'My God Alfie, they said you were dead. Wilfred. Wilfred,' she called. 'Come here. It's Alfred.'

'All right Jane. Calm down. What is it?'

Alfred heard his father's words getting louder as he approached. He took one look at Alfred and gasped like a fish. He couldn't believe what he was seeing. He shook his head to clear the illusion.

'Hello Dad.' Alf dropped his bag to the floor and hugged his father. 'I'm not dead Dad,' Alfred cried and he slapped his father playfully on the shoulder.

'I don't believe it. I swear!'

'Go and sit yourself down love and tell us all about it,' said Jane. She bent to retrieve the pieces of plate but Wilfred stalled her.

'Come on love,' he said gently. 'That can wait. Alfred's come back to us from the dead.'

The kitchen was as he remembered. The table was set for three. Three worn dinner plates with hairline cracks and the gold trim half worn off, three sets of knives and forks with bone handles and three sets of cups and saucers that matched the dinner plates.

'Expecting Ron?' asked Alfred hoping to see his brother. It would be easier to ask him about Sophie.

'He's over at the Baker farm doing hay. No, your aunt Daisy comes by after Women's Institute once a week,' his mother replied. 'Tell us what happened Alfie. Why did they send us a death certificate?'

'I got caught up in mortar fire. Got knocked unconscious and Gerry picked me up and put me in their tank. The boys would have thought I'd taken a direct hit. I woke up in hospital.'

'Where?'

'Italy.'

'Why didn't you write Alfie?' Jane's voice was plaintiff.

'I did. I guess you didn't get the letters. I was moved from camp to camp.'

'Camp?'

'Prison camp love,' Wilfred explained.

'I see.' Jane busied herself with bread and cheese. Tears were forming behind her dark gray eyes. 'Were you hurt?'

Alfred smiled lightly and rested his hand lightly on hers. 'It's all right Mum. Nothing that couldn't come right.'

She nodded and wiped the tears with the back of her hand.

Wilfred said nothing. Alfred sensed his father's discomfort. He'd never displayed much emotion.

'So, Sophie...' Alfred ventured, 'thinks I'm dead?'

His parents looked at each other.

'What?' he asked, looking at each of them in turn.

'Well, um, Sophie, she,' his mother stuttered nonsensical silence filler.

'She took up with someone else son,' Wilfred interjected.

Alfred bowed his head.

'Who?' he asked as he faced his father. He was a man now, not some love struck boy. He would take the news as such. But it was his mother who answered.

'We had a lot of Americans over here Alfred. They offered our girls chocolate and nylons and chewing gum.'

'She left me for chewing gum!' Alfred snapped.

'Of course not love. Like you said, she thought... we all thought you were dead.

'I'm sorry Alfred,' Wilfred began, 'but you'll hear it anyway. You may as well hear it from us here and now. She got in the family way.'

175

Alfred couldn't believe it. Sophie had been nothing but purity personified when he had left. She promised she'd wait for him. He remembered their summer picnic and the glorious swim and the delicious wet dress. She had written to him during the war – until his capture anyway. He had kept all her letters. They were stowed in his army pants in his duffel bag.

'Where is she now?' he asked.

'He took her back with him,' explained Alfred's mother.

Alfred excused himself from the table. Jane jumped up and flustered around behind him. 'Why don't you settle into your room love? Your room's just the same Alfred, just the same. I knew you'd be back love. I knew you'd want it just how you left it.'

'Leave him Jane.' Wilfred's gravelly voice slowed her and she let Alf go.

'Thanks Mum,' said Alfred. He paused at his bedroom door. It was exactly as he left it. His mother had kept the room for him expecting, hoping for his return. But now he could see it had been a shrine to him for all that time. It unsettled him. He could not stay. He would leave as soon as he could. How could he explain to his mother? But he could not wind back the clock. He had outgrown this house. He set his bag on the high bed and sat down next to it. He slapped his palms on the crocheted wool cover, savouring the touch and smell. How his senses had craved this. For two years he had wanted nothing more than the luxury of his own soft bed and Sophie beside him.

He didn't bother to kick off his shoes. He lay with his hands behind his head staring at the ceiling. Had he misread the intent of her letters? Had she drifted from him before she thought he had died? What did it matter now if she thought he was dead? Of course she should fall in love with someone else. Who was he to deny her happiness? He pulled the letters out of his bag. Six of them; all of them when he was alive. They'd been read and folded, then refolded so many times they were furry along the folds, the paper almost parting. He had thought the worst when the letters stopped coming. But then so had his parents'. That had made it all the more puzzling, but that's why there was also hope. He had been fortunate to receive as many even if a couple had arrived at the same time. Some of the boys were not nearly so lucky. He held the tattered envelopes for a time recalling the pleasure and anticipation he felt when he first received them. They had flooded him with love and hope, desire and ultimately satisfaction. In the end he conceded that the letters had served their purpose. Sophie had kept him going, fuelled his mettle and provided the impetus to come out of that crap alive. He didn't open them, but stood them on his dresser against the mirror. He wasn't quite ready to let her go.

***

Alfred stepped down from train onto the concrete platform. The day was warm and steam from the JA 8-4-2 engine filled the air above the carriages as it caught a wafting breeze. The station was situated behind the township and rows of tiny railway houses regimentally lined the tracks. Alfred walked beyond them to more substantial housing, Californian bungalows. The style had not made it to his rural homeland, the farms all being established before the Californian fashion, although one or two streets in town sported the new style, accommodating shop owners and professionals. They were pretty little houses with wide covered verandahs to the front. Each had a single garage and the yard was fully fenced with wooden pickets or a stuccoed low concrete wall. A central path led to the front door, usually with a flower garden either side.

Alfred wondered what the occupants were doing. Did the owners go to war? Or did they stay at home and look after other lad's girlfriends? Did they all mimic the sameness that the houses displayed? Did they all house a family with three children and a devoted wife at home all day while her husband worked in an office?

He reached the centre of town and sought out the haberdashery. He paused on the footpath outside the shop's window and used the glass as a mirror. He straightened his collar, ran his fingers over his hair and slapped down the sides of his shirt. As he entered the shop a bell rang above him. He felt eyes on him as he surveyed the shop.

A dark haired girl was laying out a roll of cloth on the counter and a buxom woman with a handbag slung from her arm was straightening the cloth with her other hand. They both turned to Alfred although the girl quickly returned to her work and furtively lifted her eyes to Alfred.

Alfred realised immediately that this was Harold's Lily. She was beautiful. He could only see half of her but that was enough to see how lovely she was. He shuffled from foot to foot.

She was expecting him so it was pointless to pretend to browse the shop. So he just stood.

'You must be Alfred,' she said coyly after the buxom woman left. She smiled shyly. He held out his hand to her and she took it much like a queen would receive a servile.

'Hello Lily,' he said. 'I feel as though I know you already.'

She blushed and lowered her head.

'Oh, I'm sorry. I didn't mean to offend,' Alfred added hurriedly.

'Don't be silly,' she laughed. 'I know a little about you too. Harry was a good letter writer.'

Alfred pulled out Lily's letter to Harold from his top pocket. She saw that it was opened and water stained. She looked questioningly at Alfred before taking it slowly from him.

'Thank you,' she whispered. 'I'm on lunch in a few minutes.'

'Then let me treat you to tea,' Alfred offered.

'That would be lovely.'

***

'I did love Harry so much you know,' she began over lunch. 'I would have married him. I waited for him.'

Alfred was surprised but didn't give Lily any indication of it.

'We exchanged many letters, although I'm sure we didn't get all of them so just to make sure he had my love I told him every single time,' she explained.

'The letter I brought back. He had it in his pocket

when he died,' said Alfred. 'It was raining at the time. I only read the signature Lily. I didn't read your letter.'

'It's all right Alfred. I'm sure it's no different from the letters you got from your girl,' she smiled at him and placed her hand lightly on his. He mutely looked at her delicate hand. He liked the feel of it. It would be nice to keep it there.

'Alfred?' Lily pressed him for a reply.

He realised she was asking about Sophie. What had Harry told her about Sophie and him?

'Um,' he stammered. 'My girl couldn't wait.'

She startled and immediately removed her hand from his.

'Oh,' she remarked. 'I'm terribly sorry.' She reached for her tea cup.

Alfred watched her blush pink lips kiss the cup. He marvelled at their plumpness and imagined them on his own lips. Her soft green eyes scanned his face from over the top of the cup and her silky dark hair bobbed freely around her oval face. The silence was too long. He realised he was staring at her. Now he struggled for something to say.

'Tell me about Harry,' she broke the uncomfortable silence. 'Was it awful? The way he died?'

He knew it would come to this. He'd struggled with it during the long train journey: how to tell Lily how Harry died. He hadn't had to describe it before. His mates all had their demons to carry, they'd seen death and disfigurement and the severing of limbs, but none of them spoke about it. He wouldn't describe Harry's death to his family because he couldn't narrate the Monte Cassino battle. He relived it in the dead of night, every night. He didn't need to recall it and sully the memory of innocents. No. He would keep such memories to himself. Now she had asked, as would Harry's parents. He sanitised the dreadful awful truth. He had to sanitise it for his own sake, for all their sakes. He wondered if in time the pictures in his mind would fade.

'I'm sorry Alfred. I should not have asked,' said Lily. 'You're upset.'

'Nonsense, you have every right to know,' he replied. He went on to explain the battle and Harry's part in it. 'His last words to me Lily, he said tell Lily I love her.'

Lily fought back tears but they sat in her eyes anyway. She tried to blink them away but one or two escaped down her cheeks. Alfred reached over to her and with his bare finger gently wiped one cheek. He desperately wanted to put that finger to his mouth and taste her salty tear. She smiled at him and wiped the other cheek.

'So,' she said. 'It's lovely to meet you Alfred. So kind of you to look after Harry, and now me.'

Alfred shuffled in his seat. He hadn't really regarded this mission as one of guardianship. But her comment gave him courage.

'Lily?' he asked quietly.

'Yes?' she stared intently at him.

'May I see you again?'

'I would like that very much Alfred.'

***

Alfred laid the plaid woollen blanket on the rough grass. He had chosen this secluded spot along the river

181

for their picnic with meticulous care. The river was tranquil and clear and the delicate rapids were a way downstream. He didn't want the sound of the river to dominate his loving of Lily. He wanted to hear every whisper she whispered, every murmur she murmured and every breath she breathed. Mature podocarp forest grew right down to the river's edge and gave partial shade over the water and the small embankment. It was quite a walk in to this hideaway but it was easy enough underfoot for him and for Lily. She sat on the rug and opened the wicker picnic hamper.

He had brought his cane trout rod with him as he always did but he had a feeling that today he wouldn't use it. They had been here many times over the past few months and while he fished Lily had sunbathed or read the *New Zealand Woman's Weekly*. They had kissed the second time he brought her here and subsequently had modestly given themselves over to heavy petting. But today, Alfred thought, today Alfred hoped, would be different. Had Lily sensed it too? She was restless and a bit giggly.

'Leave the picnic Lily,' said Alfred and he moved the hamper to one side so he could sidle right up next to her.

'Not hungry?' she teased.

'Oh yes. I'm hungry Lily,' he growled deeply. 'I'm hungry for you.'

She giggled as he took hold around her waist and gently nudged her back to lie on the blanket. She embraced his passionate kiss rewarding him with her hot exploring tongue, urgent and wanting. She wriggled away and settled her form to mould to the ground.

'Mmm,' groaned Alfred. 'You want me.'

182

'Maybe. I'm just trying to get the sticks out of my back,' she said with a gentle slap to his shoulder.

'Then come to me,' he said as he lay back on the blanket deftly pulling her onto him.

She kissed him back and became aware of the fire that stirred within him. She moved her hips over him pressing, pushing against him, and he groaned.

'Oh Lily. Oh Lily, Lily, Lily,' he intoned.

'Shall I stop?' teased Lily.

'No.' He clenched her buttocks and with one hand lifted her skirt and slipped it inside her underwear. He closed his eyes and breathed deeply as he pictured the fleshy white buttocks he was kneading.

'Oh Alfred,' she murmured.

He rolled her off him and she lay there for but a moment anticipating his masculine touch.

'Kiss me Alfred,' she begged.

He leaned over her and tenderly kissed her nose while his hands grasped her tender body, feeling, inspiring, and urging his desire on. She giggled. He kissed her full lips and she parted them for him. He paused and gently slipped the thin wool cardigan off her shoulders. She helped him shed it. Then she took his head with both her hands and guided his face to her breasts. He buried his face and rubbed his hands up and down the sides of her body and rested them at the side of her perfectly formed full round breasts.

'Mmm,' she moaned. 'How many buttons darling?'

Alfred enjoyed the cue and undid each one as he counted aloud.

'Oh Lily, Lily,' he sang. He carefully threaded each of her arms out of her blouse and he quickly nestled his face into her trussed up breasts. He looked at her questioningly.

'Yes,' she whispered an answer without him needing to ask. He pulled away her undergarment and lifted it to her face deeply breathing in her scent before he discarded it. 'Mmm,' she moaned using her own hands on her body feeling her nipples stand erect. 'Come to me darling.'

He bowed his head above her and tenderly sucked on a nipple deftly flicking his tongue over and around it while fingering the other one. 'Lily,' he panted. His hips writhed above her, driving onto her.

'Alfie?'

'Mmm?'

'I want you today,' she whispered with an air of seriousness afraid of breaking the spell with the full force of her voice.

'I want you too,' he replied mumbling into her soft flesh. He nibbled his way up her smooth skin to her neck. She wriggled.

'Yes I know, but I'm telling you that you can take your pleasure today. All of me.' She stroked his head.

He pulled back. 'Are you sure Lily?'

'I love you Alfie, I'm sure.'

'Oh Lily. I'll love you like you'll never forget. My lovely little Lily.'

She laughed and raised her hands above her head so her nipples pointed directly skyward.

'Grrr,' Alfred murmured and he sat astride her rubbing his flat palms over her breasts and stomach, exploring, searching, and loving. She rocked her hips beneath him ensconced in a desire never before felt or understood.

He undid his shirt buttons and felt the gentle breeze rustle through his sparse chest hair. Lily rubbed a hand over his chest and pulled his shirt down over one shoulder. He took it off. She brought her other hand around to the top of Alfred's trousers.

'Let me help you,' she whispered as she used a finger to trace a tickling line from his tummy button to his fly. He undid his belt.

'Let's see,' she teased, 'how many buttons?' She undid them counting each one off as she went.

Alfred stripped off her shirt and underwear and soon she lay naked on the blanket in the midday sun of autumn. Her face was expectant, her eyes large in her sensual smooth face, intoxicating Alfred under her spell.

'Scared?' Alfred asked her.

She nodded.

'Don't be scared Lily. I'll make it perfect for you. He peeled off his trousers then buried his face in between her breasts before tracing a line with his tongue down her body. She startled under his teasing touch but succumbed to the sensual pleasure he gave her, parting her legs for him. His hot tongue explored her licking lightly and softly then urgently probing until she began to writhe desperate for a deeper, harsher pleasure.

'Mmm, Alfie,' she moaned.

'Yes darling.'

'Oh, Alfie.'

'I know darling.'

She rubbed her breasts groaning loudly and pinching her nipples. 'Alfie, you're torturing me.'

'Not yet darling,' he whispered.

185

'When?' she cried.

'Soon.'

He buried his head again in her silky dark mound until he evoked groans of pleasure from Lily. She raised her head to watch his thick hair bobbing between her writhing hips. She reached out to clamp her hands on his head, to prevent him from stopping. He stroked himself, extending his desire, prolonging his loving for Lily.

She spread her legs for him and he guided himself into her. She muffled a cry and bit her clenched fist.

'Oh Lily,' he moaned, his hands pressing down on her shoulders.

With the stab of pain she stopped moving her hips. Her eyes were wide with fright. He laid his entire body along the length of hers comforting her in his strength.

'It's all right darling.' He kissed her softly, reassuringly, and she kissed him back but it was absent of desire. She focussed on the fire in her groin. He moved his hips gently and slowly while he caressed her breasts and licked her face.

'You're beautiful Lily,' he said.

'I don't know what to do Alfie,' she whispered.

'It's good Lily, its good. Do nothing. Did I hurt you?' He continued with a slow back and forth dance of his hips, never wavering, never faltering in his hip dance.

'A little,' she confessed. 'Is it okay?'

'Yes, yes, my little Lily,' he soothed her.

She reached around to his buttocks as he rode her. He became lost in his aching quest for sensual fulfilment. With his eyes closed he gave himself to Lily wholly and completely. He picked up his pace until a crescendo was reached and he groaned loudly with every surge until he collapsed, panting at Lily's side. Lily lay still not daring to move. Then she tentatively placed a finger between her legs and confirmed that her virginity was gone. Gone forever to Alfred, whom she loved very deeply. Alfred leaned over and kissed her delicately on her lips and they lay naked on the bank of the river until the cool air dried the sweat from their spent bodies.

***

After a lunch of egg and bacon pie and blackberry nip they lay back on the blanket in the mid afternoon sun.

'I've never been so happy Alfred,' Lily confessed.

'Good,' he beamed at her, gently pushing back a lock of dark hair behind her ear.

'I'm not scared now,' she volunteered as she sat up.

'You don't need to be scared of anything with me,' he replied.

She bowed her head and coyly glanced sideways at him. He lay propped up on his elbows with no shirt on and his young muscles rippled under his skin. His stomach was flat and a trail of dark hair led from his stomach to the top of his button fly. His chest boasted a crop of dark hair just desirable enough for her to want to bury her face in it.

'Can we do it again?' she asked shyly, not lifting her head, afraid the answer might be no.

Alfred faced her, lips stretching to such a wide smile it threatened to split his face. She sat in her blouse and underwear with her knees pulled up and her arms wrapped tightly about them.

'Why don't we swim first?' he asked.

'Okay,' she agreed.

'Humour me.'

'What?'

'Walk into the river naked.'

She blushed. 'Just me?'

'Yes.'

'Naked?'

'Yes. Please Lily. You're so beautiful. I want to watch you walk into the river naked.'

'Like this?' she teased, removing her blouse but keeping her bare back to him as he lay on the ground.

'Yes, like that Lily,' he whispered.

'And this?'

She crawled onto her knees to face him and she knelt at his side caressing her torso, her hands moving seductively along the sides of her body, teasing him as her nipples hardened. She glanced to his trousers and smiled. She bent forward swinging her breasts in the gentle autumn air as she deftly removed her underwear.

'Oh. Lily,' Alfred groaned and sat up.

'Okay,' she said pertly and swiftly stood up quickly pulling out of Alfred's reach.

Alfred watched Lily skip to the edge of the river daintily picking her way around sharp sticks and stones on the riverbank. The trees dappled the sunlight hitting the water and sparkling the surface blue and yellow. He watched Lily's skin speckle with the light. As he sat up on the blanket he admired her. She had an hourglass figure and a shock of charcoal hair which floated freely above her milk white shoulders. Her body angled in from her shoulders, pinching in at her dainty waist and flared out generously to her luscious inviting hips. He didn't know how long he could simply sit back and watch her.

'Ooh,' she shivered involuntarily.

'Cold?' called Alfred.

'A bit,' she said as she bent forward and splashed water onto her arms.

'You shouldn't do that,' warned Alfred.

'What?' she turned her head and peered over a shoulder at him. With the movement one breast swung around teasingly. He wanted to go to her but restrained himself enjoying the show, the challenge of resist heightening his desire.

He smiled. 'Bend over.'

She playfully turned around to face him and bent forward, splashing her arms with the fresh water.

'Why not?' she cooed. 'Why not Alfred?'

He could resist her no longer. He fixated on her as he arose from the blanket, and peeled himself out of his trousers. She stood straight and watched him come to her, naked, dashing to the river. He saw her focus on his manhood and she squirmed in anticipation. He skipped into the water and dived in.

'Aah,' she squealed as he splashed her, cold droplets of clear river water giving her goosebumps. She dived in after him revelling in the freedom of the water on her bare skin.

'Oh Alfred. It feels wonderful. This is the best ever.'

She stood up cupping her breasts in her hands and laughing, her hair plastered to her head and dripping down her face. He swam back to her enjoying the licking tongues of cool water dancing around him. He stood in front of Lily and held her hips firmly against his. She rested her hands on his shoulders and kissed him hard and deep. He moved against her and she swayed with him and against him and with him some more.

'Oh, Lily, Lily, Lily,' Alfred murmured.

He lifted her up and she screamed with joy as he entered her. He felt her relax.

'Oh Lily I want you,' groaned Alfred locking his arms around her wet body.

He squeezed his eyes tightly shut and sucked his tongue to the top of his palate as Lily took him to heaven and back.

'Mmm,' he groaned as he moved over her. She understood his need and pleasured him harder, harder until he was afraid of losing control.

'Is that what you want Alfred?' she whispered.

'Yes, Lily.'

She tightened her grip around his neck and submitted fully to his skill. He took her ripe nipples into his hot wet mouth.

'Oh, oh my God, Alfred.'

'Move on me Lily,' he instructed.

She tentatively rocked her hips back and forth with Alfred deep inside her then warmed to the pleasure of it.

'Alfred,' she gasped. 'It's beautiful.'

'So are you Lily. My beautiful, beautiful Lily,' he replied.

'Mmm. You know how to pleasure me Alfie,' she panted.

Finally she screamed and he could feel her clamping and releasing over him. Then he tightened his buttocks and dug his fingers into her back as an enormous release swept over him.

'Oh God,' he groaned holding himself prone until the

last of the cataclysmic sensations swept through him. Lily splashed backwards into the water and then they lay at the edge of the bank with the clear water rippling over their exhausted bodies until the sun moved off the river.

Chapter Eight

Lana descended into a yawning cavern of blurred dreams where her subconscious fought with her mind. She thought she could fight back but with the weight of the sky on her body and the past fogging her mind she was no match for the brain spirits. She needed this long repressed memory to wash over her and envelop her in its sanguine embrace. She was sixteen at home surrounded by all her favourite things and Paul sat at her bedside holding her hand. There was a poster of Leif Garret pinned to the yellow papered walls and a macramé hanging basket with an aspidistra set in it to one corner. On her dresser was a coloured photo propped against the mirror of her and Paul with their arms around each other's waists, both in shorts, she in a bikini top and he with no shirt – a day at the beach taken earlier that summer. She tried to wake herself from the dream. What was Paul doing here? Why was she in bed in the middle of the day?

She felt no pain as she lay still under the single sheet. Until she went to move her knees up. 'Aah,' she cried. 'What happened?'

'Dog attacked you. Do you remember Lana?' asked Paul. He lifted her hand to his mouth and kissed it gently. She watched him bow his head to her hand and he looked at her with liquid brown eyes from under hooded lids.

'Oh yeah.' She tentatively lifted the sheet and peeked under. She was wearing pink cotton summer pyjamas.

'I feel a bit stupid,' she confessed shyly.

'Because of the dog?' Paul asked.

'No, the pyjamas,' she laughed. 'Ooh,' she winced and lifted the sheet off her knee.

'I like your pyjamas Lana,' Paul murmured. 'Can I have a look at your knee?' He delicately pulled the sheet back and pursed his lips as he studied the wound. It was not bandaged, merely butterfly clipped together. He pointed out the puncture wounds to Lana.

'See here?' he said.

She sat up and looked to where Paul was pointing.

'Teeth marks. Does it really hurt bad?'

'Uh huh,' she whimpered pushing out her bottom lip and nodding.

'I wish I could kiss it better for you,' Paul whispered. 'You're the bravest girl Lana. Not many girls would try to outrun a greyhound.' He stroked her shin.

'Well that's just stupid isn't it?' She collapsed back on her pillow and shut her eyes as she recalled her terror. She'd been at the water's edge on a flat sandy beach on a perfect blue summer day when a creature began running towards her. At first glance she thought it was a rabbit it was running so fast and it was all hind legs. She looked around for its owner, or some other unlikely object of its desire. There didn't seem to be any. It was definitely intending to make her its primeval kill. She screamed as she bolted from it.

Paul was up on the shell bank putting on his wetsuit getting ready to surf. He heard Lana's screams and saw her running along the hard sand where the tide had retreated, arms flailing trying to outrun the dog. It was beautifully graceful. Muscle and sinew rippled beneath its short coat and its ribs undulated under the movement of it. It was impossible not to be caught in the spell of its beauty. The dog appeared to run in slow motion. Paul stood mesmerised. But Lana's screams spurred him into action. He picked up a piece of driftwood and careered down the beach kicking up sprays of sand behind him.

'Don't run Lana. Don't run,' Paul cried out flailing the driftwood but she continued to run and scream.

'Paul, Paul.' She could not maintain a sprint. Her legs were hollow, every scrap of energy spent. 'Paul.' Lana lunged to the ground and the next thing the dog was on top of her. She felt its hot breath on her neck. And then its wet tongue and hard teeth. It kind of went numb after that. She tried to burrow her head into her shoulders, to hide her neck. She flung her arms and legs wildly, screaming all the while. Her fingers sunk into the dog's furry face and it pulled away with a yelp, some of her blood on its jaw. Suddenly she felt its sharp incisors crunch at her knee.

The pain shot through her leg and by this time Paul had thrown himself upon the attacking dog and whacked the side of it with the piece of driftwood. The dog yelped and backed off. Lana retreated into a ball hugging her knees and crying. Blood ran down her shins and she had wet herself with fright.

'Oh Lana.' Paul carried her back to their picnic blanket.

She sat up in bed to find Paul had replaced the sheet.

'Why did it come running at me like that?' Lana whimpered. 'I don't even know where it came from.'

'I don't know,' replied Paul. 'Thank goodness it's your knee and not your beautiful face Lana.'

He pulled a strand of her hair back behind her ear. The wound on her neck was small and red raw. The doctor said she was extremely lucky not to have severed an artery and when it healed the scar was likely to be slight.

She smiled. He really was the sweetest and hunkiest boy a girl could have for a first ever sweetheart. She was the luckiest girl in the world.

Conscious was fighting with subconscious and slowly gaining the advantage. For some obscure reason she knew she wasn't recovering in her room with her sweetheart. But she was in a happy place long, long forgotten. She wanted to stay there with Paul at her side holding her hand.

But she stirred with the cool breeze. Suddenly the sky was very heavy on her slight body. She became aware of a biting cold in the ash-swirled air. Her lips were numb. She tried to clean them of the ash that had built up by running her tongue over them but she could hardly feel them. She sputtered instead. She went to move but everything felt stiff. Nothing would do as she commanded. She managed to lift her head an inch off the ground before she fell back with a groan. She squeezed her eyes shut and sighed. She pictured the dog, a summer's day and Paul. It was nice. Why couldn't that be real, and this be the dream?

She wondered how long had she lain out here. She shivered and tried to shake off the brown dusting of ash that had settled over her. A dull ache throbbed at the back of her head. If the mountain would stop spinning she'd be able to get up. She knew she should get inside and warm up but if she shut her eyes and stayed real quiet she might get to her happy place again. It wasn't far away, within grasping distance and she would be warm and safe. Just a few minutes more and then she really would get up.

The mountain continued to spin. It spun her into a blissful darkness – before the dog. She exalted at his touch. She had anticipated this date for nearly a week. Paul had asked her out by sending her a note in maths class. He had sat at the back of the room on tenterhooks as she, seated at the front, finally received it and opened it beneath the desk. As soon as the teacher faced the blackboard she turned her head and half smiled her ascent to him. He sat with his head bowed slightly, a shock of dark hair covering his face and his doe eyes peering out expectantly. Her smile confirmed his hopes and he quietly smiled his reply.

He had bought her an ice cream before the movie, hokey pokey. It was her favourite even now. Hokey pokey ice cream was synonymous with summer love and if she chose another flavoured ice cream it would dissolve those special days of innocence. The lights in the picture theatre lowered so that the only light came from the flickering screen. Lana longed for Paul to reach out for her hand and when she finally felt his warm fingers touch her thigh a bolt of lightning surged through her. She had never experienced such an intense rush of hot pleasure before and she felt her throat redden. She offered him her hand and he took it. It was warm, bigger than hers and she wanted to leave her hand there forever.

They had taken their time in walking to Lana's house. At the front step they felt awkward as they faced each other wondering if there was a right and a wrong was to approach the kiss. The air was cool and she shivered. But it was different to how she remembered it. It wasn't cold at all, or Paul would have warmed her in his arms.

She could hear someone calling her but not using her name. It should have been her mother but it was a man's voice.

'Lady, lady,' called the voice.

'Paul?' she murmured.

'Lady, wake up,' the voice said with urgency, a bit gruff.

Lana was waiting for Paul to kiss her on the lips. How could he kiss her while calling lady at the same time? She stirred but could not open her eyes. She would not open them until she felt his tender lips on hers. A sweet promise, so close, so close.

'Lady,' called Bill again as he approached her. The voice was not one she recognised. She grunted as she forced her eyes open. A figure, blurry, was making its way towards her slowly, clutching its side.

'Oh,' Lana moaned. 'What happened?'

'You must have fell girl.' He offered her one hand and grimaced as he held the other one fast to his side. She didn't take it but struggled into a sitting position.

'Oh, my head,' she groaned, gently rubbing the back of it. 'No wait, I remember. Your mates attacked me. Where are they? What's going on?'

'Come on lady, let's get you up and in the warm,' Bill replied.

'How long have I been here?' she asked.

'Well I guess it's near enough the middle of the day. I don't know. I've lost a few hours myself,' he confessed. He stroked his chin and now that her eyes had refocused Lana could see that normally he would be clean shaven, but after a couple of days laid up he'd sprouted a brownish red tinge that made him look scruffy.

She struggled onto her hands and knees and hauled herself upright. A dizzying sensation swept over her and she took a step backwards on the uneven ground. Bill stepped forward to steady her placing an arm around her waist.

'Why are you doing this?' Lana asked.

He shrugged.

'I'm not going with you until you tell me what the hell's going on.' She struck his arm away and dug her feet into the ground. 'Your name's not Bill is it?'

He hesitated and for a second Lana thought he was going to protest, but he gave in to her.

'No,' he said. 'It's Bing.'

'And Dave and Jim?' she pressed.

Bing shook his head. He'd already done the wrong thing in giving his own name. He wasn't about to risk the wrath of Joe by grassing on them.

'Well, where are they? Why did they try to kill me?'

'They've gone. I'm sure they weren't going to kill you. It was just a warning.'

'Just a warning?' she screamed. 'Not enough to knock me unconscious, after beating me senseless, they left me outside on a volcano where I could have been killed by a flying rock, or failing that, died a slow death from hyperthermia!' She tried to catch her breath and unwittingly reached out to Bing for support. She was trembling. She wrenched her arm away and rested both hands on her knees. 'What the hell were they warning me about?'

'You seem to have recovered lady. You better get inside,' said Bing. He turned and hobbled back to the hut.

Lana watched him from her bent stance which she straightened only when she saw him go inside. She looked around her. Scuffle marks in the ash told of the attack and several trails of boot prints led to the hut. Bing was right – she needed to escape the weather and she had little choice but to believe him that her attackers had left. Still, she couldn't quite bring herself to trust him and she sneaked back down the slope not to the front deck but to the side window. Peering through the glass she saw Bing working at the bench. There was no sign of Dave and Jim, who she was quite sure, were not their real names.

The door creaked as she stepped into the room. It was gloomy and the yellow plastic at the window belied the dark mood. The packs and sleeping bags of her attackers were nowhere to be seen. She relaxed a little.

'Paul!' she suddenly exclaimed. A sudden constriction caught in her throat. He should have been foremost in her mind. 'Where is he?'

Bing shrugged. 'Nobody here but you and me.'

'But he should have been back hours ago,' she cried. 'I have to find him. He must be hurt.'

'You get yourself sorted first lady,' said Bing. 'You can't be roaming around a live volcano after a beating like that. You've been knocked out anyhow. Your brain's been rattled. Sit there. I'll get you something to drink.'

'I don't need any help from you,' she spat at him. But the idea of a hot drink was tempting and reinforced how cold it was inside the hut.

She shivered and rubbed her shoulders. 'It's cold in

here.'

'Fire's gone out,' he replied.

'So you've been in a fever all morning and your friends deserted you while you were delirious.'

'That's about the size of it lady.'

'Will you be straight with me Bing? You said some stuff this morning. You're not weekend trampers are you? And my name is Lana,' she added.

'Ask me no questions...'

'Why did they leave you then?' Don't seem like very good friends to abandon you like that.' She knew she was pressing a sore point and hoped to open up the wound just enough for Bing to inadvertently blurt out some truths.

'That's enough lady,' he barked. 'It's none of your business.'

'Fine.' Lana sulked.

He slammed two steaming mugs of tea on the table. Lana cupped both hands around one and cautiously lifted it to her lips. The liquid was sweet and welcome and the steam wafted over her face, bringing some feeling to her lips and cheeks.

Bing took a sip of tea then eased back over to his bunk and lay down.

'You're not in a good way are you?' she asked him.

'I'll survive,' he replied.

'I'll light the fire.'

As she went to stand Lana reeled forwards overcome by a dizzying sensation in her head. 'In a minute,' she said as she fell back on the form.

Lana felt the mountain tremble underneath them and metal pots on the sink clattered. Seconds later a fresh pelt of volcanic debris clattered on the roof. She glanced through the front window that overlooked the deck. The wind had increased and thick swirls of grey and white ash raced around the hut. The yellow plastic sucked in and out of the frame relentlessly thudding at the end of its reach.

Lana lost any energy the drink had restored. Her head, stomach and legs were hollow. She tried to concentrate on Paul and Emma and the predicament they might be in. Something must have gone wrong or they would have been back by now. She was scared of her inability to cope with a rescue, particularly if she was physically compromised.

She looked over to where Bing was lying prostrate on his bunk, his breathing laboured, eyes closed. He seemed to be an okay person and she didn't feel threatened by him but was furious at him for being friends with her attackers and therefore guilty by association. If he had meant to hurt her he would have left her lying concussed in the cold to contract hyperthermia. She would have died, no two ways about it. But he had not done that. He had made a big effort to awaken her and get her to safety, wounded like a stuck pig as he was. But he wasn't telling her everything, anything in fact, not by a long shot. At least she knew his name, and that Dave and Jim weren't the real names of her assailants. Come to think of it, what sort of name was Bing? People weren't called Bingham these days – not since Jane Austen.

'How do I know your friends haven't gone after Paul and Emma?' she asked.

Bing groaned.

'You don't know do you?' she challenged him.

Suddenly the consequences of such an event loomed large in her head. The thought of Paul lying unconscious and vulnerable, maybe bleeding jolted her. She might be the only able bodied person left on the mountain, heaven forbid.

'Lana,' Bing gasped. 'They wouldn't waste time looking for your mates. They were out of here like a dose of salts. They're scared of the volcano. You saw what they were like.'

She considered this. She couldn't think of any reason Bing might lie to her. He had everything to gain by keeping her on side. Who else could see to him if his wound turned septic?

'I guess you're right,' she murmured.

She very delicately squatted in front of the firebox keeping her head high so the blood wouldn't rush to it. But that had its own problems. Her body stiffened as it lay in the cold and now she ached all over. She reignited the fire then brought in more split firewood, setting it next to the firebox.

'I'll change your bandage before I go.'

'Na, I'll be right,' Bing replied.

'Nonsense. That one's soaked. Must be bad.'

Lana padded into her bunkroom and returned with a modest first aid kit which she emptied onto the table.

'You should save that for your friends,' said Bing nodding at the bandages, tape and scissors.

'You know maybe I should.' Lana bristled.

'Although I'd say those two can take care of themselves, wouldn't you say?'

'I wouldn't know.' He was playing her at her own game – needling her, but for no good reason that she could see. Well, she was in the box seat.

'Sit up please and take your shirt off,' she directed. He struggled into an upright position and Lana tugged his fleece over his head.

'Good grief lady, be careful,' he winced.

'That was the easy bit,' she replied. 'I'm not experienced at this sort of thing. It's a pity for you Emma isn't doing this. She's vastly experienced.' She spat the words out and instantly regretted it. Even as she said it she imagined Emma curled safely in Paul's arms as he shielded her from the spewing volcano.

She clenched her teeth as she unfastened Bing's bandage and unravelled it around his clammy pale body. Blood had soaked right through to the top layer and changed to a rusty brown colour. A thick cotton pad held fast with tape covered the wound.

'Someone did a good job here,' Lana remarked.

'Tom's a quack,' Bing replied.

No sooner had the words left his mouth than the two of them locked eyes and simultaneously smirked.

'Two down, one to go,' Lana mumbled.

She ripped the tape off his midriff.

'Aah. Shit!'

Thickly coagulated blood had stuck the pad to Bing's wound. 'I think this will start bleeding again when we lift it.'

'Then don't lift it,' Bing gasped.

'Can't leave it on.' She was surprised at how authoritative she sounded. She gently prised the pad off and frowned at the now weeping wound. She leaned in closer to inspect it.

'What's this?' she asked Bing.

'I fell and got stuck with a branch,' he explained weakly. He hadn't expected to be interrogated.

'You know what's wrong with that?' asked Lana. 'First, there are no trees up here and therefore there are no branches. And secondly, that's no puncture wound is it?'

Bing pursed his lips and kept silent.

'In fact, if I'm not mistaken,' she continued, 'I'd say it's a knife wound. And that would be the second knife wound I've seen in two days.' She sat back on the form and waited for him to explain. He considered his reply at great length.

'Look. Lady. Lana. I'm not going to hurt you.'

'You're right there.'

'I just want to get out of here as soon as possible. The less you know about me the better.'

Lana harrumphed as she cleaned the wound and reapplied the dressing. It was clear she wasn't going to get anything else out of Bing right now so she left him to lie on his bunk.

The room was warming and she felt mellow as her bones responded to the heat. She was surprised to feel a little light-headed. Perhaps a quick nap to clear her head would be okay before she went searching for Paul and Emma. Before long she descended into a light slumber.

***

Lana snapped her eyes open and tried to focus on the timber slats of the bunk above her. There was a clarity that hadn't been evident when she went to bed. In fact she felt so much better she couldn't be sure if she'd slept for two hours or twelve. She could hear the crackle of the fire and the disturbed irregular breathing of her charge, but there was no movement; no Paul or Emma. And there was silence outside.

She tip-toed into the main room. Although the fire had died down the room retained a pleasant warmth. She peered into the firebox and estimated the two or three hours had passed. After all, there was still natural light. The yellow plastic was slack in the window frame and no ash swirled past the windows. It was eerie – like she was the only one left alive and the sun was about to disappear forever.

She gently pressed her fingers to the lump at the back of her head and grimaced. It was the size of an egg and tender to touch. How could she have come out of the attack so lightly? She knew from the outset she would have a job taking on two men on the sloping ground but she had put up a good fight. It seemed the most natural thing in the world. After all, it was what she had trained for all these years?

Without waking Bing she dressed swiftly, her bruised body screaming as she manipulated her limbs into wind-proofs. She went outside and stood on the deck. It reinforced the isolation she felt, standing there donned in mountain clothes, hood pulled low on her head, jacket zipped up to her chin, thick mittens preventing her carrying out the simplest of motor tasks. The mountain looked docile, not at all like the angry pretender it had been hours earlier. But for how long would it rest? And how long would the sun share its rays with her? It was already low in the sky, struggling to filter through the fine ash. Lana dreaded losing it to the chill night that would immediately follow and she shivered at the thought.

Paul. He was her priority. And Emma, of course. She was all they had. She felt sorry for them that she was their only hope. She conceded she knew this part of the mountain, but she'd always been up here with a colleague. It was daunting to even take one tiny step off the deck and thereby commit to being a one-person – a one bruised and battered person – rescue party.

She put herself in Paul's shoes. He was fit and probably hadn't intended to be out for long. If he wanted ash and lapilli samples he could easily have gathered those from near the hut. Lana wandered around it. No footprints or bodies, as expected. In that case he had probably gone as high as he possibly could, perhaps on the south side of the outcrop that gave the hut some protection from volcanic blasts.

Lana tried to remember the forecast. She knew the weather was to hold for the duration of her time on the mountain. She was due out today and so far the prediction was correct. Beyond that she did not know. She was aware however, that roughly every six days a front passed over the country. Sure as eggs, looking out on it now, the weather was taking a turn.

She walked a little below the hut where she gained a good vantage of the valleys and ridges ahead of her and tried to determine the route that Paul may have taken. The map of the landscape was imprinted on her mind. A myriad of streams ran off the unruly peaks sometimes big enough to warrant a footbridge, other times not. Already shadows were cast into the valleys. She hoped Paul wasn't lying injured in a valley developing hyperthermia. It was anybody's guess where he was, *where they were*, she reminded herself. She scanned the ground for footprints and looked back at hers which were dark brown amongst the fine dark brown powder. Paul and Emma's footprints should be as easy to see as hers.

She determined a reasonable route to the upper slopes and in time discovered what she assumed to be Paul and Emma's trail. Her pulse quickened as she followed it and constantly paused and looked back in the direction of the hut, reassuring herself of her lifeline. As long as she could see it she was safe. Well wrapped against the cold, she had equipped herself with a backpack containing a small first aid kit, a silver life blanket, water and thermal shirts for each of them. She trudged on soon losing sight of the hut to eventually come to a halt. Her heartbeat echoed in her ears, a combination of exertion and fear. She didn't like not being able to see the hut, even if it was only a spot on the horizon.

She pushed on and soon ascended into cloud which clung to her. It was damp and it settled thickly and uninvited, transforming into tiny translucent bubbles that appeared to side a shade above her clothes so they looked fuzzy all over. Heavy and clogging, it gagged her. It deadened everything within it: the air, the ground, her breath that emitted in thin white streams. When she looked behind her she could not see the distant desert, only her last few footprints. And the hut had long since disappeared. She wanted to lie down and let the cloud envelope her like a blanket.

'Lana Marshall!' she exclaimed aloud. 'Pull yourself together. You can't get lost. You're following their footsteps. You are not scared!'

She stamped her feet hard on the ground and it squeaked as she scuffed the glass ash. 'You're not frightening me!' she shouted into the nothingness. She hummed Gluck's Dance of the Blessed Spirits. It helped stave off the fear of being alone as she concentrated on following one ragged boot mark after another.

After a short time the trail became confused. There seemed to be two sets of prints descending. Or was it descending and ascending? Was one set ascending? A different gait. She surveyed the ascending trail closely for a few metres gently touching the outline of boot prints, trying to fathom who had passed which way and why. Then she did the same on the descending trail. Finally she chose to follow the ascending trail and strode uphill with a heroic sense of purpose now that she believed she was on the right track.

'Oh good grief,' she cried halting abruptly.

Her phone buzzed in her trouser pocket. She'd forgotten all about it. A hot flush settled on her throat as she anticipated Paul's message. She fumbled under layers of thick clothing and dragged it out. Alex! She peeled off her mittens which were by now quite damp. She read Alex's message but it was out of context and she realised that he had not heard from her. But she had texted him. He must have received it. She had sent it before the eruption. There could not have been atmospheric interference, not then. She checked her sent box but the message was not there. Poor Alex she thought. She scrolled to the outbox and found it there. She pushed send then rapidly searched Paul's number and pressed talk.

***

Paul could hear a bird in the distance. Its melodious call lulled him into a warm summer's day in the cool air of lush green forest. Dappled yellow light filtered through the leafy canopy speckling the moist forest floor. He could not see the small olive bird and its call was a long, long way off. He didn't remember being in the forest. He didn't feel as though he was. There were no other forest sounds and his body felt stiff, racked with cold. Where was the bellbird?

And if Bain would just get off his leg then maybe the feeling would come back to it and he could get up. This is the last time you talk me into abseiling into a sink hole, he thought. Strange that he wasn't wet. They'd fallen into a subterranean stream but he felt dry, and the bird was down here.

He thought about opening his eyes and deliberated over the consequences of that. He could feel pain in his shins, back, and head. His shoulders felt stiff and his palms tingled. If he opened his eyes the pain might go away. He shivered then grunted. The bird stopped singing and he opened his eyes.

No sweet smelling forest clothed in sunlight. No dark hell-hole from which he and Bain would have spent days to extricate themselves. Instead, a shrouded barren landscape enveloped in damp cloud gave him up. He shivered to full consciousness and recalled how he came to be here. He had climbed up the slope to obtain samples of volcanic debris and been caught out not only by the force and frequency of the explosions but by Emma. Where was she? Hadn't he rescued her? – man-

209

hauled her broken body up the slope to the shelter of an outcrop? Or was that a dream too? Why wasn't he with her, keeping her safe? She shouldn't be on her own. He should be with her holding her, warming her body and telling her everything will be all right. But he wasn't. He'd let her down. And then he remembered he had set her down against a rock and told her he would get help. Lana was right. It was too dangerous to be out here. Lana! The phone! He dug into his pocket and pulled it out. Missed call, the bird. Lana. He pressed call and held the phone to his ear.

***

Lana had just slotted her phone into her inside breast pocket, resumed Gluck and followed about five boot prints when Debussy's Clair de Lune flute solo pierced the air. She startled to a halt and with mittened hands fumbled with her zip and grabbed her phone to her ear.

'Paul?'

'Lana!'

'Where are you?' she asked.

'Just below a ridge about thirty minutes from the hut,' he replied.

'Are you hurt?'

'A bit.'

'Can you walk?'

'Dunno.' He struggled to get onto his hands and knees. 'Aah. I've twisted an ankle.'

'Is that all?' asked Lana.

'What else do you want?' he quipped.

'What about Emma?'

210

'She's got a broken leg. She's not with me.'

'Broken leg?' Lana screamed into the phone. 'Stay there. Don't move. I'm nearly there. I'm following your footsteps. If I'm not there in,' she looked back estimating how long ago she had left the hut, 'twenty minutes, call me.' She snapped her phone closed.

She was torn. On the one hand she was relieved that Gluck's Blessed Spirits had delivered her Paul and she really didn't have to pretend to be brave anymore. But the two of them unable to walk! Unthinkable.

She imagined what she would find when she got to Paul. If he could not walk by himself how would they rescue Emma? And what other injuries had he sustained? If he had only a twisted ankle he would have hobbled back to the hut hours ago, surely.

She concentrated on her tracking which wasn't too difficult now that she had her eye in. Paul's size tens had gouged a black print into the dark brown ash. Presently she raised her eyes to the horizon which was the ridge and from here looked like the top of the mountain. The cloud was low and the line that defined the horizon and the top of the mountain was blurred. What was more obvious was a flat green shape hunkered into a round form. She peered harder and deciphered a brighter green on the sleeves where Paul had brushed off some ash. Immediately above him the rocks retained a nutty dark brown colour, the terrain being so steep that even ash could not gain purchase. Lana groaned at the prospect of having to negotiate a steeper incline.

She paused. Paul had said that Emma was not with him. She scanned the hill all around where Paul lay. No sign of Emma. Perhaps she was the owner of the messy prints that trailed off below the track.

'Paul,' she yelled, and waved both arms in the air. 'Paul.' Her words sounded dull and bounced back at her. But she saw him lift his head and wave an arm in reply. He shuffled she quickened her pace.

'Lana,' cried Paul as she approached him. 'I'm sorry.'

She rested her hands on her knees and bent forward panting but quickly became aware of a dizzying sensation and was forced to squat.

'You did well to find me,' said Paul.

'I wouldn't have had to if you had used common sense and not gone exploring an erupting mountain,' she chided him.

He mocked a wince. 'I asked for that.' He attempted to stand up. 'Ouch!'

'What is it?' asked Lana.

'Ribs, head, back, shin, ankle,' he rattled off.

'Brain?' Lana asked.

'Emma,' Paul replied ignoring her, 'she's hurt.'

'Where is she?'

Paul nodded in the direction of an outcrop. 'I left her beyond this hill near an outcrop.'

'How is she?'

'In a bad way. Can't walk. You'll have to get Dave and Jim to bring her down.'

'That's not possible.'

'Why not?'

'They've gone,' she explained. 'But not before they set upon me and left me outside to die. I broke a nose and squashed a groin before they knocked me out though.'

'I can't believe it! Lana, it's my fault. I shouldn't

212

have left you there. Are you all right?' He screwed up his face with anguish then draped an arm around her shoulder but she brushed him aside.

'I'm fine. Just a bump on the head.' She noted the confusion in Paul's eyes and was happy to leave it there. 'Bing saved my life. They left me to freeze in the snow. I was supposed to die.'

'Bing?'

'Yes, not Bill. And not Dave and Jim,' Lana explained. 'Don't ask. We have to get you and Emma back to the hut. Time for chit chat later.'

She stood up and peered in the direction Paul had said Emma was. 'I'm not sure if she's got a broken leg, I don't know what to do.'

'Find Emma,' said Paul. 'See if you can make her comfortable. She'll tell you what to do. Then come back to me. Here,' he rifled in his pack for his survival blanket, 'take this.'

Lana pulled a thermal shirt out of her own pack and dropped it in Paul's lap. 'I've got one for Emma. Put this on.' And with that she scooted over the brow of the hill out of sight of Paul and made directly for the outcrop.

It was closer than it looked and at its base she noticed a splash of dark blue accentuated by the crisp white snowdrift on which it sat. As she drew nearer she realised that Emma had been there a long time. There wasn't a skerrick of colour in her face except for her blue lips. Her eyelids fluttered open, dislodging the ash that threatened to stick them together. 'Emma,' Lana said as she squatted alongside and tapped her firmly on the arm. She was answered with a groan. 'What happened? Is it your leg?'

213

'Yes,' Emma gasped. 'One is broken, I'm sure.'

'Don't try to move. I'll make you more comfortable then come back to get you.' Lana helped Emma put on a warm shirt and wrapped her in the reflective blanket.

'Where's Paul?' asked Emma.

'Just over that brow,' Lana replied. 'He didn't make it to the hut when he left you. He got struck by a bomb.' She stood up and studied her handiwork. 'For clever people you two sure are stupid. Fancy leaving the hut in the first place.'

'Paul struck? Is he hurt?'

'Of course he's hurt.' Lana was short. 'He would have rescued you otherwise wouldn't he? Don't worry, he'll live.'

'God, it's my fault. If I hadn't gone with him and fallen, and stupidly broken a leg...'

'You think it's your fault Paul got hit by a lava bomb? Save the dramatics and tell me how to fix you. You did make it to paramedic didn't you?'

'Of course I did,' Emma grunted her reply. 'You need to splint me. Paul should have left me where I was, shouldn't have moved me. I wasn't thinking straight.'

Lana looked around them. There was nothing that could be fashioned into a splint. Everything near them, the rocks, the low scrubby vegetation, was rounded as if they'd been ducking for cover from the ferociousness of the mountain's weather for decades. 'There's nothing to make a splint with. Are you in terrible pain Emma?'

'Of course,' she gasped through gritted teeth.

'I've got Voltaren.' Lana punched open the blister pack and emptied them into Emma's hand then held her water bottle out for her. 'It's all I have. I'll be back soon with a splint and some way to get you out of here.'

'Please, please Lana,' Emma cried. 'Give me some more drugs.'

But Lana had already turned from her and didn't see Emma slam her clenched fists onto the ground. She retraced her steps back to Paul.

'Here,' she said. 'Take my arm.'

'Did you find her?' he asked. 'How is she?'

'Apart from at least one broken leg she's remarkably robust.'

Lana offered Paul her arm and propped himself into a hunched standing position tentatively lifting one foot off the ground. 'Where does it hurt most?'

'Ankle, ribs,' he gasped.

'Breathing?'

'Yep, hurts.'

'Do you think you could have fractured your ribs?' she asked.

'Could have. Took a couple of direct hits.'

'Lean on me. I wish I had a stick for you. And that brings me to a problem we've got when we get back to the hut.'

'It does?'

'I told you Bing saved my life.'

'I changed his dressing and he does not have a stick wound. Isn't that what they told us? It's a knife wound.'

'Ah,' said Paul. 'That fits then doesn't it?'

'With the dead man at the lahar?'

'Yeah.'

'I think they were fighting because Bing was saying things while he was delirious and he made thrusting movements, like you would if you had a knife.'

'What's he doing now?' asked Paul.

'Sleeping. He's pretty sore. Paul, I'm not scared of him. Obviously he won't tell the truth but it seems his mates have abandoned him. He's putting on a brave face about it, saying they're afraid of the mountain.'

'But why did they attack you sweetheart?' Paul lightly touched her upper arm this time Lana let the small action comfort them both. But only briefly.

'I tried to talk to Bing in his sleep,' she explained. 'It didn't make any sense to me but Dave saw us and I guess he thought Bing had said something to incriminate them. I really don't know what though. I keep going over it in my head.'

'Let's get out of here Lana. This daylight won't last much longer and it's getting a little breezy. We have to get Emma yet.' Paul took a tentative step testing his weight on the twisted ankle. Lana positioned herself alongside him so he could lean on her.

A heavy drop of rain hit Paul's sleeve followed by another one and then another. His lightly powdered sleeve soon spotted grey and green and his dark eyelashes were delicately powdered with the silicic ash.

'I don't want this stuff in my eyes Lana. Hang on.'

He took his bandana and flicked it across his face.

'That's better,' Lana smiled. 'I thought I was rescuing Casper the friendly ghost.' They both laughed but it was too much on Paul's ribs. He checked himself and held Lana's gaze.

'Do you remember when we used to laugh Lana?' he asked.

'Yes,' she said quietly. 'I do Paul.'

'I'd like us to laugh like that again.' His eyes held

216

hers.

She tightened her lips into a thin line and said nothing but Paul did not press her.

'Come on Florence Nightingale,' he grimaced, 'get me out of here.'

The rain began to steady reducing visibility and the thick ash was slushy underfoot. Lana laboured under the added weight of Paul and progress down the hill was awkward although with his loping strides it wasn't much slower than her usual gait allowed. Soon the rain dripped off her hood into her eyes and down her cheeks and nose.

'This isn't good for Emma,' Paul announced.

'What are we going to do Paul?'

'We haven't got time to waste. We're going to have to make some kind of sledge. You'll have to drag her back. At least it will be downhill some of the way.'

'A sledge?'

'Maybe a mattress. The vinyl will slide relatively easily. It's just a matter of finding some rope to attach to it.'

Lana slipped into her own thoughts. Paul talked as if she alone could haul Emma to safety. What faith he had in her. Didn't he see the fuzzy light inside her head? Couldn't he feel the bruising all over her body? If he did, would he send her back out here to attempt a rescue? He's conceding defeat, she thought. He's in a lot of pain and he knows he can't help. But he hasn't admitted the pain, not likely to, not while he thinks he can still impress her. She smiled to herself. Doesn't he know he's not sixteen anymore?

'Not long now Paul,' said Lana. 'I've got the fire

going so you can hang your wet clothes on the rack above it. Come on. Less talk, more walk.'

Presently the little hut came into view, the narrow stainless steel chimney emitting puffs of smoke. It was a sanctuary amidst the white sky and the brown ground and Lana felt warm just looking at it. Already she could smell the piquant wood smoke and thought how good it would be to relax in front of the fire, not to have to go back outside in the rain and wind, alone.

'When we get to the hut,' said Paul, 'you dry off and grab some food.'

'I have to make a sledge,' Lana argued.

'I can do that.'

'With fractured ribs?'

Before long they'd hobbled the last hundred metres over the already disappearing footsteps to the hut.

***

The interior of the hut was gloomy but the warm respite it offered was immediate and Lana felt the weight of worry lift from her the minute she stepped inside. The yellow plastic sucked in as she opened the front door and the rain made a dull pitter patter on the tin roof as it negotiated its fall through the ash. Bing snored on his bunk unwittingly adding a staccato to the soothing rhythm.

Paul limped to the centre of the room shivering, leaving a wet trail behind him. He shrugged off his mountain jacket and attempted to lift his damp merino thermal over his head.

'Aah,' he cried and dropped his arms back to his sides. He turned to Lana. 'Could you help me?'

218

'Again?' she said. He dipped his torso and she gently pulled off his two layers so that he stood bare-chested in wet trousers so close to her that she could feel his hot breath on her cold face. The sight of him made her gasp. She longed to trace her fingers over the bumps and hollows that made up his shoulders, rib cage, pectoral muscles, stomach. Surely he had planned to trap her like this. Finally she dragged her eyes away and saw him staring at him and she checked herself. She hoped her face didn't betray her sudden lust. Paul started to undo his belt and fly. Lana quickly turned away and walked to the bunkroom, where she changed into dry clothes.

Clad only in wet underwear Paul arranged his clothes on the rack. As Lana returned to the room she remembered she hadn't retrieved a towel and turned back to get it. Paul grinned and in a few short steps followed her. As she came back through the door holding a small travel towel she collided straight into the chest that just minutes before she had willed herself not to touch.

'Aah, Lana,' Paul pleaded. He held her by the arms and smelt her damp hair. She clasped the towel between them and he gently prised it from her. She reluctantly gave it up and he draped it over his shoulder. He held her close to him. She allowed herself to breathe in his masculine scent and nuzzled her face into the side of his neck. It was a little bit rough, like sandpaper. It couldn't be more perfect. She wanted to stay nestled into him, to nibble his neck with her hot lips and exploring tongue. He felt warm and strong and if she stayed there any longer she would melt under his touch. But as appealing as it sounded it was not an option.

'Oh Lana,' murmured Paul.

She breathed deeper, forcing each breath to travel to and from her lungs without the interference of her staccato heartbeat. She couldn't trust herself to speak. She knew if she did it would be to say yes. She felt his desire stir against her hips and she moved against him imperceptibly.

'Mmm,' groaned Paul.

'No.' Lana pushed Paul away but she couldn't look him in the eyes. She dragged the towel off his shoulder and handed it back to him dangling it between their bodies. He lifted one corner and used it to dry the rain off Lana's face and hair.

'Paul,' she whispered. He continued to delicately wipe droplets from her. She coughed. 'Paul.' Her no-nonsense tone severed their intimacy. 'Get yourself dry and put some clothes on. You said there's no time to waste. I have to build a sledge.'

***

Emma couldn't remember the last time she'd been in so much pain. Although she could and did recall the time she broke her ankle on her second geology field trip in the Canadian Rockies. They'd been put into groups of three and she didn't mind the group she was in although Jabba was inclined to be a bit lazy. His mind was sharp enough, but strangely for a student of the earth sciences, he preferred to play computer games thus contributing to his portly stature. Funny she should remember him of all people now. It gave her no comfort, in fact, felt sullied by the memory.

It was six days in and they'd finally got off the mountain range and for what was deemed a treat they'd swapped teams and were taking instruction at the bottom of a sheer cliff face on how to use a Jacob staff and record the observations as they scaled the cliff. A narrow stream trickled around them and the lecturer, Alan, who could have been a sports commentator in another life, was leading the group around the stream to point out a reverse thrust. Emma seized the opportunity to show off her athleticism and decided to jump across the stream. But it didn't go as planned. The rock she landed on rolled sideways and she tumbled flatly into the stream screaming her head off. So that was the end of the whole field trip for her. She was hopping mad with herself but she did take to Jabba and the others being especially attentive to her. By then she'd already been a first aid cadet for six years and beaked out instructions between outbursts of writhing gasps.

She felt hot as she recalled the broken ankle. She wasn't sure if it was actually her broken leg that provided the warmth or the memory of the hot July day of the field trip.

A breeze stirred her from her reverie and suddenly she shivered. She tucked the life blanket around her and cursed at the situation. It wasn't looking good. Even with the survival blanket conditions were becoming ripe for developing hyperthermia. It would be so easy to just breathe through the pain, let it go and drift off to sleep. But she knew she wouldn't wake up. That was the sneaky thing about it. It lulled you into a nice cosy place and you'd think, yes, a quick nap, while away the boredom, kill the pain, and next thing you know, it's black forever. So she embraced the agony. As long as she could feel it she was alive. She even went so far as to adjust her buttocks which had become decidedly numb. The action accentuated the acute stabbing in her leg.

She was ashamed of herself. Her reaction to the popping explosions was unprecedented. It had never happened before. As she lay there she anguished over its cause. The eruption had sounded frightening and the dislodged debris raining down all around them had filled her with terror, but from where had such fear manifested? She strained to pick something out of her past that may have triggered it but came up empty. Paul would ask, she was certain. He deserved an explanation, especially since her actions had put his life at risk.

She warmed as she felt his kiss on her mouth. It wasn't how she envisaged it but they were alone and it would have passed for passionate. Dare she imagine the sequel? She would only get frustrated and a broken leg was not conducive to amorous relations, although certainly she would affect a good deal of attention from him.

The rain fell sparsely initially, plopping lightly on the silver blanket then rolling quickly off to be sucked up thirstily by the dry mountain soil. Emma shivered and groaned. Time dragged. She had no idea how long she'd been there; probably not as long as it felt. How long before Lana returned? She was sick of this agony.

***

Lana dragged the mattress along the now familiar track. Behind her it looked as though the track had been

222

graded. It was a slow process. The rain made the vinyl slippery to grasp and Lana's mittens frequently let go, only to have the heavy mattress wallop onto the ground while she lurched ahead without the weight of it. At least she didn't need to follow the jumbled boot prints anymore, so recognizable were the landforms around her. But they comforted her in her aloneness.

Emma was in imminent danger of hyperthermia, something not lost on Lana. She had no time to waste. She cursed the rain and hoped Emma wasn't getting wet. She didn't want to have to strip them both off and share body heat.

Paul had bundled Lana up and saw her off at the door. She wondered where he found the confidence in her and hoped it wasn't misplaced. Or maybe he didn't have confidence at all. But she was the only one who could bring Emma back, so naturally Paul bolstered her own belief in herself. She imagined herself as a five year old going off to school all by herself. Her mother wouldn't have let her go if she hadn't thought Lana could do it. And nor would Paul.

She trudged on, mittens now gripping the rope attached to the mattress. She made good time to the brow of the hill that once traversed the hut could no longer be seen from. They'd discussed strategy while Paul hastily put together the sled. Lana must make haste to Emma because the journey back would be slower and darkness could, if they were unlucky, beat them home. Hopefully by the time night fell Lana would be back on the siding track and if the atmosphere was forgiving, a scant moon might illuminate the trail.

She stole a quick glance behind her. The hut was tiny

in the distance and she could see puffs of smoke above it. She adjusted Paul's bandana over her nose and mouth and pulled her beanie hard down over her ears.

As she broached the crest of the rise she was struck by a gust of icy wind which blew rain directly at her. Rain drops settled on her dark lashes before becoming so swollen they rolled off and were absorbed by the bandana. Suddenly, if she hadn't felt miserable before now, she was overwhelmed. She was tired, she was battered and bruised. Damn the stupidness of Emma, she thought. Of Emma and Paul. She grew angry which manifested an increase of adrenalin. For now she didn't just trudge and drag herself forward, she stomped. And she continued to stomp up and down the small ridges and all the way up to the outcrop where she had left Emma.

Thankfully Emma was completely covered by the silver sheet. There was no movement from it. Lana was too tired to yell and didn't try to rouse her until she was directly at her feet. Emma gave no indication that she'd heard Lana approach.

'Emma,' said Lana. Nothing. 'Emma, can you hear me?' Lana jostled Emma's shoulder but Emma's only response was to groan. 'Wake up. I'm going to get you out of here.' She tugged the cover away from Emma's head.

'Where's Paul?' Emma moaned.

'In the hut.'

'Paul's gone to get help?' she pleaded.

'Sorry to disappoint you, but I'm the help.' Lana dumped her pack unceremoniously on the ground and rubbed her aching shoulders. The track markers she'd commandeered for splints rattled as they landed. She ripped off Emma's survival blanket. 'At least you're dry. Will I splint you before or after I get you on the mattress?'

'Before,' Emma gasped. 'Loosen my laces.'

Lana did as she was instructed. 'I've got some clothes to roll up to support your leg and track markers for splints and two belts to hold it all together,' she explained. 'Okay?'

Emma nodded.

'Emma, help me. Tell me how to do this.' Lana spoke loudly and clearly knowing that to engage Emma increased the woman's chance of survival.

'Place the padding between my legs and feet.'

It should have been a simple task but Lana was cold and she was intent on working quickly. Even rolling the clothing seemed impossibly difficult but eventually she managed without causing Emma too much discomfort. That done, Emma continued.

'Get a bandage and make a figure of eight around my feet and ankles.'

Lana unwrapped the bandage.

'No don't unroll it,' Emma snapped. 'Too late, look at it. What a mess.'

In her haste Lana dropped it and already it was damp and dirty. She was aware of a slight tremor in the movements. Emma was making her nervous and with each wrap she swore it was either too tight or too loose. Emma belted out instructions while Lana wrapped the belts and bandages around Emma's knees, and lower and upper thighs. Lana forgave Emma's rambunctiousness on the poor woman's agony, but it didn't help her confidence to be barked at like some imbecile.

'Now slide onto the mattress,' Lana instructed. She dragged the mattress alongside Emma. 'Lift your buttock onto here then I can pull you on.'

'I can't,' Emma gasped.

'You can and you will,' Lana answered tersely.

'If Paul was here...'

Lana bit her lip as she recalled Paul's warm arms holding her less than an hour since. Emma's complaining got lost on the breeze. How would Paul handle this woman? Humour her to gain the best outcome probably. Well Lana wasn't so empathetic.

'If I have to haul you onto this mattress myself you'll be in more pain than you are now,' she told Emma.

'Are you mad at me?'

'No,' Lana answered. 'I'm not mad. You have to help yourself Emma. And the first thing you can do is shut up. Just to save your energy, you understand?' Lana stopped short of making the attack personal. She needed Emma to work with her, not against her and if they had a spat it would prolong their time out here. Lana would get the job done, safely, efficiently. She didn't have to like what she was doing but she must channel her entire energy into the task. It was all or nothing right now.

Emma did as she was told, screaming when the jagged bone jostled away from its resting position. Tears streamed down her face as she threw herself prostrate partly on the mattress.

'One more little jump Emma,' Lana commanded. She leaned forward to help.

'I can't,' Emma cried.

Lana grabbed her under the arms and hauled her body fully onto the mattress which by now was fully wet. Her screams echoed off the rock face into the valley below, but Lana soon had her lying on the mattress with the survival blanket tightly wrapped around her and covering her face from the rain.

'I'm sorry for your pain,' Lana said matter of factly.

But there was no answer from the sled.

Emma knew enough to save her energy; besides, she'd slipped into a sulk. She'd much rather it was Paul who came to her rescue. It would make a much more romantic story when she went back home with him on her arm.

Lana didn't want Emma to be upset with her, and whilst she had told her she was sorry for her pain she'd only said it so Emma wouldn't think her too hard. In truth, she couldn't have cared less, because her job was to bring this woman home alive. Pain didn't come into it. Emma's or Lana's.

She hauled the sled downhill with its broken cargo as she had hauled uphill; with anger for fuel. Her sides ached where they'd been overstretched during the fight and her muscles fought the new tasks Lana was asking of them. But she did not complain to Emma. It was a stop start exercise that strained her arms, legs and back beyond what she thought possible. She alternated between walking frontwards and backwards and never once spoke to her patient. Emma screamed intermittently as Lana dragged the sled over rocky terrain. She didn't mean to drag her over rock, she could barely see them; the light was fading and she was tired. But she kept on, hot and perspiring under her windproofs.

As Paul feared, dusk fell by the time Lana reached the siding track. Only now did she waste a little energy and utter a few words of comfort to Emma. The evenness of the track allowed Emma to hold onto the mattress more easily and at last the rain began to ease.

'The hut's just up ahead,' Lana shouted. 'Not long now.'

Lana knew that dusk would take a long time to fall, but even so, at the higher altitude with all the snow and some moonlight able to penetrate the thick air, it would never get pitch black. She began to think about the hut, the warmth, the fire, food and Paul. Her stomp eased back into a trudge and she chanted a mantra in her head: trudge drag trudge drag. Before long she'd broached the final brow and made out the dark shape of the hut. A tiny spot of amber light was all she needed to give impetus to the final leg.

'We made it Emma,' Lana cried. Trudge drag, trudge drag. It was relentless but not never-ending. She could smell the wood-smoke now, and as she sucked it in she let it bring with it the smell of Paul.

She trudge dragged the last few steps to the hut and exhausted, dropped the sled's ropes and crawled onto the deck where she collapsed.

***

Paul lay across a bunk in the warmth of the main room wearing long johns, thick socks and a mid-weight merino thermal top. His body ached and he was exhausted with the pain of breathing but his mind hadn't settled. He'd sent Lana back out into certain danger and the guilt of that sickened him. She wasn't experienced, he knew that. It would be his fault if she had an accident.

It was his fault anyway. She had every right to be angry with him. So far she hadn't vented much anger. He wondered what she was like when she flared up. He found he was mildly excited at the prospect. If only he hadn't been injured he would have slung Emma over his shoulder and been back in the hut hours ago.

He was disturbed by a shuffle then a thump and with a limping hop he rushed outside to see Lana lying face down on the deck. Beyond her Emma was on the sled, completely covered by the silver blanket. She groaned.

'Lana,' he cried, squatting alongside her. 'Sweetheart, you did it.'

'Isn't anyone going to help me here?' Emma's drawl sang out into the night.

Paul helped Lana into a sitting position. 'Come on, let's get you inside.'

'No. I'm okay.' She crawled onto her hands and knees. 'Get Emma first.'

'Paul,' Emma called. '*Please* help me.'

'We're right here Em,' Paul called back, and then to Lana. 'Lana, can you manage one last push?'

She nodded and taking hold of Paul's hand dragged herself to her feet. Together they took hold of the rope and on the count of three hauled the sled in short bursts up the steps and into the hut. Then they made a bed of a dry mattress and laid it near the fire.

Bing meanwhile had risen from his fever induced slumber and made a billy of tea.

'You got some painkillers?' asked Emma.

'Sure,' Bing replied.

He brought a mug to Emma who lay propped against a pack for support while the others perched on the edge of the platform bunks. She downed the drugs and let her body relax. The hut was quiet for a time while they recovered from their ordeal and allowed the warmth of the tea to work its way to their cores. Eventually it was Emma that broke the silence.

'I'm sorry I was a worry to you Paul,' said Emma.

'It's all right Em,' he smiled at her. 'I was unconscious the minute I left you, so I wasn't too worried.'

Lana smiled inwardly. Emma hadn't expected that.

'But still, I guess I shouldn't have gone,' Emma replied.

'Too late to worry about that. Well done for hanging on in there.' He congratulated Emma then patted Lana's thigh. 'And well done you,' he added softly.

'Yes,' Emma joined it. 'Well done. We could have died up there. You made a good sled Paul.'

'It's Lana that needs compliments, not me,' said Paul.

Lana brushed off the comment with a shake of her head. 'It's your turn now,' she said to Paul.

'Sweetheart, I'm fine,' he replied. 'You should rest.'

She ignored him. 'Tell me when it hurts,' she said pressing her fingers to the sides of his torso. He flinched and grimaced. 'Sorry,' she murmured under her breath. 'I could have been more gentle. They're fractured aren't they? Don't know how many. Are we supposed to strap them or leave them?'

'You have to strap his upper arm over the injured side of his chest,' Emma interjected.

'Lucky we've got a first aider.' Paul toasted Emma with his cup of tea and she responded likewise.

'Make a sling Lana,' Emma demanded. 'A triangle. If

we don't have one, use a blanket. Then lay some padding on the injured side and position Paul's arm at forty five degrees across his chest.'

This time Lana worked slowly and methodically, partly because the warmth of the hut didn't convey the same urgency as working out on the mountain and partly because she enjoyed the intimacy with Paul. She was aware of him watching her work, studying her face. She imagined she knew what he was thinking and refused to look into his eyes. She was grateful that Emma recited step by step instructions.

Emma continued. 'Now Paul, shuffle into a supported position like I am but lean towards the injured side. I think you should come down here by me, by the fire.' She patted the ground next to her.

'I haven't finished,' Lana announced. 'What about your ankle?'

Paul manoeuvred his leg to allow Lana to easily work on it.

'It's very swollen and it's hot. We should strap it,' she said.

'I can do that for you Paul,' said Emma.

'Actually Em,' he replied, 'thanks, but Lana will manage.' He saw Lana's eyes sparkle and she smiled to herself as she peered intently at Paul's foot.

'Can I roll up your legs and check out your shins?' asked Lana.

She daintily lifted the thin woollen leggings off his shins and bunched them at his knees.

'Oh.' She clutched her stomach as she caught sight of white skin flapping around the blood red wounds. 'Sorry,' she said, turning her head.

'Bad?' asked Emma.

'Yep,' she gagged.

'Sprinkle iodine on it,' Emma instructed. 'It will heal quickly but nastily. Not much skin on shins.'

Paul sucked in his breath between clenched teeth as Lana applied some. It had a reassuring hospital smell to it.

'You knocked your head when you fell,' she said. 'Let me have a look.' She took his head in both her hands and gently massaged her fingers through his hair.

'Ah,' Paul whispered, barely audible as Lana scraped over a matted area above his forehead. She sprinkled iodine on it.

'I'm surprised you got off as lightly as you did,' said Lana. 'You said you took a direct hit. Where?'

'It struck my back pack,' he replied. 'A big bugger. Pack saved my life.'

'Were you knocked out Paul?' asked Emma.

'Yeah.'

'Concussion,' she continued, 'is not to be taken lightly. You could have recurring bouts of dizziness or memory loss. Or both.'

'How bad can that be?' challenged Paul.

'She's right,' said Lana. 'I've had dizzy episodes.'

'Why are you dizzy Lana?' asked Emma.

Lana hushed her voice to a murmur and scuttled closer to Emma. 'Because his mates,' she nodded to Bing who was back resting on his bed, 'beat the living daylights out of me!'

'What?' Emma screeched.

'It's all right, they've gone,' she said. 'He's okay. He saved my life.'

'Shit Lana, I'm sorry. And hey, guess I should say thank you for saving mine,' she said.

'No problem. Get some rest.'

Lana doled out painkillers to everyone except herself and soon it was too much effort to talk.

Paul allowed Lana to fashion a pillow from clothing and tuck him into his down sleeping bag. He snuggled into its puffy folds and drifted off with the sound of her sleeping breath in his ears.

***

The explosion was accompanied by a thunderous crash through the roof of the hut. Lana screamed and dropped the metal plate spilling hot rice all over the floor. She lurched hard against the sink bench, her heart beating hard against her chest. The hole revealed the night and it was raining, straight through the roof. She stared at the dark boulder imbedded into the wooden floor, steaming as the rain vaporised on its surface.

The hut filled with the sounds of Emma's screams, for the boulder came to rest only inches from her mattress. Flecks of rice peppered her.

'Cripes! Emma!' exclaimed Paul. 'You okay?'

She struggled to sit up flailing her arms at the rice. Paul scrambled to his feet and hopped to her. The rain was all over the place, pushed in by the wind.

'Lana, help me pull Emma away from the hole,' Paul ordered.

For a moment Lana heard nothing and clung fiercely to the kitchen bench, her back to it.

'Oh,' said Paul finally noticing her. 'You're not hurt

are you?'

She threw her hand to her breast. 'Gave me a fright, that's all. My heart is in my mouth.'

'Can someone get me out of here?' It was Emma, by now soaking up the worst of the rain that was driving in through the hole in the roof.

Lana and Paul quickly dragged her aside and Bing helped to make her comfortable.

'You seem to attract bad luck,' Bing remarked.

Lana squatted over the rock. She held her palms above it feeling the heat of the volcano surge through her. 'How hot will it be?' she asked.

'It probably left the crater at around eleven hundred degrees,' Paul calculated, 'but as you can see it's already crystallised during its flight. It's fairly rounded, quite vesicular so it's got a lot of air in it. That speeds cooling. In 1996 they found a boulder the day after it had been ejected and it was over sixty degrees centigrade after rolling down a snow slope. The coolest this will be is about one hundred degrees I'd say.'

Lana couldn't draw herself away from it. She kept her hands above the rock and settled herself into a kneeling position. She was oblivious to the drops of rain that plastered her hair to her head.

'It's beautiful,' she whispered.

'We're not safe are we?' asked Bing.

'Depends,' said Paul.

'On what?'

'Whether you think lightening strikes twice in the same place,' he quipped seriously.

The hut shook under more guttural explosions. Pots on the bench rattled.

'Look,' said Emma. She pointed to the side window. 'The sky is glowing.'

'Surtseyian eruptions,' Paul explained. 'Hot, big, highly explosive and infinitely beautiful.'

'How long could this last?' asked Lana.

'Unfortunately it could be hours or days or weeks,' Paul replied. 'I have no way of predicting.'

They all looked at each other in silence. The primeval growls of the volcano reminded Lana of lions she had seen in reserves. It was a sound that you felt at the lower end of the audio spectrum rather than heard. The glass in the windows rattled in their frames and the metal cups on the table clattered. The yellow plastic sucked in and out as a gust of wind funnelled down the hole in the roof and blew out the solitary candle leaving the pale sliver of yellow firelight from the firebox the only light to filter onto the floor.

'I'll get it,' said Lana, finally dragging herself out of her mesmerised state.

Paul put a hand out to her and lightly touched her arm. 'Are you sure you're okay Lana?'

'Of course.'

She managed a weak smile and swallowed down her rapid heartbeat. Her legs felt hollow and as she lit a match she realised her hands had not yet stopped trembling.

Volcanic debris blasted down onto the tin roof and with each volley no one in the hut could utter a word. The bombardment was irregular but each was consistent in that first there was a loud thud followed by a jagged tumble, sometimes bouncing off the roof to land with a thud on the ground, or at other times coming to rest in

235

the gutter. All ears were trained on the missiles and as each volley receded everyone let out a collective sigh of relief. The floor beneath the hole became scattered with the rain and flecks of fine rock. It became cool.

'If this goes on we're going to be stuck for food and medical supplies,' said Lana.

'I've got rice,' Bing volunteered.

'Not anymore,' Lana replied. 'I went through your pack when you were asleep. I was just dishing up when the rock struck.' She looked at the rice on the floor. 'Sorry.'

'There will be food in the warden's quarters,' Paul reassured them. 'And hopefully a radio.'

'Warden's quarters?' asked Emma.

'The outside room,' grunted Bing.

'Well if there's a radio in there why the hell haven't we used it? Geez guys. Hello!' Emma flopped back on her mattress with a melodramatic flailing of arms. 'Honestly!'

'I'll break in there tomorrow,' said Lana, 'unless you've got a key.'

'Of course I don't have a key,' he replied, then added, 'I don't know why you think I would have.'

Lana watched the exchange, the way Paul seemed to smile but not smile as he said it and the way Emma held his eye longer than was necessary.

'We'll have to have cheese and biscuits tonight,' said Lana. 'We're okay; where we were?'

Paul lowered his head a little and looked at Lana beneath heavy lids and smiled lightly.

'Maybe,' he replied.

***

The day dawned dull with cloud sitting heavy in the air, but at least it wasn't raining. There had been no reprieve in the explosions all night but the last couple of hours it appeared calm. It was another long night. Lana had at one stage got the urge to relieve herself but was so terrified to go outside that she convinced herself she didn't need to go. But then, if she was ever going to get to sleep, if by some miracle the mountain stopped terrorising her enough to relax, she couldn't because all she could think about was her bladder. In the end she chanced going off the deck and even then was caught so short that she scuttled back inside with her pants around her knees. Slamming the door behind her and shaking she was sure she'd woken everyone up, but they all reassured her that they weren't asleep.

She lay curled in her sleeping bag facing Paul and listened for a change in his breathing to tell her he was awake. Finally he opened his eyes.

He turned to her, shuffling slightly before he was reminded of the pain.

'Good morning angel.'

'I'm not an angel,' she replied. 'Did you get much sleep?'

'Nope.'

'I heard and felt every single explosion,' he replied.

'Paul,' Lana whispered. 'I'm the only one able to get out of here under my own steam,' she said. 'I have to go and get help.'

'If the mountain was behaving Lana,' Paul corrected her, 'then maybe I'd let you go, but it's not. And there's the small matter of the lahar. You couldn't traverse it anyway.'

Lana bristled. 'You'd let me go?'

She tried to control her whisper. She didn't want the whole hut to be in on their conversation. He rustled his arm free and stroked hers. His touch was becoming familiar to her and it was nice but even so she debated whether to shrug him off.

'Oh come on sweetheart, I didn't mean it like that and you know it. I don't want anything to happen to you.'

'Maybe you're right,' said Lana, 'and I had forgotten about the lahar. So why don't I go the same way the others did? Straight down. I could Paul. I'll cut through the army land.'

Paul shook his head and grasped Lana's hand. 'You still have to cross the stream down below and it will be more dangerous than you realise. Trust me Lana. I'm not risking your life. Don't argue with me. The mountain hasn't finished with us yet.'

Lana flung her head back onto the thin pillow she'd fashioned out of her clothes and stared at the bunk slats above her. *Matt loves Marie* said a scribble in a heart with an arrow through it. *Pink Floyd was here* said another. Suddenly she was back in 1979. *We don't need no education, hey, teacher, leave us kids alone.* What a mantra to be sitting school certificate under. The wonder that she and Paul had scraped through at all. That plus the hours they'd spent on the phone talking about nothing.

'You can radio for help if there is one in the warden's quarters,' she said. 'Otherwise I'll have to use our mobiles and I have to go outside for that. We need to get airlifted since no one around here can walk.' She squeezed his hand. She almost forgot it was there it felt so natural.

'Even if we could walk we wouldn't make it over the creek with the bridge out,' said Paul. He rolled towards her. 'Do you think its fate Lana?' he asked quietly, his voice dropping an octave.

'What?'

'You and me. Here. Now,' he said.

'Let's see,' she said picking his hand up and placing it back down on the bunk between them. 'Manipulation and cunning just so you can see me again, lahar and volcanic eruption – you might think you're in control but I like to put this one down to Mother Nature. Extensive injuries resulting in my having to care for you. Could be a little bit of fate.'

He smiled. 'Careful planning so you find me the highly irresistible, good looking single man that I am, eruption forces extended stay in close quarters. I couldn't arrange that myself I have to concede. But put them all together Lana, fate.'

'Paul,' Lana whispered tersely. 'I am seeing someone. I told you.'

'And I respect that you need time to finish with him.'

She frowned and this time raised her voice. 'You have a nerve.'

'Oh Lana, please don't be mad at me. I see how you are with me. You want what I do.'

He reached out for her hand and stroked her fingers. She closed her eyes and felt a stirring deep inside her. Reluctantly she reclaimed her hand. She rose from the bunk and ran her fingers through her hair. She had slept in her clothes in case of the need to evacuate, as they all had.

She picked her way around Emma who stirred as she did so and walked over to the jagged hole in the tin roof. Light grey cloud moved past and a tiny gleam of blue presented far beyond it. The rain on the floor had reduced to a damp dark stain, having partially dried from the heat of the fire.

She squatted again in front of her rock, for that was how she thought of it. She knew exactly how it came to be and how it got there. No one appreciated it like she did. Paul was right. It had cooled rapidly and now she touched it, cloaked it with open palms. She shut her eyes and imagined the heat within.

'Meditating over your rock again?' Emma shuffled into a sitting position.

'How's the leg?' Lana refused to be rattled.

'Got any painkillers?' Emma grimaced as she spoke.

'Here,' Paul cut in, digging around his sundry items splayed all over the bunk. 'You can have these.'

It didn't escape Lana's attention that Emma held Paul's hand longer and fixed his gaze deeper than the exchange normally should have taken. She stood abruptly and put a block of split timber in a plastic bag and stepped out to the front deck.

Attached to the main hut was a separate room with access only from the deck. It had no internal access and was used exclusively for wardens. As such these rooms were always locked and generally well provisioned.

'I'm going to break into the warden's quarters,' Lana announced.

No sooner had she walked outside than explosions

240

started up again. Debris rained down, hitting the deck and cracking the timber under the shock of the hot rock. She flinched.

'Here goes,' she said as she swung the plastic bag. With a resounding crash the glass shattered spraying glistening shards inside the room. Paul appeared at the door of the hut and watched as she used the wood to smash out any chips remaining in the frame.

'Go Lana,' Paul grinned.

'First time I've had to break a window on purpose,' she frowned. 'Quite liberating.'

She hauled herself in through the window and unlatched the door from the inside. The room was tiny. There was a double bunk, a two hob gas burner connected to a nine kilogram gas cylinder, a wooden desk, a shelf and a set of shiny silver dumb bells.

'Can you believe that?' asked Paul incredulous.

'What?' asked Lana, looking around the room.

'A set of dumb bells! What the heck?' He rolled one aside to read the end of it. 'Ten kilos.'

'Must be a super fit hut warden,' Lana suggested. 'Maybe a body builder.'

'Well there's no special body building food in here, unfortunately,' said Paul as he analysed the contents of the shelf.

'Rice, tinned food, milk powder, rolled oats. Thank goodness,' said Lana. 'It's better than nothing.'

'Can't see a radio,' said Paul.

Suddenly the ground lurched beneath them. Lana lost her balance and slumped to the floor and Paul attempted to brace himself in the door frame. The timber walls creaked and buckled and the glass in the remaining window in the tiny room shattered spraying Lana with shards. The room took on a thirty degree lean and part of the floor at the higher end pulled away from the inner wall. Lana clung to the floor as it moved beneath her and from within the hut she heard Emma screaming.

'What was that?' Lana asked in panic. She scrambled to her feet taking the hand that Paul offered.

'Our foundation's been smashed. A boulder's taken it out,' said Paul. He limped to the edge of the deck and peered under the hut. The front corner of the hut was resting on the ground. Parts of the walls were smashed and timber lay smashed and spread all over the ground. A dark brown steaming boulder sat at the corner with the hut perched on it.

'Quick. Inside,' he directed.

The floor of the hut now angled from the front door to the rear of the hut and the door would not close properly in its jamb. Lana picked up a piece of firewood and rammed it against the door.

'What happened?' called Emma.'

'We got struck again,' answered Paul.

'My God,' she fretted. 'We have to get out of here.' She tried to get up, grunting with every move she made.

'Stay there Em,' said Paul.

'Don't you tell me what to do!' she suddenly spat. 'Just, just...'

'Steady lady, calm down.' It was Bing. He helped Emma into a sitting position.

'We're all a little on edge eh?' he said. 'We didn't get much sleep.'

Paul turned his attention back to Lana.

'You're bleeding sweetheart,' said Paul.

She looked at her arms and legs and noticed blood on the right thigh of her long johns.

Funny, there was no pain.

'Oh,' she exclaimed. She picked out a tiny shard of glass with her thumb and index finger and placed it on top of the firebox.

'Lana,' said Paul. 'We have to ring for help.'

'I know,' she replied. 'I'll go outside when this lot dies down.'

'Sweetheart, let me go. You're scared,' soothed Paul.

'I am not,' Lana replied indignant. But she choked down her fear and stamped on the hollowness in her stomach. 'I want to do it. You're already badly injured.'

'So one more direct hit to me isn't going to matter is it?' he challenged.

She gave up arguing with him. Everyone was frightened and they were all likely to say things they might regret. It was academic anyway. There was nothing anyone could do until it stopped raining molten lava. They sat in the gloom of the hut wondering if one good hit would finish them off before she had a chance to ring out.

***

The night morphed into a long morning with no reprieve that would allow a dash outside. Lana frequently stood in the doorway exasperated and wishing it to stop. The air was damp and cloud hung thickly white over the mountain often engulfed by brown toxic gases. Volcanic debris swirled around the hut and banked up against rocks and tussock. Little sun and much less warmth penetrated this shield to the earth.

Biding her time Lana fidgeted with the phones rechecking the messages she would send. Her heart beat harder than usual and she could feel it thumping high in her chest, almost in her throat. Her mouth was dry as always happened when she was nervous. It happened before every concert she ever played. Now she wondered why she had always been so nervous before a concert. What was the worst that could happen? A missed note. Now she really did have something to be nervous about. She reflected upon the risky task ahead of her and watched for Paul to give the all clear.

She found it difficult to concentrate although there was very little activity in the hut to distract her. Emma had calmed down and Lana couldn't blame her for being scared out of her wits. The rock had nearly landed on her. Lana imagined how it would be for her. A competent outdoors woman suddenly incapacitated and to lose control of everything around her. It was bad enough that she couldn't walk unaided and was in constant agony, but to rely on Lana as a nurse, well, Lana was very aware of her shortcomings in that area. She conceded that Emma had every right to grumble. Lana glanced to where Emma sat scribbling in a journal.

Every so often she would stop writing and raise her head bolt upright and stare right through the far wall of the hut. Then she would close her eyes as if allowing the thoughts she'd conjured up flood through her body. Lana envied her serenity.

She turned her attention to the fire. It pulled her into its vortex, crackling muffled sparks within the sooty cast iron box, competing with the fire in the mountain.

Finally she tore her eyes from it and looked across at Paul. The movement made her light-headed, a delayed symptom of the concussion. She squinted to focus on the dial of the phone. Lana composed one message to send to both Alex and Julie. She tried to allay any fears they may hold for her safety and she asked for an airlift at the first opportunity.

Paul was occupied writing up notes and timing the lull between explosions. Lana was reminded of a husband timing the contractions of his pregnant wife. She supposed he'd done exactly that and for a split second she was overcome with intense jealousy. She'd never felt a burning desire to give Yuri a child and she didn't have any regrets but as she pondered Paul's attentiveness to the woman who bore his daughter she suddenly felt less of a woman.

It was quiet now. It had been for a few minutes. Paul set his pen down and stared blankly at the firebox. Lana felt him mentally calculating. They locked eyes.

'It's giving us a window,' Paul said to Lana. She breathed deeply and rose from the table then picked up a frying pan and made for the door. Kicking the firewood doorstop to one side she stood hesitantly in the door frame.

'You can do it Lana,' Paul reassured her.

'I know,' she exclaimed and ran from the hut picking her way down the slope until she was about sixty metres away. Then she squatted and cowered under the frying pan. With her free hand she dug into her pocket for the phones and checked for coverage. One searched but the other found a connection to the network. She pressed send then ran downhill a little further until the second phone picked up coverage. Above her she could see how the hut nestled against the ancient lava outcrop affording some protection from the wild ejections of the mountain. And high above that the mountain continued to vent its steaming mass. She felt very small.

She hurried back to the hut but paused to inspect the damage. She stooped at the collapsed corner and peered under. Many of the footings were smashed and floor boards were suspended like demolition timber not connecting to anything. Lana could hear the soft sounds of chatter inside the hut and Paul's limping footsteps across the floor. A little way beyond the damaged area and under the main living area was a sock with what appeared to be something in it. Something about it gave the impression it hadn't been there long. She weighed up whether to retrieve it but the mountain chose for her. As a guttural blast echoed through the thick air she scrambled to her feet and feeling a hot debris pepper her back, ran inside.

Chapter Nine

Colleen pushed open the casement windows of her fifties weatherboard bungalow and felt the day's stale air waft past her. She had cobbled together the finances for the property after her divorce and had spent the last few years putting her stamp on it. She delighted in the solidness of the workmanship; the narrow golden floorboards, the plaster ceilings with embellished cornices and the heavy terracotta tile roof. And nothing pleased her more than coming home after a long day and letting the breeze swish around the net curtains. It reminded her of her grandmother's house.

She slipped out of her office clothes into jeans and a tee shirt then bent to the mirror to remove her jewellery and scrutinise her face. She held the skin taut at the sides of her face eliminating wrinkles and turned side on to check the set of her dark hair dye. Satisfied, she wandered into the kitchen to fix her tea.

She had a poached egg on toast and peered over her fork at the television news.

'The second night of volcanic eruptions from Mount Ruapehu is preventing any rescue of three scientists and several trampers believed to be sheltering in a hut on the North Island mountain. The eruptions come only a day after the tephra dam at Crater Lake was breached causing a lahar to spill down the Whangaehu Valley. It's thought that one person, possibly a tramper, was caught in the lahar. A person was spotted by a helicopter near the Round the Mountain Track south of the lahar path on Tuesday. Our reporter is on the scene.

'Thanks Mallory. I have with me volcanologist Bain

Conway who has done extensive research on Mount Ruapehu. What do we know about the stream of events we've seen over the last few days?'

'Initially the dam of Crater Lake breached enabling the full amount of lake water to surge down its path as a lahar.'

'What caused the breach?'

'Given that the mountain is now erupting it's highly likely that a small volcanic eruption provided enough impetus to move the lake water and thus break through the tephra rim.'

'Tephra?'

'The ash that was deposited around the lake in 1996. It's reasonably loosely packed.'

'What can you tell us about the path the lahar took?'

'It behaved well, following traditional lahar paths.'

'Was there any doubt it would?'

'Always doubt, which is why so much effort went into the construction of a bund.'

'The eruptions. Impressive?'

'Yes. Luckily we have significant research on Ruapehu styles, but no two eruptions are the same.'

'There are people trapped in Rangipo Hut. What sort of danger are they likely to be in?'

'Significant. But of course, that would be the safest place to be.'

'Have you had contact with them?'

'No. But given the relentless eruptions I wouldn't expect phone coverage.'

'What sort of rescue can we expect?'

'You'd have to ask search and rescue.'

Colleen let the interview fade as she mopped up egg

off the plate with her toast. She tried to remember the 1996 eruption. It was difficult to recall. At that time her world had imploded as she witnessed her husband moving furniture out of the house to set up home with his fancy woman and her six kids. No, she just couldn't recall it.

'In other news, police are no closer today to solving the medal heist from the country's premier military museum. The missing medals include four New Zealand Memorial Crosses, three 1914-1915 Stars, four South Africa medals, two New Zealand War Service medals and three New Zealand medals. Police are refusing to comment on whether the theft was an inside job.'

That was the news she really wanted. She muted the television and let the thirty-something blonde with the unnaturally serious face mime the auto reader.

In a way she didn't mind the events of the last few days. It was an unexpected excitement for her and one that didn't place too many demands on her. After all, there was nothing she could do to find the medals. Suddenly she was the centre of attention at work. Discussion in the tea room turned from Colleen's association with the medals to general war stories as the older partners relayed family stories.

The medals would go on the market. Perhaps not so soon. She hoped they weren't destined for overseas. They may never be recovered in that case. She let herself remember her mother's stories. She had not thought of her parents in quite some time and now in a way her parents' took on more importance. The proud moment of her grandmother receiving the New Zealand Memorial medal was told by Colleen's mother Clarice at least every Christmas. It was one of the family legends. When Colleen inherited the medal, as was proper, being the eldest daughter, she had thought long and hard about what to do with it. Her friends told her it was an unselfish act to donate it to the museum on permanent loan. But deep down she felt a bit of a coward. She had balked at the responsibility of holding such a treasure. Now, as the television news showed a picture of the medal she felt a pang of loss followed by a tremendous bout of guilt.

***

Alex retrieved the text message from Lana upon his return from lunch. He was hot and ruddy and still perspiring having just played a lack-lustre game of squash with a colleague. He grabbed a coffee before settling back down to work for the afternoon. On his desk his mobile phone flashed a tiny red light alerting him of a message.

He snatched at the phone. Lana was okay, but three people were injured. She wanted to be airlifted off the mountain. He sank into his chair and considered what she had said. It would be just like Lana to say she was fine so he wouldn't worry.

He composed a message back hoping she still had the phone on. There was so much he wanted to say. He wanted her to know and understand the depth of his love but at the same time he didn't want to burden her with unnecessary distractions. In the end he simply told her that he loved her.

He called Julie. 'I just received a message from

Lana.'

'How is she?' asked Julie.

'She says she's fine. The others have injuries.'

'What sort?'

'She doesn't say. Bad enough to request a Helivac.'

'I see.'

'She won't be too good at playing nurse.'

Julie laughed. 'Oh I'm sure Emma's telling her what to do.'

'Do you know if there's a chopper ready?'

'There's a team standing by. We just need the mountain to cooperate.'

'I want to be there when she's lifted off. Where would they fly to?' Alex asked.

'They're talking about choppering them down to the army base. They've got a glorified field hospital.'

'Okay. I'll be ready for it.'

Alex signed off and told his secretary he'd be unavailable for the rest of the day, possibly the week.

***

Tom walked into the sparse lounge carrying two cups of coffee. Even with the fire roaring the room looked and felt cold. Joe had little interest in anything other than function, thus had furnished it with nineteen seventies green lounge suite, a second hand wooden coffee table and a couple of beer crates that served as a book case. To one corner was a flat screen television, much too big for the room. The timber floorboards were pitted and stained, more so in front of the hearth where black burn marks spotted the floor.

Tom squinted, the skin around his eyes puffed and blue. His nose was swollen and his glasses perched unnaturally high up on the bridge. He set a cup down on the table in front of Joe and backed toward the fireplace to stand on the hearth.

He took a sip and shook his head. 'I still can't believe how so much could go so wrong,' he said. 'The robbery was the easy bit as it turned out.'

Joe sat with his head bowed. 'We need to get Ant.'

'And do what with him?' asked Tom.

'Hide him of course,' Joe snapped at him. 'He's got a stab wound in him, the stupid bastard.'

'How the hell are we going to hide him?' Tom replied. 'It's not like no one's seen him. Christ, the helicopter's probably got a GPS on him. You know we have the problem of the whereabouts of the Memorial Cross. He wanted it for himself. Why else wasn't it with the others? He was going to double cross you Joe.'

Tom spoke with authority. He'd given this a lot of thought. Certainly Joe hadn't been forthcoming on theories, or solutions come to that. Tom felt uneasy that he didn't know Ant and Bing as well as Joe did. Maybe Bing has it anyway. Who's to say he can be trusted?'

'I say it,' Joe spat.

Tom pressed the issue. 'Why did he take it Joe? He must have had his own agenda.'

Joe shrugged. He'd brooded over when to reveal to Tom their familial relationship all the way down the mountain. With every close call the mountain threw at them he swore he'd tell him. It was only fair. If it wasn't for him Tom wouldn't be in this mess. And if Tom got killed like this, well, it wasn't what the man deserved.

But equally, if Joe himself were to die then he'd be denied the pleasure of seeing the pain wrought by his plan. Finally he spoke, blandly, as if it was not his voice behind what had yet to come.

'Sorry?' Tom thought he had misheard.

'I said I told him to take it.'

Tom's mouth dropped as he comprehended what Joe said. 'Why?'

'Because your grandfather is my grandfather.'

Tom reeled back against the mantelpiece and his hands instantly flailed to his swollen face. How could that be? He looked nothing like Joe, nothing at all. 'No,' he cried. 'Prove it.'

Joe recounted Tom's family history while Tom absorbed the accuracy of it. He'd never told Joe some of those details; probably wouldn't have if they'd been mates for ten years. Yet, he'd recited names and dates confidently, which made what Joe say entirely credible, if not wholly believable.

'You've never heard of Sonya have you?'

Tom shook his head by now his eyes wide stretching the squint. He was too shocked to speak and as Joe spat out the narrative Tom found himself studying every aspect of Joe's physique wondering where in the family Joe's stocky build had come from. Differences aside, perhaps there was something about his mouth and eyes that did fit Tom's family genes. The more Joe revealed the more Tom was forced to believe him.

'Sonya is your aunt, my mother, Alfred's love child.' Joe enunciated each syllable so Tom fully understood.

Tom spluttered. 'Love child? Alfred?'

Joe explained how his grandmother Sophie had an

affair with Alfred and the result was Sonya, born 1956. Alfred was already a father to four boys and Sophie, married to an American, a mother of four children. It wasn't until 1963 that Sophie's husband realised that Sonya wasn't his child and so incensed was he that he sent the little girl to Alfred.

Sonya was presented to the family as the daughter of a widowed friend. Alfred was besotted with the little girl. She had Sophie's soft features and in every way she reminded Alfred of his first true love. Initially Sonya was something of a novelty, especially for the four boys. She charmed them with her endearing American accent and they took to looking out for her. But over time, instead of warming to the little girl, Lily found that having Sonya in the house was too painful. She knew of course, whether Alfred had told her the truth or she'd guessed, didn't matter. Every time she looked at the girl she was reminded of her husband's infidelity. So Lily sent little Sonya to boarding school. Alfred would not argue with Lily or divorce her. And boarding school wasn't supposed to be punishment for Sonya. It was Lily's way of hurting Alfred.

Sonya became estranged from Sophie and from her American step-father, who never acknowledged her from the day he sent her away, and had a strained relationship with Alfred and Lily. School holidays were difficult. Sonya always felt like a guest. She knew she wasn't wanted and gradually the stays home became less as she invited herself to friends to sit out the long weeks until school started again. By the time she was seventeen she found herself pregnant and the father long gone. 'The child she gave birth to was me,' Joe concluded.

Tom felt heavy under the weight of the news. 'We're second cousins,' he whispered. 'You sought me out. Why? You didn't need me.'

'Make revenge sweeter,' Joe replied slowly through barely moving lips. 'Oh don't worry, we'll still split the proceeds. Three ways, not four.'

'You bastard!' Tom leaped to his feet and swept the table clear of everything. Cups crashed to the floor spilling warm coffee which found its way quickly to the gaps between the floor boards. 'What revenge?'

'Okay, maybe I didn't need you and you've made such a cock of it I shouldn't have let you in as it turns out,' Joe spat.

'Granddad Alf's nothing to you. You think swiping a stupid medal's going to stick him in the ribs?' Tom reeled. Then the realisation dawned on him. 'He doesn't know about you does he?'

'He should have looked after my mother better,' Joe screamed. 'There you all were playing happy families, going on camping holidays and sharing presents around the Christmas tree and there was me and mum making do on a cleaner's wage.'

Joe paused as he reflected on the scene he'd just described then barely whispered. 'I just wanted him to remember my mother. And I wanted him to hurt.'

Tom flinched at the depth of Joe's maliciousness. He suddenly appeared evil. One minute he genuinely appeared circumspect and the next he could see the anger rise all the way up Joe's body until his neck clenched and the carotid artery flexed. He didn't want to fight Joe – for one thing he could hardly hold his head up thanks to the injuries Lana had bestowed on him, and secondly, he didn't think Joe would let him simply walk away, his own injuries notwithstanding.

'You've given me a lot to digest Joe,' said Tom. 'I should walk out on you right now, but that's not part of your game is it?'

Joe smiled at that. The sick leer of a psychopath. At that minute Tom realised, Joe cared little for anyone except perhaps his mother – Tom's aunty, an aunt he didn't even know he had. What poison had she fed the young Joe?

He didn't have the energy to know more. It was twenty four hours since they had made the break to safety. As they descended the mountain, volcanic lapilli rained down on them and even though the lahar had discharged as much as it was going to, a safe crossing place wasn't available until they were nearly off the mountain and back out to the Desert Road. The river was thick with eroded sediment and muddy with turbulence.

They were comfortable with river crossings and their army training allowed them to believe that they were indestructible. However, the traverse did not go smoothly when Joe lost his footing part way across and tumbled heavily into the fast flow. He'd been swept ten feet before Tom had the presence of mind to scramble to the far back and run alongside Joe. Ordinarily Joe should have been able to swim to safety, if he didn't get trapped in an eddy or get flushed over a rapid, but yesterday there had been too much debris in the water. Each time he tried to get a foothold on the river bottom he was knocked flying. Joe tried to scream to Tom over the din of the dying lahar and Tom screamed back how he was going to save Joe, which was to beat Joe to the bend in the river where it narrowed and try to catch him. He had limited options – he had no rope and there were no trees to snap off a pole.

As he neared the bend Tom shed his pack and leapt onto a large rock that jutted into the river. He threw himself flat onto it at the exact moment that Joe came tumbling down. He thrust one arm out and immediately connected with Joe who clutched at it. He was able to slow Joe's trajectory enough for Joe to scramble up the rock and for several minutes they sat there until they caught their breath.

Joe's body had taken quite a battering, especially his shins which now had skin off. He had cuts on his lip and bruises on his body. He refused Tom's ministrations and they pushed on off the mountain.

Yes, now he was suddenly exhausted. Joe had used him and laughed at him from day one. He felt a fool. He'd certainly been played for one.

Chapter Ten

Lana paced the hut. It did her no good for the mountain was relentless in spewing its fire. She moped from window to window hoping to see a change but it remained threatening. Visibility was low and she felt not only the mountain but her mood closing in on her. She looked at her phone on the table and sighed. Help seemed so close but without coverage it was far away.

Emma, now promoted to a proper bed with her leg strapped and splinted was taking as many painkillers as was necessary but she'd given Lana strict instructions to administer them according to a schedule and try not to give in if Emma asked for more. So far she hadn't. But at the current rate of consumption she could only medicate for two more days.

Luckily Emma spent a great deal of time connected to her MP3 player. And when she wasn't absorbed by that she kept an eye on Bing, something Lana was grateful for.

Bing wasn't giving any trouble – couldn't come to that. He was still in pain but had probably pulled through the worst of it. His fever had broken and at least he could walk. He kept to himself mostly, partly because that was his nature but also he didn't want to say the wrong thing and let slip the truth. He was as familiar with the mountain as Paul seemed to be but to give them that impression would only invite unwelcome questions.

And Paul, Lana knew, was in more pain than he let on. He spent most of the time sitting straight-backed at the table to ease his breathing. The swelling around his ankle had receded a little but he still couldn't put any weight on it. It had turned blue already. He'd fashioned a crutch out of the broom and he and Emma shared the use of it. He insisted on not taking painkillers, preferring that Emma had them.

'Sit down Lana,' said Paul. 'Nothing's changed out there.'

She flung her arms out and let them slap the sides of her thighs. 'I'm sick of waiting,' she moaned.

'At least you're not sick,' Emma reminded Lana from her bunk. 'Is it time for another pill?'

Lana recognised the pain in Emma's voice as the words caught short in her throat.

'No,' Lana replied, a little harder than she intended.

'Are you hurting Em?' Paul asked her gently.

Lana saw Emma's eyes light up as she whimpered in response. Paul shot a glance at Lana, his eyes begging on Emma's behalf, but Lana was firm.

'Your next pill is about two hours away,' she said. 'In the meantime I'm going to have a wash. Oh,' she added grabbing the first aid kit. 'I'll take care of this.'

She padded over to the sink and filled a large pot with cold water, added some warm water from the pot on the fire and took it into the bunkroom. She felt a bit selfish. The others hadn't managed a wash. No doubt it would make the waiting more bearable, if they didn't all have layers of sweat and ash and sticky out hair.

Lana made a washing space on the floor in the narrow space between the wall and the bunks. The window below which she was positioned faced south and her view was reined in by a near vertical ancient lava flow. She manoeuvred herself in the narrow confine and stripped off placing her clothes meticulously on the bunk. She laid a tiny travel towel on the floor to kneel on it then dipping a bandana into the warm water she sponged herself down. She shivered but revelled in the tingle of newly clean skin. Finally, she knelt on her hands and knees and with a tiny piece of soap lathered her hair.

The eruption was no louder than she'd heard for the last twenty four hours but with the tremor came a barrage of artillery that she hadn't heard coming. The window above her shattered causing her to scream but a split second later all she could feel was the searing pain in her calf. She was caught off guard and couldn't put any more breath into a scream. Her lungs emptied and all she could manage was a primeval moan.

The rock landed behind her and rolled to rest against her calf singeing the flesh so that she could now smell herself burning. She leapt, gasping in cooling breaths, but it did nothing to ease the pain. She tried to shuffle out of its reach but so focussed was she on the searing flesh of her leg that she was oblivious to the shards of glass embedded into her back and buttocks.

She jolted forward scared to move; there was broken glass all over the floor, on her hands and on the towel under her. A cool breeze across her back and thighs caused her to shiver.

Paul threw open the door and took in the scene shocked to see her ivory body marred with tiny red beads bubbling to the surface.

'Oh my God. Lana,' he exclaimed.

Still on her hands and knees facing him, she looked up to see him frozen at the door, his eyes drinking in her nakedness. Too late Lana tried to cover her breasts with one arm. She whimpered.

Limping, Paul stepped forward. 'Lana,' he said. 'Don't move, there's glass. Stay still.'

'It's my leg, my leg!' she cried through gritted teeth. 'Get the rock off.'

'It is sweetheart. You're burnt. It's blistered already.' He grabbed her shirt off the bed and used it to roll the rock aside, pushing it under the bunk.

'Oh, sweetheart,' he said through pursed lips.

She whimpered. 'Is it bleeding?'

'No,' he replied. 'It's seared the skin. Cauterised it.'

She twisted her head behind and caught a glimpse of the wound. It was smaller than it felt, no bigger than a golf ball. The shattered window let in cool air so that at once she was both hot and cold and hurting and close to tears.

From the other room Emma called for Paul, asking what had happened. Lana tried to stand as Paul became distracted. 'No, Lana.' Paul put a steadying hand on her shoulder. 'Don't move honey. Too much glass.'

'We've got a burn,' he yelled back to Emma then turned to Lana.

'Hang on sweetheart,' he said softly and dashed out to Emma who advised how to treat the burn. Soon he was back with a large pot of water and a bottle.

'What can I do?' Lana asked.

'Nothing. Don't move. I'm going to cool the burn for ten minutes then tape Emma's bandana over it. Then I'll start on your body. She saw him gaze longingly at her and once again tried to cover herself. He threw her shirt to her but it was a hopeless exercise in modesty. She focussed her energy on the small shot of pain in her leg and it was nigh on impossible to stay still, but her weight was heavy on her arms.

Paul cooled the burn and covered it. 'Now for the glass. How are your knees Lana?' But he didn't wait for an answer.

He left the room and returned with the head of the broom. He brushed away the shards and pushed them beneath the bunk. Lana felt goose-bumps on her arms and shoulders and was embarrassed to feel her nipples hardening. Paul crawled around to Lana's rear and positioned himself on the floor.

'Sweetheart,' he said. 'I'm going to pull out the glass. Try not to move okay?'

'Yes,' she replied. 'Paul?'

He concentrated. 'Mm?'

'This goes no further than these four walls. Okay?'

'Okay sweetheart.'

She couldn't see Paul grin but she heard it in his voice. 'I mean it Paul.'

He did not touch Lana's skin whilst extracting the first and largest piece of glass from her left buttock. She held her breath as she anticipated the process. She closed her eyes as he worked on her. How she wanted to feel his warm hands against her and his hot tongue nibble her freshly scrubbed buttocks. Paul handed the glistening triangular shard to her. It was smeared with her blood. She took it with the hand that shielded her breasts and laid it on the bed next to her.

He continued to extract piece after piece of glass from her. She was aware of his breath, heavy but measured for the mountain had gone quiet for a moment. Paul shifted uneasily on his knees. She heard him sigh but then he continued.

He worked his way up her back, delicately extracting the fine slivers until none remained. She could hardly feel his touch.

'Lana,' he whispered and caressed his flat warm hands over her buttocks. Lana groaned under her breath and closed her eyes, the pain in her leg mysteriously abated. His hands moved up the sides of her body, teasing the swell of her breasts but she held fast without moving. She didn't give him the slightest encouragement. She fought her body to remain rigid so near it was to melting.

'Stop,' she said in a guttural voice that came from so deep within her it surprised her as her own.

'Do you want me to stop?' he groaned and pulled her buttocks to his face. She felt his hot breath on her cool skin, then his wet mouth, stubbled and rough around his soft lips as he nuzzled into her. She couldn't pull away from him, even if she was physically able to. For now she was sixteen and in love with the most gorgeous boy in school. He licked then nibbled her buttocks, kneading her slowly, deeply.

'Want?' she cried. 'What I want and what will happen are two different things.'

'They don't have to be sweetheart,' Paul countered still nibbling.

'That's enough Paul.' She squirmed out of his reach knocking the small bowl of soapy water all over the floor. 'Blast!' She sat on her knees with her back to him and stretched an arm out for her clothes. Paul handed the pale blue merino to her and she slipped it over her head then slipped on the leggings he held for her. 'Ow.' She flinched as she threaded her legs in then sat cross-legged to face him. The fine wool hugged her slim body to reveal her aroused breasts and her flat belly. She noted Paul's desire and reluctantly met his eyes.

'You can't keep teasing me like this Lana,' Paul said quietly.

'I hardly did it on purpose did I?' she retorted.

'Do you really not want me sweetheart?' he asked.

She thought she detected genuine grief in his voice. How to tell him she wanted him more than she'd wanted anything in her life, but it was too late. He was too late. Thirty years, five years too late. How to tell him that she was once crushed beyond what she never thought she could live through and to be with him now struck her so deeply in her heart that she couldn't remove the arrow. And if she did remove it the barb would take a piece of her heart with it, just like before.

She looked away, to the floor, to the window, to the greyness outside the window.

'Look at me sweetheart,' Paul implored. 'Look what you do to me. Tell me you want me.'

She stared at his primed body, rested her eyes for a moment on his groin and then met his impossibly dark eyes. Those eyes. Those hooded brooding eyes. She could drown in them if she wanted to, if she wasn't strong. He held his hand out to her but she only stared at it. He dropped it to his lap and edged closer to her. He spoke quietly and let his deep silky voice penetrate her.

'Lana, look at us. We're made for each other. We just shared something special. Didn't you feel it? Don't you feel it?'

She remained mute, tortured, twisting and wringing

her hands in her lap until they sweated.

'Won't you talk to me?' he asked her.

She opened her mouth and gaped, but no words came out.

'I... I can't.'

'Why not sweetheart?'

'Because,' she began then shrugged. 'Oh I don't know.'

'Because you'll give in to your true feelings? Because you'll give in to your beautiful body?' he pleaded.

'You caught me in a compromising situation,' she said matter of factly. 'You did what was required.'

'Lana, Lana,' Paul intoned. 'Don't leave it like this.'

'I can't give you what you want,' she said.

'Well then, I'm sorry,' he replied tersely. 'Sorry for both of us.'

She watched him silently leave and cringed as the door slammed shut behind him.

***

The broken window in Lana's bunkroom was too large to be fixed and as night closed in she hauled her sleeping bag into the adjoining bunkroom.

'You in the dog box mate?' Bing called to Paul from his bunk.

Lana glanced at Paul from the corner of her eye.

'Huh!' Paul grunted.

'What happened in there?'

'Broken window.'

Lana felt Paul shut down any conversation before it started. Not that there'd be much conversation with

Bing, but it set the tone in the room. Paul was mad and she was obviously to blame for his black mood.

She dragged a form up to the firebox and delicately sat down stretching her legs out. She took several deep breaths. She didn't want the others to learn of the glassy splinters in her posterior. She focussed on what she still had to do, as the only fit one. No matter how sore the burn on her leg, she could walk. No matter how many punctures of flesh rippled under her soft skin, she would not reveal the discomfort it caused her. But she was tired. Her muscles felt soft where they'd been battered and she knew the bruising would show itself by tomorrow. Her leg stung and it would only be a matter of time before it began to throb. And then she'd have to negotiate for Emma's painkillers.

'How is your pain Emma?' she asked.

'Bearable I guess, if I don't move,' she replied. 'Let me see your leg.'

Lana shuffled softly to her and let her lift the bandana.

'God Lana, that's horrible.' She sealed the cover back over the wound. 'You mustn't let it get infected. You should be on anti-biotics. So should Bing.'

'We don't have any,' said Paul.

'It's about time you had those ribs strapped Paul,' said Emma patting the bed next to her. 'Come here. I'll do it for you.'

Paul was hesitant to move. He seemed to be waiting for Lana, but when she didn't object he sat down next to Emma.

'Take your shirt off Paul,' she gushed.

He grimaced as he tried to but fell short of success.

'Let me.' She wriggled to help him. He smiled tightly at Lana who took it as a gesture of embarrassment. Surely he wasn't uncomfortable half naked on a bed with the gorgeous blonde Canadian. It didn't escape Lana that a gasp escaped from Emma's mouth as she surveyed Paul's muscled chest. She watched Emma trace her fingers over his chest. He relaxed under her touch. Lana's stomach tightened. Now that she'd given Paul the brush off he was keen to show her that there was always someone else for him. She noted pleasure in Paul's face as he let Emma stroke him, much more than was necessary for a medical assessment.

'Cough Paul,' Emma demanded.

He gave a feeble splutter.

'Not good enough,' she said. 'If there's any fluid on the lungs you have to shift it. It might hurt but I want you to cough properly.' She added, 'for me.'

It was too much. Lana bolted to her feet and dashed to the door. As Paul coughed he was surprised by Lana's flight and he genuinely spluttered. If Lana had stayed she would have witnessed Emma soothing Paul by rubbing her hand over his back.

But she couldn't stay a moment longer. She kept running, out of the hut, up and over boulders. She didn't care where she went. Unfortunately there was only one place she would feel a little bit safe – the little plastic box up the hill. She slammed the door shut and sat on the seat. This was the place to be alone with her misery. Paul could enjoy himself with Emma, of course he could. Hadn't she just five minutes gone told him that there was no future for them? And now it was plain that he had accepted that. She kicked open the toilet door and stared at the landscape. It was more moonscape now. She saw none of her beloved vegetable sheep or the lime green and orange lichens that survived prostrate on the warm rocks. The mountain was devoid of colour except brown. It was almost not of this place. It was a place not recognised by her. She was suddenly overwhelmed by the enormity of the mountain, its power, and her tiny place on it. She wished more than anything she wasn't here.

'Bugger it!' she yelled as she kicked the fibreglass wall. She should bloody well walk out right now. That's what she should do, except she couldn't. Apart from being too scared to be alone she knew she wouldn't make it. She banged on the wall with her fist and flopped back down on the seat. She couldn't go back inside yet, not until she calmed down. In a couple of minutes she began to cool and judged that perhaps now would be a good time.

Reluctantly she made her way back down the slope, clomping much louder than she needed to, giving fair warning to those inside the hut. When she scrambled inside with a flurry of ash Paul was struggling to put his shirt back on over his newly trussed chest. No one said a word but Emma had a self-satisfied look on her face.

'Could you...' Paul began.

'Could I what?' Lana cut him off and stoked the fire, poking it like it was the enemy.

'Help me with my shirt.' He smiled uncertainly.

'I'm busy aren't I? Ask her.' Lana spoke quietly. She nodded in Emma's direction without engaging the eyes of either of them and then quite deliberately turned her back on everyone in the room and lay down on the form in front of the fire.

She was light-headed. Had to rest. Couldn't let on. Must be the concussion. She knew she should talk to Emma about it. But there was nothing that could be done for it, right? Besides, she knew any words from her would stick in her craw. She let the warmth of the fire flood her aching body.

When she woke it was to the gently clink of metal on metal as Paul made a meal for them. A single candle flickered a dull amber light into the room. She stiffly rose from the bench and looked around. Bing dozed. It was black outside. She was sheepish, embarrassed for her churlish behaviour and tossed Paul a surreptitious glance from beneath her tousled fringe. He tactfully ignored her so she opened the firebox and started poking around again.

***

After a scant meal of boiled rice and baked beans rifled from the warden's supplies, Lana turned into bed in the front room. A self imposed exile she felt, while the others were in the warmth of the main room and had each other for comfort. Not that she didn't deserve to be alone. She did. It was best all round if she removed herself from the main room for a while. But she didn't feel alone as the tilt of the floor meant her door would not shut so she could hear most of the conversation.

She stared out the little window and sighed. If the days seemed long enough, the nights were infinitely longer, unbearable. She wondered if she'd sleep tonight. At least it had stopped drizzling but the eruptions were as frequent as earlier in the day. However, it only seemed to be spewing ash for the moment. Suddenly she was reminded of what she had read about Scott and his men in the Terra Nova hut nestled under the shadow of the fiery Mount Erebus. Of course, subsequent events overshadowed much geological reporting. In fact it was easy to believe that Erebus was benign, so little effect did it have on the expedition or its outcome. Nevertheless, it was omnipresent, as smoking backdrop to Scott's quandary and gaining only cursory mentions in the diarised drama.

Thankfully, Lana thought, Alex knew she was here. A lot of people did. At least for her, for them, it was only a short walk out and an even shorter helicopter flight. What must it feel like to know that your lover is not only twelve months away, but another twelve months from getting help to you?

Lana didn't get a chance to ponder that. An explosion threw her out of bed. She tried to gain purchase on the floor but her feet kept sliding out from beneath her. She scrambled back onto her bed.

'Aah,' she screamed.

Paul limped to the door which now hung loosely in its frame and clutching his headlamp directed the beam across Lana and around the room.

'Cripes look!' Paul aimed the light at the corner of the hut where a massive volcanic block had come to rest.

Lana pressed her back against the wall. 'That's too close to home,' she spluttered.

'You're sure attracting trouble,' Paul replied.

'The whole hut is on a lean. Are you okay?' he asked.

'I am,' Lana replied. 'But the walls! The floor!

Everything is falling apart.'

'Help.' A weak moan came from below Paul's feet.

'What the?' said Paul. He shone the halogen beam to the floor and splashes of dull colour bounced back between the gaping boards.

'Help me,' said a breathless voice.

'It's Bing,' he said.

Lana was aware of movement behind her in the main room. Emma had dragged herself upright with the broom handle and had lit a candle which flickered in the disturbed air.

'What's he doing there?' she asked. 'He couldn't have fallen through the floor.'

'What happened Bing?' Paul yelled through the floor.

'My arm's trapped.' His words were laboured and airy.

'Cripes Lana. I'm of limited use with these ribs,' Paul whispered. 'Don't worry mate,' he called to Bing. 'We'll get you out.'

'What was he doing under the hut?' Lana whispered.

'Search me,' Paul replied.

'I suppose it will be me who will be rescuing him,' she huffed. 'Do you know what it's like under there? Of course you do. Shit!'

She scrambled off the bed and went outside with Paul limping behind her. Even Emma staggered to the door. They paused at the edge of the deck and surveyed the crumpled room.

'You could have been killed,' Emma said to Lana. It was a fact. A statement only, but then she added, 'are you all right?'

It was only then that Lana noticed how she trembled.

271

She thought it was the cold making her jaw jabber. Emma rubbed Lana's shoulder and for the moment it gave her a bit of comfort.

'Yes,' she answered abruptly.

'Help,' called the far away voice again.

Emma and Lana looked at each other.

'Yeah mate,' Paul called back and then to Lana, 'Ready?'

He led Lana off the deck and knelt at the collapsed corner. The rock was steaming. It was sobering to imagine it could have landed five feet further in, killing Lana for sure. He gave a silent prayer of thanks.

'Up here Paul,' said Lana a little uphill from him. 'There's more space.'

Paul shone the light into the void and played the beam over the damage. Timber foundations were smashed and lying horizontal on the ground at the failed corner and further under timber supports were split and angled having been wrenched away completely from the bearers. Bing lay spread eagled on his stomach on the dry ground with what looked like the whole weight of the hut resting on one forearm.

'Oh my God, Bing,' cried Lana. 'Hold the light on him,' she directed then threw herself onto her stomach and wriggled into the space, drawing alongside him. Paul shone the light along Bing as Lana searched for injuries, finally letting the beam rest on his trapped arm. 'Oh God,' she whispered. 'What are we going to do?' She rubbed his back as much to sooth her as Bing. 'Can you move?'

He let out a grunt as he forced his muscles to flex then relaxed back into the ground exhausted with the intensity of it.

'No,' Lana murmured. 'It's all right Bing. We'll get you out.'

She wriggled back out.

'Well?' asked Paul.

'Not good. It's stuck pretty good.'

'It's okay mate,' called Paul. 'We'll get you out.'

'How?' Lana asked.

'Bing?' Paul spoke reassuringly into the void.

'Uh,' Bing replied.

'We're going to make you comfortable for now, okay? You'll have to spend the night there while we figure out what to do,' Paul explained.

Lana assembled Bing's sleeping bag, a bottle of water and the silver life blanket then dashed back to Paul who was trying to comfort Bing. He grabbed her arm as she prepared to crawl under.

'Thank you Lana,' he said. 'It's not easy, I know.'

She shrugged. 'We're wasting time.'

She dropped to the ground the shoved the equipment in front of her and unfurled the silver blanket.

The timbers above her creaked as the foundations railed against the groaning weight of the hut. Lana froze.

'Careful sweetheart,' warned Paul.

'There's movement here Paul.' Her heart beat hard in her chest. Now she really was scared, much more than before.

'Lana, use the broom handle to push it to him,' Paul instructed. 'We can assess it tomorrow.'

Then he directed instructions to Bing. 'Lana's got some warm stuff for you. And water. Okay? Take it from her. The blanket will save your life. Lay it over you and try to wrap yourself in it.'

Lana poked at it with the broom handle and managed to drape it over Bing's head.

'How did you come to be under here?' she asked him smoothly without a hint of accusation.

'Went to toilet. Heard possum,' he gasped.

Paul pulled the light away from Bing and led Lana away from the edge.

'Did he say possum?' Paul asked.

Lana nodded and together they smiled.

***

Two minutes. Two minutes and he would have been out. Of all the luck. Luck hadn't been on his side since the robbery. Two and a half minutes ago the only thing to bring tears to his eyes was the stab wound. Now his eyes filled not because he felt like crying but it was his body's release from the excruciating pain. It wasn't like he could rub his arm until it felt better. Now he couldn't even feel his arm. He sure as hell couldn't move it.

The blanket was a help. He was thankful Lana had managed to put it over him for he could feel the warmth of his breath around his head. It was an impossible position to do anything. At the best of times the thick set of his shoulders made actions above his head difficult. His shoulder stiffened under the unnatural angle and the only way he could massage it was to lift his head to allow his free arm access to it. And that wasn't an option. It was all just too hard.

He allowed himself to think of home. How ironic that he'd left the dog chained to her kennel with a bowl of water and some biscuits. She'd have knocked the water over by now and eaten the biscuits straight away. He was confident he'd be gone only twenty four hours. He cursed that he wasn't more lucid when Joe and Tom left. They could have seen to her. She was a quiet dog, not prone to barking just for the sake of it. It wasn't likely the neighbours would notice her; he tended to keep to himself.

There was a good chance he would die here. Damn it, he wasn't ready for that. Maybe after he was stuck here for a week, dehydrated and starving, his mind might come round to the idea that death would be a pleasant release. But not now. Joe would think he's done a runner.

Why would he think that? No one could escape the mountain while it's still erupting. For all he knew they hadn't made it. Lana wouldn't leave him. He saw that in her. She would if he was dead though.

His thoughts started to blur, running together in a way they never would if his body wasn't full of infection and his mind full of fear. There was no help coming until morning. Nothing else for it but to drift off to sleep, if he could just roll onto his side...

***

Lana and Paul sat at the table which now listed towards the door. The single flickering candle filled the hut with false cheer. There were now so many gaps in the woodwork that the air pushed through and fanned the flame in all directions. Paul stoked the fire and watched it crackle quietly.

275

'What's a possum?' Emma asked from her bed. She'd endured the ordeal because she rifled through the first aid kit and downed a couple of painkiller while the others were outside. At the moment she felt quite comfortable. There would be hell to pay when they found out, especially now Bing might have first demands on drugs, but that was something to worry about later.

Lana explained. 'Scourge of the forest. Imported Australian mammal.'

'Forest being the point,' Paul added.

'They don't live on the mountain – nothing to eat,' Lana continued.

'Oh I see,' said Emma. 'He lied about what he heard.'

'He didn't hear anything,' said Paul. 'I haven't believed a word that man's said in two days. No reason to believe him now.'

'He's in a good predicament for interrogation,' Lana calculated.

'If we don't release him from his predicament he could expire,' said Emma. 'We're talking about a crush wound.' She gave them a moment for the implications to sink in. 'The longer the arm is crushed the higher the risk of toxins flooding his body when the arm is released. That will kill him. But aside from that look at his other problems. The knife wound untreated could turn septic, potential hyperthermia tonight with death to follow. He's in a very precarious situation.'

'What do you think he was doing?' Lana asked.

'Look guys, forget that for a minute. You gotta get him out of there,' Emma interrupted.

Paul gave the fire a thrust then slammed the door closed on it. 'Not tonight,' he stated. He turned to Lana

276

as he spoke to Emma. 'I'm not having Lana go under there until we know it's safe, and we know what we're dealing with.'

Paul ignored her and picked up where Lana left off. 'What did you see under there when you looked before?'

'Just a sock. There was something else, like crumpled old clothing but nothing to make me think twice. Like it had been there for a long time.'

'What about the sock?' Paul asked.

'Not old,' she replied. 'And it could have had something in it.'

'We'll look tomorrow.'

'It's pretty creepy under there. What's to stop the whole hut sliding?' Lana hugged her arms and gave them a rub.

'It probably will take another jolt to do that.'

'Do you really think we're safe?'

'Better in the hut than under it,' he said and touched Lana lightly on her hand. 'And better in the hut than outside it.'

She felt the instant warmth of his hand and for a split second she wanted him to keep it there but she involuntarily gave the wrong signal and he pulled his hand away.

'I owe that man you know,' she said quietly. Paul waited silently for her to continue. 'You weren't here. I was unconscious, lying on the cold ground. I was beaten and left for dead. I know I was supposed to die. Those guys thought I heard something Bing said. Trouble is, what I heard, I didn't understand. So they beat me for nothing. I would have slipped into hyperthermia if it wasn't for Bing calling out to me and waking me up.'

She paused and dropped her voice even lower, to barely a whisper.

'Do you remember?' She shouldn't, she knew she shouldn't go down this track. Not when they'd closed the gate. 'Do you remember the dog?'

She barely raised her head to him but when their eyes met Paul's eyes crinkled and the corners of his mouth set in.

'I remember a screaming girl, a big bad dog and pink pyjamas,' he replied. 'I remember everything Lana,' he whispered. 'Everything.'

'When I was on the ground,' she continued, 'I remembered.' She gazed at the fire. 'It was a good time wasn't it?'

'The best Lana.'

'Now it's my turn to look after you. Call it even,' she said matter of factly trying to quell the emotion that had welled up in her then she arose briskly and turned her back to him as she pretended to be busy at the kitchen sink.

***

Bing had vacated a particularly desirable bed, one that Lana filled. At that end of the hut the floor and walls were still adjoining and the only sign of bombardment was the hole in the window and the roof. It would have to be fixed soon if they were trapped here for much longer. She had grabbed snatches of fitful sleep amidst the intermittent rain of debris and now a dull grey light pervaded the hut telling her that dawn had finally broken.

278

She glanced across to Paul. He was lying on his back away from her but close to Emma. His regular breath was punctuated periodically by short silences.

Her body was racked and aching. She'd lain awake for ages waiting for dawn and at least now she could see the pebbles shoot through the roof and bounce onto the floor. The yellow plastic didn't move. She felt as if she had had no sleep but recalled a dream, so concluded that she must have slept at least long enough to have at least that dream. She stirred quietly trying not to wake the others but Paul stirred and winced as he hauled himself into a sitting position. The two rounds of insulation tape were stuck fast, a raw red contrasting against his pale chest. Lana wondered how difficult it would be to remove the tape; it would take half his chest hair with it.

She peeled herself out of her sleeping bag, padded across to the skewed front door, and peered out holding the door open wide enough only to put her head out.

'What's it like?' asked Paul.

'Overcast, cold, barest of breeze.' She jammed the door shut and walked over to the fire, poked the embers and blew into it. Then she stoked it with the split firewood from the stack on the floor. She loved the mornings in a mountain hut. It was a shame this wasn't an ordinary day with the anticipation of a good hike and exciting discoveries. She sighed. Today was likely Bing's only hope for rescue. God, what a mess! She didn't look forward to being the main act; she was a better support person. She tip toed to roughly where she thought Bing lay below.

'Bing,' she called softly bending to the floor. 'Bing, can you hear me?'

'How is he?' Emma sat up in her bunk clutching her bag around her.

'Shush,' Lana demanded as she knelt down and put an eye to the floor boards. Daylight filtered up but no movement from Bing, and certainly no sound from him.

She shrugged. 'Nothing.'

Paul struggled to extract himself from his bed and shirtless, joined her above Bing.

'How are the ribs?' Lana asked him still with her head bent to the floor.

'Good,' Paul replied. He lightly fingered the tape.

'And the ankle?' Lana sat back on her haunches and studied both his ankles. 'Looks like the swelling's gone down a bit.'

'Yeah it feels good.'

'If you're so good you can free Bill,' she said getting up off the floor. Paul put a hand out to help her and without thinking she took it and found herself face to face with him. He scanned her body and his eyes came to rest on her breasts which were snugly outlined in the thin wool, her nipples teasing him. She pulled herself away and quickly dressed, pulling her trousers and shirt over her thermals.

From under the sink bench she pulled out a frying pan and hauled on a half filled pack. Then when the mountain gave the all clear she dashed around the corner of the hut and squatted under the frying pan.

'Bing. Bing,' she called urgently. She peered under but it took a few seconds for her eyes to adjust to the dark. Eventually she made out his prostrate form. It was worse than last night. She could make out that his right arm was obscured from the elbow down, buried beneath

280

a mangled bearer and floor joist. The angle of the floor had transferred a significant load of the hut onto this portion of timber. And Bing was trapped right beneath it.

'Cripes Bing,' she cried again. 'Can you hear me?'

'Uh,' he grunted.

'It looks bad. Can you move your left arm?'

He wriggled his fingers and lifted his elbow a centimetre off the ground. He was weak. She had to keep talking, at least that would give him the impression that she was in control, helping him. She hoped he couldn't hear the waver in her voice.

'Good man,' she encouraged him. 'Are you warm enough?'

'Uh.'

'Is that a yes or no? Give me one grunt for yes. Two for no,' she directed. 'Are you warm enough?'

'Uh,' he grunted.

'Good. I'm going to get Paul.'

'Bing's well and truly stuck,' she said as she banged her way back inside. 'It's like he has the whole load of the hut tilted down onto his arm. I don't know how we are going to free him, I really don't.'

'Is he conscious?' asked Emma.

She'd set herself up, or at least Paul had, with packs and clothes behind her to prop her up. She was brushing her hair, slowly, as if she had all day to do it.

'Yes,' Lana replied. 'There's not much air in him. He's finding it difficult to talk. I told him Paul would be out to see him.'

'Let me finish doing breakfast and then you can get this porridge into him. But only if I say it's safe enough to go under Lana,' he warned her. 'Okay?'

They ate in silence and listened to the mountain vent its spleen.

'When is it going to stop?' asked Lana.

Paul held her gaze. 'We'll be fine. You'll see. You are doing very well by the way.'

She pressed the corners of her mouth together and Paul instantly covered himself.

'For a flutist that is,' he said with mock seriousness. She couldn't help but notice a twinkle in his eye.

'Yes, I am doing well for a flutist,' she agreed.

'Okay,' said Paul clunking his empty bowl on the table. He picked up Bing's cup of porridge which sat warming on the firebox and headed outside with it. 'Let's go.'

They squatted at the side of the hut under the dubious protection of a fry pan.

'Hey Bing,' called Paul. 'How are you doing mate?'

'Uh.'

'Hurt to talk?'

'Yep.'

'Can you feel your arm?'

'Uh-huh.'

'That's no,' Lana explained.

'Got some porridge here Bing,' called Paul.

'How safe is it?' Lana whispered to Paul.

He shuffled close to the void and listened then shone his torch under.

'No creaking,' he replied.

'I can crawl to him,' she whispered. 'It's only a wee way.'

'Do it slowly Lana. No sudden movements,' Paul instructed.

'Tell that to the mountain,' she scoffed and dropped flat to her stomach. As she edged herself closer to Bing she could smell the damp patch before she saw it. Should have expected it, she guessed. She scuffed the dusty earth and continued to haul herself alongside Bing.

'Here,' she said softly and handed him the cup with a spoon in it. 'Lots of sugar on it. Keep your energy up.' Bing gasped as he struggled to manoeuvre his left arm into a position to feed himself, but it was impossible. He flopped back where he lay.

'Let me,' said Lana. She rolled onto her hip and spooned porridge into Bing's mouth.

'Lana,' called Paul in his deep smooth voice. 'Look for a crevasse that a lever can be set into.'

She was alarmed at his even tone. It frightened her into a freeze. Did he think merely talking would dislodge the timbers? She looked above and around her. 'It looks tight as a drum,' she murmured

'I was afraid of that. What colour is Bing's arm?'

'Can't see,' she replied. 'It's too trapped.'

When Bing finished eating she wriggled back out and followed Paul back inside. The yellow plastic sucked in and out with the repeated opening and closing of the door. They stood at the fire and held their hands out to it.

'Symptoms,' Emma stated. 'Tell me his medical condition.' Her tone spoke authority and Lana was glad of it.

'He ate his porridge. And he's urinated,' Lana replied.
'Cold?'

'No. I don't think so,' Lana added.

'Good. That buys us time. Can he be freed?'

Lana looked to Paul. He would answer for her. He

would know if she could free Bing, for she alone would be the one to do it.

'Have you ever changed a car tyre Lana?' he asked.

'No,' she answered surprised. 'Why would I?'

'We'll try to jack the floor up an inch,' he explained. 'We need a lever and something to rest the hut on while his arm is freed. The only thing we've got is boulders.'

'You can't lift boulders Paul,' said Emma. 'And you should be coughing, by the way.'

He gave a chesty cough and clasped his midriff then went on. 'Lana, assemble some flattish boulders to build a small cairn as close to his arm as possible. Build it up to the bearer then as we jack it you can slip more into the space.

'Shall we use the broom handle for a lever?' asked Lana.

'Not strong enough,' he replied.

'Frying pan handle?' Lana suggested.

'Not long enough. No leverage,' Paul explained.

'Axe!' Lana exclaimed. 'The steel end will slip in a narrow gap and the handle is stronger than a broom.'

'Good, keep thinking. Not quite enough leverage,' Paul paused for a beat. 'Outside plumbing.'

'What?' Lana asked.

'Galvanised pipe is what we're after. Strength and length. I don't want you under there when we lift it. Let's investigate the pipe to the outside sink.'

He limped to the door and flung it wide open. The stainless steel sink was situated to one side of the open deck on the opposite side from the warden's quarters. From where he stood he could see the pipe screwed into a single tap through the back of the sink.

'The tap end is the easy bit,' Paul explained.

'Is it?' Lana stretched on tip toes next to Paul in the door jamb and peered over his shoulder at the sink.

'The other end is the tricky end. Come on.' Paul limped outside and followed the pipe back to its connection at the plastic water tank. It was attached to the wall of the hut with galvanised U-clamps screwed into the timber and at the water tank it screwed into the bottom.

'We have to unscrew the clamps off the wall,' Paul explained. 'We need about two metres of pipe.' He patted his trouser pockets. 'I have a Swiss army knife with a screwdriver.'

'Of course you do,' Lana remarked expressionless. 'And the other end?'

Paul disregarded her sarcasm. 'We don't have a saw to cut the pipe unfortunately so we'll unscrew the tank connection here and plug the outlet,' he explained pointing at the outlet.

'With?' asked Lana.

Suddenly Paul flung himself at Lana landing heavily on top of her as he shielded her from a light spray of volcanic pebbles.

'Aah, shit!' He took the full force of the falling rocks on his back and she muffled a cry of shock. Then Paul, as he rolled off her, squirmed clutching his midriff.

'Oh Paul. God, I'm sorry,' Lana cried.

'Not your fault,' he gasped.

'You didn't have to do that for me.' She crawled underneath the water tank. 'Here.' She held out her hand which he declined but struggled to his hands and knees to shuffle in beside her.

It was cold under here. The sun was a long way from making its way around to this side of the hut. She rubbed the cold from her arms.

'Not a good place to shelter sweetheart,' he advised.

'I don't suppose it is,' she agreed. 'So what now?'

'Wait it out. Only be a few minutes,' Paul hoped. 'You know how much this weighs?'

'It's full,' said Lana.

'This is a one thousand litre water tank. One litre of water weighs one thousand grams, so a full tank weighs one tonne, plus the weight of the tank and the support structure,' Paul calculated. 'If this goes, Bing won't be the only one stuck. We'll be dead.'

Lana hunched on the ground hugging her knees. Her breath faltered as she exhaled and Paul, aware of her distress, put his arm around her shoulder. It reminded her of how it used to be with him. It was pleasant and this time she didn't shrug him off.

Soon the mountain offered a reprieve. 'Come on,' said Paul. They leapt up and made their way back into the hut. 'Take my army knife and start unscrewing the clamps. I'll start on the tap.'

Lana pried open the knife and battled with the screws with less dexterity than she could possibly have imagined. She had never used a screwdriver before let alone one that was only four centimetres long and set in a cumbersome contraption that made it impossible to turn in the hand. She cursed under her breath at the stupid design. It made for a laboursome exercise, albeit, ultimately successful.

She met Paul at the sink. 'Oh you're done,' she exclaimed with amazement.

'Yep. How'd you do?'

She grinned proudly and held the four clamps out for him to inspect.

'Fantastic, now find me something to plug the water tank.'

Lana was buoyed by their small success. And if she were completely honest with herself she was just a little bit pleased that Paul had praised her.

She recalled her laundry tub in Sydney. Yuri had lost the plug so she used the plug from the vanity which was much smaller, but had wrapped it in a facecloth. It was annoying, but as a temporary measure it worked. In fact it was so effective it was a good six months before they got around to replacing it. As she walked slowly back inside she surveyed the ground for an appropriately sized rock. Preferably a flattened one and one smaller than the hole, say no wider in diameter than twenty five millimetres. She picked up several and went inside with them.

She grabbed her panties off the bed and held them in both hands contemplating firstly what the loss would mean to her and secondly, how effective a stop gap they would make. She had been thinking of washing them anyway if another day was to be spent up here. She caressed the fabric; red gauze with little pale blue and white flowers embroidered on the front panel. If she wrapped the rock in the soft cotton gusset the rest of the material would easily jam into the hole, plugging it and preventing their precious water supply from escaping.

Lana ran back to Paul. 'Got it,' she announced.

Shock was clearly visible on Paul's face when she held out her panties and a small brown rock.

'Really?' he queried.

'Yes, I used to have a laundry tub...' she began.

'Okay, I believe you,' he interrupted her. 'I need your help to unscrew this. Can you go half way down the pipe and lift it off the ground. I'm trying to unscrew this end. You need to take the weight for me. I can't use a hell of a lot of body torque.'

She strode to the mid section of the pipe.

'Okay?' Lana called to Paul.

'It's turning,' he replied. 'Good girl.' Paul grunted and wheezed a few more turns of the pipe then paused. He reached to the ground and picked up the rock with the panties. Lana peered over at him. He seemed uncomfortable and she was a little bit smug. She hadn't meant to tease him. He held them up between his thumb and first finger as if he was afraid to touch them. 'You sure?'

She nodded.

'They seem a bit... nice for this,' he said.

'It's okay. They needed washing anyway,' she quipped.

Paul rested the partially unscrewed pipe on his shoulder and wrapped the rock in Lana's panties as drips from the outlet turned into a steady dribble.

'One last turn Lana,' he yelled to her.

Then the pipe came free and the outlet momentarily spewed into a deluge. Quickly Paul plugged the gap and curbed the flow then turned to Lana to find she was beaming widely at him.

'Let's take the pipe around to Bing's side,' Paul instructed.

Lana edged along to the corner and dropped the pipe

with a clang.

'It's all right mate,' Paul shouted into the dark subfloor space. 'We've got a lever here. Soon get you out.'

***

'Lana! Lana!' It was Emma calling from inside. Lana clomped to the door of the hut and pushed it wide open.

'What?'

'You have a lever?'

'Yes.'

'Look.' Emma dropped her voice. 'I need to impress on you the importance of freeing Bing. Because if you can't, you'll have to amputate his arm.' She spoke frankly. Any joy Lana had felt at their small successes soon turned to gravity.

'No,' she whispered. 'Isn't there any other way? I can't cut off a man's arm!'

'I'm laying out all the options for you, that's all,' said Emma. 'I don't want to scare you.

Lana nodded soberly and slowly walked back to Paul.

'What's up?' he asked.

She choked on her reply. 'If we don't free Bing we have to amputate his arm.'

'Ah,' he sighed. 'That's not unexpected.'

'We have to free him Paul. I can't cut the man's arm off,' she wailed. Paul took her by the shoulders. 'Oh God Paul. I feel sick.'

'Now look. We're not there yet Lana,' said Paul. 'First things first eh? Let's get this building off him. We're wasting time. We have to build a jack. I'll find a

289

nice flat piece of timber for a platform and you start finding large rocks.'

Lana assembled half a dozen rocks that could be stacked and stashed them in the void.

'Okay Bing?' asked Lana, not expecting an answer.

'Uh,' he grunted.

'We're going to jack up the floor and you're going to pull your arm out,' Lana explained.

Bing blew out an exasperated sigh through parched lips. Lana crawled onto her stomach and pushed the first of the boulders ahead of her. Then she carefully began to stack them next to Bing's trapped arm.

'Very quietly now Bing,' she soothed. 'No sudden movements.'

She grunted as she rolled the boulders into place on top of each other. She didn't seem to have much strength in this confined space and even manoeuvring onto her hip didn't give much purchase to the lift.

'Can you manage Lana?' asked Paul.

'Nearly,' she grunted. 'I need a couple more. They look bigger under here.'

'Good girl.' Paul encouraged her. 'Go easy now.'

She positioned the four rocks into a cairn leaving about a twenty five millimetre gap between the cairn and the bearer.

'Can you hand me the pipe?' Lana called to Paul.

He passed in one end and she slipped it into the gap.

'It's in!'

'Position the pipe parallel with Bing's arm,' instructed Paul, 'then take this piece of wood and wedge it between the pipe and the pile. Don't let it drop. It's going to give us the amount of lift. All right?'

She eased the pipe and wood into position and wriggled out backwards.

'This better work,' she sighed. 'Can you try it now?'

Paul pushed his weight down on the pipe and it moved easily with almost no discomfort to his chest.

'Too much flex,' he said. 'It's too long.'

'What if I go under?' asked Lana.

'Not while I'm trying to lift. Too dangerous,' he replied. 'Add a wedge to the block.'

He limped around to the firewood stack and returned with a fairly flat piece that could be used as a wedge.

'Add this or swap it,' he said giving it to Lana. 'And position the pipe to go uphill. We need more purchase space and to do that I'll have to go up here,' Paul explained taking a couple of steps uphill.

Lana again slithered beneath the hut and carefully added the block of wood to the cairn and maintaining the tension on the pipe.

'Don't worry Bing,' she murmured through clenched teeth as she worked. 'Paul's got it figured out. We'll soon have you free.'

She didn't wait for Bing to reply. Besides, he might have detected the smell of fear about her, like the dog on the beach. She knew she would reek of it. Quickly she backed out.

'Better?' she asked Paul.

Paul grimaced as he pushed down on the bar. He suddenly jerked and they both knew the blocks of wood that Lana had so carefully positioned had failed. From inside Emma was yelling, demanding to know what was happening. A sharp clunk hit the floorboards as Emma dragged herself across the room. Paul lost his footing and collapsed over the bar, yelling obscenities as he hit the ground. He struggled for breath.

'You okay Bing?' called Lana.

'Uh,' he grunted.

'Try again,' said Lana scrabbling back to the subfloor space. She edged the blocks back into position.

'Bing, we're trying to create some space for your arm to slip out,' she explained. 'At the slightest give pull your arm out okay? As soon as you feel any movement above you drag your body or roll it. The arm will come with you. Okay?'

Bing blinked his understanding.

'It has to come free Bing,' Lana said soothingly. 'If it doesn't we will have to cut the arm off to save your life.'

'No,' Bing gasped.

'It's true Bing,' she continued. 'You will die if we don't cut you out. So, any movement we manage, you pull.'

She shimmied out backwards.

'Okay?' asked Paul.

She nodded.

Together they pressed down on the pipe.

'What's happening?' Emma called from the deck.

Lana clenched her teeth and threw her whole body onto the pipe. 'Grr,' she grunted, only to feel absolutely nothing move. 'Nothing,' she yelled. 'Nothing's happening!'

In despair she let herself flop onto the ground and rested her back against the wall. Paul let the pipe drop and stared into her eyes for what seemed an eternity. There was nothing they could say. They both knew what had to happen next. Paul helped Lana to her feet and they slowly made their way inside.

***

Lana slumped at the table and covered her head with her hands. If she could just shut out what they were saying about cutting Bing's arm off maybe it wouldn't really happen. What did Emma really know anyway? What gave her the power to tell Lana to chop Bing's arm off? Surely she could get a second opinion. Only she had seen the frightful predicament that Bing was in. She wanted someone else to see, then it wouldn't feel like her responsibility. But that was unrealistic. Neither Paul nor Emma could shimmy under the hut. At least Paul had seen that lifting the weight of the hut even a millimetre was an utterly impossible task.

She let her mind back into the room. Emma and Paul had quietened and all she was aware of was the billy hissing on top of the fire. Paul limped over to her and set two cups of tea in front of them. He took another to Emma who was back on her bunk.

'We have to amputate,' Lana announced. 'Don't we?'

'Afraid so,' Paul conceded.

'Do you think if you weren't injured we'd have lifted the floor at all?' asked Lana.

'I don't know,' he replied. 'There's a huge weight bearing down on that corner. Probably not.'

'Amputation! God, how am I going to do that?' Lana cried. 'I don't even like cutting meat. I always cut it partially frozen so I don't have to feel the flesh on my fingers.'

'You can do it Lana,' said Paul.

'You have to do it,' said Emma. 'I'd do it if I could get under there, honest I would.'

'Oh yes,' Lana replied angrily, 'I bet you would.' She sulked for a bit and the others let her. She just needed time to come to terms with it. But not too long, Emma figured, if they wanted to give Bing the best chance of survival.

'Knife?' Emma broke the silence.

'I've only got my Swiss army knife,' said Paul.

'Bing should have one,' said Emma.

Paul rifled through Bing's pack. 'Yes, here's a better one.' He held up a short heavy knife in a leather sheath. It had a thicker than usual stainless steel blade tapered off sharply to the edges and a delicate curve to the blade. The point was a sharp triangle. The handle was encased in worked leather. 'Looks custom made,' he remarked. 'Quite beautiful.'

He turned it over in his hands toying with the balance and Lana noted how gentle he was with it.

'I bet there's blood on that,' she remarked.

He put the knife on the table and cleared a space.

'Is it serrated?' asked Emma.

'No,' Paul replied.

'Shame,' she mused. 'Get your first aid gear and put it on the table.'

Paul assembled one bandage, a few sticking plasters, pain killers, disposable gloves, a tiny packet of fold up scissors, a cotton pad and anti-inflammatory pills. Lana added her sarong.

'It's clean and yes, I always carry one with me,' she said.

He ignored her remark as he flicked through the

294

items. He frowned.

'What?' asked Lana.

'I thought we had more painkillers than this,' he replied.

Lana scanned what was left then directed a fierce look at Emma. She held up one packet, its blister nodules half empty. 'You want to explain this?'

'Ah shit,' said Paul. 'You've been cheating on us Emma? You only had to ask.' He was more disappointed than mad. He'd have given her his share.

Lana slammed the packet on the table. 'We're in this together Emma. I'm sure Bing will be grateful for the few you've left him, you stupid, selfish bitch!'

Paul grabbed Lana,' Leave it sweetheart. We've got work to do.'

He poured a measure of whiskey into a tin mug. 'The least we can do is give the man a drink. Come on Florence.'

'Good luck Lana,' said Emma. 'You yell out to me anytime, okay? Just anytime you're not sure what you're doing.'

Lana rushed for the door with the knife in her hand and slammed it behind her. The cheek of that woman and now acting as though she's the oracle and it's Lana with the attitude. She leaned on the wall of the hut and let her spinning head still. She felt the weight of the knife in her hand. Paul was right; it was a thing of beauty. It must be special to Bing. Perhaps she could talk to him about it as she sliced off his arm. Probably not. She didn't expect she'd be very comforting at all to him. She noticed a dullness in her stomach but as she went to sit Paul came out carrying the sarong and whiskey.

'You all right sweetheart?'

She tried to speak but couldn't. She nodded.

'Come on.' He led her back to Bing.

Paul squatted at the corner talking at Bing in a matey bloke's way, desperately trying to comfort the man.

'I don't suppose you've done anything like this before?' Lana asked Paul.

'Afraid not sweetheart.' He handed Lana the mug of whiskey. She swirled it around the sides of the cup and lifted it to her nose.

'Go on. Have a sip,' said Paul gently.

It felt like fire in her mouth and she pushed it to every corner and crevasse then let it go. She felt it move slowly but the hotness stayed in her mouth, around her teeth, below her nose, down to her belly. Then she scrambled onto the ground and eased herself alongside Bing.

'Some firewater for you Bing.' She cradled the cup to his mouth. 'This is not easy for either of us Bing,' she said. 'I'm sorry to have to do it. I really am. I'm truly sorry for the pain.'

''S'okay,' Bill grunted.

Lana fished into her jacket pocket for the knife and sarong.

'I'll cut as close to the dying arm as possible,' she explained. The bone will be a problem. I don't have a saw. I'll try to cleave it using a rock against the blade. As soon as it's free I'll tamp it with the sarong.'

Lana felt her mouth go dry and she sucked her tongue hard against the palate. Her breathing had become shallow and her breath struggled to leave her lungs, jerking its way out, fighting with the mineral laden air going in. She pulled back the blanket and cut Bing's

296

sleeve at the elbow and then held the cool blade of the knife against his skin. She intoned a prayer under her breath and felt Bing's body tense as he recognised the implication of the cold steel. Her mind reeled as she tried to dredge some practical butchering skill to the fore. She'd never even filleted a fish. She always bought fillets, never even brought them home with the heads on, or tail, or fins, or scales. Meat was a luxury, not a necessity and always came in unrecognisable pieces. Lana's meat never resembled a biological form. She was about to cut into another human being's arm, a living arm on a living man where blood was coursing through the very veins she expected to sever. There would be blood, muscle, sinew, gristle, skin and bone. She doubted she would ever eat a steak again.

She turned the knife to its edge, screwed her eyes tightly shut and contemplated the cut. And then with a weak scream she did it.

Bing screamed too and Lana jumped back lifting the knife off him. She watched the blood well up into a fire-red line as the skin gave way, revealing pink flesh on either side of the crimson river. She turned her head aside and her stomach churned. She gagged as hot saliva filled her mouth.

'Good girl Lana,' called Paul.

'Has she made a cut?' Emma yelled from the hut. Lana was aware of Paul relaying the scene to Emma.

'Emma says to cut around the bones,' he relayed instructions back to her.

Blood welled up and dribbled around the arm. Lana gritted her teeth and cut around the radius and then the ulna. The knife was sharp and she had no difficulty cutting through the skin, muscle and the interosseous membrane that connects the two bones. Her difficulty was physiological. She gagged. The smell of fresh blood was fouling her senses and she hated it. The iron smell reacted with the fillings in her teeth. She could feel them, metallic and smooth. She wanted to bury her head in hot soapy water. How to escape the smell? She couldn't seem to. The blood was swimming all around her, creeping up the blade of the knife, coming for her, sticky, hot and someone else's. It pooled on the ground and she lay in it, dank and putrid. She pulled herself aside from Bing and dry retched.

'Come on Lana,' called Paul. 'Pull yourself together. Save Bing's life for him. He saved yours, remember?'

'Yep,' she gasped, choking back tears.

She scrabbled around for a fist-sized rock to use as a short sharp jolt against the blade of the knife.

'Bing,' she called loudly to him even though she was close.

'Uh,' he moaned. His body wriggled all over the ground.

'I have to cleave the bone. It might shock you. Have your whiskey Bing.'

She sidled back into position resting on her side. The blood had become a brown stain in the dry ground. The knife's leather handle was soaked in it, warm and sticky. Lana wiped the blade on her sarong then positioned a tapered edge across the bones. With her other hand clenched with the rock she smashed down on the blade. Bing screamed as the knife bounced off his bones.

'Ah, sorry, sorry, sorry, Bing,' screamed Lana. 'Paul?'

No Lana. It's fine,' he yelled back. 'Try again. Think about your karate okay? Short sharp shock and deal to it. Do it once, hard. One good blow. All your energy.'

Paul said the right thing. Karate focussed her. She summoned her chi energy from deep within her core and spread it to her nerve ends at the skin with renewed strength and purpose. She breathed in deeply and repositioned the blade.

'Arrgh,' she screamed with an expulsion of energy as she bore the rock down on the blade. She felt the bones shudder as they cracked under her hands.

Bing's scream was blood curdling. He writhed his hips and splayed his kicking legs then curled himself into a ball clutching his severed limb, dragging it away from its night trap. Suddenly it was if a fountain had been turned on. Thick red blood pulsed to the severed end and spurted out.

'The sarong Lana, quick,' called Paul. 'Bing, give me your legs. Straighten yourself out.'

But Bing was deaf to Paul's instruction and Lana quickly grabbed the gold cloth and sidled up to him. Her hands trembled as she peeled the stump from Bing's other hand and held the crumpled sarong on it. Bing held fast to it for a second then fainted.

Lana wriggled backwards and grabbed Bing's feet but he was heavy, a dead weight. She let go and backed out fully into the daylight away from the foul smell of Bing's blood. Paul bent to help her.

'No,' she panted and swung herself around and shimmied back in feet first. The manoeuvre gave her more purchase and this time she wriggled like a caterpillar as she pulled Bing out of the space by his feet.

'He fainted,' Lana announced. But before she could assist Bing further she bent over resting her hands on her knees and again tried to vomit. She spat out the saliva that welled up in her mouth.

Paul squatted next to Bing, took the crumpled bandage, and folded it neatly before repositioning it against what remained of the arm. It was already soaked in Bing's blood.

'Come on mate,' Paul rallied him. Slowly Bing came to. 'You're doing really well. Stand up Bing.'

'Aah,' Bing cried as Paul helped him.

'You and me both mate,' said Paul wincing.

Bing's legs didn't want to work. He kicked them out in front of him and tried to ground his feet but it wasn't working for him.

'Lana. Help,' instructed Paul as he supported Bing underneath one armpit.

She took Bing's other side and together they staggered into the hut and lay him on his bunk. Lana handed Bing painkillers and a mug of water.

'Sorry Emma, no more for you,' Paul said to her.

'Guess I deserve that,' she answered matter of factly.

'Get those drugs down you Bing,' said Paul. 'Let me look at your arm.'

'It's imperative the wound is kept clean,' Emma said. 'Let me see it.' She edged towards Bing. 'Hold it high above his heart.' She took the weight of the arm. 'Paul prepare a bandage please.'

As Emma held the stump up in the air and Paul followed Emma's directions, Lana looked away. She had seen enough blood and felt enough nausea, tasted enough vomit and smelt enough of other people's blood and urine. She suddenly felt an overwhelming desire to cry, or sleep. Or both. She let the sound of Emma's drawl wash over her. Suddenly she didn't care about the stolen painkillers. She didn't care about Emma's broken leg or Paul's cracked ribs. Her body ached, stretched with the bruising and tired from lack of sleep.

A fresh bombardment of volcanic debris hit the hut rattling the pots and pans. Something inside her snapped and she threw herself on the bunk alongside Paul with her hands over her ears. Paul let Emma finish off the sling and kneeling, he ducked his head level with Lana's and whispered to her.

'It's okay sweetheart. It's all right.' He caressed her shoulders which racked uncontrollably.

She sat up and wiped tears from her eyes. Paul sat back on his haunches and wiped her wet cheeks with his finger.

'It's the shock,' he explained. 'You did an amazing job Lana. You saved Bing's life.'

Lana crawled off the bunk and took a corner of the room to change, trembling as she stripped off her outer wear. Then she took her blood stained trousers and shirt to the veranda and dumped them outside.

By the time she returned Paul had poured four shots of whiskey. He handed her a mug. Her eyes brightened when she saw the smooth amber liquid and her head lightened as she inhaled its intoxicating bouquet. She let the whiskey and the warmth of the fire wash over her, cleansing her.

'I thought the mountain had stopped,' she explained. 'I don't know why I did that. Feel so stupid.'

'You're traumatised sweetheart,' Paul answered.

Lana sipped at her drink and caught Emma's eye. She raised her mug to her without smiling. 'Thanks for your help.'

Emma returned the gesture. 'Glad to be of some use.'

Chapter Eleven

Late into the afternoon the mountain still hadn't let up. Just when Lana thought there was a lull in activity and she'd relaxed a little, just when her mind was vacuous enough to entertain non-volcanic thoughts, a fresh eruption would rain down. Drinking teas was the only activity that kept things normal. At least it was something to do. No one much wanted to talk. Lana felt the tension. She'd been snappy and that was out of character for her. But these were extraordinary circumstances and not one of them was trained for this.

Her stomach growled though she didn't think it was hunger. The thought of yet more rice and beans curbed any appetite she might otherwise have developed. It was a knot of anguish balled in her gut, unable to unfurl.

Paul seemed always to be hungry. Of all of them he seemed to cope the best. But he tended to keep his own counsel too. He seemed to understand that no one could talk without flying off the handle at some trivial remark. It was a waiting game. Waiting. Waiting. He kept a billy of water on the fire which spit rhythmically, a tiny cymbal of percussion to the mountain's bass tremor. He passed the time recording notes and taking photographs.

Lana felt sorry for Emma. She hadn't done anything to Lana to receive her wrath. Besides, if it wasn't for Emma's first aid knowledge they would all be much worse off. Emma only had three months left in New Zealand. She'd met Lana for the first time in Iceland for the conference where they'd roomed together. Lana was charmed by the younger woman's confidence. Marvelled at her in fact. She was everything Lana would have wanted to be had she had her time over again. Emma could hold an audience, something Lana was still too shy to do. For the short time they'd been together in Iceland Emma swept Lana along with her and Lana enjoyed it.

Julie saw an opportunity for Lana in having Emma around. It would add an academic dimension she wouldn't otherwise be exposed to. It also added a personal dimension neither Julie nor Lana could have anticipated. Emma was loud but she was fun and generous. She was forthcoming with all sorts of personal information, whether it was sought or not. She had been captain of the school hockey team and so popular that all the boys wanted to date her. But there was only one boy for her and she enrolled in geology to pursue him. Finally they dated and graduated together only to split up because she found out he'd been two timing with a girl since their first week long field trip three years earlier.

Emma claimed she'd never known true love but Lana pointed out that she had known it or she wouldn't have been so hurt by it. Emma brushed it off telling Lana she was a romantic and anyway, hadn't she been lucky with Yuri.

Lana didn't even blame her for sneaking the pills. A broken leg probably was the most unbearable injury out of them all, and no one could have predicted Bing's amputation. No one could have been more surprised at Lana's nasty attack on Emma than Lana. She put it down to stress, and thankfully Emma seemed unaffected by it.

'God, how much longer?' Lana moaned.

She snapped her phone open and shut willing the battery to spring to life. Somehow she'd forgotten to turn it off and the phone had been roaming, hastening the battery to die.

'Nothing,' she said grumpily.

'Me neither,' said Paul. 'Mine died ages ago. Don't worry. A chopper will come.'

'But you said last time the mountain erupted it went off for weeks,' she retorted.

'Yeah,' he agreed. 'But no two eruptions are the same Lana. You know that.'

'Of course I know that,' she said. 'I'm fed up cooped in here, dirty, hungry.'

'Thought you weren't hungry,' said Paul.

'Just not hungry enough for more rice and beans,' she replied. 'Probably be hanging out for rice and beans at gee, let's see, dinner time and we've got nice candle light. What about music? Bing's groaning should do nicely.'

'I wish I could tell you to go for a walk sweetheart,' said Paul. 'We're all going stir crazy.'

'At least you can walk Lana,' Emma added.

Lana felt the slap on her face. 'Yes. I'm sorry. I was just thinking about your predicament. You'll be in plaster casts won't you?'

'God, I hope it's only one!' Emma shot back.

'Do you do yoga?' It was Paul.

It seemed such a ludicrous suggestion and Paul was so serious that Lana and Emma burst out laughing. It wasn't so much the idea as the man behind the idea. It wasn't the sort of suggestion they expected.

'Yes. No,' she said not willing to pursue the subject of yoga. 'You're right. We're all in this together and I'm not even injured.' She raised both her arms out from her sides and let them drop heavily onto her thighs with a slap. She flinched as her hands connected with her bruises. They'd come out a rich black and blue but she wasn't about to let on.

'It's clear there'll be no rescue today,' Paul remarked. 'It will be dark in an hour and the mountain wants us to stay the night.'

He padded out to the warden's quarters and fossicked around for a can of beans.

'You're walking better Paul,' said Lana as he set about preparing the beans.

'Yeah. It's not too sore,' he agreed.

'Shall I restrap it?' she asked.

'Remove the strapping before you go to bed,' Emma said. 'Otherwise it will start to swell.'

With her back to Emma Lana rolled her eyes and caught Paul's amused expression.

She piled heaps of rice onto plates.

'Bon appétit,' said Paul. 'And here's to another day.' He lifted a mug up as a toast, took a sip and then passed it to Lana. She smelt the whiskey before she tasted it and it filled her mouth with fire. She caught the look in his eye which told her to keep the whiskey secret.

They ate in silence and listened to the rumble of the mountain, the crackle of the fire and Bing's laboured gasping between mouthfuls. Lana shuffled over to Bing and helped him with his meal.

'Are you managing Bing?' Lana asked. 'Your body needs energy to cope with the trauma. It can't repair itself if you don't give it fuel. You understand?'

'You think I'm going to grow another arm?' He smiled a crooked smile but his eyes belied his agony. 'Can I have painkillers?'

Paul took a couple off the table and handed them to Lana along with his mug. She stared questioningly at him and he raised his eyebrows. Bing took the pills in his mouth and Lana held the cup to his lips. He took a gulp and kicked back his head with a swallow.

'Aah,' he sighed and lay back on his pillow of clothes.

'Early night for us all,' Lana declared. 'It's been a hell of a day.'

She set her sleeping bag next to Paul's and put her sleepwear on top. She caressed her camisole with the lace trim. She imagined the sensual feel of it on her skin, but how practical was it? What if she had to evacuate in the night, she wondered. The day's dust had filtered through to her skin and made her dark hair stiff. She was even more uncomfortable now than when she took her wash. Commonsense told her she should wear sensible clothes to bed.

She glanced across to Paul who was wiping dishes at the bench.

'You think we're safe in here tonight?' asked Lana.

It was a stupid question, she knew. Prepare for the worst and hope for the best. Wasn't that a solicitor's mantra?

'Well, where would you rather be?' Paul replied. 'In here or out there?' Then he saw her dilemma.

She balled the cami into her fist and walked to the door. It was safe enough at the moment to make the tiresome dash up the hill to the toilet. She headed out into the rapidly cooling evening. The last of the day was retreating, slinking into slumber by an advancing red dusk. She scrunched her way over the ash-laden ground to the putrid smelling box for what she hoped was the last time that day and slipped into the camisole. It felt good, no matter that the day's grime enveloped her.

By the time she returned only one candle was left flickering and everyone was in their sleeping bags. She blew the candle out and Paul flicked on the thin white halogen beam. She slipped into her bag and peeled off her bush shirt. She deftly removed her long johns inside the bag.

'Did you remove your ankle strapping?' she whispered.

'Oh no,' Paul replied. 'I should though.'

He unzipped his bag and unfurled his legs. He wore only boxers. Lana wriggled to his foot and sat cross legged. She had not yet zipped up her bag and she saw the light play over her body.

She placed his foot on her bended knee and found the edge of the bandage. Lifting his foot with each round she tenderly unwound the strapping.

'Shine your light on it,' she instructed.

Paul aimed the beam on his foot but not before he played the light over her upper thighs. She pretended not to notice but when she saw a flicker of movement beneath his shorts she smiled to herself, her head bowed studiously over her work.

'Looks fine,' she announced and as she let it down she gave it the tiniest twist.

'Aah!' Paul flinched and jolted away from her.

If Lana hadn't crawled back into bed so quickly she would have seen Emma reach out to take Paul's hand.

***

A dull clatter woke Lana. Strangely it had a rhythm to it unlike most of the tremors. Then it grew louder until she could feel the noise of it in the top of her chest.

'Lana. Emma.' It was Paul.

She opened her eyes to see Paul leaning over and shaking Emma's shoulder.

'It's a chopper,' he said. 'We're getting out of here.'

Lana leapt up forgetting she had next to nothing on.

'I hope it's not the last time I see that,' Paul mumbled under his breath.

She dragged her clothes on hopping as she threaded her legs into long johns, lurched across the room and flung open the door to the displaced air from the helicopter blades. She watched it hover then ran to the edge of the deck. Two men were talking into their headsets and pointing at different spots on the ground. They were looking for the spot marked as the helipad. Lana ran off the deck without stopping to put on her boots and pointed to where she remembered seeing it. It didn't resemble a helipad now, covered in brown muddy ash and strewn with debris. She shivered as she watched it land and the men took their time in getting out.

She looked around her. The clouds had changed, no longer fat with moisture and the air was lighter, cleansed by thick droplets of moisture which now sat swollen on the ground. She noticed Paul slowly limping towards her.

Finally the passenger door opened and a paramedic clamoured out clutching an enormous medical bag. He ducked under the two spinning blades.

'Hello,' he said. 'In a spot of bother?'

He was a slight man and wore a scruffy salt and

pepper beard which emphasised his twinkling blue eyes. His manner was so relaxed that Lana instantly felt a heaviness lift from her shoulders.

'You could say that,' she replied. 'I'm Lana and this is Paul. We have injured people in the hut.'

'And you have a bad ankle,' he said to Paul loudly over the din of the blades.

Lana led Maurice inside.

'This is Emma,' Paul said to Maurice. 'She's a volunteer paramedic in Canada. She's been giving us advice. Unfortunately she has a broken leg.'

Maurice immediately conversed with Emma and quickly ascertained the priority of injuries. He dispensed morphine for her then started on Bing.

'We amputated his arm at lunchtime yesterday,' Paul explained. He was trapped under the hut. Can you do anything for him?'

'What painkillers has he had?' Maurice set his bag down on the table and opened it.

'Paracetamol and whiskey,' Paul stated.

'Bing. Can you hear me?' asked Maurice. 'We're going to fly you out by helicopter.'

'Uh-huh,' Bing moaned.

'I'm going to make you a bit more comfortable for the journey,' Maurice explained. He fished in his bag for more morphine then spread a large white triangular bandage out on the table.

'Would one of you help me to sit him up and I'll get this bandage on and strap his arm to his body. You've done a good job but we can do a better one with the right equipment. We need to keep the arm still and elevated.'

Lana climbed into the bunk and with Maurice on the

310

other side raised Bing to a semi-sitting position.

'Poor Bing,' said Lana. 'He also has a deep knife wound to his side. He's been bed ridden for about three days.'

Maurice lifted Bing's shirt and inspected the wound. Then he expertly fastened the triangular bandage around his shoulder and arm.

'I won't remove the bandage on the stump,' Maurice said. 'Someone's done a lovely job there.' He raised his eyebrows at Lana.

'Wasn't me sorry.'

'There. That should make you a bit more comfortable,' Maurice announced.

Lana leapt off the bed and started to gather up her possessions.

'We have to do two Helivacs I'm afraid. Can only fit four people.' Maurice was apologetic. 'I have to take the injured.'

'So who?' asked Lana. She knew it wouldn't be her and dropped her sleeping bag to the floor.

'Has to be Bing and Emma,' Paul suggested.

'Sorry, no,' said Maurice. 'You have priority over Emma.'

'How can that be?' he replied. 'I'm fine.'

'Don't be silly Paul,' said Emma. 'You need x-rays and proper strapping for your ribs.'

'She's right,' said Maurice, 'and we don't want to risk punctuated lungs so pack your bags.'

'We'll be back for you as soon as we can Lana,' Maurice said brightly. 'You can have the sightseeing trip. Let's get these injured men sorted first. Pack your bags and be ready.'

'How long?' she asked.

'An hour,' said Maurice confidently.

She helped Paul pack his gear then did the same for Bing. Maurice assisted Bing onto his feet and together they helped him out of the hut to the waiting Robinson R44 which still had its single engine running.

Lana left him with Maurice and the pilot to manoeuvre into the back seat while she ran back to the hut where Paul was struggling with the weight of his pack.

'Put that down,' she said. She heaved it off the ground and slung it over her shoulder.

'Oh, Lana,' Paul cajoled her. 'I wish you could go.'

'Don't be silly,' she retorted with bravado she didn't feel. 'I'll be with you in an hour.' She forced a furrowed smile but Paul turned to her and planted a kiss on her forehead. She felt awkward. It was almost like being on her front doorstep again, but not quite. Suddenly Paul saved the moment and as he walked away she stood flummoxed, wondering what had happened, if indeed anything had. She caught him up ducking well outside the reach of the rotors.

Paul climbed in grimacing with the effort and Lana passed his pack to Maurice for him to squash between the seats. Paul buckled himself in and put headphones on then gave her a quick wave. She backed away ducking her head as the pilot revved the engine and the blades whipped into a frenzy and lifted off.

Lana felt sick. Alone. She stood on that spot and watched the chopper fly out of view until it was a tiny dot that she couldn't differentiate from all the other tiny dots that made up the wide volcanic landscape.

Slowly she walked back to the hut and stood on the deck amongst the ash and volcanic rocks, staring at the horizon. And below it, a thin line that delineated the space between the mountain and the ring plain, between danger and safety. She recognised the churning in her chest as a precursor to tears and took several deep breaths, letting her shoulders rise and slump. But it didn't work. Hot tears welled up behind her eyes and at the first blink squeezed to fill her bright blue eyes until they became so many they flowed down her cheeks. She let them fall, salty and heavy.

After a time she went inside and surveyed the hut. It didn't look as messy as before. She smiled at the yellow plastic window. It was somehow comforting and finally she wiped the tears from her cheeks and dabbed her eyes, careful that Emma didn't notice then she packed her bag and dressed appropriately for a flight off the mountain.

'Well,' she said to Emma. 'This is it. Brr,' she rubbed her arms. As she strode across to the door to shut it she noticed silent white flakes falling. 'Oh,' she exclaimed excitedly.

'What?'

'Oh no,' she groaned as she realised the significance of snow. 'Snow,' Lana replied.

'Oh God,' Emma exclaimed and flopped back onto her bunk. It seemed the waiting wasn't over yet.

Chapter Twelve

Alex couldn't settle and the bare walls of his office allowed his mind to wander. He shuffled the GST returns into a neat pile and pushed them to the other side of the desk and turned to his computer. He typed in Paul Harrington, PhD. It's a wonder he hadn't thought to do it before, given it was all he could think about. He figured he would meet this Mr Harrington when he picked up Lana and that being the case it might make him look a bit better if it was obvious he'd done some research of his own. He double blinked. Multiple entries filled the screen, all of them which led to academic papers he had published either alone or in collaboration with other scientists. There were no photos of him nor any personal information but Alex calculated the guy must be about a hundred years old given the amount of research he'd conducted.

He clicked on a few. The oldest paper dated to 1987 and was collaboratively written. He clicked on more, and still more, but there was nothing published earlier than that. Beads of perspiration peppered his forehead. He bit back the slithering snake of jealousy as he realised that Paul Harrington PhD, was not an old man at all. Quite possibly he was the same age as Lana. It suddenly made sense that she hadn't told him about Paul. What had Julie said? They met in Iceland? Obviously they'd formed some sort of relationship. He kept clicking on Paul's academic papers.

His early research focused heavily on volcanic activity around the Pacific Rim. At least he seemed to have a grasp of his subject. Alex hoped it was enough to keep Lana out of harm on Mount Ruapehu. Then he noticed an obvious change in research objectives. He had contracted to public health bodies in various non-English speaking countries with a focus on advising on the effects of volcanic eruptions on the community and agriculture. Lastly his papers turned to the study of lahars back in New Zealand.

'Huh,' Alex grunted.

These dated to only a couple of years old. Had Lana been seeing him since then?

Alex was quietly impressed. *Well bully for you Mr Paul Harrington*, Alex thought as he shut down the screen, *you haven't met Alex Cliff, chartered accountant!*

***

Alex couldn't concentrate. All afternoon he imagined meeting Lana as she stepped out of the helicopter. He would present her with a ring and she would slip it onto her finger and admire it before flinging her arms around his neck.

He drove to Lana's house and let himself in. It felt odd being there without her. He padded down the hall to her bedroom. It was so feminine, so Lana. He assembled a bag of clothes for her, then hovered over her dresser to look for a ring. He found one that he had seen her wearing and put it in his pocket then headed straight to the jewellers.

***

Finally Alex got the call from Julie advising him a

helicopter rescue was imminent and now the sun shot soft yellow rays into the side of his eyes as he headed north. Within half an hour of easy travelling the mountain came into view. He'd always thought that as mountains went, Mount Ruapehu was not the prettiest mountain around. It was so unwieldy. Why could it not be conical like the little Mount Ngauruhoe on the side of Mount Tongariro?

He turned up the volume on Ashley Halley's violin concerto and let himself be consumed by its uplifting melody. Nothing could spoil his mood for he was about to meet the woman he loved and ask her to marry him. Not even the thought of Mr Harrington could dull his mood.

Eventually Alex approached the truck stop town. Its redeeming feature was the Army Museum. He drove slowly around the back road until he found the entrance to the army base as he expected Lana to be delivered there. A barrier arm was down across the private road where he stopped at the sentry's box.

'Alex Cliff,' he said to the guard. 'I've come to pick up Lana Marshall. The lady airlifted off the mountain.'

The sentry directed Alex to the medical unit and bade him a nice day.

***

The tree lined streets within the compound led Alex to a nondescript one storey cream weatherboard building with a ramped access to the centre. He walked through the double doors to carpeted foyer which in turn had double doors to an open plan reception area. Behind a curved desk a young woman in army fatigues was taking a phone call. As she finished Alex approached her.

'I've come to pick up Lana Marshall, the lady airlifted off the mountain this morning,' he said by way of introduction.

She tapped the name into her computer. 'She's not been brought here sir. Was she definitely being flown into the base?'

'That was my information.'

'Wait,' she said. 'There were two people admitted an hour ago airlifted from Mount Ruapehu.'

'That's right. She was with them,' Alex said. 'She wasn't injured so she wouldn't be admitted.'

'Wait here sir. I'll see what I can find out,' she said.

She left him standing alone in the centre of the reception area. Corridors extended in either direction from this central hub. Alex noted how eerily quiet it was. The carpet looked like it had been ripped out of a picture theatre thirty years ago although the building itself was undoubtedly nineteen fifties.

The woman returned.

'Lana's colleagues are here at the base. Follow me please,' she instructed and swiftly disappeared down a corridor. She stopped at a four bed room much like a modern hospital with curtains neatly pulled aside each bed and grey vinyl on the floor.

'This is it,' she said and left him at the door.

Alex stepped into the room and assessed the men.

The man with the bandaged arm who was asleep was clearly in his thirties and the other one, well, mid forties? It would be pushing it to say he was fifty. The man still had plenty of colour in his hair and he didn't carry any

317

extra fat around his face. Alex noted the fine lines at the corners of Paul's mouth and eyes. He stirred as Alex entered the room.

'I'm Alex, Lana's partner,' he announced as he approached the bed.

'Ah, pleased to meet you,' said Paul shoving himself into a half sitting position. He offered his hand. 'Pull up a seat.'

Alex fetched a chair from the other side of the room and sat alongside Paul.

'Where's Lana?' he asked.

'Still in the hut. Not enough room on the chopper,' Paul explained.

'Oh no! Is she all right?' Alex bit his lower lip.

'Apart from a burn on her leg, she's fine,' replied Paul.

'A burn? How?'

'She took a hit from a small lava bomb,' Paul explained.

Alex reeled as Paul relayed the events surrounding Lana's injury. Unable to keep his glasses from sliding down his nose he removed them and dabbed his face with a handkerchief.

'There's nothing to worry about,' Paul explained. 'She's with Emma, a paramedic. Besides, Lana did her best rescue carrying that injury,' Paul added.

'What do you mean?' Alex detected a smugness in Paul's reply.

'See that guy there?' He nodded in the direction of Bing. 'Cut his arm off to save his life.'

A look of horror etched into Alex's face and his mouth contorted with revulsion.

318

'Had to do it,' said Paul. 'Either that or die.'

'Has the chopper gone back for her?' asked Alex.

'I don't think so. Weather changed on us. It's snowing up there.'

'What about her phone?'

'Flat battery. Bugger to get coverage anyway, without getting pulverised that is,' he added.

'So I still can't contact her.'

Alex sat quietly trying to take the measure of this man while digesting the awful news that Lana would have to spend yet another night on the mountain. The silence was uncomfortable. He had to break it.

'Have you known Lana long?' he asked.

'We were at school together,' Paul volunteered.

Alex flinched like he'd been shot from an arrow. He hadn't expected that! He caught Paul smile imperceptibly and it seemed to Alex that Paul had directed the shot at his heart, hinting at secrets not for him.

'You were helping her with her glacier research?' He spat the words out of his dry mouth.

'Helping each other,' Paul replied. 'She was helping me with the lahar survey but all hell broke loose and we didn't manage to get to the glacier.'

Alex nodded slowly, impassively. He wore a mask as he scrutinised the friend Lana had neglected to tell him about. The man who lay in the bed appeared unassuming, comfortable and confident but his eyes were piercing. They bore into Alex extracting information without Alex's permission. His carefully clipped stubble had just about been overtaken by four days of five o'clock shadows and now he looked scruffy, older than his forty six years. He appeared fit, certainly not overweight. Alex grudgingly admitted that Paul would be attractive to women. But was he attractive to Lana?

'How are you hurt?' he asked Paul.

'Couple of fractured ribs, twisted ankle,' Paul replied. 'Nothing really. But my vehicle is up the mountain and I'm here so I may as well be here until I can reunite with my vehicle.' He shrugged.

'If Lana isn't hurt she won't stay here,' Alex mused aloud. 'They might not even bring her here.'

'Find out and let me know.' Paul made a demand into a request. 'Please,' he added.

Alex screeched his chair against the vinyl floor as he got up. He padded back down the hall to the woman at reception. He was glad of the task. Paul was too casual about his situation and all too casual about Lana. They had both played it cool, close to their chest, like a pair of male dogs meeting each in the park for the first time, circling and sniffing each other before a fight.

'Excuse me.' He interrupted the woman. 'Could you tell me when my girlfriend will be rescued and where she will be taken to?'

She dialled an internal line, explained to someone what she wanted, paused and hung up. 'You need to speak to mountain rescue in the communication building. Best thing is to drive. Go out of this complex and take the first left into Gallipoli. Coms building is second on the left,' she explained.

'Thanks very much,' said Alex as he turned and walked back to his car.

Paul had thrown him. He wanted to like him. There

was nothing not to like prima facie. He could understand Lana omitting to tell him about Paul. She would have thought that he might feel threatened by him. She was protecting him. Well he would be the man Lana expected him to be. He would thank Paul very much for being there for Lana but make it clear that he was here now so he'd be taking charge.

He drove through the semi suburban lichen encrusted streets to the communications building. It was also a one storey sixty year old cream weatherboard building but this time with a concrete ramp to one end. He stepped inside to find the same outdated carpet that the medical unit had. There was more activity here with switch boards beeping and lighting up. Army personnel were too-ing and fro-ing. He approached a stout middle aged woman behind a desk.

'I'm Alex Cliff,' he began. 'My partner Lana Marshall is to be helicoptered off Mount Ruapehu shortly. Can you give me any information on that?'

'That flight is delayed due to snow sir,' she replied. 'We are monitoring the weather as well as the volcanic hazard. As soon as practicable the flight will resume.'

'So it's a waiting game,' said Alex.

'Correct sir.'

'Can you tell me, where she will be dropped off?'

'You can collect her from the heliport,' said the woman.

'Which is where?'

He visualised the instructions as she explained how to find the heliport then drove over. On the tarmac sat a stationery Hughes helicopter. He glanced back at the mountain. Even at this distance he could tell that it was snowing up there – the clouds were a different colour.

He drove back to Paul who dozed in the army bed, the weak sun banded across the floor and bedspread.

'Lana's flight is delayed. Snow,' Alex added. 'Look, Paul. Thanks for looking after Lana. We both are grateful.' He offered his hand and Paul shook it with a fierce grip that Alex hadn't wholly unexpected.

'Can I have your mobile phone number?' asked Paul. 'So I can reach you later. I might have to speak to Lana and her phone's flat.'

'Of course,' Alex replied. He pulled out his wallet and rifled through his cards before choosing one to hand to Paul. 'It's on here,' he said pointing to the bottom of the card.

Alex shuffled uncomfortably from foot to foot. He cursed himself for not being familiar with either the mountain or Lana's research. It made it difficult to ask the right questions. 'There's nothing I can do here. I'll see about getting a motel room. I'll leave you to recuperate. Thanks again.'

As he took his leave he glanced across at the other bed. Bing had his eyes open and had watched the exchange. Alex gave him a tight smile and hurriedly left the room.

Chapter Thirteen

Alfred waited on the patio with his overnight bag for Colleen to collect him. He had been up for hours, excited by the forthcoming trip. He wore narrow cord brown trousers and a rusty-coloured brushed cotton shirt with the sleeves rolled up. The morning sun caught the grey hairs on his still strong tanned arms.

Colleen too had been up for hours. She'd had a good run; there wasn't much traffic. She bumped into the drive and slowed to a stop in front of Alfred, then bounced out to greet him.

'Hello Alfred. All ready then?' she asked.

Alfred didn't have time to catch his breath. No sooner had he stood and gained balance with his stick than Colleen had him hustled and buckled into the front seat. It was a pleasant change to be in the company of a decisive female and to be doing something out of the ordinary.

'Got everything?' she asked buckling herself in and graunching the gearbox into reverse.

'Hope so,' Alfred replied.

The day was fine and puffy white clouds punctuated a perfect blue sky.

'It will be cold up there,' said Colleen nodding to the hills in front of them.

'Don't I know it?' Alfred replied. 'I spent months training there before I left for the war.'

'Is that where you met Uncle Harold?'

'Yes. And many other good men. We were only kids you know, when we arrived at training camp. We thought we were men. But we weren't men until we returned.'

'Was it awful?' Colleen asked.

'Oh yes and no,' he answered casually. 'When I came home I thought I had my Sophie waiting for me. But that wasn't to be. That was really hard, not the war. It was the thought of my Sophie that kept me going, gave me hope and purpose. Kept me going.'

Colleen stayed silent but nodded in all the right places.

'War brings out the best in men you know,' Alfred continued almost to himself. 'Characters intensify. You live for the day because tomorrow might not come, so the person you are strengthens. For example, if you're a natural clown you ham it up all the time so that the act becomes bigger than you. It's a cover of course.' He smiled. 'That was Mickey Tusker.'

'What sort of character do you have?' asked Colleen.

'That's for you to work out Colleen. I wouldn't try to. I hope my comrades saw some special qualities. But they wouldn't tell you and I wouldn't expect them to.'

'I bet you couldn't wait to come home though.'

'Oh, I don't know. I hadn't really started life had I?' he said. 'I finished up in I don't know how many prison camps and life wasn't bad if you weren't in a hurry to get out. But that's a story for another time. I ended up in Trieste. You know? Right at the top of Italy. Port town full of tall stone buildings. Used to be part of the Austro-Hungarian Empire and a beacon for literature and music. Anyway, I digress. We got there second of May. I always remember that because the day before we crossed the Izonso River and I remember thinking that Dad and my younger brother would be at river at the back of the farm in the hide for opening morning.'

'What?'

'Duck shooting!'

'Oh.' said Colleen. 'Carry on. You were in Trieste.'

'Gerry had just surrendered and it should have been the end of the war for us but Italy's neighbour to the north, Yugoslavia, and an ally I might add, decided they wanted Trieste for themselves. Well that put the cat amongst the pigeons. We thought we were going to put our feet up and wait for the next boat home. No such luck.'

'So the allies started fighting each other?' asked Colleen.

'Not really. For six weeks Yugoslavia shared occupation with the western allies. Luckily the Yugoslavs withdrew in mid-June leaving Trieste to Italy and then finally we could leave. But there was a log jam. Too many men, too few boats. By the time I got home Sophie had high tailed it with a flash American.'

'Oh, I'm sorry.'

'Don't be,' said Alfred. 'No one to blame. Things happen. At the time I did dwell on the fact that I could have been home to her sooner if the nonsense at Trieste hadn't happened. But it probably wouldn't have made a scrap of difference. When I finally got home it felt like I hadn't been fighting a war. I was just there. I didn't feel my absence could be justified and I'd lost my girl because of it.'

'Do you still feel that way?' Colleen asked quietly.

Alfred thought how easy it would be to open up to Colleen. But he wasn't used to that. He'd been unusually revealing already. Maybe age was catching up with him and it really didn't matter who knew what anymore. He felt on the verge of telling her about Sophie but it just stuck. He wondered why he couldn't tell her. It was right there. But no, he wasn't ready to share Sophie just yet.

'Oh no.' Alfred laughed easily. 'I soon met Lily. She was promised to your Uncle Harold and I thank Harry every day for giving me Lily.'

'You said you had four boys.'

'And ten grandchildren,' Alfred beamed. 'Tom went into the army too. As a medic.'

Just as Colleen was about to ask yet another question he diverted her attention to the approaching town. Seems like time had flown. How long was it since Alfred had been here? He had little reason over the years to visit and living in the east like he did almost never needed to drive through it. But for the long absence it seemed as familiar as yesterday, like time hadn't really touched it.

'You getting peckish Alfred?' asked Colleen as she slowed approaching the centre of town.

'I could go a mince savoury,' he replied.

'Let's have a break then.'

Alfred breathed a sigh of relief as Colleen abandoned her conversation and drew the car to a stop.

***

After a quick bite to eat they pulled into the car park of the fortress that was the museum. If it gave the impression of an impenetrable tank then the designers had done their job. But Alfred appreciated the frankness of the building. It was no-nonsense, box-like and imposing on the gently rounded landscape. The colour

326

was a sensible, subtle shade of green. He shook his head as he pondered the breach in its defences on the night of the robbery.

Strong winds buffeted the car and red and yellow tussocks around the car park and base of the museum swayed wildly. He strained a look up through the front window as if he'd see where the wind came from. But all he noticed was piles of pale grey ash piled in skinny rows and stacked in crevasses where the wind had moved it. Now the wind picked up the fine top layer swirling it once again into the air.

Colleen was right. It was cooler here. She could feel it without even getting out of the car. And there was a hollowness to the atmosphere that you only noticed on the plateau, probably less oxygen at altitude. Ordinarily the mountain would be clearly visible from the township but not today. It was obscured by cloud, tendrils settling deep into the valleys, and sinking into the rivers below. A thick yellow-brown plume billowed above and fanned out to the north east, fading into transparency as it dispersed as far as the eye could see.

'It's the first real sign of the eruption we've seen isn't it?' Colleen remarked peering through the windows at the ash piles.

'Apart from the pasture having a white tinge to it,' said Alfred. 'Let's go.' The wind pushed the door out of his grasp and he braced himself with his stick, shocked for a minute at the force of it. Colleen rushed to him and with heads down against the wind they staggered to the museum's entrance.

At the ticket counter Colleen explained that it was her medal that had been stolen. The young lady took

Colleen's hand in her hands, holding it far longer than a handshake.

'I'm *so* please to meet you,' she said. 'I was the one who noticed the theft. I didn't know you were coming.' Introductions were made. 'Did the police ask you to come?' asked Sandra.

'No. Alfred and I want to get more of a picture of things. Can we see where the medals were?' she asked.

'Let me escort you,' said Sandra as she led the way into the museum.

There was so much to take in already. Alfred had barely shuffled up the ramp when he paused in front of a great wall of granite etched with names which had a thin film of water trickling over it. Red poppies adorned the floor of the display where people had written a loved one's name and tossed it in. He ought to do the same but the ladies had gone on ahead.

'Alfred was in the same battle that my uncle received his medal for,' Colleen explained to Sandra. 'But Alfred didn't get a medal. Sadly,' she added.

He caught them up where they were paused at a world war two diorama. The mannequin took him by surprise. Silly really. He'd worn that uniform for two years and there wasn't a day went by that he couldn't feel the itch of the green serge on his skin. But to see it there pressed and clean in front of him suddenly gave him heart palpatations.

'Alfred, what is it?' Colleen steadied him. 'Can you get a chair?' she asked Sandra.

'I'm fine,' he insisted.

'Then why are you perspiring?' Colleen dabbed his forehead with her handkerchief. 'Here, sit down.'

Alfred sat but protested. 'This is silly, I'm fine.' But he rested for a minute and in his mind's eye he was smack in the middle of the battle for Monte Cassino. The blood over his uniform was not his. And nor were the bits of flesh; the black hair, half a cheek, an ear and a blue eye. Shattered teeth imbedded into the weave of his sleeve. It was the last thing he saw before he blackened into unconsciousness.

Alfred wiped at his clothes. The ladies were fussing over him. He didn't like that. He got up from the chair and straightened himself.

'Was that your uniform Alfred?' Colleen whispered slipping her arm through his.

But Alfred didn't answer her, not right away. He gave himself a moment and finally nodded, but he didn't look at her. She'd think he was traumatised, that he might need looking after. He was having none of that.

They stopped in front of the medal cabinets. 'Here we are. Which was your medal?' Sandra asked Colleen.

'The New Zealand Memorial Cross, George VI,' Colleen replied.

'Ah, yes,' said Sandra and turned to face the wall. 'It hung here.'

The gap remained exactly how Sandra had discovered it.

'They got in, how?' asked Colleen.

'The same way you and I did,' she replied. 'Then hid in here somewhere and didn't go back out. They must have had a computer expert because they fooled the security systems.'

'Any leads?' asked Alfred.

'Afraid not. Look, you have a look around. Sir, if you

get tired I can arrange a wheelchair and please, come and see me soon and I'll arrange afternoon tea for you.'

'Thank you,' said Colleen. 'We don't expect special treatment.'

'Well, you've got it, so just make yourselves at home.' With that she turned on her heels and strode back the way they'd come.

Alfred didn't mind the memories that surged forth. He felt dreamy; the present and the past rolled into one. He'd survived the past and the present was good for now.

It had been a blessing to lose consciousness after the explosion. He could tell straight away it was Mervyn. The brown freckles were distinctive. He was part Maori. He had no idea how many more of them had taken the hit. He'd been lucky. The hospital was quiet and the Italian nurses were pretty. But he wasn't there long before he was moved from one grim camp to another.

Alfred stared into the medal cabinet and let the present envelope him. He read the cards and silently paid respect to the fallen. Colleen left him. It seemed to her that Alfred should be left alone with his thoughts. He might share them with her, or he might not but she would not push him.

She perused the ribbons and medals on the wall. One was a New Zealand Memorial Cross, George VI, just like hers. It was awarded to the mother of a soldier lost in Tobruk. The purple ribbon had faded to mauve. Strange that it had not been stolen. She wandered around and from time to time cast a glance back at Alfred.

He hadn't expected that it would take such a toll on him. After all, didn't he respect the lives of the dead every Anzac day? Wasn't he, in full military dress, always present at not only the dawn service but the mid-morning service?

The palpitations came again when he recognised the American uniform. If he hadn't remained in the army for a few years after the war he may never have found out what had happened to her. The ANZUS alliance had seen him visit the American base in the Philippines for international manoeuvres. He couldn't help but ask around. He just had to know she was all right and if he could get word to her that he was alive, well, that's all he could hope for.

Sophie's husband had worn that uniform. He was a career soldier, not like Alfred, who had only clung on until something better came along. Alfred was due to return home the next day after having spent six weeks on manoeuvres. During that time he'd spoken to dozens of American soldiers who had New Zealand war brides. Or it would have been dozens if their friends hadn't mistaken Australian brides for New Zealanders. It was a long shot at best. He despaired that he would leave without finding her. Then a tall burly man named Willard sought him out. Heard he'd been asking round. Sorry to have left it so late but he'd just got back from the German base. His wife was a girl from New Zealand. Sophie she's called.

Alfred's heart leapt into his mouth. It had to be her. He couldn't get leave at this late stage and Willard promised to bring Sophie to the ship tomorrow to see him off. And so it happened. He waited on the dock for nearly an hour before she came, stomach full of butterflies. Silly. Someone else's wife. Nothing could

331

come of it. As soon as he saw her it was like they'd never been apart. He could see it unspoken in her eyes. They kissed chastely and he touched her tiny waist for a split second. She wore her hair fashionably bobbed and her cotton dress had coiffure French poodles around the bottom. Impossible to believe she was already a mother. Impossible to believe, she retorted joyfully, that he was not dead. He explained the misunderstanding and she apologised for it.

It was the quiet way in which she apologised that unsettled Alfred. Was she trying to tell him that she was sorry he hadn't made his life with her after all? Was she happy? Did she have regrets? He wanted to tell her he didn't blame her for leaving but he couldn't, not in front of Willard. The ship's horn sounded over the bay. Soldiers jostled them as they hurried to the ship. Willard grabbed Alfred's hand and shook it heartily, slapping his shoulder with the other. Suddenly there was no more time to say anything, not even to gaze upon Sophie's tender face. Alfred watched Willard take Sophie by the shoulders and steer her away from him. For years afterwards Sophie's mournful eyes pierced him as he recalled her looking back at him over her shoulder.

He hadn't heard Colleen's approach and he startled when he felt a soft touch on his elbow.

'Penny for them,' she said quietly.

Alfred cleared his throat gruffly and squared his shoulders. He suddenly felt quite tired and suggested they call it a day.

***

'Thank you for meeting with me Paul.' Sarah offered her hand to Paul.

'No trouble,' he replied. 'Pull up a seat.'

Sarah surveyed the room. Bing was asleep.

'Don't worry about him,' said Paul. 'He can sleep through anything.'

'I'm pleased to finally meet you,' Sarah began. 'I've heard lots about you. Sorry the circumstances couldn't be more pleasant.'

She settled on the hard chair and studied Paul. She liked what she saw. Although he wasn't displayed in the best light he was ruggedly good looking, hiding shy eyes beneath thick lashes, and she could tell from the firm handshake the conviction of the man.

'You may be aware,' Sarah continued, 'that Lana received a grant from the Tongariro Natural History Society to fund a conference trip to Iceland and to assist with research that she is carrying out on Mount Ruapehu. I feel responsible for the predicament she's now in.'

Paul frowned a question.

Sarah continued. 'You see when Lana came home after Yuri's death I asked her to stay. Just as a trial really. We've been friends since school. You'd already moved on by the time I started at school but Lana and I were inseparable. She took it hard, you leaving. We eventually went our separate ways but stayed in touch. Anyway, I'd hoped that Lana and I would just pick up where we left off and to a certain degree we have. But there's no denying that time changes us all. So if it wasn't for me...' She let the premise hang.

'Lana is capable of making her own decisions,' replied Paul.

'Society members are worried about her. Is she all right Paul? Is there anything we can do for her if she has to stay a few more days?'

'She's got a nasty burn on her calf,' Paul explained, 'but it's under control. She's not alone. Emma's stuck up there too.'

'So I understand.'

Paul looked over at Bing and Sarah followed his gaze.

'Lana amputated his arm in order to free him from under the hut,' he explained quietly.

'Oh my God,' exclaimed Sarah. 'How did she cope with that?' She watched Paul relax back on the pillow as he recalled what Sarah could only imagine.

'She's stronger than we give her credit for,' he finally said.

'So she's comfortable?' asked Sarah.

'For the time being,' Paul replied.

'Paul,' Sarah said. 'I've had discussions with a local volcanologist, Bain Conway. Do you know him?'

Paul grinned. 'Bain! Haven't seen him in a while.'

'He's on his way here now,' said Sarah. 'His assessment is that...' She flipped open her notebook. 'Here it is; that the mountain has gone through several eruptions styles from a wet Surtseyan one that cleared the vent to a hot gas subplinian Strombolian phase. The lake likely held ten million cubic metres of acidic water but as you know a large amount of that expelled as a lahar.'

'Yep. Good. Agree with that,' Paul concurred.

'He said eruptions could last weeks!'

'I know,' said Paul. 'That's why I wanted Lana to get on that chopper.'

'The type of eruption we are seeing now,' said Sarah. 'What can you tell me about them?'

'They are subalkali. That is, a basalt with silica,' he began enthusiastically. 'It's a function of tectonic plate boundary subduction in a shallow upper mantle environment. You will have witnessed high explosivity in the form of fire fountains. Unfortunately I couldn't witness the best of that while I was on the wrong side of the mountain. I got some glimpses of it though. The high explosivity is a function of the release of water which has come from the subducting plate and also from sea water.'

Sarah tried to concentrate. She'd asked the wrong question. She interrupted Paul. 'I'm thinking about Lana and the implications for her.'

'I'm afraid we have to cross our fingers that the mountain gives a window to send the chopper back,' said Paul.

'I don't mean to sound harsh but what about her research? How will the Tuwharetoa Glacier be affected by the eruptions?' asked Sarah.

'Last time this happened all the major glaciers survived. We need to be worried more about the effect of climate change on our glaciers than a little eruption,' Paul added. 'Our temperate climate means we could lose seventy five percent of our glaciers to the greenhouse effect by 2100. Lana is studying the lag effect of carbon dioxide in the atmosphere released last century and how that contributes to diminishing glacial areas. So, as far as Mount Ruapehu is concerned eruptions of this size are mere burps. And we can be thankful that it vents occasionally because a massive andesite eruption that covers half the North Island is not what we want.'

'Yeah. But what does it mean for Lana's research?' Sarah pushed the point.

'Effectively she's stuffed this season,' said Paul. 'So don't expect anything from her this year.'

'I see,' said Sarah. 'Well I won't put any pressure on her. I hope she gets off there soon and I hope she doesn't get gun shy.'

'Don't blame yourself,' said Paul. 'She's a big girl.'

Sarah began to take her leave but reconsidered. 'Look Paul,' she said. 'I know Lana. We talk. She's scared of being hurt. First Yuri and now you. Not that you mean to hurt her, she knows that. But she's with Alex now and like I said before, she never really got over you. But she's changed and so have you. Good Lord, I've changed! What I'm saying to you is that our relationships can never be what they were.' She let Paul absorb her words and this time she did take her leave.

'Before you go, can you do me a favour?' Paul asked catching her in time.

'Sure.'

'My phone. Can you charge it for me and get it back soon as?'

'No problem. My husband's got one the same.' Sarah pocketed Paul's phone and no sooner had she turned to leave there was a familiar voice from the door.

'Well, well, what have we here?'

'Gidday mate,' Paul grinned.

Bain stepped past Sarah to shake Paul's hand.

'Bain,' said Sarah. 'I've just been explaining to Paul how Lana fits in with us. She's still on the mountain you know.'

336

'Is she? Why?'

'Not enough room in the chopper,' Paul explained.

'Ah. So, it wasn't you I saw from the helicopter,' Bain confirmed.

'Was that you? Did you get it on film?' asked Paul.

Bain grinned. 'It's my footage they used on television.'

'How did ERLAWS work out?' Paul asked.

'Like a dream. No disasters, no incidents,' said Bain casually. Then he dropped his voice conspiratorially. 'Did you see the body?'

'At the lahar? Yeah.'

'How did he die?'

Paul looked across to Bing who was still dozing. Bain and Sarah followed his gaze.

'Not sure,' said Paul.

'Look, I'll leave you two to catch up,' said Sarah. 'I'll be back later with your phone Paul.'

Chapter Fourteen

Lana was fed up. The snow set in as a late spring flurry. It was beautiful in itself, silently gliding to earth and building up in little ridges, floating through the hole in the roof and partially melting before the next snowflake landed on it. Pity it was spoilt by the eruptions resuming. The magical feel of snow quickly gave way to a foreboding that she'd never get out of here.

There was no pattern to the explosions that Lana could determine. She flinched at every bombardment.

For the most part Emma was easy enough to cope with. She mostly dozed although she was constantly plugged into her ear phones so it was impossible to tell most of the time if she was awake or not. Lana knew she was trying to be a good patient. Evidently sitting still for long periods was something foreign to Emma. And if it weren't for the morphine they'd probably be at each other's throats by now, such was the norm of forced confinement.

Lana cranked up the fire then tidied the hut and swept the floor. The huge hole in the bunkroom window allowed freezing cold air to funnel underneath the door to the main room and draughts whistled through the cracks in the floor at the collapsed corner. Housekeeping was a way to occupy her but it didn't occupy her mind.

She tried to rationalise the range of emotions she had gone through in the last few days. She had been nervous with Paul at first and fretted that she might not live up to his expectations. Reuniting with him had unearthed memories that she didn't want. How she had hated those freckles. It was years since she'd thought about that – the hating of them. She'd devised a way of dealing with it though. If people looked at her she quickly spoke to them to deflect their focus from her face. She made them concentrate on what she said instead. After all, there was nowhere to hide; you had to talk to people. It didn't change her from being shy on the inside. Thankfully over the decades the freckles had faded and merged so that she always looked as though she had a healthy tan. She was obsessed with her looks, and she hated that weakness. She wondered what Paul saw in her, as she gently stroked her cheeks with her fingertips. Surely he couldn't help but notice the fine lines around her mouth and eyes. She sighed. What irony. Finally she had the skin she wished for when she first knew him, but now it came with ever diminishing elasticity.

In later years she'd learnt karate. There was no deep and meaningful reason for it. She'd turned up at the hall expecting to learn Scottish country dancing but had the wrong night. Coincidently she knew the instructor and he persuaded her to do the class since she was already there. And that was it, she was hooked. Scottish country dancing never did get the benefit of her two left feet. For ten years she diligently learnt karate and over that time it did become deep and meaningful. It gave her the confidence to trust herself. She became aware of her life force. The teachings of the masters down through generations was of supreme importance to her and she felt humbled to carry on the craft in its pure form. Karate didn't require beauty of the practitioner, for to Lana, karate itself was a beauty. But for all that she was relieved not to have a mirror in the hut.

She thought Paul was trying to recapture the past. He was in love with an idea, not a person. Their time together had come and gone and he should just accept that.

She brushed the ash into a pile, scooped it up and tossed it off the deck. Anyway, what the hell was she doing thinking that she had to please Paul? She was already in a perfectly happy relationship! Why Alex would this very minute be fretting. She kicked the door open as she entered the room and it crashed into the wall, bouncing on its twisted hinges.

'What the hell?' Emma yelled tugging her earphones out of her ears..

Lana slammed it shut behind her and jammed a log against it.

'What's rattled your cage?' asked Emma.

Lana thought better of starting a conversation. She was only mad at herself. She dragged the bench to the fire screeching it across the floor and sat down heavily. She picked up the poker and fiddled with the fire.

But Paul liked her – that much was clear. Or else in his mind he had moulded her to his idea of her. Well, she couldn't crawl inside his head to be sure. What she could do now that she had time to think was to work out her own feelings. She did like him. Being with him gave her butterflies and a dry mouth. She became excited by his touch and when he came too close she breathed in his masculine smell until her lungs nearly burst.

He had been frank with her and she could see that she may have led him on which wasn't fair because as she had told him more than once, she was in a perfectly stable relationship. She kept coming back to that. She had never explained to Paul that she loved Alex. Why not? She analysed the fact, tore it apart, and put it back together. Maybe she didn't actually love Alex. There! The thought materialised.

Alex was a pleasant habit. That was all. She certainly had deep feelings for him. But not madly, wildly in love feelings. In fact thinking back she couldn't recall ever having butterfly feelings for Alex.

She shut the firebox and idly dragged the hot poker across the concrete pad watching the charcoal leave a mark on it. The question of Alex. Whatever happens, Lana thought, she finally had faced the truth about Alex. And she would deal with it sooner rather than later. She felt a weight lift from her shoulders. It was like a fog had cleared inside her head. She would have to end it with Alex. It wouldn't be easy explaining to him that they had come to the end of the road but the thought occupied a singular place in her mind. He would be crushed, subdued like a whipped pup. He most likely would retreat with his tail between his legs. She imagined they'd still be friends though. They'd get over the sadness and move on.

She cast her mind back to the beginning of their relationship. It was always comfortable, like they had known each other for years and quickly settled into that familiar routine when nothing is a surprise. Alex called her his black widow. And he was right. She'd always referred to herself as a widow when she was with Alex. Not black exactly; she'd gone beyond that in the grieving process. But now she felt like a single woman. It felt right to shed the mantle of widow, at long last.

Lana stood up abruptly and let her hands walk down

her sides and around her waist. She wondered if she had lost any weight. Had her body started to consume its muscles to keep her alive? She conceded that she had probably lost a few fat reserves. That would accentuate the wrinkles. She screwed up her face at the thought.

'What now?' Emma groaned.

'Nothing.' Lana answered too quickly. 'Thought I heard something.'

'I didn't.'

Lana made tea, deliberately turning her back on Emma. But this time Emma forced her into conversation.

'I was thinking,' Emma continued, 'when this is over, maybe I'll write a book about it.'

'Could be a short book,' Lana replied.

'What do you mean?'

'Well you were unconscious on the mountain for I don't know how many hours and then for the rest of it you've been asleep.' Lana cringed as soon as she added the second remark. It wasn't strictly true and Emma would probably not let that pass.

'You cow,' Emma retorted. 'You're jealous! You're sick to your stomach that Paul likes me!'

'Paul likes everyone.' Lana whirled around to face her.

'Well he's given up on you, you cold fish. You weren't there with him,' she continued, 'out there thinking every minute might be your last. He kissed me Lana, good and hard.'

Lana didn't even feel the cup leave her hand. It careered through the air before she'd thought better of it and struck Emma on the shoulder.

'What are you doing you mad bitch?' Emma's scream

pierced the air. She rolled over and retrieved the cup heaving it back through the air at Lana. It ricocheted off the chimney and Lana ducked as she saw it coming.

'I don't have to listen to your lies!' Lana screamed. She grabbed her pack and strode outside. It wasn't so cold. She welcomed the chilly snow-filled air to cool her down. She was trembling. What's got into her? How had a seemingly innocuous remark by Emma been so affecting that it had led to that?

'I'm self destructing,' she whispered. She must be stir crazy. It hadn't taken long – five days. Pathetic she thought. Perhaps Emma was right. She must be jealous. Why else would she fly off the handle at the mention of Paul. So much for the years of self control she'd practiced at karate. She couldn't go back in. She wouldn't. She had to stop dwelling on herself, and Paul, and Alex. She leaned forward on the seat under the window and let her breath calm her.

Finally she pulled pen and paper out of her pack and rested it on her knees. She forced her brain to overpower her mind. She drew a sketch of a lahar and labelled its components. It was possibly post eruptive and once off the flank of the volcano it would have travelled faster than a normal stream flow. It pushed water ahead of it bulking up and entraining sediment. She drew a cross section to show slower heavier particles at the base of the flow and lighter smaller particles at the fastest top part of the flow.

The exercise occupied her for an hour as she captured every little detail to put into the diagram. So occupied had she been she failed to notice it had stopped snowing. Now the noise of a helicopter not much more than a speck in the sky gradually got louder as it neared. She threw down her work, dashed to the edge of the deck and waved her arms high above her head. The passenger waved back.

Lana ran back inside. 'Hurry,' she shouted. 'They're back for us.' She shoved her belongings in her pack and lifted the heavy rock that had fallen through the roof into her bag. Given that she didn't have to walk out with it she figured it was a luxury she deserved.

As she doused the fire the door kicked open and Maurice stood in the doorway.

'Hi Lana,' he said. 'All set to go?'

'Am I ever,' she exclaimed.

'Not a minute too soon,' Emma grumped from her bed.

Maurice made a quick inspection of Emma's leg. 'I'll get the pilot to help me lift you,' he told her then he picked up Lana's bag. 'Blimey Charlie, you got rocks in here?'

She grinned at him. When he left the silence was uncomfortable. Lana sullenly stuffed Emma's belongings in her pack. She felt Emma's eyes drilling her but Lana had calmed down on the deck and she was so buoyed by the rescue she wasn't mad with her for the moment. When Maurice returned with the pilot the two of them slung Emma between them and shuffled her to the waiting helicopter.

Then Lana climbed in and put the headphones on. It was her first time and she was determined to enjoy it.

***

Lana smiled inwardly from the moment the helicopter took off to the minute it landed. Even the acute pain in the back of her leg didn't dampen her joy. Although apprehension now sat in the top of her gut as she contemplated meeting Alex. If he wasn't waiting for her here then it would be tomorrow. She gazed out the window. She had a bird's eye view and was relieved she didn't have the world beneath her feet like the pilot did.

The mountain took on a new demeanour. She had felt a part of the mountain when she was on it and had assumed some control over her fate. But now, looking at it from the air it sat like the giant behemoth it was and suddenly Lana felt very small. The mountain was her master, as if it had ever been anything else. It was a restless heaving giant, not wholly understood and her heart ached for it.

As they approached the township the day was drawing to a close and the sun streamed its last watery rays onto the parched plateau. From the air Lana spotted Alex standing next to his red Mazda. A green pick-up drew alongside and Lana watched a woman get out and move straight towards Alex. It was Sarah. Alex waved at the helicopter and Lana slowly lifted a hand in acknowledgment. Her first contact with him for a week. She was glad to see Sarah; she'd be a rock for her now. She gulped down her nerves. How long had it been since she had ended a relationship? Not that she had done the endings. Well over twenty years.

Lana scanned the compound. Low weatherboard buildings made up the army base. It looked to be a functional no frills place. A few trees mostly on the roadsides, and lots of asphalt.

The chopper hovered over one spot for a spell then gently kissed the earth. It seemed an age before anyone in the front seats made a move to get out. She unbuckled her seatbelt and climbed down. Maurice passed her the pack grunting with the weight of it. He shook his head grinning.

By now two army medics had arrived and were working at extracting Emma. Lana shook Maurice's hand. 'Thanks so much Maurice. Thanks for everything.'

She ducked her head beneath the rotor blades and strode out to Alex. He ran to her and holding her arm led her to his car. Then he took her in his arms and hugged her, squeezing her tightly.

'Oh Lana, Lana,' he cried. 'Oh, I've been so worried,'

She stood limply inside his hug and suddenly, inexplicably began whimpering a tear or two, unable to hold back. His tenderness towards her scared her for what she was about to do to him. Inwardly she seethed indignation at Alex's timing. She wanted a bit more time to consider how to break the news gently.

Over her shoulder Lana winced at Sarah who lunged at the two of them with a bear hug.

'Thank God you're all right L,' Sarah gushed and it was just the term of endearment that made Lana smile. It conveyed the trust and dependence of a long term friendship. It also conveyed Sarah's no nonsense pragmatic approach to life.

'I'm pretty glad to be here too,' Lana sniffed a reply.

'It's okay now darling,' said Alex. 'You're safe now. Are you hurt?'

'Gash in my leg. It's all right – painkillers,'

'You should get it checked out Lana,' said Sarah,

'then you can come home with me. You both can.'

Alex looked taken aback. 'Oh no, thank you,' he said, 'but I've got us a motel.'

Lana switched her gaze from one to the other but it was Sarah who made the decision. 'Of course you must go with Alex.'

Alex shuffled Lana's pack to his car.

'I didn't expect a welcoming party,' said Lana. 'How long have you been here?'

'All day,' Alex replied. 'When I heard this morning that the first helicopter was leaving I drove up. And then of course you weren't on it. As the day progressed I got us a room hoping that you would still be rescued today.'

'Where's Paul?' asked Lana.

'He's fine,' Alex deflected a reply.

'But where is he?' Lana pushed.

'He's in the infirmary,' he replied. 'It's not far from here. I've been to see him.'

Lana's eyes grew like a rabbit in headlights. 'Have you?'

'Yes,' Alex replied. 'You were lucky Lana.'

'Ah, yes, I was,' she said cautiously. Was Alex being deliberately provoking, feigning goodwill or was he genuine in his comment?

'An old school chum?' Alex asked.

She nodded mutely.

'Let me take you to the motel,' Alex suggested. 'You're dead on your feet.'

'I'll let you two get on with it,' Sarah announced. 'I'll see you tomorrow L.' Then she added turning to Alex, 'look after her.'

Lana shook her head. 'Take me to Paul. Please?'

Alex hesitated.

'If you won't take me I'll get a ride with Emma. I need my leg looked at anyway.' She walked towards the van where the paramedics were strapping Emma in. Alex ran after her and put an arm around her.

'Come on Lana,' he said. 'We'll get your leg seen to and if there's time we'll call in to see Paul.

She shrugged him off but about turned and marched back to Alex's car. 'Paul will be worried about me. Please take me to him first and then I will get treatment.'

She opened the door of the Mazda and parked herself in the front seat leaving her pack where it lay. She flicked the rear vision mirror towards her and inspected the image, wiping her eyes dry. She watched Alex struggle with the ridicuously heavy pack and dump it into the boot. She looked straight ahead as Alex sat alongside her and started the car. He readjusted the rear vision mirror and buckled up. Then he sat idling the engine until Lana realised that he was waiting for her to put her seatbelt on. Only when she clicked the belt into its receptacle did he move off.

'Thank you,' Lana said smiling softly at him. Alex patted her thigh with his left hand and gave her a quick closed smile. He left his hand there and after a time Lana felt obliged to place her hand over it.

Alex followed the ambulance to the medic unit. The day was drawing to a close and the yellow sodium street lights had just flicked on. While the ambulance delivered Emma to the back entrance Alex pulled in to the front of the old weatherboard building. Lights were on inside.

He led Lana up the concrete ramp through both sets of double doors to reception. The same young woman was busy at a filing cabinet behind an enormous desk.

'Hello,' said Alex. 'This is Lana Marshall, just Heli-vacced off Mount Ruapehu. She needs medical attention for a gash to the leg.'

'No,' Lana intervened. 'I've come to see Paul Harrington, Dr Paul Harrington,' she added.

She felt Alex glare hot pokers through her but she maintained calm as she smiled at the woman.

'Oh, very good. Well done Miss Marshall,' the woman said efficiently. 'Go on through. You know the way sir.'

Lana followed Alex along the corridor. Suddenly the pain in her lower leg manifested. She hadn't really noticed it before, not with every step anyway. She favoured the leg slightly. Their footsteps barely registered on the thin carpet as they walked along. They stopped suddenly at an open door. Alex did a double check that he had got the right room and cautiously entered.

Paul was dozing but sitting more or less upright and Bing was much the same. Paul opened his eyes and grinned boldly upon seeing Lana. She beamed in return but was careful to measure her excitement in deference to Alex. Nevertheless, she strode to his side and kissed him chastely on the cheek.

'Hello angel,' said Paul. 'Good to see you.'

'How are you?' she asked screwing her face into a wince at his term of endearment.

'Oh, I'm just fine. Only here because I've got nowhere to go, what with my vehicle up the mountain,' he explained.

'Mine and yours!' Lana laughed with him. 'I believe

you've met Alex.' She stepped back to allow Alex into the conversation.

Paul nodded. 'Alex.'

Alex stepped forward and offered his hand. 'I didn't thank you for looking after my little girl,' he said.

Lana bristled. Paul detected Lana's cringe and his eyes locked with hers to share a secret smile. He knew she was embarrassed and that Alex's innocent comment marked her as his chattel, his lover – not Paul's.

'If there is anything I can do to make your stay here more comfortable,' said Alex, 'just let me know. You have my card.'

Lana expressed surprise and she looked at Paul questioningly.

'Oh yes,' Paul said confidently, 'we've had a pleasant morning discussing your welfare sweetheart. Have you had your leg seen to?'

'She insisted upon seeing you first,' Alex cut in testily.

Paul smiled. 'Quite right too.'

Alex put an arm around Lana's shoulder. 'Come on Lana. Let's find a doctor. Then you can have a hot shower and dinner.'

Lana wished Paul hadn't said sweetheart. He was trying to wind Alex up and she knew it. And what's more, he had succeeded.

'Lana,' said Paul. 'Do as Alex says. Don't worry about me.'

He had dismissed her and he was right to do so. Hadn't he promised not to pursue her? That was what she had insisted after all. She suddenly felt retched. She would finish with Alex tonight and there would be no

Paul either. Still, she owed Alex the right to take care of his girl, just for now. Turning her back to Alex she took her leave of Paul and gave his thigh a gentle squeeze as she kissed his cheek. It conveyed everything that was in her heart and it was contrary to everything she had said to him.

***

Lana stood under the delicious hot spray of water and lathered soap all over her body. The water was as hot as she could stand it and she lifted her face to the stinging jets. It streamed over her face and hair, and pricked at the skin of her shoulders, back and buttocks until she glowed red. She scrubbed so hard her skin tingled and the more she rubbed it to soothe it the more she needed to rub it. She delayed getting out of the shower as much as from the pleasure of being in it as much as the dread of confronting Alex.

After leaving Paul they had sought medical advice for her. The gash was in her calf and treated as a burn. They told her she was lucky it hadn't penetrated the muscle, although the area under attack had singed badly and cauterised. Unfortunately she could expect it to blister and it was imperative she keep it sterile. By the time she'd finally let Alex take her to the medics the pain relief had virtually worn off. 'Don't give me anything too strong,' she had protested. 'Nonsense,' they had dismissed her and prescribed a course of anti-biotics and enough painkillers to ensure she didn't wake up in the night. She realised now that she'd been running on adrenalin for too long. That alone had kept most of the pain at bay, since she'd doled out the drugs to the others, short changing herself.

Reluctantly she turned off the faucet and stepped out of the shower into the small steamy bathroom. She towelled herself dry and pulled on her jeans and pink V-necked skivvy. She threw a dress scarf around her neck and fingered her wet dark hair into shape.

Alex had set the small table for dinner and on it was a chilled glass of chardonnay. She couldn't deny that it felt good to be looked after. It was a relief to be out of the constant dust and draughts, the temperature extremes and the gloom of the hut. Even now she pictured the yellow plastic window and wondered whether it was wildly sucking in and out. She supposed it was. Alex busied himself in the small galley kitchen clattering pots and clinking china.

Lana lifted the glass to her lips savouring the floral bouquet before she drank then carried it with her to the couch where she sank languidly into its deep folds.

'You look lovely Lana,' said Alex as he crossed the room and sat down next to her cradling his own wine.

Lana smiled sadly and gazed at the floor in front of her.

'Penny for them,' said Alex.

'Sorry,' she said. 'Miles away.'

Alex put an arm around her shoulder and Lana stiffened.

'It's been traumatic for you, hasn't it?' he asked. 'You amputated that man's arm.'

'I had to do it. He would have died.' She was defensive. 'We were a team up there you know. I didn't act alone. Emma told me what to do.'

She continued to stare at the floor, unblinking. A heavy silence ensued and finally Alex broke it.

'Lana. Lana, you and I,' he began, 'that is, we make a nice couple don't you agree?'

She turned to face him. His eyes implored her to agree with him but when she said nothing he dug into his shirt pocket and pulled out a small ring box. Lana's heart missed a beat as he offered the box to her.

'Lana, these last few days I've been frantic with worry,' he said. 'I came to realise that I'm nothing without you. I couldn't bear it, not knowing if you were dead or alive. We should be together. Every day, not three days a week. Marry me Lana.'

'Alex,' Lana gasped. 'I didn't guess.' She felt the blood drain from her face. I didn't know you felt like that.'

'I didn't know either, really, until I thought I might not see you again,' he replied. 'Then I knew.'

'Knew you wanted to marry me? Or knew that you loved me?' she asked.

'Both of course,' Alex replied.

'No Alex. Not of course. You have to love me first. You have to say it first. You didn't say it first.'

'Do you love me Lana?'

'I thought I did. I care deeply for you. But, in love? I don't think I've ever been in love with you. And if you're honest you'll agree that you only want me to marry you so you don't lose me. That's not the same as marrying me for me. Do you see?'

'Cripes Lana. You're twisting this all out of shape,' Alex cried.

'I've had a lot of time on my own to think. To think

about me. Alex, it's about me. I don't want you to think it's anything you've done, or haven't done. It's me that's changed,' she explained.

She held the box in her hand.

'You've chosen a ring for me,' she said sadly. She knew what an undertaking that must have been. Once Alex decided to go through with it his deliberations and research for the appropriate ring for her would be been extreme. She slowly opened the lid. A glistening solitaire diamond on a gold band sat squarely in the middle of the plush velvet cushion.

'Oh Alex,' she whispered. 'You shouldn't have.'

'Marry me Lana,' he said.

'I can't. I can't,' she groaned. 'I'm so sorry Alex. I just can't.'

She felt his pain. He retrenched and she almost put a hand out to comfort him.

'Is it him?' he asked.

'I had a lot of time to think on the mountain,' she reiterated. 'When I met you I was still grieving for Yuri. My whole world changed when he died and I continued to change it making my own decisions. I was ready to cope with the sort of loving you provided. We fell into an easy no strings relationship. I never felt it was going anywhere and that was fine. I didn't need it to or want it to. I wasn't ready to replace my Yuri.'

'And now?' asked Alex.

'Although I care deeply for you Alex I've never been head over heels madly in love with you. And I assumed you felt the same. You seemed comfortable in your freedom after your divorce. I think we have been two people perfectly suited to each other in a moment in time. But not for all time.'

She fidgeted with the box, turning it in her hand, opening and shutting the lid.

'But it is *him*, isn't it?' Alex pushed, determined that there would be a reason other than his own failings for not holding onto Lana.

'Not precisely,' she replied. 'But I can't deny that meeting him again has forced me to assess my feelings for you. I've never been unhappy with you. But I've never had butterflies in my stomach either.' She smiled apologetically. 'Sadly,' she added.

'And Paul gives you butterflies,' Alex spat bitterly. 'Obviously.'

'Nothing happened. I haven't betrayed you,' she averted her reply.

'But you have feelings for him don't you?' he pressed. 'And as soon as you leave me you'll be off with him.'

'I don't know,' Lana replied. 'He was special once but that was a long time ago. We've been through a lot up there that's all. You bond with people in ways you don't imagine.'

'You're not facing the same truth that I see Lana,' Alex spat. 'I've just seen the two of you together. And remember, you neglected to tell me about him. You always tell me who you go away with but this time you didn't. Why was that I wonder?'

'I wasn't being deceitful,' said Lana. 'I didn't want you to get jealous about nothing. Nothing was ever going to happen and it didn't. I swear.'

Alex half laughed and shook his head. 'I knew you were protecting me from myself. I said to myself, she doesn't want me to be jealous of him so she didn't tell me about him. I invented that lie to kid myself, to ignore the truth.'

Lana placed a hand on his. 'I'm so sorry. Please, believe me.'

Alex reclaimed his hand then rubbed his tortured face.

'I think I do believe you Lana because you see the world through the eyes of a sugar plum fairy. It's all lovely in your world isn't it? Can you really be so stupid to believe that Paul doesn't want you for himself? I saw you. And you want to be with him.'

'Alex,' she replied. 'I'm saying that our time has come. We've reached the end of the road.'

'But Lana,' Alex wined. 'The ring?'

'Take it back,' she said. 'I'm sorry.'

'Please. Darling. Is there no other way?'

'You know there isn't,' she snapped. 'And I just want to make one thing clear. I'm not anyone's little girl. I make my own decisions.'

'Where did that come from?' Alex asked.

'Never mind,' she retorted. 'Forget it.'

'Well sit down then,' said Alex. 'I'm not getting into a slanging match, although it seems like a good time to spell out your faults.'

'What faults?'

'Lana, it doesn't matter now does it? I was prepared to marry you warts and all but it just doesn't matter now,' he replied. 'Apparently.'

'What? Prepared to marry me! How gracious of you. Warts and all? Did you feel sorry for me?' she cried. 'Is that it? How dare you Alex!'

'See? Look how you twist what I say,' he retorted and

356

with that slammed the ring box on the table.

'I'll get another room,' she declared and left slamming the door behind her.

***

Lana returned to the motel unit to find the door locked. *Must have self-locked after me she thought.* She tapped lightly on the glass. No reply. She tried the handle again.

'Alex,' she called softly. Still no reply. She looked about her sure that he must have nipped out for something though she could not imagine what. No sign of him outside. She tried the handle again and rattled it trying to rouse him.

'Alex,' she called more urgently. 'Open up will you?'

There was silence from within. The curtains were drawn but Lana noticed a movement behind them. She stepped toward the window and tapped.

'Alex,' she cried. 'What are you doing?' She suddenly realised that he was ignoring her. 'Alex, let me in. Let me in,' she whispered hoarsely to the curtained window. Nothing.

She stood back from the unit uncertain what to do. She wasn't prepared for a confrontation and certainly hadn't expected this irrational behaviour from him. In a way it was a delightful discovery that she didn't actually know everything about him. She was secretly thrilled that he had a bit of spark. But only for a short time. She sat on the bonnet of Alex's Mazda with her feet resting on the front bumper and wrapped her hands around her forearms, rubbing them against the chill. She wore only socks on her feet and she could feel the cool from the metal seep into her soles.

There were no other units available and the proprietors had exhausted all avenues of alternative accommodation for her. The township was crawling with television and print media covering the lahar and the volcanic eruptions. There was simply no alternative but to stay the night with Alex.

She slipped off the bonnet and tried the door again.

'Alex. There's nowhere else for me to go,' she appealed to him. 'Do you hear me?'

'I hear you,' he answered.

'Thank you. So unlock this door for me,' she pleaded.

'Why should I?' he asked.

'What?' Lana thought she had misheard.

'You want rid of me Lana, so go.' There was a tone in his voice Lana had never heard before. He spat out the words as if he despised her. Like a wounded cat hissing.

'I've got nowhere to go,' she snapped.

'Should have thought of that before you walked out.'

'Are you serious Alex? 'What's got into you?'

'Ask yourself Lana,' he retorted.

'Alex.' Lana stiffened and lowered her voice to a low murmur. She spoke firmly with her forehead against the door. Alex was directly behind it. 'Alex, this is ridiculous. Open this door. Let me in. At least let me ring for Sarah.'

'No Lana. Go away,' he answered.

'I can't change how I feel,' she said. 'This is all very immature,' she said.

'How can you leave me now? Why now? The ring? Us?'

'There is no good time to leave,' she said. 'I don't want to hurt you but that's how it goes. I'm hurting doing this to you. Don't you see?'

'No.'

'For goodness sake,' she appealed. 'I've got nowhere else to go tonight. I have to sleep somewhere.'

'Go to him,' Alex spat. 'Lover boy.'

'Don't you bring him into this. It's not about him.'

'Seems like it to me.'

'Well it isn't. It's about me. And you,' she added.

'Don't deny it Lana. And him. Mr secret.'

'I'm not standing on this doorstep having a conversation about my relationship with you or my relationship with him. Now open this door or,' she faltered.

A muffled sound echoed through the door. Alex had taken a step back. Suddenly the curtain at the window flickered revealing the warm amber light of the room. He opened the window a few inches.

'I'm not letting you in Lana. Unless you say you're not serious. You weren't thinking straight. You're not leaving,' he said calmly.

'I've never seen you act like this,' said Lana. 'You're upset. Just let me in so I can get my clothes.'

She was frightened. She wasn't convinced now that she wanted to spend the night with him. The Alex she knew was never irrational. Measured calm, consideration and reasoning were the qualities she had always associated with him. Is this what she had missed on the nights she didn't share his bed? This was a green eyed monster talking. Not Alex at all. She briefly wondered how she would react in a similar situation.

'Here,' he spat.

Clothes came flying out the window onto the asphalt. She retrieved them and dumped them onto the bonnet of his car. Night was falling and the day had disappeared but it was the starless middle time, where the night was not yet so settled that it displayed its glittering jewels.

She was at once indignant and determined, but fragile and scared. She felt the familiar ball in her stomach begin to heave and the choke of her chest as she tried to suppress upwelling tears. Sobbing through heavy indigo eyes she slid into her thick jacket and tied her feet into her runners.

Alex shut the window with a slam and roughly pulled the curtain back into place. Now it was over. It really was over. Alex had made it over. If ever she imagined she might have changed her mind it was done now. Alex had shut the door and shown her a side of him he had never revealed before.

Her thoughts were disturbed by the noise of the motel door being wrenched open. Out flew her bag far out onto the hard asphalt. She heard the door slam back into its timber jamb and watched in slow motion the glass in the central pane shatter onto the step. Several motel doors opened, their occupants peering at the source of the shattered glass.

Lana stared at the door, not daring to move, unwillingly to become part of the scene. She waited. There was no movement behind the door, no sound. The lady next door stood timidly on her front step, peering at Alex's door, trying not to make her curiosity obvious. She appealed to Lana with questioning eyes.

'Are you all right?' asked the woman.

Lana stepped back from the vehicle to reveal herself.

'Yes thanks,' Lana replied. 'I'm fine.'

The kindly looking woman stepped towards her and Lana quickly wiped tears from her eyes with the back of her hand.

'May I use your phone?' Lana blurted out. She spontaneously blurted out tears and they fell quickly, hot and salty down her face and into the corners of her mouth. She bit her lips in an effort to trick the contorted mouth muscles out of their silent scream. Her shoulders racked with great heaving sobs and she threw her clothes to her face.

'Oh dear,' said the woman who had introduced herself as Colleen. 'Oh dear, dear. Come on love.' Colleen put an arm around Lana's shoulders and let her cry.

'Sorry,' Lana heaved through body racking sobs. 'I'm so sorry.'

'Now, now. It's all right,' soothed Colleen. 'You come with me and I'll make you a nice cup of tea.'

She gently steered Lana towards her unit and noticed a flicker of the curtain at Alex's window.

***

Lana sat quietly at the small Formica table trying to shrug off her tears while Colleen prepared a pot of tea. Alfred cleared away the dinner plates.

'I'm sorry to be a nuisance,' Lana began. 'If I could just use your phone I can get a friend to collect me.'

'You're not a nuisance,' Colleen replied. 'Get that tea down you first then your friend might be able to understand you without your blubbing.'

Lana tried to engage in conversation but every time she opened her mouth nothing happened.

'Don't rush.' Colleen smiled sadly at Lana. 'You take your time love.'

Colleen set three cups of tea and a saucer of chocolate biscuits in the centre of the table. Alfred took his tea into the lounge clattering the cup on the plate as he shuffled. Lana took her cup and held it in both hands warming them and taking comfort from it. She managed a false smile. It was the very least she could do, show gratitude to this angel of a woman.

'He wouldn't let me back in,' Lana explained haltingly.

'I could see that,' Colleen replied.

'I tried to find somewhere else to stay, but there isn't anywhere. The whole township is full,' Lana continued. 'My friend is a half hour drive away. She met me off the helicopter today.'

'Are you sure you want to trouble her?'

'Well…'

'You can stay here for the night if you want to.' Colleen nodded at Alfred. 'He's in his own room next door, so there's plenty of room.'

'That's very kind, but…'

'See how you feel after that tea.' Colleen took a sip of her own.

'I, I upset him. I've left him,' Lana quietly volunteered.

'Sweetheart if that how he reacts then you don't need him,' Colleen reasoned. 'The man you thought he was just got trampled by the mean spirited man he really is.

362

Although I'm sorry to have an opinion and it's none of my business but you have to respect yourself. I'm sure you saw a lot of love in him and it's upset you to see him like this. Is that right?'

Lana nodded. 'He's not mean spirited.' It was an affront on her, an attack on her judgement.

'Oh dear,' Colleen began. 'I'm sorry. I had no right to say that. I just wanted to say that you mustn't blame yourself for the way he acts.'

'I might have done the same in similar circumstances,' said Lana.

'Lana,' said Colleen. 'I feel as though I should know you. But I don't do I?'

Lana was pleased at the sudden change of subject. She shook her head.

'No, I haven't met you before,' she said. 'I've been on Mount Ruapehu for the last five days. We got trapped and helicoptered out today.'

'Ah,' exclaimed Colleen. 'That's it then. Your picture has been in the paper and on the television news.'

'Oh has it?' Lana asked.

'There was a man with you. Is he okay?' Colleen asked.

Lana dropped her eyes at the mention of Paul.

'He's got fractured ribs and he had a sprained ankle,' Lana explained. 'He's spending the night at the army base.' She smiled. 'What about you? What brings you here?'

'Did you hear of the medals theft?' asked Colleen.

'No.' Lana shook her head.

'A few medals were stolen from the museum, probably while you were on the mountain. Anyway,'

Colleen explained, 'one of them belonged to my family. I donated it to the museum on a long term loan when my mother handed it down to me.'

'What sort of medal?' asked Lana.

'It's called the New Zealand Memorial Cross. It was given to my grandmother for the loss of her son Harold at Monte Cassino in 1944,' said Colleen.

'So you came up here to see where it was stolen from?' asked Lana.

This time Alfred spoke. 'And to reconnect with the past.'

Colleen shot a look of surprise at him. He'd been uncharacteristically sombre all afternoon. Now she thought she understood.

Lana nodded, not focussed on Alfred at all. 'Yes, the past. It's always with us isn't it?'

Alfred coughed to clear his throat. That was all. Nothing else. He sipped his tea. Colleen pushed the biscuits towards Lana.

'Alfred was the brave young man who tried to save my Uncle Harry. I thought it would be nice for him to accompany me. And nice for me I hasten to add.'

'I really should ring Sarah,' said Lana.

'Nonsense. There are two beds here.' Colleen spoke with finality. Her tone said that she knew best and she would not be argued with. Lana made a small protestation, an obligatory one, for she was very comfortable with Colleen and was very happy to stay.

'I don't want to put you out,' she said. 'I'll split the cost of course.'

'Whatever makes you happy,' said Colleen. 'Now, I'll make you some dinner.

Chapter Fifteen

Paul was right. He confirmed it when he saw them together. Even if Lana didn't know it he knew it. She needs time to see that she's not serious about Alex. He'd give her that, but how much? That was something he couldn't be sure of but he had promised to leave her alone and so he would. If Lana wanted Alex over him then that's what Lana shall have. How did the saying go? If you love something set it free and if it returns then it's meant to be? But goodness knows, he had made his position clear enough. It was up to her now.

She was a long way from the shy girl he first knew and the more time he spent with her the more he wanted to be with her. She was wrong. He could love her again. And she could love him too, if she would open her heart. Just because they'd spent all these years apart didn't mean they'd become different people. Of course not. Lana had a reticent streak, he could see that; a remnant of shyness never quite shed. And she was kind. That trait hadn't disappeared. And she was still uncomfortable analysing her emotions. After her younger brother had drowned when she was fourteen Lana withdrew into herself. There wasn't counselling for kids in those days. Paul had only just appeared on the scene and everyone else in the school knew about the accident. But even when she and Paul became close she couldn't talk about it. All these years later he could see the barrier she put up. He sighed. God, she made him feel sixteen again, surely she felt the same.

He dwelt on the touch of her hand on his thigh. Had she changed her mind about him? Had he imagined it?

Had she squeezed his thigh or not? If he shut his eyes he could conjure up the smell of her, the vision of her milky white skin so close to his. He was aware of a stirring beneath the sheets. He could think of nothing but Lana. But she was probably right this minute making love to Alex and any thought of Paul would not even enter her head.

A trolley clattered along the corridor and stopped, shaking him out of his reverie. Paul was glad of the distraction as an orderly delivered their meals first to Bing and then to Paul. After devouring the roast lamb he pushed his plate aside, stepped out of bed and pulled a chair up alongside Bing. He used Bing's knife and fork to cut some meat for him.

'Thanks mate,' said Bing.

'No sweat,' replied Paul. 'Dunno what they're thinking giving you that to eat. Idiots.'

With his left arm Bing skewered bite-sized pieces of meat and vegetables onto his fork. He had slept a lot since his rescue thanks to the pain killers and had built up a fierce hunger.

'What was your lady doing with that bloke?' Bing asked Paul between mouthfuls.

'She never was my lady,' Paul explained. 'Always was his.'

'Could have fooled me. Didn't look it today neither. She wants you mate. Any fool can see that,' Bing scoffed.

'She can't,' Paul replied.

'Umph,' huffed Bing. 'Then she's not as clever as I thought. Didn't have the chance to thank you mate. For freeing me and looking after me before that too.'

'Don't mention it.' Paul rose and patted Bing on the shoulder.

He lay back on his bed and let his mind wander to the events of the past few days. Lana had run hot and cold, sometimes leading him on and sometimes turning him off. It seemed like she didn't trust her own feelings towards him. She had visibly relaxed when he agreed to stop pursuing her. Ironically, that's when she seemed to tease him, flirt with him almost. She didn't appear to know she was torturing him more than before.

And coming to see him with that fastidious accountant in tow. Did she have to bring him! And Alex playing the big man thanking him for looking after Lana. Indeed! What he didn't know! But for all that, it was Alex Lana was with tonight, not him, and he felt the hungry snake of jealousy curl into his gut.

***

Paul stirred in the saffron dawn. He could hear a hushed conversation in the room but he lay still with his back partially to Bing and let the voices wash over him.

He was surprised to see Emma in the bed alongside. But she was asleep, her chest heaving a steady rhythm.

'Bing,' someone whispered. 'Is it safe to talk?'

'How are you Bing?' asked the second voice. He recognised it as the one with glasses.

'How do you think?'

'Geez, what happened to you?'

There was a pause, then he heard Bing explain. Grunting more than whispering. 'Corner of the hut got hit with volcanic boulder. Collapsed. I was underneath.

Crawled under to get the medals and it collapsed further. Arm got trapped.'

Paul could hear one of the men suck in breath.

'Who cut you out?'

'The girl.'

'Do they know why you were there?' The voice was steady, in control. The shorter one, of course.

'No. Told them I heard a possum. They bought it.'

'You sure?'

'Yeah. It's sweet. They believed me.'

'Where are the medals now?'

'Still under the hut.'

'What about the cross?'

'That damn cross.'

'Keep your voice down!' The shorter one giving orders still.

'Well you didn't have to get so het up about it. Wasn't worth killing over. Don't you see the irony? So where is it?' The man with glasses; the voice of reason.

'I guess it's on Ant. Isn't that bleedin' obvious?'

'Where's Ant now?'

'Dunno. Guess he's still there.'

'Could have been swept away by the lahar.'

'Didn't the scientists drag him out of the way?'

'So they said.'

'That knife wound Joe. That will seal it. We're stuffed.'

'Why the hell didn't you search him at the time?'

'Geez, I was already stabbed and bleeding like a stuffed pig and he had practically fallen into the lahar. Was I supposed to drown as well?'

'Why didn't you have a look before you scarpered?

We need to retrieve them. All of them.'

Paul heard a shuffle sound, like a bag being rifled through.

'What are you doing?' whispered Bing.

'Just making sure we're still on the same side,' Joe murmured. The bedside cabinet door clicked shut. The drawer slid open and closed.

'You bastard.' Bing again. 'Here.' Paul heard the bedclothes fly back. 'Satisfied?'

'Roll over.'

'Geez Joe,' whispered the one with glasses.

'I said roll over.'

'Ah,' Bing groaned. 'Satisfied?'

'Had to be sure. You understand.' It was Joe. His voice betrayed no emotion.

'It's dangerous up there,' Bing said.

'If the hut's demolished they'll be found and if Ant's got the cross then it will be found when they realise there's something worth looking for.'

'No one can link us though Joe.'

'What about him?'

Paul could feel three pairs of eyes boring into his back. He faked a soft snore and welded his eyes tight shut.

'He can.'

'No he can't. Not with the medals. He can with the girl though. And that was an accident. Understand? Her word against ours. I wish you'd brought the medals back Bing. We'll have to go back. These eruptions can't last much longer.' There was menace in his voice. Surely he didn't intend Bing to go with them?

Paul kept breathing systematically and audibly. He

heard the conversation pause. A chair scraped and footsteps approached his bedside. Then the footsteps receded.

'It's a battlefield up there. Don't be so hasty.'

Paul was getting stiff but he didn't want to draw attention to himself. But a pang in his ribs forced his hand. He stirred. The conversation halted again as he relaxed onto his back and opened his eyes. The visitors excused themselves quickly barely engaging eye contact with him. Paul silently queried Bing but the man gave nothing away. Paul left it at that.

***

Lana woke to the smell of toast and the pale white light of pre-dawn. She inhaled the scent of crisp cotton sheets and snuggled down a little further under the covers. She was surprised she had slept at all given her raging emotions. Then she remembered. Colleen. The medal. She dragged herself out of bed and pulled on her clothes.

'Morning,' said Colleen. 'Tea's in the pot.'

Colleen put a plate of toast on the table and Lana pulled up a chair. Her stomach was in knots. She was fizzing to get away. It had taken a while to work it out, what with everything whirring through her head. She'd made a phone call to Sarah telling her not to visit today after all. Sarah was desperately disappointed but didn't pressure her to change her mind and allowed Lana the time to work things out with Alex. Lana hated to lie to her but she told herself it was only a little white fib which Sarah would understand.

If only Lana had known about the robbery then certain events wouldn't have been so enigmatic. She was annoyed at her misjudgement of the situation. God, it surely wasn't that difficult to see! Her distraction had been Paul. And Emma. She'd had plenty of time to retrieve Bing's package but no, she could only think of herself then she had to pick a fight and let things get blown out of proportion. And that left no option now but to go back.

'I'll be off after breakfast Colleen,' she said. 'Thanks for your help.'

'Oh.' Colleen was surprised.

'I have unfinished business,' Lana explained somewhat lamely. She quickly downed a cup of tea and a piece of buttered toast then picked up her bag to leave. As she opened the front door the newspaper on the step caught her eye.

'Oh,' said Lana bending to retrieve it.

She handed it to Colleen and peered over to Alex's front step. No newspaper. And the curtains were drawn back. Colleen hovered inside the front door.

'Where will you go?' she asked Lana.

'To get my car back,' she lied. 'I need to borrow Alex's car.' She set her bag next to the driver's door and threw herself flat on the ground beneath the engine bay. She felt along the metal shelf. There was nothing there. She shimmied to the other side and repeated the exercise. Nothing. It had to be here, she thought. Alex would never risk locking himself out of his car. She strained to gain a look inside the engine bay but the light was unforgiving. She flopped back onto the concrete. She had to get a move on. Alex could catch her at any

371

moment. She inched her fingers along the chassis again, and there it was; a small metal box with the spare key inside.

She flung her bag in the back and as she whispered goodbye to Colleen she heard the shrill ring of Alex's telephone. By the time Alex crossed the room to answer it Lana had gunned the car out of the motel block.

**

Alex rushed out of the bathroom ruddy and glistening from the shower with steam billowing out behind him as he rushed to pick up the phone.

'Alex! It's Paul. Is Lana there?'

'No.' He listened to the pause at the other end. He could tell his abruptness had surprised Paul. He was about to make up some lie, that she'd gone to get bread for breakfast or something. Anything that might delay admitting to the world the inevitable, when he glanced outside. 'Hang on,' he said. He strode over to the window. His car wasn't there. He threw open the door and stood on the step naked and wet grasping the phone. His car was nowhere to be seen.

'She's gone!' he cried.

'Where?' asked Paul.

'I don't know,'

'What do you mean?'

Alex clenched his teeth and calmed his voice to a monotone. 'I mean she stole my car and I don't know where she's gone.'

He could hear Paul digesting the information.

'I think she could be in danger,' Paul finally replied.

'She's gone back up the mountain.'

'Shit,' Alex said as he heard Paul click off.

***

'Mind if I keep this for the day?' Paul asked Emma as he snapped the phone shut. She took it with a twist of her torso giving Paul a flash of white breast. She made no attempt to straighten her gown. She glanced at the battery life. 'I suppose so. Why so worried?' she asked.

'Lana's gone,' he replied.

'Of course she has,' said Emma, 'into the loving arms of her chartered accountant.' She looked smug. And sexy. And she knew it. She patted her hand on the bed that Paul should sit. He shook his head.

'No, she's gone.'

'Where?'

Paul looked across to where Bing lay sleeping. Or pretending to sleep. 'Don't know.'

'There's nothing you can do Paul,' Emma murmured. 'Why don't you help me get better?' She rubbed his thigh.

'Emma.' Paul dropped his voice to a low murmur. 'You're a lovely girl, you really are.'

'But.' She cut him off.

'But you're not the girl for me. I'm sorry.'

She grabbed his hand faster than he knew what was happening and the next he felt was her nipple hardening in his palm. He closed his eyes as he savoured the warm plumpness for just a moment. He felt her relax her grip and he moved his hand over her breasts, before pulling back and wiping his hand on his sleeve.

373

'Sure?' Emma whimpered.

Paul turned his back on her. She had stirred him and he wasn't going to give her the satisfaction of seeing it.

'Looks like I've got a ride home,' Paul announced with mock cheerfulness. He swapped his hospital gown for cotton trousers and a long sleeved thermal top, neither of which were clean.

'I appreciate your help up there,' said Bing through a mouthful of muesli.

'Okay mate. Best of luck with the arm. I'm sorry for it,' said Paul.

He slung his pack over one shoulder and with a half turn to Emma told her to look after herself then walked out. He padded down the carpeted hall with only a hint of a limp to reception where a middle-aged woman made him sign discharge papers. He stepped out into the morning chill and gazed up at the mountain. A dirty yellow haze hung around the top but the sky was blue around it, deepening in colour further from the volcano. Thick white clouds occupied the distant sky.

He cursed at the madness of his anticipated journey although he secretly admired Lana's courage. He walked through the compound which had street names for New Zealand battles fought on foreign soils and out to the state highway. He thumbed a lift north in a long haul articulated truck. After convincing the driver that he was not the guy in the paper who was on the mountain at the time of the lahar and subsequent eruptions they settled into an uneasy silence. After twenty minutes the truck driver eased the rig to a halt at the track to the ski field on the east side of the mountain.

'There's a volcano alert on the mountain mate,' the

driver warned. 'You're taking your chances.'

'Thanks a lot,' said Paul stepping down from the cab. The stretch caught his ribs and a thin sliver of pain shot through his back. 'I'll be careful.' The driver jerked the truck into gear but Paul didn't give a second glance as it threaded into the north bound traffic.

Chapter Sixteen

Lana constantly checked the rear view mirror. Not that she expected to see Alex hot on her heels. She knew she shouldn't have taken his car but it was her only option. It was surprisingly easy and she couldn't deny a small thrill at the accomplishment.

She didn't think she could face him now. She made a mental checklist of clothes she had at his house. How long should she wait to collect them? She shivered. It was new territory, breaking up like this.

He would be furious finding his car gone. At least he didn't know she was taking it up the mountain. She wasn't sure how far she'd get for the track would be thick with ash. She pictured the high gloss paintwork pockmarked with a film of acidic debris. No, Alex would not at all be pleased with her.

But of course he wasn't following. Eventually the ski field road appeared out of the desert landscape on her left. The morning's passing traffic had swept ash from the adjacent vegetation so that the road was now skirted with the purple of heather and the brown of tussock grass. But beyond that, all over the mountain the ash lay sterile and dirty. The mountain was formidable, like a grand old lady awaiting the return of her glory days, a dowager of all the lower landscapes. Right now there was ample blue sky plus patchy cloud and just then, just for a moment it seemed she was allowing Lana to return.

'Told you I'd be back,' she said aloud to the mountain.

Paul had said the eruptions were unpredictable. It might be calm now, even for the rest of the day, but equally, it could explode right this minute. Lana recalled her fear. But fearful or not, she wouldn't turn back now.

'I just need a few hours of calm,' she pleaded.

She turned the car into the narrow rutted dirt road. Suddenly she was closer to the track surface. Perhaps Alex's car wasn't up to the task. This sewed the first seed of doubt on the whole expedition. She picked out the fairest route she could but still was catapulted around as she traversed the potholes and ridges. The chassis bottomed out intermittently and gouged along hidden obstacles. No doubt lava blocks and bombs. The ash was thick as she expected but there were no vehicle tracks ahead of her. The further along she crawled the less obvious the track became and she could barely recognise it. If it were not for the tussock grasses and coprosmas that grew either side, the track would be indistinguishable from the rest of the mountain ring plain.

Ahead of her several vehicles were parked all clothed in the same brown blanket of ash. She recognised her car and Paul's utility, and there was another double cab utility which she assumed belonged to the men. By now the track opened to a sloping exposed ridge that dropped off gently to both sides, but not so gently that she could afford to get it wrong. It was windy up here and ash had swirled in the cool air, before eventually piling up against the vehicles. Lana revved the Mazda hard to power it up the slope. She felt the wheels skid beneath her and panic flooded into her as she realised her loss of control. The rear of the car jutted out from underneath her and she clung knuckle-white onto the steering wheel as she fought the front wheels to stay on the ridge. She shot on the handbrake and threw the car into first gear all the while pumping the throttle. At last she felt the wheels make purchase and she rode the last twenty metres on adrenalin. By the time she pulled the car to a stop she was shaking like a leaf.

She gave herself a few moments to still her heartbeat. It was eerily quiet. Tiny ash particles sailed on the breeze, already starting to settle on the windscreen. She rattled around the glove box for anything that might come in useful. She smiled. There was a cake of chocolate. Then she donned her mittens, beanie, scarf and thick jacket. Into the pockets she stuffed her life pack and the chocolate then locked Alex's car and started along the Round the Mountain Track. She would have to concentrate, for it wasn't going to be the easy walk of a few days ago.

She reflected upon that day. Did she honestly think that she was going to spend a night in a mountain hut with her first ever sweetheart without feeling something for him? She'd been pleased to have Emma's company. It provided her with a shield. She was supposed to just be a pair of ears that Paul would be tempered in speaking in front of. She wasn't meant to charm him. Lana felt herself getting angry. She thought their past would not count but it seemed it counted for a lot. And she didn't expect to have any residual feelings for Paul but again she was wrong.

She kept her head down against the stiff wind. Whatever Paul thought of her now, he could not surely think of her as a coward. She wondered if he had figured it out yet. Had that been him ringing for her as she left the motel?

She squinted at the track ahead of her. It was obscured but she could make out the orange painted timber poles that marked the route. She wished she wasn't alone. All things considered the day provided bearable mountain conditions for a traverse. The unknown factor of course was the state of the mountain's plumbing. It wasn't rumbling at present but Lana was aware that it possibly wouldn't last.

She knew it should take her approximately one hour to reach the lahar path and another half hour to reach the hut. It had taken longer than that to walk in the other day although she had deliberately walked slowly then. But this time there was not the insignificant factor of the bridge being smashed to pieces.

The lahar comprised most of Crater Lake's acidic water and the explosive eruptions would have taken care of the rest. Therefore, she calculated, there shouldn't be any water coming from that source. But she wasn't sure whether any other tributary fed into the creek. She hoped that only a trickle of mountain water, if any, would be meandering downstream.

She pressed on. Each footfall left a deep boot imprint and with each step a bit more ash stuck to her boots. She was aware of only her clumpy footsteps. There were no insects buzzing or passerines chirruping. In fact, there were no insects or birds at all. It was eerily moon-like. She almost thought she would be glad to reach the body. At least she wouldn't be alone.

Presently she found herself on the north side of the Whangaehu Stream. From here she couldn't see the crossing place but she should have been able to hear the gushing water. She listened. Nothing. She recalled the trek in. They'd had lunch only a few metres ahead, on a lava outcrop above the swirling waters of the river. It was a noisy spot, but there was something that always drew you to stop by a flowing stream. From there the swing bridge across a particularly deep turgid rapid could be viewed.

Lana took in the scene ahead of her, from the green and yellow warning sign that advised trampers not to cross the river in times of a lahar, right across to the other side of the valley. She stood well above the stream on a level floodplain. It would have been thousands of years since a raging torrent had breached its course and flowed over the ground she now stood upon. She looked upstream to the headwaters where a thin trickle of grey water channelled down from Crater Lake high above it. The glacier above the lake was caked in muck, hardly recognisable now as a glacier. Still, Lana longed to be up there working out its secrets.

She watched the water fall silently to disappear into the channel below her. She drew nearer until she stood above the stream and peered across to the far side. The body was still there, covered in ash. She shuddered at the thought of searching it and she hoped she would find what she had come for quickly.

She cautiously picked her way down the slope beyond the warning sign. Suddenly she was out of the breeze and below the level of the ancient floodplain it was also warmer. Enormous boulders perched above the river, testament to the power of the torrent required to move them. Some had been expelled by historic eruptions just as surely as some had come from further upstream and been deposited a few days ago.

As Lana neared the stream she noticed greyish andesitic rocks with canary yellow sulphur deposits on them. She picked some up and not being convinced of their provenance stuffed them into her pockets to take back to the university.

She turned her attention back to the task of crossing the stream. The bridge that once traversed this section had been demolished, splintered into unrecognisable fragments and carried downstream to the river's mouth on the west coast. An upright support remained, as did a couple of pieces of wire rope which were bolted into concrete foundations on either side of the creek. There was no point in crossing there now since the site would have been chosen for its benefits on the approaches, not for the ease of crossing the stream.

She scanned the river upstream and down. Ideally, she didn't want to get her boots wet. She wondered what Paul would think of her dithering around looking for a crossing point that wouldn't give her wet boots. With that motivation she instead concentrated her efforts on finding a crossing place where the water would not go over her knees.

Finally she settled on a spot and put a well placed boot in the stream. A clamp of steel braced around her lower leg and she gasped. She placed her second foot between two boulders behind which the frigid waters were swirling creating a mini whirlpool but it was only knee deep and she put all her weight onto it. The iciness of the water made it tempting to rush her crossing but she tempered her enthusiasm and painstakingly took a third step steadying herself on the wet boulders. She had chosen a narrow crossing and as yet proved, not too deep a one.

The longer Lana stood mustering courage to complete the crossing the more acutely aware she was of the icy clamps around her legs. She couldn't afford the luxury of a detailed investigation of the rest of the crossing. She pushed ahead, cautious but not confident. She tentatively placed one waterlogged boot down, secured the footing and then put all her weight onto it. She was across in three more steps.

On the other side of the creek she paused and slapped at her legs to get the blood flowing again. Already the water soaking her lower trouser legs was creeping higher.

She scrambled over to the body. She could smell it from ten metres away and gagged. She hadn't anticipated decomposition. She had assumed that the thick layer of ash would somehow have preserved the body intact, like the bodies recovered from Vesuvius. She screwed up her nose and put a wet mittened hand over her mouth then wound her scarf around her face. It did little to mask the putrid smell of rotting flesh. She wondered why it would be in this advanced state of decomposition when she hadn't observed any insects on the walk in. Then she recalled the day of the lahar. That was the same day as they found the body. There were no eruptions that day. Flies and other insects, perhaps even birds could have fed upon the body. Certainly flies would have laid their maggoty eggs.

Lana had never seen a body before. It was stiff and the eyes were open. The body was fully clothed and as she approached she could tell he wasn't as old as her. His face was line free and his fingers looked like swollen chipolata sausages. But he wasn't fat. She revised her judgement on his age, conceding that maybe he was older than he looked, that the swelling of the body had plumped out his lines. She squatted over it and rifled through the pockets of the jacket then all the pockets of his shirt and trousers.

Her hand clasped upon a small metallic object in the hood lining of the jacket. She popped the plastic rivets and fished it out. It was a cross on a mauve ribbon. She quickly tucked it into her jacket pocket and zipped it shut. Then she rose from her crouching position and stood solemnly over the body. She wished she could do something respectful for him. She looked up to the sky and back down at the body. What had gone so wrong that he ended his days in the lonesome spot, wounded and quite probably up to no good?

Slowly she climbed out of the river valley up onto the ancient river plain on the other side. Immediately she noticed the chilly wind cutting her face. It should only take her a half hour to the hut. Her elevation afforded her a view over the mountain ring plain. She could see all the way out to the road she had come in on. There was still patchy snow at her present elevation but none down on the ring plain. She fancied she could see a dot or two of moving colour on the horizon but as there was no track down that way she dismissed it.

The walk to the hut became easier and she realised now how tense she'd been anticipating the river crossing. And the ease with which she'd found Colleen's medal buoyed her. The vegetation was thickly covered and still there were no fresh footprints. Everything was pockmarked with brown volcanic bombs, some larger ones soft and cooling. Her boots squelched and the water in them soon warmed up. She settled into an easy gait. The trail around the mountain was fairly level punctuated by steep ascents and descents where old streams had carved channels off the side of the mountain. Every now and then an ancient lava flow blocked the easy track and she would have to scurry up and over. She grew to expect cool winds on the ridges and no breeze whatsoever in the valleys.

Lana thrust her hands deep in her pockets and fingered the thin metal cross. She imagined returning it to Colleen; just to see her face would be reward enough for this endurance. Now she was certain what she would find beneath the hut.

Time seemed to drag and the hut didn't appear. On and on she trudged. She was sure she'd been walking long enough to reach it. Eventually she halted in her tracks and looked to the west towards the mountain top. Something didn't look quite right. The tops were too high, too far away. She groaned. She realised she was too far down the mountain. She must have walked right past the hut which would have been obscured from view thanks to its location on a relatively flat piece of ground. Locked onto her spot for fear of getting anything else wrong she looked back at her dark brown footprints. The trail slowly but surely descended the mountain. She squinted above and behind her for the orange marker poles she should have been following. She considered her options. Retracing her footprints might not guarantee she would come out exactly where she went off track. She would have to be on her guard not to end up all the way back at the stream. If she headed straight up above her she surely should recognise the track and pick up the marker posts from there. There was a chance she could trudge straight on over the track and keep plodding up the mountain, but any mistake should be easier to rectify than the retrace option. If that happened she may be able to spot the hut, if she hadn't walked too far south. She noted the position of the sun. How long had she wasted? She had allowed herself only half a day and already she had mucked up.

She started walking straight up the hill above her. It never bothered her to walk or scramble straight up a slope. She was always overjoyed at how quickly a hill could be scaled by taking the direct route. She honed her senses. She remembered that she and Paul had more or less jogged this section of the track the day the lahar started.

Just then an orange topped marker pole appeared like a lighted beacon in the gritty landscape. Lana let out a huge sigh of relief. She staggered to it, paused and scanned the northern horizon in the direction of the hut for another one. There it was, tiny in the distance but recognisable as a marker pole. For the second time this day she felt the tension leave her shoulders as she realised she wasn't lost.

Presently, after a weary slog, the hut edged into view. The sun was high in the midday sky and it cast a short sharp shadow over the ground in front of the hut. A rush of familiarity swept over Lana and she picked up her pace. The hut looked sad and broken as it leaned unnaturally to one corner. But even so Lana felt comforted. She wished the skinny steel chimney was puffing a silent white smoke into the air.

Finally she reached it. She crawled onto the deck and dangled her legs over the side as her breathing resumed its resting pulse. She psyched herself up for the crawl under the hut then finally squatted near the collapsed corner. The brightness of the day made it hard to see anything. She crawled onto her stomach. Already she could smell the rotting flesh of Bing's severed arm.

Gagging she clasped her scarf over her nose and mouth. The ground had sucked in Bing's blood as a dry brown stain. Ahead of her was the sock. She wondered why she hadn't taken much notice of it before. It was clear now that it was not an old sock. She wriggled in and stretched out to it until her fingers touched it. With a big push she propelled herself forward and grabbed it. The contents clinked. She smiled to herself.

She wriggled out backwards relieved that this would be the last time. She glanced across at what remained of Bing's forearm and wondered if it would over time become flat and dehydrated. When her legs reached the exterior of the hut she crawled onto her hands and knees. She was faintly aware of a shuffle behind her and she started to turn around. But the painful whack to the back of her head prevented her seeing anything but a set of boots and all of a sudden everything went black.

***

Paul didn't follow the rough track that Lana used but instead set a visual bearing more or less straight for the hut up the desert ring plain and the mountainside. He didn't have the luxury of time. He walked a few hundred metres in off the road and shrugged his pack off his shoulder. He fished out his small day pack and transferred what he required into it then scouted around for an appropriate bush camouflage with which to hide his main pack.

He walked easier with a lighter weight on his shoulders and if he cast his mind away from his body he could almost believe he didn't have fractured ribs. His ankle had lost a lot of the fluid which had previously made walking difficult and the enforced rest over the last twenty four hours had gone a long way to healing the tumescent sprain.

It was relaxing in a way, the repetitious crunch underfoot. Too easily his mind played images of Lana. One minute she was smiling, ephemeral, like in a dream; talking to him but not talking, beckoning. Next he felt the pinch that was all too real but then she was sixteen again. Always beautiful and always wanting him. That's what he wanted. He may not get it but it was worth trying. In the distance he could see two coloured dots so small they appeared not to be moving.

His ankle pinched. By now he'd gone back to a bit of a limp. He looked up ahead. The coloured dots were still there. He cursed Lana. Damn her for putting them both in danger, as if they hadn't escaped with their lives already. But he had to admit, she showed bottle. Only she hadn't thought it through, obviously. Was she aware that she was being followed? When did she develop the fortitude to do this? He rued the lost decades. Maybe he didn't know her at all. Lana was right – they didn't know each other. But that didn't mean he wasn't going to try.

Ash covered almost everything. It smothered the sparse vegetation and rocks. But not the new rocks. They were dark brown and red and littered the mountainside, gleaming and proud, absorbing the weak morning sun, free of lichen. Earth's newest treasures would grace this desolate spot until they flowed back to the sea and one day in another epoch when man was wiped from the geological record, be swallowed into the cauldron of magma from whence they came.

Ahead of him far in the distance against the snow backdrop he couldn't see the two dots. He tightened the straps of the small pack hard against his shoulders and increased his loping pace into a light jog.

***

Lana came to inside the now familiar hut. It seemed dark but that could have been her eyes not able to focus. Her head spun. She wasn't sure if it was the mountain trying to waken her with its insistent grumbling or the urgent voices of her assailants that had spirited her to consciousness. She went to clasp her hands to her head but her movements were hindered. She wriggled on the plastic mattress but still her hands wouldn't move. They were tied behind her back. Panic now, she kicked out, but her legs acted as one. They too were bound tightly with tape. And her mouth was dry, stuffed with a cotton bandana. She squealed behind the restraint and hauled herself into a sitting position just as the roof clattered with volcanic rock. The men she knew as Jim and Dave sat at the table with the gleaming medals spread out in front of them. She groaned when she saw them.

'Ah, you're awake,' said Jim.

Lana blinked her request for assistance and she squealed for them to remove the dry obstruction in her mouth. Jim started to get up from his seat but Dave quickly put an arresting hand on him and he sat back down again. Lana knew she'd already won Jim over, broken nose notwithstanding. His face had started to yellow around the nose. He didn't seem too phased by it. Perhaps he respected her for that. Inherently she felt he was a good man, he kept showing that side of him to her. No, it was Dave she had to work on, or Bob or George, or whatever his damn name is. She settled quietly to lull them into a false reality. She bowed her head a little and looked at her captors beneath hooded lids.

'You found our medals for us,' said Dave evenly. 'Even the Memorial Cross. Did Ant have it? Huh? Was the cross on him?'

Lana nodded, wide-eyed.

Dave walked to the window casually and appeared to be thinking hard. Or was it a ruse? Wasn't this whole ridiculous situation a play? He stared hard at her, menacingly, quietly. He unnerved her.

'What made it your business?' he asked her.

He said it with such vehemence Lana didn't even attempt to speak. What caused him to be consumed with such rage?

'Lana,' he snapped. 'That's your name isn't it? What the hell makes it your business to come back up to this mountain and put your nose in where it's got no business to be?'

A rhetorical question, given her current position. He was angry. At her. For giving him a problem to deal with. They had to do something with her now and that wasn't part of their plan. Her heart beat hard against her chest as fear crept over her. Suddenly she had the urge to use the bathroom. 'Joe,' Jim pleaded. Joe shook his head to him. Lana recognised the slip. Why didn't Joe react violently? They must be going to kill her. Joe stood in front of Lana, legs apart, camo trousers tucked into his boots, biceps flexing under his black tee shirt.

'Okay,' he said. 'The situation we have here is this. You can link us to the medals. We don't want you to do that. So, we have to kill you. So maybe we don't want to do that. We're not murderers are we? So we bought a little insurance.'

Lana frowned and looked from one man to the other. Did Jim know about this insurance? Was it a ploy he'd just thought up or had they both made up a story and discussed it while she was unconscious? Or was he telling the truth? She couldn't discern any truth in Jim's face.

'If we aren't back at Bing's bedside by six tonight with all the medals your boyfriend is toast. Remember Bing has already killed a man.' Bing. She pictured Bing – lying helpless for days on the same bunk that Lana was now trussed up on. She remembered him saving her life and being kind to her and giving her comfort. She recalled how she and Paul had ministered to his grievous wounds after his so-called friends abandoned him. She thought of him lying in the hospital bed, drugged up against the unbearable pain of amputation and considered the truth behind Joe's words. She had given a little of herself to Bing during those long days and nights in the hut and she felt a hotness in her throat at the thought she'd been used like a fool.

Lana's sapphire eyes took on an indigo hue as they grew wide and she looked across to Jim. He sat still as a statue at the table, staring resolutely at a spot in front of him. Still she could determine no truth from him.

Joe pulled out his phone and lay it on the table. 'If you don't play ball Lana, Bing will do what I tell him. Now, are you going to give us any trouble?'

Lana shook her head. She had to give them the benefit of the doubt. Something in her heart prevented her believing that Bing would kill Paul, but that was not a risk she could afford to take. All it would take was a stab to the heart while Paul slept. Even a one armed man could manage that.

'Ungag her Tom,' ordered Joe.

Tom walked over to Lana and paused in front of her.

'Hang on,' Joe shouted urgently. Joe threw Tom a bootlace. 'Tie her wrists with this.'

'But Joe, she's already tied enough with tape,' Tom countered.

'She can bite through that,' Joe replied.

Tom gently tied her wrists, his green eyes engaging with Lana's through his glasses. He took her hands in his own and tested for movement between her wrists, then placed them on her lap. He removed the gag from her mouth.

She sputtered, 'Do you really think you will get away with this?'

'Lana, men don't like women who nag,' said Joe sadly, tut-tutting and shaking his head from side to side. 'Put the gag back in Tom.'

Tom did as he was commanded.

'Where's Bing's number?' asked Joe loudly to himself scrolling through his phone.

Lana squealed in protest inside her gag. Joe casually

made a show of finding Bing's phone number. Lana squirmed out a pleading cry of protest.

'Oh?' said Joe. 'What's that? No more silly nagging?' He snapped the phone shut.

'No no,' he said to Tom who was about to remove the gag again. 'Leave it. Lana just agreed not to go to the police or cooperate with the police. She agreed not to identify us or admit to any knowledge of the medals. Guess your boyfriend's safe. For now.'

Joe and Tom stared at her. She nodded slowly.

***

Tom stepped out into the bracing air and let the toilet door shut behind him with a slam. He heard it bounce once against the door frame and echo its crash against the smooth clean walls. It had been clear when he ascended the hill. He needed time to himself as much as the toilet. What hold did Joe have on him, really? He was sick to his stomach seeing Lana treated the way she was. She didn't deserve it. It was different when it was just about the medals, about money. But Joe displayed a dark side. How was it possible this man was related to him? He should walk away now. Confront Joe, tell him he can have the medals, all of them. No strings. He's out.

Now eruptions had begun in earnest and he could feel the rock pepper the battered toilet. No sooner had he taken a step outside when he felt a whack to the back of his head. He plunged face first into the thick ash that covered the ground, burying his obscenely bent and bruised nose into it. His glasses flew off landing away from him. His mouth connected with an obscured rock and his front teeth smashed through his soft pink upper lip causing blood to well inside his mouth. He didn't taste it. He was already in a pleasant vortex of darkness when he hit the ground.

***

Paul dragged Tom's dead weight around the uphill side of a huge boulder. He pocketed Tom's glasses and noted the man's good quality serge army clothing. The drag marks left a wide channel in the ash. He scooted down to the hut with stealth taking a wide route so as not to leave any footprints. He stole a glance through the broken window of the bunkroom and could see through the internal door into the main room but not the bunk Lana was on. He could clearly hear the hiss of gas burning. No one was speaking. Paul slunk around to the opposite side of the building. The window, still intact, was situated between a single bunk and the multiple bunk platform. He peered in to see Joe with his back to him at the sink bench and Lana curled into a ball lying on the bunk, bound. He was relieved to see her alive.

His heart swelled. She could have been sleeping if it weren't for the constraints. Her boots had been removed, roughly he could tell, because her socks were sloppy at the ends, like it wasn't important that they fit right. He couldn't see her face properly, her hair hung lank over it like fresh licorice straps. He wanted to stroke it out of her eyes.

Paul squatted on his haunches and leaned his back against the timber wall. He estimated how long Joe might wait before he realised that Tom was taking too long in the toilet. He reckoned Joe would look for Tom firstly in the toilet. He'd be best to deal with Joe there too. With his fitness compromised he knew he had only the element of surprise to give him the advantage. But he worried about the drag marks. If Joe explored an area wider than the direct route to the toilet he would notice Paul's boot prints and Tom's marks. He had to take Joe out before he noticed the drag tracks.

Paul crept onto the deck and slunk to the side of the verandah where a stack of split firewood filled the tiny space. He ducked below the level of the front window and reached into the wood pile to grab the axe then like a shadow scrambled back up the hill approaching the toilet from the top. He sat in the toilet and waited.

***

Paul shivered against the cold. He had been moving quickly all morning. A light perspiration bathed his muscles inside his warm mountain clothes. Even after the river crossing, though initially bracing, he had quickly warmed. Even then his boots had barely got wet and his feet soon warmed any trapped moisture. The air was thinner at 1556 metres and the fresher for it. His hands were cold and he plunged his hands in his pockets and fetched out his gloves. For good measure he tucked his hands under his armpits. After a time he hunkered down behind the toilet leaving the door open and peered through the crack between the door and the door jamb in the direction of the hut. It seemed an age before Joe appeared at the edge of the deck. He watched him scan the mountain searching for his friend.

Paul slipped back into deeper cover and presently heard Joe's scrunching boots approach and then stop. He could feel his heart thudding in his chest. When he judged Joe to be on the other side of the open door he sprang up and pushed against the door. He met with resistance for a second before Joe tumbled onto the ground then he leapt on him and delivered a crushing blow to the head with the axe before the man even had a chance to look around.

Joe landed where he fell, crumpling into a broken nest of arms and legs. Paul stooped over him and put a hand to Joe's head. The man's eyes were closed and Paul breathed a jagged sigh of relief. A dark ooze began to well up through Joe's cropped dark hair.

Paul scrambled up to the boulder where he had left Tom. The man was still out to it. He dashed back to the hut and burst through the partly open front door.

'Lana!' he cried.

She startled at the outburst and squirmed on the bunk raising herself to an upright position. Paul rushed to her and gently cradled her head in both his hands.

'Oh Lana.' He removed the gag and embraced her, smoothing her hair back from her face and tucking it behind her ears.

'Sorry,' Lana whispered. 'So sorry.'

'It's okay,' Paul replied. 'But I need your help.' He freed her wrists and ankles. 'Quick, your insulation tape. We have to tie those guys up before they wake up. Where is it?'

'In my life pack,' she answered and shoved her hand deep into her jacket pocket and gave it to him. He emptied its contents onto the bed: mirror, matches, pencil, paper, condoms, ear plugs, sheep wool, trout fly, nylon, boot laces. He picked out a roll of red tape.

'Can you follow me? Are you hurt sweetheart?' asked Paul.

'Just my pride,' said Lana.

Paul led her out of the hut and up the hill to where Joe lay.

'We need to tie his wrists and ankles and gag him then drag him to the hut,' Paul explained.

'Wow, Paul!' exclaimed Lana. 'I'm impressed.'

He grinned. 'Thanks.'

'He's not... he's not dead is he?' she asked.

'Na. I was afraid of that myself,' Paul confessed. 'He's concussed big time.'

'Where's Tom?' she asked.

'Behind that boulder.' Paul nodded in the general direction. 'Here sweetheart. Start tying his wrists together while I check the other one.'

Lana heaved the unconscious Joe so his arms lay more or less together. She reeled off some tape and held the end in her mouth while she scrunched up his sleeves to reveal his white wrists.

'See how you like this,' she spat at him as she wound the tape several times around his wrists. Satisfied, she hauled Joe's legs together and wrapped his ankles. Paul returned and positioned Joe's head for Lana to wrap a gag of insulation tape.

'How does it feel to do this to him?' asked Paul.

'Not as good as I thought it would.'

'Come on,' said Paul. 'One more.'

She followed him to Tom. The man lay on his back, his face covered in muddy ash, specs gone.

'Tom's actually quite nice Paul,' Lana said smoothly.

Paul stared at Lana and amazement set into his fine features, melting into a light smile.

'They say that about kidnap victims you know.'

'What?' Lana demanded defensively.

'The victims start to empathise with their captors.'

'Oh don't be silly,' she countered. 'He just tried to make it a bit easier for me, that's all.'

'Okay sweetheart. I'm sorry. Talk about it later.'

Paul bound Tom's wrists and ankles and wrapped a length of tape around his head.

'Where are his glasses?' asked Lana.

'Here,' Paul replied as he dug into his pocket for them. He handed them to Lana and she gently secured them behind Tom's ears.

'He would have done that for me,' she said to Paul when he gave her another look of mute amazement. Then he lurched forward thrown by a tumultuous explosion.

'Ah shit! Can you help me drag them downhill?' Paul yelled over the thunderous noise.

Lana positioned herself at Tom's feet while Paul lifted him from the arms. But they'd only managed one step when Paul dropped the arms and doubled over, lightly supporting himself on his knees.

'What is it? asked Lana.

'Nothing.'

'Oh don't be a hero,' she retorted. 'It's your ribs isn't it? Swap ends.' She pushed him out of the way and took hold of Tom's arms and together they dragged him to the deck.

'No time to lose,' cried Paul as they dumped Tom.

'Let's go.' He bounded up the hill with broad strides and Lana followed head down dodging rocks and rock fall like a rabbit in a field.

'Same again Lana,' said Paul bending at the knees to pick up Joe's feet. She hurried into position and soon they had Joe dumped alongside Tom.

'We need to move them to safety then tie them together,' Paul explained.

'Where?'

'Under the corner of the hut,' said Paul.

'Are you mad?' Lana challenged him.

'First they leave you outside to die, then they tie you up Lana,' Paul reasoned.

'But shouldn't we put them inside?' she asked.

'Definitely not.' Paul was adamant.

'On the verandah then,' suggested Lana. 'Paul it's too dangerous under the hut. The building could collapse further and crush them. Do you want that on your conscience?'

'Guess not.'

Lana dragged Tom up to the covered part of the deck then went back for Joe. Paul used the single rope clothesline behind him and tied the two men back to back at the chest and thighs. Satisfied he stood above them. They deserved to be kicked.

Lana felt her left knee buckle and she would have fallen had Paul not caught her.

'Steady sweetheart. What's wrong?'

'I don't feel so good,' Lana replied.

'Do you want to be sick?'

She nodded. Paul supported her to the edge of the deck where she bent at the waist over the side. She felt the hot water build up in her mouth and her stomach heave, but, nothing.

'What's brought this on sweetheart?' asked Paul.

'Maybe another knock on the head.'

'They knocked you unconscious again? Oh Lana. I'm so sorry. Come on, let's get you inside.'

Chapter Seventeen

Lana sat on the edge of the bunk with her arms wrapped around her middle and let Paul fuss over her. The adrenalin that had been fuelling her had just about worn off and suddenly she felt she couldn't do this anymore. What had possessed her to come up the mountain again? And on her own. Stupid.

'Rescued me again,' she muttered to herself.

'Again?' Paul asked.

She shrugged. 'The dog.'

'Oh,' he laughed. 'The dog, of course.'

He remembered. It was going to be all right. She instinctively reached down to her leg. The wound hadn't stopped stinging. It would leave a scar. Just like the dog bite had left a scar. She let her shoulders slump. It appeared she couldn't look after herself. Not really. She thought when she hauled Paul off the mountain that day that she could be proud of herself. But now he had saved her. Again.

That's what he was supposed to do wasn't it? She'd put him to the test and he passed. He was there for her. It wasn't the plan, but it had turned out like that.

'You followed me,' she said.

'I knew you were in danger.'

'It was you ringing the motel. Alex will be furious with me.' She tried to smile. 'I took his car.'

'I know,' Paul replied.

'It's not just that.' She hesitated as Paul held her gaze. 'I've left him.'

'For me?' Kneeling on the floor in front of her he gently caressed her legs. 'Honey, for me?'

'Maybe,' she whispered. 'I don't know.'

Paul untied her boots and removed them. He rubbed his hands over her socks, caressing her feet then gingerly lifted her trouser leg. The wound was wrapped. 'Hurt?'

She nodded. 'Stings.'

He gently massaged around it. She let him. Stabs of pleasure pierced her as she succumbed to his touch. She could tell he was hesitant.

'Lana,' Paul whispered.

'Mm-mm,' she murmured.

'We're staying put,' he said.

She nodded and smiled.

'You sit there and relax,' he ordered.

She nodded again. Paul lit candles and set them on the table then opened the firebox and prepared some kindling.

'I threw water on it when I left,' Lana explained.

'You did a good job.' Paul smiled at her.

He neatly set the fire and set a match to it. A pleasant amber glow flickered against his face illuminating his dark eyes. Soon the piquant odour of wood smoke pervaded the hut and flecks of blue caught the early afternoon sun. It felt like winter but instead of rain or sleet pelting the roof it was soft, hot volcanic debris and instead of the constant patter of a wetting rain there were intermittent explosions and a deep-seated rumble that reverberated through the room.

Paul set a pot of water on top of the firebox to warm and turned his attention back to Lana. She sat silently with her knees up to her chin and her arms wrapped around her legs.

'I'll have to keep the fire well cranked up tonight,'

said Paul as he came to sit alongside Lana. 'I've only got a silk liner.'

'Silk liner?' exclaimed Lana.

'Yeah, well you never know when you might need a silk liner,' he laughed. 'I see you went for the lightweight adventure travel option.' He scanned the room which was devoid of anything useful Lana might have brought with her.

'Did you actually bring anything with you?' he asked.

Lana dug into her pockets and pulled out her life pack and some chocolate.

'Everything a girl needs,' Paul quipped.

'I wasn't planning on staying,' Lana replied.

'Never mind sweetheart,' he said, 'we've got warm clothes. And each other.'

Lana smiled at him and tentatively put a hand on his thigh.

Paul reached across to her and took her face in one warm hand guiding her closer to him. She lifted her face to his and their lips met, tenderly. She parted her lips and delighted in the taste of Paul's hot wet mouth and the feel of his tongue exploring hers. She couldn't remember it being this good last time. She was aware of a stirring deep inside and she hungrily kissed him back.

'Mm, sweetheart,' Paul murmured. 'You want me?'

'Yes,' she whispered.

'Are you really free?'

'Yes.'

'You sure?'

'Yes, Paul,' she panted. 'I'm free to love you.'

'Mm, God, you're beautiful,' Paul groaned.

He pressed her shoulders gently back onto the cold

vinyl mattress and kissed her long and tenderly. She felt his soul in the depths of his kiss. It was all of him. It wasn't just a kiss. It was his very being he was giving her.

'You'll have to help me sweetheart,' he murmured.

'Why?'

'Ribs,' he replied. 'But it's okay. They're only fractured. The doc loved your tape but I don't need it. I could have killed you when they took it off me.'

'Oh, of course,' she replied.

Paul rested back on his haunches and removed his jacket. Then he took off his shirt leaving only a thin wool merino top to cover his chest. He folded his shirt to make a little pillow for Lana and tucked it under her head. She smelt him so close to her face. It was that masculine smell that consumed her with desire. She reached up to his face with both hands and kissed him passionately, urgently then pulled away and rubbed her cheek against his face. She felt herself fall into a pit of hot pleasure and let the feeling consume her.

Paul unzipped Lana's jacket and threaded his hands around her waist. She felt the warmth of him on her cool skin and she arched her back to his delicious touch. He caressed her back exploring its curves. It felt like he couldn't get enough of her. His hot palms rubbed over her body, slowly, tenderly, back and forth then faster, more urgently, exploring feeling, caressing her. He slipped the jacket off her shoulders and she felt the air of the hut hit her skin where Paul exposed it.

Lana reached to Paul's waist and undid the top button of his trousers. She took hold of the zip and slowly dragged it down exposing the top of his underwear. She peeled his trousers down to his knees and smiled when she saw that his boxers did nothing to hide his burning passion for her.

Paul slipped off the bunk and kicked his feet free of his trousers all the while taking care not to make any sideways movements that might aggravate his ribs. He removed his remaining top and threw it to Lana who caught it and held it to her face, inhaling deeply to capture all of his scent. It was warm and it was Paul and she buried her face in it giving a little moan. From the end of the bunk Paul leaned in and undid Lana's trousers. She arched her back for him lifting her buttocks off the bed and he pulled her trousers off leaving her in hot pink lace panties. He smiled.

'Don't laugh,' Lana said, embarrassed.

'I'm not sweetheart, I'm delighted,' said Paul chuckling.

'You're more than delighted. You're pleased to see me,' she laughed.

'I am that.'

He crawled back to Lana and rubbed his hands under her top and all over her body. She felt electric, on fire.

'God, I want you,' she whispered. She took off her top to reveal a hot pink lace bra to match the panties.

'Perfect,' teased Paul and he lowered himself over her and buried his face in her cleavage.

'Take it off Lana,' he moaned.

She stretched behind her and unfastened her bra and felt instant relief as Paul used his teeth to pull it away. His stubble moved frantically over her smooth skin, tickling her. His mouth found her hard pink nipples and with a sucking tongue he pleasured her, flicking and teasing. She writhed under his touch and succumbed to a pleasure only he could give.

She ran her fingers through his hair, eyes closed and hips writhing anticipating the heaven he would deliver. Had she waited a lifetime for him? She didn't want to wait, couldn't wait any longer.

'Paul,' she moaned.

'Mm?'

'Lie down,' she said and softly nudged him.

He lay on his jacket carefully, wincing only sparingly. Lana kneeled alongside him glowing white in the gloom of the hut. She ran her hands tenderly over his warm hairy chest up and down his torso, teasing, feeling his hot body under her touch eventually slipping her fingers into the top of his boxers. His desire was great and she took hold of him with a skillful hand.

'Mm, sweetheart,' he intoned.

Lana panted. She rubbed Paul, watching his closed eyes in his sweet face, delaying undecided as to what to do. Finally she dragged his shorts off and took hold of him with both hands caressing him, wanting him.

'You're beautiful too Paul,' Lana whispered.

'Come here sweetheart.'

He reached an arm out to her and pulled her into him kissing her tenderly on the lips.

'Make love to me Lana,' he murmured.

'I will,' she replied.

'You can't lie on my chest,' he said.

'I know.'

Lana slipped off her underwear and straddled him. Stabs of pleasure shot through her as she gently ground over him and he writhed and groaned with her. Lana played her hands over her own body exciting Paul, his darkly brooding eyes lighting with fire, and Lana became more wanting at seeing his desire. He held his warm hands on her hips and she let him guide her as she rocked back and forth over him then swallow him into her innermost sanctum.

A jolt of electricity surged through her. Paul caressed her breasts causing Lana to grip her hands on his rippling biceps as she continued to move slowly up and down on him. He moved his hips beneath her, matching her sensual movements until he drove a sense of urgency. She watched him give himself up to her, squirming with enjoyment at the touch of her hot exploring hands rubbing his sides, his chest, his hips. She picked up the rhythm now keeping time with Paul's urgent desire. She ground back and forth on him, feeling him, wanting more, lifting her face high with her eyes tightly shut exalted with pleasure. Paul's hands drove her hips manfully, and she was pleased to have them on her, firm and masterful.

She watched him panting, sometimes eyes open drinking in her nakedness, sometimes closed giving himself over to intense sensual pleasure. She noticed a subtle change of rhythm, and with one hand caressing her body she placed the other between her legs and helped Paul to pleasure her. Suddenly he tensed and groaned loudly. Lana squealed then enjoyed her own contraction and release over him. She screamed with each one and when she relaxed it came again shocking her into a heightened state.

Paul went to sooth her racked and perspiring body but her hands met his before he could touch her.

'No,' she said abruptly.

'No?'

'Don't touch me,' she panted and rolled off him. She glowed a blush pink in the blue light of the room and flopped back onto her jacket and the little pillow Paul made for her. They lay in silence forever.

'All right?' she asked finally.

'Not bad. Might need a bit of practice,' Paul quipped.

She laughed and nudged him on his shoulder.

'Come here sweetheart,' he murmured. 'Snuggle into me.'

She rolled onto her side aware of the hot sensation between her legs. She inhaled Paul's irresistible odour and let it permeate her senses. She draped a light hand over his clammy chest and trailed her fingers through his dark silky hair.

'I know you didn't do that lightly sweetheart,' Paul said and he kissed his index finger and placed it on Lana's lips.

'You seem to know a lot about my feelings,' said Lana. 'Am I so transparent?'

'Yes you are darling. And I know you never stopped loving me.'

'Even when I'd forgotten of your existence?' she challenged him. 'When I never in a lifetime gave you so much as a passing thought?'

'You felt it the minute you saw me and I knew then I was right to see you again,' he replied.

'I think I did feel it but I didn't believe it and I didn't want to give in to it,' she said. 'Never in my wildest dreams did I expect to see you again Paul. I was so shocked. It spun me into orbit. I wanted to see you, yes.

But I wanted what was impossible. I wanted to fall in love with the unflawed man I had last known and I expected you to want the same. It took me a long time to come to terms with the affects of us aging.'

'Lana, you've aged better than most. Look at you sweetheart,' said Paul, 'you're, well, you're beautiful.'

'I'm not beautiful. Look at these lizard hands. Ugly face and hands I grew up hearing,' said Lana. 'Well there's not much I can do about that but I soon learnt that I could control my body.'

'Lana, baby.' Paul was stunned. 'I never realised.'

'Why would you? I've only just figured it out myself. Always striving to prove something aren't I? I mean, when I start something I get fixated on it and take it as far as I can. Compensates for being ugly.' She smiled tightly and cast her eyes downward, embarrassed.

'I'm sorry. I don't mean to be sorry for myself,' she said softly. 'I never have been.'

'No. Not at all,' said Paul soothingly. 'It does explain how difficult it has been for you. Seeing me again that is. I unwittingly brought those memories back and you didn't want that. I'm sorry Lana. I didn't mean to hurt you.'

'You didn't hurt me Paul,' she whispered. 'It's my own stupid head I had to sort out.'

'You are not and never have been ugly sweetheart,' he said, gently rubbing her arm. 'Especially to me.'

She felt a giant ball of emotion welling up in her chest. She gulped it down and simply nodded.

'And as for those clever hands Lana,' he said as he picked up her hand. 'These clever beautiful hands.' He brought her hand to his mouth and he sucked each finger slowly, lovingly one by one. Lana shut her eyes as Paul's hot mouth took a finger and slowly expelled it. She opened them to see him lost in sensual pleasure, head relaxed and eyes firmly shut.

'I love your hands sweetheart,' he whispered and gave her back her hand. 'I love you Lana.'

She paused, scared to say it back. She had been through a lot in the last few days; self analysis, the Alex realisation and the break-up. No. She couldn't verbalise her love for Paul even if it was at the top of her heart to do so. It was a bit much, a bit soon.

'Lana?'

'Mm?'

'You know how when you start something you need to go all the way with it?' asked Paul.

'Yeah.'

'You've started on me now,' he said smiling lightly. He wiped a thread of silken hair from her face and tucked it behind her ear. 'Can I take it you'll go as far as you can with me?'

'Have to see won't you?' Lana teased and kissed him on the nose.

***

Lana hummed an Ashley Halley flute concerto as she made mugs of tea. The hut was warm, almost hot from the heat of the roaring fire and the early night had stolen the weak spring sun from the room. A solitary candle glowed above her workspace and cast her shadow into the room. It flickered ever so slightly drawn by the cool air passing above the hole in the roof. Eruptions

409

continued intermittently.

She played a game to keep the fear of eruptions at bay. Every time a fresh volley of explosions started, she pictured the red cascading fountain as her body being ignited by Paul. It gave her butterflies and she was smugly pleased at that.

Paul had boiled rice for their tea and sharing a spoon they ate straight from the pot. Now he was checking on their charges, trussed and bound on the front verandah. Lana could not set eyes on them.

She heard mumbling from the deck. Paul was talking and the men were grunting. He came back into the room.

'They're awake,' Paul announced.

'Give them some water Paul,' said Lana and she poured cold water into a mug and handed it to him.

When he returned Lana had two mugs of piping hot sweet black tea sitting on the table. Her block of dark chocolate sat in the middle like a prize and the medals were spread out around it.

'Dessert,' Lana announced, laughing at the chocolate.

'You're my dessert Lana,' said Paul. 'My entree, main course and dessert. How lucky I am. Am I lucky sweetheart?'

'Yes. You are lucky Mr Harrington,' Lana confirmed.

She sipped her tea silently. 'I didn't thank you.'

'Oh, think nothing of it,' Paul quipped. 'I should thank you but I tell you this, you'll really have something to thank me for once my ribs are mended.'

'Not that,' Lana laughed.

'What then?' Paul asked, genuinely puzzled.

'For saving my life.'

'I don't think they would have killed you Lana, but if

you're sure I saved your life you can thank me again and again and again.'

'Are you going to leave those guys there all night?'

'Yeah,' he said. 'Won't do them any harm. They're army boys. A night out there is just training to them. Forget it. Focus your attention in here.'

'You're right.' Lana conceded. 'It's a waste of my energy worrying about them. Paul, these medals. I met a woman at the motel. She spoke of a cross. It was given to her grandmother for the death of the woman's uncle at Monte Cassino. And amazingly the old fellow who tried to save the man's life was with her. They'd come to see where the medals were stolen from. And here it is.' She picked up the cross reverently and turned it in her hand. 'I want to be the one to return it to her.'

'You are amazing Lana Marshall,' said Paul. 'You put yourself through all this danger to return a medal to a woman you don't even know.'

'You and I are possibly the only people who know about them,' she replied. 'As soon as I worked it out I had to come back. They could have been spirited out of the country and never seen again. I didn't want that on my conscience.'

'Well they're safe now. And so are you my angel.'

'Oh,' Lana exclaimed. She fetched her jacket and pulled out a rock. 'I want to ask you about this.' She handed it to him. 'Why does it have sulphur on it?'

'It's andesite,' he said weighing it in each hand and turning it all around. 'Where did you find it?'

'In the river.'

'This rock came from the floor of Crater Lake. It tells us of volcanic activity. It's purged out with the discharge of lake water,' Paul explained. 'That's a good find Lana. When you think about it you're only going to find this once in a blue moon. When the mountain erupts, that is.'

Lana beamed and set the rock on the table with the medals. She broke the chocolate into squares and popped one into her mouth. A hissing sound interrupted her.

'The water's warm enough for a wash,' said Paul lifting the lid of the billy which sat on the top of the firebox.

'Oh, I don't know,' said Lana. 'After the last time, do you think it's wise?'

'I think it's very wise sweetheart,' he replied. 'Come over here.'

She rose from the opposite side of the table and stood before the fire. Paul cleared a space on the floor and stood directly in front of her. Unbidden, she lifted her arms above her head and allowed Paul to peel off her thin woollen top. She wore nothing under it and her breasts and flat stomach shone amber in the half light of the solitary candle. He knelt down and pulled her trousers to the floor. She stepped out of them leaving her wearing pink panties. Paul put a finger inside each side seam and peeled them off.

Lana sighed as she expected Paul to rub his face against her or rub his hands across her buttocks and down the outside of her legs but he didn't touch her. He stood up, took her by the shoulders and turned her on the spot. With her back to him he stretched around to the pot of warm water on the fire. He dipped his bandana into the pot then applied it to Lana's neck, draping the cloth down the length of her neck and across the tops of her shoulders allowing cool rivulets of clear water to trickle down her torso, her back and her breasts. Then he wiped her back gently dabbing the cotton cloth all the way down to the top of her buttocks.

He rewet the cloth and washed her back gently to begin with then firmer, harder, working himself into a frenzy. He became attentive again and dragged the cloth softly over her firm white buttocks and the backs of her thighs.

Without a word he stood and she felt his forceful hands take her by the shoulders and turn her to face him. His chocolate eyes were attentive to her face and she watched him delicately wipe around her nose and eyes, and dabbed her eyebrows in the direction they grew. Then he held her gaze as he worked on her cheeks, chin, forehead. She parted her lips aware of the hot silently panting breath emanating from her. She stood perfectly still. She saw herself in her mind's eye as if she were in a dream. She didn't want to spoil it by moving or it might prove to be a dream and disappear in a flash.

Paul wet the cloth again and lifted Lana's arms to wash under them then moved across her chest to her perfectly white plump breasts. He lifted them tenderly and wiped under them while Lana held her breath and felt her nipples react to his delicate teasing touch. She exhaled as Paul let her breasts relax and he dabbed at her stomach and tickled her tummy button.

He knelt in front of her, wet cloth in hand, gently dabbing it below her stomach. He wet her soft hair and he raised his face to her. She understood him and silently parted her legs. Paul wiped her and seductively washed in long unbroken movements from her inner thigh to her ankles.

'Don't stop,' she murmured reaching out to his dark head with her white hands. He repeated the action on her other leg. Lana directed his face back to her centre where she held him to her savouring his flicking tongue on her, around her. He nibbled the fleshy inside of her thighs and came back to her pleasuring her until she moaned. She could smell her sweet scent which triggered a growl from her. He trickled his fingers down the outsides of her buttocks and thighs so lightly it felt like rain.

'I haven't finished angel,' Paul whispered.

He shuffled back and wiped the cloth between her toes.

'Ah,' she said. 'Tickles,'

'Does it now?' he teased. 'Like this?'

'Yes,' she laughed, lifting her foot off the floor. He took it placing it on his lap and threaded the damp cloth between her toes.

'All done.' Paul stood up in front of the naked and newly washed Lana. The magic was broken. But he held the cloth in front of him and pleaded with his eyes for her to do for him as he had done for her. Lana took the cloth and put her hands gently on Paul's hips to turn him. He stood where she had stood with the heat of the fire directly onto his back.

Paul lifted his arms up and Lana peeled his shirt off. She stretched onto tip toes to do so and felt her breasts brush against his chest. The candlelight cast a golden whiskey colour over him and his rippled muscles cast a series of short shadows on his upper torso. She didn't think she would be able to keep her hands off his chest and biceps. She wanted to taste them and bite, bite hard.

'Oh,' she moaned. Her passion was excruciating and

414

obvious, hard to restrain and she groaned a guttural cry of pleasure. She knelt in front of him and peeled his trousers off dropping them to the floor. He stood naked in front of her and he was beautiful. His manhood leapt at Lana like a jack in a box. She was desperate to tame it, dying to take him into her burning mouth but instead sat back on her haunches and lifted his feet out of his trousers.

'I do like you there sweetheart,' he cooed.

'I haven't started Paul,' she said standing naked in front of him. She slipped the cloth into the warm water and started cleansing Paul's neck then dragged the warm cloth across his chiselled tanned shoulders. She wanted to bite into his muscles and nuzzle into his neck, but she dutifully wiped him clean instead.

She dragged the cloth slowly in unbroken movements from his shoulders and over his biceps to his forearms, wrists and fingers. Then she came up to his face which was only two inches higher than her own. Their eyes locked. Lana tried to concentrate but Paul's molten liquid eyes were sparkling in the firelight, almost laughing with glee. Slowly Lana's mouth cracked into a small smile and together they giggled.

'Stay still,' Lana murmured.

She edged the wet cloth around Paul's eyes and his strong nose and cheeks. She remembered the feel of his face on her breasts and her body shivered with hot desire as she anticipated his touch. He held her stare so deeply she felt him read her mind.

She turned her attention to his chest and wiped away the perspiration of their lovemaking in long singular strokes down to his belly hair where she provocatively

415

stopped. She turned him and used the same seductive movement down his back and buttocks. They were tight buttocks fashioned by plenty of field work and she didn't know what else. And they were white and pure and for now, they were hers.

He parted his legs for her and she knelt behind him. She delicately held the cloth to his soft inner thighs, a white oasis in a tanned forest. Then she squeezed the cloth allowing cool rivers of water to trickle the length of his legs, negotiating hair and knees to drip onto his feet and ankles. She watched him flinch, but remain brave, staying true to the passion of the moment. She relented and with firm strokes rubbed the cloth from inner thigh to foot.

She put her hands firmly on his hips and turned him around. She dipped the cloth in water, lightly wrung it and knelt in front of him. He was teasing her, moving himself in spasms. She wiped all around his hard member and slipped the cloth to his inner thigh. He parted his legs a little and she deftly manoeuvred the cloth up and took him in it. He panted silently and put a hand out to the table to steady himself. Lana squeezed droplets onto him teasing him and suddenly, forcefully, she took him hard into her flaming mouth.

'Oh my God, Lana,' Paul groaned. 'God, don't stop.'

She was thrilled at Paul's outburst and gave a series of hard thrusts with her head before she stopped as suddenly as she had started.

'I haven't finished,' she whispered.

She wiped the cloth down the front and outsides of his legs using the same sensual technique as he had used on her. She finished with his feet, massaging each one in her lap then sat back on her haunches to review her work.

Paul held both hands out to her, palms up. She rose taking them and stood face to face with him. Eyes locked, she held the cloth out to him. He took it from her never breaking eye contact and stepped a half step toward her to bridge the gap then took her in his arms. She was dry and warm while he was cool and damp. She felt her nipples press against his chest and his manhood pressing urgently against her.

He kissed her long and hard embracing her body, rubbing his hands all over her porcelain nakedness and running his fingers through her hair before he manoeuvred her round to the table. She sat on the hard edge for him and he lightly feathered his hands over her milky white breasts and arms. She tingled at his touch, goose bumps rising on her arms and her cherry nipples hard with desire. He nuzzled his face into her breasts, found her nipples with his tongue and sucked hard. She held his beautiful thick black hair at the back of his head not wanting to let him go. But she pulled his head back and kissed him hotly and deeply while guiding him in to her.

'Oh,' she squealed and fell back on the table while Paul pleasured her. The cold hardness of the table against Paul's hot plunging body aroused her. She scraped her fingernails into the timber table top making fresh pale stripes on it as she groaned in time with Paul's regular thrusting. He kneaded her buttocks with his fingertips and grasped then released as he kept his rhythm.

The table pushed and pulled backwards and forwards,

creaking and clattering and Lana moaned as she watched and felt her breasts quivering like jelly with Paul's thrusting. He held fast onto her hips as he became more desirous, more urgent. She felt the intense movement blur into a frenzy until she was unable to tell a push from a pull. He carried her to a place she hadn't been as she clenched onto him not wanting to let him go, not able to let him go. She felt the heat, the passion, the years of desire and she felt his soul meet hers.

Then suddenly Paul screamed and held himself upright and taut like her golden Adonis, while he succumbed. Exhausted and spent he beckoned for Lana to sit up. He cradled her in his arms stroking her, loving her while she wrapped her arms around him, resting them on the top of his hips. He held her silently until his body could do no more for her. He kissed the top of her head and quietly backed away.

'You're my beautiful angel,' he whispered.

***

The dawn rays of butternut sun streamed into the room from the front window. Flecks of dust in the air glistened in a blue and yellow haze. The air was cool and still, the mood quiet, expectant.

Lana had slept nestled into the crook of Paul's arm, safe against the exploding night, safe against the cold. She'd had a cat when she was young. He used to sleep in her bed in winter. Often she'd wake up to find Boomer nestled in the crook of her arm. She used to think nothing could give her greater joy. Paul smelt good and she breathed in his masculine scent until it awoke her senses fully. She gave a little guttural groan and she heard his breathing change. She slipped a hand inside his boxers and kneaded his buttocks with her fingertips. Paul grasped the bed with his hands but made no effort to stop her. Lana scuttled down the bed and ran her hot tongue along the side of his buttock. He groaned his consent and gently gyrated his hips, seeking more pleasure. Then she nibbled and sucked and licked and bit him, sometimes soft, sometimes hard depending on the strength of desire sweeping through her body.

She rubbed her hands over him, grasping his flesh to her face until she took him forcefully in her hot mouth. She felt him expand and she moved up and down on him sucking hard, connecting him to the roof of her mouth with each downward movement. He groaned as she caressed him with one hand and cupped her breast with the other. He moved his hips slowly, in response to his fire within, writhing up and down forcing him deeper inside her perfect mouth. He stroked her head before adding downward force to hold her to him.

She wriggled back up to face him and smiled. He reached out for her breasts and her blush-pink nipples firmed under his touch. He teased her, flicking, rubbing, smiling at Lana's moaning response. She hauled herself away from him with several panting breaths. He made to rise up.

'No. This is just for you,' Lana whispered.

She pushed him back down gently and took him once again in her mouth. She felt her desire manifest between her legs and she took some of her musky liquid onto her fingers and inserted them into Paul's mouth. He sucked greedily groaning for the love of her taste. Then she did the same for herself and squeezed her eyes shut to in her mouth and kneaded the soft skin of his inner thighs. His body tensed as pleasure overcame him and he could not hold back. He succumbed to it and groaned with each screaming force of it. Finally she tasted Paul's release in her mouth and she relaxed off him while he slumped deeper into his mattress exhausted and panting.

She nudged up to his side and nestled herself against his sweaty torso. She purred like a kitten as she again lathered her fingers in her silky liquid and put them in her mouth. Then she did the same for Paul and kissed his lips at the same time. He suckled on her fingers until the taste was long gone. She supported the side of her head with one hand and rolled on her hips to face him. One plump breast rested on the other, nipples defying the laws of gravity. She draped her fingers over Paul's body, teasing him with her finger tips and he shuddered when she tickled his side. Her fingers lingered over his biceps and his muscles rippled under his taut skin, hard under her touch. Her fingers caressed his pectoral muscles. The sight of his chest, breathing, tanned, muscled and glistening with sweat was intoxicating. She opened her hand and dragged her palm across the surface and moaned. She leaned over him and suckled his chest and kneaded his biceps. She flopped onto her back and pulled the silk fabric up to her waist. Paul sat up and straddled her caressing both flat hands over her body, fingers exploring. He rubbed his stubbled face over her breasts and she held him there. Her hips writhed impatiently and Paul sat back and peeled the silk off her to reveal her white hips and soft dark mound. His hooded brown eyes reflecting the warm morning sun couldn't mask his desire. He buried his head between her thighs, groaning and panting and Lana arched softly, moaning to meet his hot mouth just as a fresh sprinkling of volcanic debris bombarded the hut. She reached out to his head, holding him, defying him to stop. His tongue came to her, exploring, taking her to Paul's heaven, to her golden heaven.

His fingers spread over her hips and round her buttocks into her skin and Lana threw her head back arching her back off the bed as Paul brought her finally, achingly to an explosive release. She screamed as her body plunged into alternate states of tension and relief, of hot and cold, of pleasure and more pleasure. She suddenly felt cold, untouchable, unable to be touched. She dropped to the bed drained and Paul draped feather like fingers across her body.

'Ah no,' she screamed as her whole body contracted. 'Don't touch me.' She dragged the silk over her body.

'Good morning to you too angel,' he grinned broadly.

He leaned over and kissed her tenderly on the lips. She could smell and taste herself on his mouth.

'Mm' she murmured softly. 'Good morning. If I'm an angel, then you're a wizard.'

'Gee thanks,' said Paul fingering his sculptured goatee. 'Do I look like a wizard?'

Lana laughed. 'You create magic.'

'Yes I do.'

'You must devise a spell to cure that conceitedness,' she said.

'Well you have to rate yourself in this world Lana,' he said. 'And I rate my chances with a beautiful raven haired angel.' He kissed her again without touching her silk-clad form. 'I wish I could stay here making love to you forever,' said Paul.

'I don't want it to end either,' admitted Lana. 'Paul? Do you think we'd still be together if we'd become lovers at school?'

'Maybe, maybe not.'

'I think not,' she continued. 'Have you heard it said that when you plant two trees close together one will overshadow the other? That might have happened. We were too young.'

'We're trees?'

'We've done our growing, just not alongside each other. And while it might have been nice to have our branches touch I feel comfortable with who I am. You can't shade me.'

'Sweetheart, no one can shade you.'

She punched him playfully on his arm.

'I'm not teasing you,' he said. 'And for what it's worth, I think you're right. But for now, we've got to think about getting out of here.'

'At least we can walk out. We have two vehicles along the track. Three,' she corrected herself.

'Does Alex realise he may not recognise his car again?' asked Paul.

'He'll have insurance. He's an accountant.' Lana instantly put her hand to her mouth. 'Oh, I didn't mean it like that. He's a nice man Paul.' She smiled weakly and lightly touched Paul's arm. 'Just not the man for me.'

Paul kissed her sweetly and crawled out of the bunk and without putting any clothes on stoked the firebox. It smoked then blazed with fury and crackled heartily.

Lana watched him with admiring eyes as he made tea

and porridge. His broad shoulders ran down to a narrow waist which flared to perfectly white fleshy buttocks. She hugged her knees and covered her nakedness in the silk.

Paul brought her a mug of black tea and sat on the form in front of the fire.

'What do we do about those two?' Lana nodded toward the deck.

Paul cradled his tea pensively. 'They'll be okay for a while. I could call the police I suppose.'

'What?' Lana choked on her tea. 'You have battery?'

'Yeah. Emma's.'

'Well, why didn't you ring before?'

'Wasn't high on the priority list, if you recall,' he said smugly.

'Well it is now, Paul Harrington.'

'Oh, Lana. You sound like a wife,' he winced. 'I'll go down the hill once it eases up. Then at least someone can come in and get these characters while we walk out.'

'And in the meantime we wait here until the eruptions stop,' said Lana.

'Long may it last,' said Paul, grinning at her like a Cheshire cat.

Chapter Eighteen

Alex fumed. How dare she! After all he's done for her! He stood frozen to the spot staring at the phone as if Paul could jump right out of it and explain what the hell was going on. Explain why she picked now to leave him and why she's gone back up that stupid bloody mountain.

He quickly dressed and tore open the front door. The cool air on his face made him hesitate for a second then he slammed the door behind him and walked out to the main road.

The air around the township glistened with flecks of ash picked up by the breeze. He gazed up to the mountain top. The heavy gas cloud of previous days had lessened to a transparent haze, more yellow than brown and at this moment the volcano softly grumbled beneath it.

In a way he hoped Paul was right about Lana's whereabouts. After all, she could have driven to Sarah's. In that case he'd be risking his life for nothing, as perhaps Paul would be, for he sensed something in the man's voice that he would follow her. If she had returned to the mountain when had she made that decision? His had been an impulse, and as he felt the deep rumble that reverberated out through the ring plain, he realised he could turn back.

There wasn't much traffic, a few trucks. He stuck out his thumb. It felt wrong. Only once before had he hitched a ride and that was when he was a teen in his first car. He had run out of petrol and hitched a ride to the next gas station and back again. He swore it wouldn't happen again.

It wasn't long before a double cab utility pulled off the road ahead of him. He hurried into a light trot and ducked to the open passenger window.

'How far you going mate?' asked the driver.

'I'm going up to Rangipo Hut,' he explained. 'Can you take me as far as the turnoff?'

'You're joking aren't you? You can't go up there,' the driver exclaimed.

'My girlfriend is there,' said Alex.

'Then she should stay there till it's clear to leave,' the driver offered.

'If you won't give me a lift I'll find someone else,' said Alex and he stepped casually away from the vehicle.

The driver was taken aback. Maybe he could talk this lunatic out of it. And if he couldn't then at least he could direct the police to the man's last sighting.

'Na, hop in mate.'

Alex opened the door and climbed into the passenger seat.

'I don't like letting you out in the middle of nowhere with the mountain acting up.' The driver looked Alex up and down, pausing at Alex's street shoes. 'Jack Baker,' he said reaching his arm clear across his body to shake hands with Alex.

'Alex Holden,' he replied shaking the proffered hand.

'How do you think you're going to rescue this girl of yours?' asked Jack.

'I have a map,' said Alex. 'My car is up there.'

Jack nodded sagely. 'She drive up herself?'

'Yep.'

'Then it will be parked at the Round the Mountain

Track no doubt. It's bound to be smashed up you know,' Jack explained.

Alex flinched picturing the shiny panel work dented with pockmarks.

'What's she doing up there?' asked Jack.

'Research.'

'Don't mind my asking mate, but have you been up the mountain before?'

'No,' Alex stayed close-lipped and they drove for the next five minutes in silence.

Presently Jack pulled off to the side of the road. 'Here we are then,' he announced.

Alex hesitated. It was warm in the ute. Jack seemed all right. Probably he'd turn around and take him right back to the motel if he asked. He looked through the passenger window. The mountain looked the same – uninviting. A narrow rutted track meandered through low scrub.

'Looks like she's up there all right,' Jack volunteered pointing out the tyre tracks.

Alex grunted. Jack could see he was having second thoughts. Alex looked ahead, through the front window, but not really seeing and not really knowing what to look for.

'Nothing wrong with turning around and going back mate,' said Jack.

Alex pictured the motel room without Lana in it, then pictured his house without Lana in it. No, he'd made his decision; life without Lana wasn't an option. He opened the door and half stepped out as Jack continued. 'Your girl might prefer you alive as dead.'

'Thanks for the lift,' said Alex and he shut the door

behind him.

The mountain loomed large over him. He was unprepared for the enormity of it. Already he felt swallowed up by its magnitude. But Lana was there and here were her tracks to prove it. He felt closer to her already. He dug his hands deep into his trouser pocket to reassure himself the ring was safe. He'd calmed down last night when he was alone. He had it all worked out, how to win her back. Only he knew what she liked, only he could give her what she needed. She wanted a shorter reign; that much was clear, just like an old fashioned woman. She was too free. So free she chopped and changed her mind and didn't know what she wanted. Look at her, two careers and not even middle aged. And then some man with supposed good looks flexes his muscles at her and she swoons and tells Alex it's all over. No, she just doesn't realise how much she wants him.

A pang of jealousy surged through him as he thought of Paul but it provided the much needed adrenalin to fuel him into action.

Pulling his jacket tightly around him he set off. His shoes squeaked on the ash when he scuffed and he quickly figured out to walk in the fresh tracks if he wanted to avoid a build up on his shoes. The track ahead was devoid of footprints. He allowed himself a smile. At least he'd beaten Paul.

But after about ten minutes of reasonably easy walking Alex's shoes were thick with clodden ash. And they were heavy. The sensation underfoot was no longer flat and easy but rounded and uncomfortable, like walking on a boulder beach without shoes. He stopped and removed a loafer clumsily pointing a sock-clad foot onto the ground for balance. He scraped at the ash on the sole of his shoe and whacked the shoe against a rock before slipping it back on his foot. He repeated the action on the other shoe then set off again, less optimistically than before.

It was another fifteen minutes further up the track before he had to repeat the exercise. In the distance up ahead he could see a red dot. It must be his car. Only then did it dawn on him how far ahead Lana was. Jack's ute would have easily handled this track. He could have already been at the track junction if Jack had offered to take him. But Jack hadn't. Alex wondered why not.

Just as he tottered on one leg the mountain gave a hiccup causing him to leap forward into a hunch. He cowered into a ball with his arms wrapped about his head. Dull plopping sounds rang around him and he snuck a peek at the falling debris. The wonder that he hadn't been struck! The pebbles were warm. He could tell because they steamed when they landed in the thick ash.

Alex stayed turtle-like for what seemed an eternity before small volcanic bombs hit him on his back and head, and buttocks and legs. Then he remembered Lana's wound and visualised the same all over his body like dirty festering mumps. Hot pains shot through him like bee stings. He gasped for breath, sucking in the electric air and when he finally filled his lungs he yelled from the shock of it. His head screamed, not emanating from his diaphragm but from the wringing in his ears and he was sure the wind was whistling through a gaping hole. He clutched at his head and pulled his hands away which were covered in red sticky blood. He gave a little gasp. Not for the first time this morning he began to doubt the wisdom of this venture.

A dark cavern opened up somewhere deep inside him. It looked soft and safe and he spiralled towards it, but the thought of Lana tugged at him. What if she wasn't in the cavern alluring and soft and lovely and wanting him. Wouldn't she hold a light? He fought it. 'Lana,' he cried. He couldn't see her but she could wait. She'd understand. He accepted the safety of the cave and gave himself to its warm embrace. Not for long, just long enough for the pain to leave and then he'd rescue her – if she wasn't already in the cave.

***

By the time Alex regained consciousness the light over the mountain had changed. He fluttered his eyes open where he lay and sputtered ash out of his mouth. It was slippery between his teeth, not like he expected ash to be at all. His nose seemed to be hot and cold simultaneously but he could breathe. He groaned with the agony of a sore head and cold seeped through his back and legs into his bones. He delicately touched the back of his head scared to move and afraid of what he might find. His fingertips stroked a swollen egg too tender to touch with anything more than a whisper. Blood had trickled from the back of his head around to his face and mouth but now it was dry and his face felt stiff. He spluttered with the taste of it.

He tried to move but that put pressure on his groin. It was numb up until then. He blindly flailed his hands over his torso until he felt a warm boulder resting on his stomach and groin. He could only whimper as he lay under it, no strength to move it.

How long had he lain there like this? What was he thinking of? Jack was right. Why didn't he listen to him? He had to reach Lana. He tried to wriggle free of the rock but his head was heavier than the rock. Strange. Never been that heavy before. He collapsed back on the ground. Hard to see. He clutched his face. It was soft. Not like the soft of a wool blanket, tangible, real. More like candy floss soft. His fingers tried to tell him that half his nose was gone, burned under a searing block while he was unconscious, that's why his head hurt. He didn't believe it. The red fingers were his, he could feel them. He just couldn't feel where they'd been.

He lay still for a long time and thought about Lana. They'd had good times. Always good. He was sorry her last minutes with him were horrible. They'd never had upsetting moments in all their years together. He'd never been mean to her as he had yesterday. Poor, beautiful Lana.

'I'm sorry,' he whispered, 'sorry.'

A shiver ran through him and he was pleased for it meant his body had the will to survive, for the moment at least. But again he tried to roll the rock off and again the effort beat him. What madness was this to run up here, rescue Lana and make her love him? But she did love him once. And that's what he clung to as he lay there succumbing to the numbing cold. He pulled the box out of his pocket and fingered Lana's ring, clutching it to his chest as the tendrils of the black cave pulled him back.

***

Colleen and Alfred had finished a light lunch of bagels and coffee when there was a knock on the motel door. Colleen wiped her hands on her trousers as she opened it.

'Mrs Colleen Hill?' asked an impossibly young policeman.

'Yes.'

'I have some news of the stolen medals ma'am,' he said.

'Do you really?' she exclaimed. 'Come in.'

She ushered the constable and his colleague into the room.

'We understand the medals are in a hut on the east side of Mount Ruapehu. We haven't sighted them but we had a report from a couple of scientists that the medals are with them. As soon as eruptions and weather conditions allow we will retrieve them,' he explained.

'Well,' said Colleen. 'Isn't that fabulous?'

'Will you be staying here another night?' asked the constable?

'Yes, for tonight,' she replied. 'But may have to stay longer now to see a resolution.'

'Very good ma'am. If I have any further information I'll be in touch,' he concluded.

'Thank you,' said Colleen. 'By the way, how did you know where to find me?'

'One of the scientists met you here at the motel,' he explained.

The constable headed to the door with Colleen in tow.

'Thank you so much,' she said and turned to Alfred

431

clapping her hands with glee. 'Can you believe it Alfred?'

'Good news indeed,' Alfred agreed. 'Who was it? Lana?'

'Must be her,' Colleen pondered. 'Oh bless her.'

Chapter Nineteen

Lana tiptoed across the floor in her thick socks and held her nose close to the windowpane. She strained to see Joe and Tom trussed up along the wall beneath the window. They looked miserable. Each time she had to leave the warmth of the hut she averted her eyes from them, shielding her face with a bladed hand. More than anything she was embarrassed that they'd heard her very vocal lovemaking. She shut out the thought that they may have even manoeuvred themselves into such a position as to be able to watch.

The day had lost its azure blue and had given way to a soft salmon dusk. The day's eruptions were frequent but inconsistent and the magnitude ranged from mere hiccups to full blown incendiary fountains riddled with molten rock from deep within the earth.

Lana's nerves had settled throughout the course of the day eased by Paul's eloquent geological explanations. He was energised by the mountain's activities and it put Lana in his head space for a brief period. She wasn't scared when Paul explained events in pure scientific terms. Even more reassuring was when he explained that for all its might the mountain hadn't actually claimed any lives, in European history anyway. In fact the most human damage Mount Ruapehu could claim was a leg four years ago when it threw a rock into Dome Shelter where two climbers were sheltering.

She crept back from the window.

'Are you going to feed those guys?' she asked Paul.

'No,' he said quickly, not giving it any thought.

'You sure?' Lana asked. 'I know it's only boiled rice

but maybe...'

'Lana,' Paul interjected. 'Let me deal with it. I'll give them tea but no food. They don't deserve any clemency, especially from you sweetheart. Besides, they're army boys. They've been trained for this. If they can't survive a little incapacitation in mild weather God help all of us.'

Paul squeezed her shoulders and she put her arms around his waist and rested them on the small of his back. He dipped his head to her and she met his lips for his kiss. She felt his tongue explore her mouth as if it was the first tender time he'd tasted it. His hands caressed her back pulling her gently but firmly into him. She pulled back laughing.

'You're insatiable Paul Harrington,' she giggled.

'Yes I am. I've got a lifetime of catching up to do sweetheart,' he replied. He stroked her arms and delicately wiped a strand of hair from her face tucking it behind her ear; something he seemed to do a lot now.

'We don't have long Lana,' Paul whispered. 'I want you to remember our time here as the best loving in the world.'

She started to reply but Paul held his index finger across both her lips.

'I want you to know me as the best lover in the world Lana.' He nuzzled into her neck and nibbled her cool white flesh. A hot pulse shot through her causing her to squeeze her eyes shut. She heard him inhale deeply and as he exhaled through the top of his chest he groaned a long murmur. She dropped her hands to his buttocks and lightly kneaded them giving a little moan, deep and guttural.

Her lower back cooled to the air as Paul lifted her

shirt and caressed her skin. His hands moved slowly then with urgency as they embraced her buttocks. Then she felt him grind her flesh as his desire became a need.

She held herself firmly against Paul's thigh as he slowly undid her top button. His hot breath on her throat sent shivers down her spine as he nibbled her. The anticipation of his mouth on her beaded nipples caused a sudden dull ache in her groin.

'Oh Paul,' she moaned.

'Yes Lana,' Paul murmured into her chest.

'Mm,' she moaned.

'You are so soft darling. I love your white skin.'

She smiled and tousled his hair, firming her hands around the back of his head. His mouth found her breast and his tongue deftly flicked across her aroused nipple. He brought his hand to it and plumped her breast in his hand. She started at the intensity and felt his manhood stir against her lower belly.

'Oh Paul,' she moaned.

He peeled her shirt off as if she were made of porcelain, threading her arms out of the sleeves. The fading afternoon light cast her shoulders the colour of dirty snow. He guided her to the little wooden table and sat her on it. She tugged at his waist and untucked his shirt. He let her remove it and she dragged it over his bowed head then guided his mouth back to her breasts, holding her there, unable to let him go, until her desire for deeper pleasure overcame her.

She propped her hands on the table behind her offering more than her breasts. As she flung her head back he kept her dusky pink nipples hard with his flicking hot tongue and fingertips until finally he moved

435

his mouth over her belly, sucking and nibbling until her trousers stopped him.

'Oh Lana,' he moaned.

'Make love to me Paul,' she begged.

'I will Lana,' he murmured. 'Like there's no tomorrow.'

'But I shall want you tomorrow Paul.'

'Mm.'

'And the day after that, and the day after that,' she panted.

He fumbled with her trousers and unzipped her hurriedly slipping his hands into the back of them. He kneaded her buttocks softly exploring at first then grasping with urgency as his desire intensified. He groaned and threw his face into her silky soft and welcoming mound.

'You smell delicious,' he groaned. 'Darling, I love you. I want you. Do you love me Lana?'

Paul gently peeled her trousers off her. He tucked his thumbs into the side seams of her lacy pink panties, shed them and ducked his head again to her. He buried his face and she felt his tongue take long sensual sweeps enticing her to the edge of explosion. She parted her legs ever so slightly for him, scared to move lest he stop; but he didn't. He probed her teasingly until she ached deeply.

'God Paul,' she whispered and pressed her hands hard onto the back of his head. She held him there and he eased her legs apart. She moaned as she threw her body back on the table and exulted in his exquisite touch. She moved her hips up and down to his tongue.

'Paul, Paul,' she intoned.

'Lana,' he groaned. 'Do you love me?'

'I do Paul.' She rubbed his head enjoying the feeling of her fingers in his hair.

'Say it Lana. Say you love me,' Paul begged.

'I love you Paul, I love you. Kiss me.'

He stood to her and took her face in his hands. She drowned in his darkly erotic liquid brown eyes. He parted her lips with his finger which she sucked until she couldn't taste her anymore. She rubbed her hands over his body, tight and muscled under her fingers. She dug her fingernails into his buttocks, scratching his smooth white skin.

'Ah, Lana,' Paul yelped then smiled and kissed her deeper. She felt his urgency as he hungrily explored her mouth. Paul lightly stroked himself then rubbed hard against her. She writhed under his touch and with delicious hands he rubbed them over her, hot and urgent, over her breasts, shoulders, arms, hips, buttocks and thighs. Then again he sucked her inner thighs, nibbling her milky flesh and inhaled deeply her intoxicating scent.

He brought his fingers to her and with his tongue and gently probing fingers pleasured Lana. He took her to a deeper place, a higher place, out of herself. She growled with contentment and moaned deeply as she threw herself back on the table, delighting in the cool touch on her bare back contrasting with the burning touch that was Paul. She rocked her hips to him.

Paul sucked on his fingers, closing his soft doe eyes to his pleasure. 'Lana, Lana, Lana,' he intoned. He pleasured her again and took his fingers to her mouth. She groaned as she suckled on them.

'Lana,' Paul groaned so deeply she barely heard her name. He leaned back a little and she felt him with an intensity she couldn't comprehend. She gagged with inscrutable pleasure as Paul entered then rode her moving her back and forth against the table. She let the table rock back and forth under her as she succumbed her whole being to him.

Paul's hands were hot on her hips as he drove into her. He cast his eyes over her delighting in her nakedness then leaned forward and took her hands in his. He placed her hands over her breasts.

'Please me,' he whispered.

She caressed her open palms over her body, her sides, her hips, her stomach, her breasts. She paused at her breasts delighting at her aroused nipples and revelling in the fire below her belly.

'God Lana,' Paul breathed. 'I want you.'

She smiled shyly and gently cupped her breasts for him. 'Pleasure me some more Paul. Don't stop,' she murmured.

Paul ground his body against her tiny button of desire until they simultaneously moaned louder and longer until Paul tensed and released taking Lana with him. Arching to him she screamed over and again until she flopped back panting.

'Oh Lana,' Paul murmured. 'I do love you. He kissed her gently on her nose then her lips. He stepped back from her, eased his arm behind him and picked up the silk fabric which he draped it over her without laying a finger on her.

She murmured. 'I don't want this to end.'

'It doesn't have to end sweetheart,' soothed Paul.

'One day it will,' she said.

'Only here,' he said. 'There's life beyond the hut.'

'For us?' she asked.

Paul shuffled a form up to the side of the table and sat on it. He lit a candle and sat it on the hearth then reached for Lana's knitted woollen scarf. He folded it and laid it under her head.

'Especially for us sweetheart,' he said.

'There's a song. It's called Candy, but I'm renaming it Lana.' He took up the tune. 'Lana, Lana, Lana, I can't let you go, all my life you've haunted me, I want you so.'

'I don't know it.'

'It's us sweetheart. Lost love found again,' he explained. 'Please don't leave me Lana, not again.'

'I don't have to leave you Paul,' she whispered.

He lifted her hand to his lips and kissed each finger one by one. His breath was warm. She let her hand stroke the side of his face. His jaw was rough with stubble.

Lana rose onto her elbows and the silk fabric carelessly slunk off her shoulders. Paul picked up a corner and covered her again.

'What's going to happen now?' she whispered.

'You can move north, transfer your studies to my university and move in with me,' he replied pragmatically.

'God, you've got it all worked out,' she said. 'Is there a rush?'

'Of course there is sweetheart,' said Paul. 'Every moment is precious.'

'I was thinking more short term,' Lana explained.

'We've got a walk ahead of us and a small river crossing. I have to return Alex's car and the medals have to be returned.'

'And then you and I go our separate ways Lana? No.'

'I didn't say no Paul. I'm not saying no,' she said. 'I'm saying yes in capital letters. Yes, I want to be with you. Why don't you believe me?'

'I don't want to let you out of my sight. My angel girl.'

She took both his hands and squeezed them and held them to her lips.

'I love you.'

***

The day dawned quiet and a heavy sun beamed unhindered into the hut. Lana stirred and turned to Paul. His hand rested on her thigh.

'Good morning darling. Hungry?' she asked with a hint of mischief.

He grinned. 'Lana Marshall,' he grumbled. 'If I didn't know better I'd say you were trying to seduce me.'

She giggled as Paul took hold of a corner of silk that draped around her shoulders. He freed it from her to expose her and before his eyes her fuchsia nipples responded to him. She caressed her hands over his hips then pleasured him with sensual fingers. He threw his head back and softly moaned.

Lana whispered, 'You like?'

'Mm-mm,' said Paul. 'Don't stop.'

She nestled into his side rubbing her breasts against his tightly muscled torso and nibbled him until her tongue found his nipple. Her hand moved rhythmically, almost of its own accord until Paul groaned louder and writhed his hips under her touch, moving faster, urgently. Lana took his cue and worked him until he was spent.

She let him recover his breath. He lay on his back glistening in the speckled morning light purring contentedly. He looked beautiful. Time really had been kind to him. She was lucky. Men his age often had a beer gut, or gone a bit bald, or grey. But Paul hadn't succumbed to these. She studied his face, his mouth, nose, eyes. Hair; there was a little greying at the temples. She liked it. How strange that she should want to make love to a man with a bit of grey in his hair. She, who felt no more than sixteen herself.

He opened his eyes and smiled when he saw her looking at him.

'Let me,' he whispered.

'Let you what?' Lana teased as she stroked his stomach lightly with her fingers.

'Oh Lana,' he groaned. He pushed her onto her back and gazed longingly at her flushed nipples sitting atop fleshy white breasts. Straddling her he buried his face between them then tickled her all over with his whiskers: over her torso, her belly, her shoulders, finally resting on the moulding of her breasts. His tongue found a nipple and he pinched the other, squeezing lightly until it would harden no more.

Beneath him Lana ached and she slowly arched her hips up and down desperate for a resolve.

'Paul,' she moaned.

'Mm-mm,' he moaned in reply.

441

'I need you,' she panted.

'I know sweetheart,' he mumbled into her neck. She parted her legs for him.

'Lana, Lana, Lana,' he intoned. He sucked his own fingers and brought to Lana's aching body the object of its desire. She moaned like an alley cat as she tensed and arched to him until she fell back depleted.

***

Lana spent the next half hour dozing on the bunk recovering from their love making. It seemed as though time had stopped. There was nothing but Paul. There was no past, no future. Only now, this minute and Paul filled every second of it. She lost count how many times they made love, sometimes tender, sometimes hot and urgent to prove it wasn't a dream. She wanted Paul's marks, his fingers and teeth, his scent. She wanted to know that his love for her was real, that when she walked off this mountain she would take a part of him. She felt what Paul felt and it felt right. She could reach out and touch her love for him. He was attentive to her, he read her, pre-empted and satisfied her. She could see it made him happy to make her happy. It felt right to do as he said; to change her whole life again. She hugged herself under the silk bag.

Paul had stoked the fire and was setting the table with two mugs of tea and a pot of boiled rice.

'Sorry, it's rice again sweetheart,' he said cheerily.

'I don't care,' she replied. 'When we're out of here you can take me out for a steak.'

'Might be sooner than you think,' said Paul.

442

'Really?' she asked. 'Eruptions have stopped?'

'Haven't you noticed?' he grinned.

'I haven't been paying much attention to what the mountain is doing,' Lana conceded.

'Well, it hasn't rumbled in at least six hours,' Paul explained. 'The police will be here soon. Then we'll leave.'

'Oh,' said Lana abruptly.

'Disappointed sweetheart?' he asked.

'You know,' she shrugged her shoulders. 'Bitter sweet.'

'I know,' Paul agreed. 'In fact, I can hear someone now.' A thuk thuk sounded in the distance, becoming louder as they tuned their thoughts into the world beyond the hut. He padded over to the front window to see not one but two Iroquois helicopters circling the hut.

'Good lord, no expense spared for thieves and scoundrels,' said Paul.

He watched as four men in uniform exited the choppers then made their way over the rocky ground to the hut. He dragged open the door.

'Good morning gentlemen,' he called to them.

'Hello there,' said the first constable.

Paul stood in the door blocking the entrance long enough for Lana to pull on some clothes. She walked to Paul's side to greet the newcomers.

'These are the offenders obviously,' stated a constable.

'This is them,' Paul confirmed. 'I haven't fed or watered them this morning. In fact I've only been watering them. They could be a tad hungry.'

Paul held his hand out to the constable. 'Paul

Harrington and Lana Marshall. We'll walk out now while we can.'

'The medals?' asked the constable.

'Sure.' Paul walked back into the hut and picked up the sock filled with the medals. He weighed it in his hand.

'Lana met the lady who one of these medals belongs to. She wants to be able to hand it to her personally. Do you think that could be arranged?' asked Paul.

'I'll keep that in mind sir and let you know.'

'Okay, we're out of here,' said Paul. He turned Lana into the room and they quickly prepared for the walk out. Clad in mittens, scarf, beanie and thick jacket, Lana stood in the centre of the room.

'I feel sad,' she said.

Paul approached her and put his arms around her waist.

'I know sweetheart, I know.'

She stepped out onto the deck and spoke to a constable.

'Do you want us to show you where the body is?' Lana asked.

'Yes please ma'am.'

'It's only half an hour from here, but the terrain is tricky,' she explained as she looked the constables up and down.

She turned to the two trussed offenders. They were being manhandled by two constables into a seated position, being separated and individually constrained. For the first time in two days she made eye contact with them and unsurprisingly she felt embarrassment. She wondered what it must have been like for them to be outside that wall listening to her groaning with pleasure. Or perhaps even watching. Suddenly she cared not. She would never set eyes on them again.

She quickly stepped off the deck and started along the ash-strewn track. Paul strode behind her with two constables in tow. She picked a path ahead following what was left of the orange markers and negotiated her way over the rocky trail.

'You two came up here twice?' called one of the constables.

'Yeah,' said Paul.

'I would have thought once was enough,' the constable panted.

'Well Nancy Drew here figured it out for you guys and risked her life in doing so,' said Paul.

Lana slowed to a stop and turned to face the following party.

'What we don't know is why the thieves fell out,' she said. 'They fought with knives and one died. You've got the other one in the army hospital. The one who died had the memorial cross hidden on him. That's the one that belongs to Colleen, the lady I met at the motel.'

She strode out again at a good pace and stopped as she approached the bottom of the ridge that overlooked the lahar path. She held back. Paul pulled up alongside her.

'Okay sweetheart?' He put an arm around her waist and squeezed gently.

She winced. 'I remember how it was two days ago.'

'Let me go Lana,' Paul volunteered. 'You don't need to see something as horrible as that sweetheart.'

'I feel like I should,' she replied.

'No,' he said. 'I can show the police. You go downstream a bit.'

'Thanks Paul,' Lana said.

'Okay,' Paul said turning to the constables. 'I'll take you to the body.'

***

Paul led the police up the ridge and paused at the crest to survey the scene to the north. Below them and to one side of the lahar path, which was now a burbling grey stream, was a bloated body. Movement caught his eye to the right. It was Lana. He watched her slowly pick her way over the stony ground. He waved but she kept walking away from him. She looked so small out there, and fragile. He had an overwhelming desire to look after her. Soon she disappeared from his view and it struck him how lonely he'd be if she never came back. He waited for the others to catch their breath before leading them down the other side of the ridge. He picked his path mindful of his ankle. If he was going to roll it this is where he'd do it. And that could lead to ribs puncturing his lungs, which would lead to no making love to Lana.

They reached the body to find it deteriorating and an acrid stench pervaded the air. Blue flies settled on the face, up its nose and in its eyes. One flew out its mouth. The fingers were puffy.

'If you roll it onto the side you'll see what looks like a knife wound,' said Paul. 'Can I leave you guys to it?'

'Yes. Thanks mate,' said a constable. 'We'll take it from here.'

'Oh by the way, I've got photos,' said Paul. 'Took

them several days ago. Thought they might be useful.'

Paul made his way downstream to where Lana sat waiting for him.

'How does it look?' she asked.

'You don't want to know sweetheart. Come on, let's get out of here.' Paul scanned the stream for a safe crossing and helped Lana across.

'Thanks,' she said flinging her scarf around her neck. She skipped on ahead, hands deep in her pockets. The walking was firm under foot but even so she concentrated, avoiding newly planted rocks that had not imbedded into the soft fine pebbles. She squinted ahead into the low sun to keep aligned with the orange route markers.

She paused to face the mountain's ring plain below and noted expansive desert: trucks trawling like ants along the Desert Road, the odd twinkle of car lights, the imposing power pylons lording it over the dry landscape and the rolling horizon that told her there was an end in sight.

'My favourite view,' she said. 'I'll miss it, believe it or not.'

'We'll come here again sweetheart,' said Paul. 'Promise.'

Lana smiled. The walk out was very different from their first walk in. She was relaxed and she revelled in Paul's company and his love for her.

'Come on,' Paul urged. 'We're still in a danger zone.'

'I don't feel in danger,' she replied.

'Another hour before we get to the vehicles Lana,' Paul warned.

She gazed ahead, sighed and traipsed off along the

trail. She couldn't help but smile. Her heart felt like it would burst out her chest and be carried away by bluebirds. In all the world the only man who truly knew the real Lana wanted to be with her. She should pinch herself. But it wasn't over yet. Alex had taken it badly. She had to return his car. There it was, in the distance, a red speck on the ridge. Now her stomach lurched as she contemplated unfinished business. She had clothes at Alex's house, as he had at hers.

She imagined him cooped up in the motel room impatiently waiting for her. He would be beating himself up, analysing both their faults, hers mostly, and making a plan to patch it all up. Just a silly misunderstanding. Look, you can see it all here on this spreadsheet. No, I didn't leave you for Paul. I didn't mean to fall in love; that came later. It had nothing to do with you. Oops – landed on a snake, back you go.

Suddenly they reached the vehicles. The two utilities and her car were covered in a thick coat of ash and were dotted with volcanic bombs. Alex's car was devoid of ash deposits but was pelted with rock. Lana approached it and rubbed a mittened hand smoothly along the panel work.

'Oh dear,' she muttered. 'Oh dear. This is not good.'

Paul opened his door and turned the key in the ignition. After a few turns the engine kicked into life. He let it idle for a bit and joined Lana at the Mazda.

'The ash could be a problem for my motor,' Paul explained. 'You follow me down the track in case I have to coast. We'll pause at the junction to the highway okay?'

'Okay,' she said.

'You look worried sweetheart.'

'Look at the state of this car Paul,' said Lana. 'Alex will be apoplectic.'

'He'll have insurance,' Paul reasoned.

'Yes he will, but he's a bit fragile at present,' Lana explained.

'Is that worrying you?' asked Paul.

'Yes it is.'

'I'll be with you sweetheart,' Paul offered.

'No,' Lana replied. 'I don't think that's a good idea.'

'But he knows about me right?' asked Paul.

'In a manner of speaking.'

'What does that mean?'

'I kind of used you as an excuse for coming to my decision in ending our relationship. Not as the reason for my decision,' she explained helplessly.

'So if he sees you and me together it will add insult to injury?' Paul asked.

'Definitely.'

'Were you being honest with him Lana?'

'I thought I was,' she replied. 'You are the catalyst for leaving him.'

'Well Alex will see that you left him for me. Straight and simple,' said Paul.

'I don't see it like that,' Lana responded.

'That's where men and women differ I guess,' said Paul. 'You return his car and give him back his house keys too, huh?' Paul advised.

'Where will you be?' asked Lana.

'Right behind you darling. I'm not letting you out of my sight.' He kissed her gently on the lips. 'Let's go.'

***

Lana engaged the Mazda into gear and followed Paul down the track keeping the revs high and the gears low. She watched Paul's exhaust drip condensation as he bumped his vehicle over the ruts. She expected they would pull into the motel and leave Alex's car with the keys in it for him to find. The state of it would send him into orbit and she had no wish to witness that.

Suddenly Paul stopped abruptly and before she realised she clunked into his back bumper. Her foot flew off the clutch and the car stalled to a halt. 'Bugger!' she cursed. Paul leapt out his door and rushed to the front of his ute disappearing from view.

Lana wrenched open her door and started to follow him. Then he loomed large in front of her, blocking her path. He laid his hands firmly on her shoulders and tried to turn her away. But she strained to look past him. He was talking to her, telling her no, pushing her. Why was he doing this? And then she saw a leg. It was Alex's leg because it had on a shoe that belonged to Alex. What was Alex doing there? Alex wasn't on the mountain.

'No Lana, no.' Paul kept saying. No what? What?

She pushed against him, shoved him, screamed. That's what broke his grip on her, the scream with the unexpected chop to his inside elbow. He crumpled into her and she scrambled around him throwing herself on the ground. Alex was cold. Alex didn't move. She stroked him, what was left of his face. He used to have a pleasing face. His eyes stared out of bloody slits, the life gone from them. She didn't recognise the rest for the gash that used to be his nose swelled up his eyes and

450

cheeks. His lips were blue and she traced them with her finger. Paul tried to move the boulder and decided a shove with his boot was most effective. Lana traced her trembling fingers along Alex's chest. His soft hand, now stiff with rigueur mortis, which he held over his heart made a fist. She gently prised it open. It seemed right to take the ring now.

Her body racked with silent convulsions. She did this to him. He was going to prove himself to her. He was going to win her back and he'd lost his life in the belief of that conviction. How could she have been so wrong? He lay there like a peaceful sacrifice to the mountain. He wasn't a bad man and he didn't deserve this.

She felt Paul's hands steady her shoulders. Suddenly all she could hear was a distant thud in her ears, all she could see was Alex imploring her to marry him. If she'd said yes he wouldn't be dead. Even if all she could manage was a maybe he wouldn't be dead. But he was, stone dead. And it was no one's fault but hers. She didn't know what to feel. A cold kind of numbness enveloped her. Then guilt filtered through the shroud. She killed Alex as clearly as if she'd put an arrow through his heart.

Paul held her tight. She wasn't sure for how long; the numbness stole time. Neither of them spoke. Then she felt herself being lifted. Paul was talking to her. His lips were moving. Now he was trying to lift Alex but she knew he couldn't, not on his own.

Then she was back in the vehicle. Paul slammed her door shut and she stared through the front window. There were drag marks in front of the ute. She knew she'd moved Alex, laid him out on the tray of the ute, like a stuck pig. She just couldn't remember.

Paul climbed in and slammed his door. She thought he turned to her and told her she was a good girl then squeezed her hand. She didn't remember the drive into town.

Chapter Twenty

Tom raised cuffed hands to his forehead and wiped the sweat from his brow inadvertently shoving his glasses down his nose. He strained one buttock off the seat then the other one. The urine was rank. It hadn't dried with the heat of his body. Paul hadn't untied them in the nearly twenty four hours they'd been trussed on the verandah.

Joe seemed to be managing better; the difference between a soldier and a medic Tom thought. Joe said nothing. His face was impassive. If he dreaded what was to come he gave no sign of it. He just stared out the window although Tom could tell he wasn't actually looking out the window, just staring out, not seeing.

Tom was on the right side of the chopper to see Lana and Paul walking to the lahar with the police. Ant's swollen body was more or less where he'd seen it last but less than five minutes later he was surprised to see a figure lying on the track to the car park.

The flight was short, uncomfortably so. Soon he would be bombarded with questions; who, what, when, where, why. That was the tough one. Motive. He didn't have an answer to that. They hadn't made a plan to cover this part; the part where they got caught. And even if they had, wasn't his motivation wildly different from Joe's? It was impossible to think over the din of the chopper. The police hadn't given them earphones so there was no way of communicating with anyone. Not that there was a need to. But it made Tom feel more isolated and it reinforced that he was a criminal. He could see the distant buildings getting bigger. He gulped down the hollowness in his gut. Not long now until he's named and shamed. Too soon he saw trees swaying under the down draught of the rotors as the chopper hovered over the base. Joe steadfastly stared out the window.

As they touched down a police jeep pulled up at the perimeter fence and two men got out. They wore army fatigues with Kevlar vests and carried arms. Tom felt his mouth go dry. The officers hurried towards them, already ducking out of the way of the rotors even though they had ten metres yet to cover.

Finally they were allowed to get out. Tom flinched at the strong grip on his upper arm as a military policeman escorted him to the jeep. He kept his head bowed long after he needed to. He wished his pants were dry.

***

'They've got them,' cried the girl behind the counter as she shoved her phone back into her jeans pocket. The cafe buzzed into life, stranger talking to stranger trying to glean any more information on the arrests. Alfred had barely made a dent in his scone. Colleen was watching her weight.

'Come on.' She grabbed her coat off the back of the chair and held Alfred's walking stick ready for him.

***

A throng of reporters milled outside the police station. Colleen had dropped Alfred off amongst them and then tried to find a park. In the end she parked the car back

454

outside the cafe and traipsed all the way back to the station. She spotted Alfred and took his arm firmly. 'Give me your stick,' she said already relieving him of it. Wielding it hip height she created space within the throng and led Alfred inside. Reporters jostled for position in the cramped foyer. A gnarled constable in badly fitting uniform sauntered out to them and patiently held up his hand. Immediately the babble stopped.

'They're not here,' he said. 'Military.'

'They're at the army base,' a reporter cried out and suddenly the room was clear leaving Colleen and Alfred alone with the officer.

'Yes love.' He addressed Colleen. 'What can I do for you?'

'We've come for our medal,' she replied.

'Ah, I see.'

She could see the man thinking. He didn't believe her. 'The New Zealand Memorial Cross, King George,' she blurted out.

'They probably won't let you take it, but you could identify it for them,' he said kindly. 'Would that do for now?'

Colleen looked at Alfred who nodded at her.

'Yes,' she answered. 'For now.'

'Well then, I think I can get my sergeant to run you over there.' He picked up the phone. 'I'll let them know you're coming.'

Shortly they were driven to the army base in a police car and after signing in at the gate house and leaving disgruntled reporters in their wake they were dropped off at the military justice building. It looked like all the other buildings, dated and tired. There was a limply hung flag on a pole around which a rose garden was planted. The first flush of spring was evident in the new red growth. Alfred paused in front of it and if Colleen hadn't already reached the door she would have seen him salute it.

On the grubby wall behind the reception counter was a photo of a young Queen Elizabeth II and a separate one of a young Prince Philip, probably taken in 1953 when this building was already two years old. Colleen approached the woman behind the desk and introduced themselves.

'May we see our medal?' she asked.

'Just take a seat ma'am and someone will escort you,' the woman directed.

At that moment a door opened and two scruffy men, handcuffed to two military police were hustled into the room. The taller of the two stopped in his tracks when he saw them. Colleen watched his face drain of all colour. She thought he must have recognised her but she was quite sure she'd never seen him before. He lurched forward as the men behind shoved him to keep moving and Colleen stepped out of his way. But not Alfred. He stood fast. His face contorted. It went from shock to rage in a matter of seconds. Instead of clearing a path he moved forward into the man until the two of them lost their footing. They landed in a heap on the floor but not for a second did either of them take their eyes off the other.

'Granddad,' Tom gasped.

'What?' Colleen screamed. 'Alf?'

Alfred's face had gone red and he struggled not just to regain his feet but with shock.

'Alfred!' Colleen screamed again. As she bent to help

456

him she and caught Tom's eyes.

'Sorry,' he whispered.

Hands jostled Tom up off the floor and the two men again faced each other. Tom's glasses had flown off in the tumble and now Alfred stood with them for a second before handing them to Tom. He merely nodded his acceptance. Suddenly the silence broke.

'Hello *Granddad*.' It was Joe. He spat out the words as if they were poison and his face wore a sneer.

'Who the hell are you?' Alfred demanded.

Joe jolted as the man behind him prodded him with a truncheon. 'You watch your lip son,' the guard warned.

'I'm just being polite to my granddad sir,' Joe replied.

Alfred looked to Tom who nodded.

'Alfred?' Colleen asked quietly. 'What's going on?'

'Wait a minute,' said a guard. He addressed Alf. 'What are you here for sir?'

Colleen interjected. 'He's with me and it's my medal that's been stolen.'

'But you know the offenders?' the guard persisted.

Alfred nodded. 'Tom. My grandson.'

'What about this one?' He shoved Joe in the ribs again.

Alfred stared hard at Joe, searching for himself in the younger man's face. Then Sophie. Yes, it was there, he could see the eyes; unmistakably Sophie's eyes. And Alfred's nose. He watched Joe smirk under the scrutiny. He would have liked to see him smile. It had the same set as Tom's.

'Don't know him,' Alfred replied. He knew it was spiteful but there could be a chance the man was completely off his rocker, not related to him at all. What would any grandson have to gain from this? Joe stood to attention. 'Joe Nutbrown born 1974 to Sonya Nutbrown, born 1957 father unknown,' he recited.

Alfred shuffled a half step back causing Colleen to place a steadying hand across his back.

'Sonya,' Alfred whispered. 'My little Sonya.'

'Sir?'

'I need a minute,' said Alfred.

'Don't worry sir,' the guard replied, 'where these guys are going you'll have years.' He marched them through reception and into another corridor.

'Ma'am.' It was the woman behind the counter. 'You can see the medals now.'

Colleen settled Alfred into a chair and told him she wouldn't be long.

***

Alfred waited until the woman had her back turned then followed the men into the corridor. He heard voices in the rooms off the far end. In the first room was Tom. Alfred stood in the doorway.

'You shouldn't be in here sir,' said the guard. Alfred ignored him.

'Tell me I haven't spawned a thief,' he demanded.

Granddad, I didn't mean to, honest,' Tom pleaded.

'Are you a thief?' he demanded again. He took a pace forward and slapped his cane on the table.

'Yes!' Tom cried. 'Yes I'm a thief. But.'

'But nothing. Haven't you learnt anything boy? Do you blame that idiot next door for your transgressions? Act like a man. You make me sick.'

'I'm sorry.'

'What did he tell you? What lies did he feed you? To do this to me?' Alfred spluttered on his words. Memories were coming too fast and he couldn't find the right words to separate them.

'I tried to stop him. Granddad, I didn't know him. I mean, I didn't know,' Tom pleaded.

Alfred shook his head. 'Neither did I.' He cleared his throat with a deep bark and pulled his shoulders back. 'Sergeant, may I see the men together? Please?' Then he added, 'Humour an old man.'

The guard held fast.

'Please,' Alfred asked.

'Oh, all right. Wait here.'

Alfred could hear the man in the next room negotiating with Joe's guard. He returned with both men.

'Still think you've got the upper hand son don't you.' Alfred addressed Joe. 'Seems like more than a coincidence that you stole Harry Jones' medal. So why'd you do it?'

Joe stood stony faced.

'Did Sonya hate me?'

Joe flinched.

'I loved that little girl,' Alfred continued softer now. 'Can you imagine, after having all those boys, to find out I had a little girl? To Sophie?'

Tom threw a puzzled look at Alfred.

'Sophie was my girl before the war,' he explained. 'She should have been your grandmother, but things didn't work out like they were supposed to.' He turned to Joe. 'When your step-grandfather realised Sonya wasn't his little girl he sent her to New Zealand to live with me. That was a cruel thing to do I grant you. I looked after Sonya in our home but it was hard on Lily. We sent her away to boarding school. It was the best thing at the time. I loved Lily. I didn't mean to hurt her, and she stood by me, God rest her soul.'

'Where were you when mum got pregnant eh?' Joe spat. 'Stuck in a foreign country, no one to help her. Where were you then?'

'If only I'd known. I would have been there for you.' He softened as he pictured his little girl pregnant. 'Sonya walked out of my life in 1974.'

'You didn't try to find her,' Joe retorted.

Alfred became red with rage. He thumped his stick on the floor. 'You know nothing. Nothing. Of course I tried to find her, but she didn't want to be found. In the end I assumed she'd gone back to America. Did she?'

Joe wouldn't answer.

'Have you spent your whole life hating me Joe?' Alfred asked. Still no answer. 'My only crime was to fall in love with two women. You know it's a funny thing, a heart always has room for love, never gets full. You think about that.'

No one said a word. He walked out of the room, down the corridor clicking his stick on the ground and back to Colleen who was waiting for him on the chair he'd vacated.

'We can go now,' he said.

***

'As you can see some of the varves remained intact.' Lana moved the red laser onto the slide. 'Which was

460

fortuitous or my research would have had to change tack, although of course after the eruption there would be innumerable proposals to put forward for research purposes.'

She addressed the group of about forty people in the common room of the lodge at the base of the mountain's western side. Sarah had organised the lecture as part of Lana's obligations under her conditions for receiving the grant. Lana had yet to publish the research. She smiled at Paul who operated the slide show for her.

He hadn't given up on her, even when she wouldn't see him after the death of Alex. That day had been a blur. She could hardly remember what happened. But she could remember the emotions and felt them as if every day had been that awful day. Overwhelming joy turned to deepest guilt in seconds. It was hard to shake the guilt. For months after she doubted herself, she couldn't decide what to do, wore dull colours. She kept her distance from Paul, but he persisted. Then one day something he wrote in an email finally lifted her out of her darkness. Something about not wanting to wait another thirty years, but if he had to, so be it. It just wouldn't be as much fun having to negotiate hearing aids, false teeth, walking sticks and God help us, continence pads. It was meant to be funny but it scared her. He was right and she up sticks and moved in with him that week.

That was two months ago. The wound on her leg had healed over but she could see the scar would be there forever. She didn't care. It was her badge and Paul was proud of it. He loved that she'd been hit by an eruption and lived to tell the tale. Each time Paul told the story the rock got bigger and she got more stoic in the face of danger, as did he in becoming the hero who saved her.

She'd got her wish and handed the medals back at a special ceremony. At Paul's insistence she wore her red dress. He said it reminded him of the night he fell in love with her. Paul stood with her, smartly casual and sporting a goatee. Lana rubbed his bicep which he flexed teasingly under his light shirt.

'You look gorgeous angel,' he said.

She'd introduced Paul to Colleen and Alfred and he'd been quietly impressed with Alfred who he knew had had skeletons rattled over the whole affair. Literally.

Lana answered a couple of technical questions before the mood in the room turned to the excitement of those days last September. She'd anticipated that and now the slide screen showed them cooped up in the hut. Paul had taken the photos and Lana hadn't paid much attention at the time. She looked at herself on the screen: slumped at the table, changing her dressing, warming her hands by the fire, her brow furrowed in every shot. And there was Emma lying on the floor, Emma lying on her bunk. She'd decided she may as well be back home in Canada with a cast on her leg as here, so once she was discharged she flew home. Lana hadn't heard from her again but she knew Paul had. There's Bing. God, what a mess all that was! There wasn't a photo of him with his arm.

'He's not a bad man,' Lana mused, then went on to explain his role in their drama. 'But he's in jail with the others. Prison farm actually, low security. Right at the base of the mountain. She tut-tutted at the irony of it.

Sarah asked the floor for any further questions then

462

thanked Lana.

'Well done sweetheart,' said Paul gently caressing her lower back.

'Was I all right?' asked Lana.

'Better than all right sweetheart,' Paul grinned.

About the Author

Lily Ennis has spent many years exploring the wild outdoors. She developed a love of geology and after a career in property she completed a BSc (earth science). She lives in Thames, New Zealand, with her husband, four cats and an elderly sulphur-crested cockatoo.

You can find Lily at her blog lilyennis.wordpress.com